THE ADVENTURES OF HOTROD AND PILOT FISH

Tom Nelson

PRELUDE

Everything must have a beginning, some kind of middle, and an end.

It's the logic of mortality. The greatest building ever made will one day come to dust. All living things first thrive and then fail. It is the same with our stories. They must start and they must end.

Even the great pyramids of Gaza have lost their capstones.

It's not about fault. It's only the nature of things.

Beginnings are the most delicate of times, and this story is beginning here.

Almost all of it is true. The parts that aren't true are the ones that I made up. Some people will be able to tell which are which, but only because they were there. For some of it all of us were there. For some of it no one was there.

The words, though, the words will be the same for everyone.

I promise you that.

I have colored all the honesty here with trickery. I've lined the lines with lies and inked the edges with falsehoods. I've filled the sketches in with deception.

You'll be able to tell that I changed the names.

You're going to meet some people soon. I expect us all to get along swimmingly.

I know it's premature to say that. I understand that it's only just starting and we have to rush into these things slowly.

First things first!

Come with me now to the desert of southern Utah, not

far from where the United States government used to test nuclear weapons.

Fifteen years after the nuclear tests moved underground and thirty years before bribes brought the flag of five rings to wave over the Utah snow. Come with me to the desert in the spirit of winter and feel how cold a desert can be.

Look out for the scorpions, they're known to sting and don't feel fear.

It is early morning with the sun just a hint on the far side of the mountains. The desert still has the cold of the night. Lying next to each other and not quite awake are a man and woman. A good couple conflicted and conjoined as only love and endurance and steel mills and deadhead runs can make.

She is not due, not for two more weeks. Except that she is due now. Time is more confusing than we care to acknowledge, and here is the end of that time. The baby isn't premature.

Call it a surprise.

The man has been to all the classes about breathing and birthing. Every time paying close attention, reading up on it at home. He has queried other fathers about what it was like for them, as though that will have something to do with how it will be for him.

Of course, he is completely unprepared, and she is screaming now though not so loud. It just sounds loud because of all that it can mean, but it's really not that loud.

Ok now it's getting LOUD!

Listen to the primeval sounds of renewal. It's a strange thing that creation is often accompanied by so much hurt. Nothing new can ever come without a struggle, without risking all. The creation of life can place two beings so close to death that sometimes neither of them makes it.

It's coming and the blankets have been shifted by the struggle of birth. There is blood on the sand. It dries as it spreads, clumps of rubies mixed in with clumps of gold.

A Scientologist would be horrified. There is no quiet

here. A Catholic or Jew or Muslim would be in joy.

A Hindu or Buddhist would be more patient about it. Some Buddhists in Japan say that it takes forty days for the soul to be firmly settled in the body. Like any new home it takes a little while to put down roots.

Those are the colorings of faith and culture.

We may not be bound by them, but we are certainly bound up in them.

There may be some truth in all of it, for the Fish is doing nothing, looking nowhere. His soul, though well aware of the falsity of the two weeks to birth claim has gotten a little lost. It's not his fault. It's just that in the desert it's easy to lose one's way. All ways look the same in the deep desert.

The surrounding mountains don't help very much either.

She looks at her child. She is worn out and beautiful.

"You are a little hero."

A mother's mandate in the first moments of life.

The soul sees and hears her and instantaneously has joined with the flesh. The Pilot Fish smiles at his mother. He is happy to be here. Then he scans the perimeter for any potential evil doers and something sharp to kill them with, but there is no evil here. There are no maidens to rescue.

It is now that the Fish begins to cry.

The sun shows us the procession of the equinoxes as it gradually extinguishes the stars. The Age of Pisces is descending slowly giving way to the Age of Aquarius.

We stand on the edges of ages.

Viewed through another perspective of time, this is the year that a peanut farmer from Georgia is elected president. He is elected on a Nixon hangover and loses to the Reagan revolution. By the time this is over, Nixon will be dead and exonerated. The statement made by Ford about the healing of the nation will finally be true. Carter will have won the Nobel Prize for Peace, and the wheel of history will continue to turn.

That is that.

The first year of our lives saw the five year anniversary of the end of the Vietnam War. The people of my country were worn out with war. Conscription had made them angry. It would take another thirty years and a national catastrophe before the politicians could drag us again into a pointless war that appeased international power balances over domestic defense.

The Great Game goes on and on and on from before Metternich to Kissinger and beyond and we understand little our part and even less the consequences of our actions.

The politics of our elders becomes our politics. We inherit them as we will also bequeath them, and we'll leave our mark on them as they pass through us. As children, as we develop, our politics are mainly felt, they are impressions without clear context. It's the same with our religions. It's unfortunate, so much of our lives are spent in the throng of things that we learned before we learned how to think.

There's such a gap between knowing something and understanding something.

We spend so much of our lives naming the places we've memorized on a map not realizing how lost we would be if we ever went there.

Let me provide some landmarks.

This is us, our generation.

Our events: the Challenger disintegrating, burning a hole in the sky of what we thought infallible and becoming for many of us the first important thing that we remember. We watch the Berlin Wall being torn down and we're overwhelmed with the majesty of freedom. We see a young girl hugging the president. The Supreme Court in Florida debates the validity of hanging chads. Then on a quiet September day we watch in horror as the two towers fall.

That is our development, and that is the end of our education. The time after that is for us to act and argue, for us to start our careers and families, and begin to take charge of our inheritance. It is then that we begin to take our place in history.

Our awareness is born in fire and our adulthood is substantiated in flame.

In Russia they say that a generation is seven years though I don't know where they mean you to stand in that, if you look behind seven years is that all of your generation? Do you sit on the midpoint of a line seven years long?

I feel it differently much more Dionysian than Apollonian, a Wittgensteinian family resemblance of the passage of time. These are the snap shots, each moment a cousin, uncle, or grandmother in the tapestry of time that makes up our lives. How well do we recognize each other? What is the strength of our likenesses? In what ways are we congruent?

We may see each other clearly while looking nothing the same.

Life has a biological continuity, but not a psychological one. Most of our time isn't worth remembering or overwhelms our capacity to remember. Much of our time is only dreaming.

I have spent much time in dreams.

But forget about politics, the Pilot Fish knows that we can't do much about that. We are only small people in the midst of great events. That's okay, we are lucky and unlucky, cursed and blessed that we should live in interesting times.

The Pilot Fish looks at all the blood and water. First water then blood, then a baby, then more blood. Our alpha and omega are blood.

We are water mixed with iron. We were made possible by the explosions of ancient stars, but that is not all we are. There are some ideas to go along with the blood from Heraclitus to Einstein to you and me.

We are iron and water and ideas. The iron and water we only have on loan. The ideas are the only things that we can really call our own and they're only worthwhile if they're shared, and that is what makes us so sad and so beautiful, but enough about what we are.

Let's get back to who we are.

Look east, out of the desert, past Salt Lake, leave the mountains behind and cross the plains to the capital of the Midwest.

Time travel with me as we move, though only a few months into the future to a maternity ward in Chicago.

There is a woman surrounded by nurses and a gynecologist, her feet are up in stirrups. She has an epidural. She is okay. After a few hours out comes a child, only a few months younger than the Pilot Fish.

It is Hotrod, but the name is something else on the birth certificate, and he is not the same now as he will be except that he is.

The very first sperm from the very first orgasm that his father had after his mother went off the pill swam ahead and away from all the rest and beat itself into the egg. That motherfucker had a job to do and he did it.

Hotrod's soul has been instilled in the flesh since that moment, and he is RARING TO GO!

The nurse swaddles him after washing off the blood, the doctor has slapped his bottom, and still he doesn't cry. He is staring at the nurse thinking: Look at the cans on this woman. Jesus Christ, these are amazing. I think I am going to like it here!

It's true, the nurse has amazing boobs.

Hotrod is not thinking about milk.

No, Hotrod's brain is spinning with lust and plans. She is like a mountain, an Everest of mammary flesh, but how to climb? Hotrod busies himself with strategy. He still hasn't cried. He is wide eyed taking in the world.

Hotrod wants to spit game at this girl, talk her up and then take her home. This is hard to do though because he doesn't yet know how to speak. It will take a couple years to get that figured out. Talking to girls will take years beyond that.

Another thought follows the first: Any girl with cans

like that must be fat, God please don't let her be fat!

He doesn't like fat girls, maybe if there is simply nothing else to work with, but never as a first choice. No, the fat ones are for last call if at all. He tries to turn his head to get an angle on her stomach, but little Hotrod's head is one third the size of his body, and he is too weak to move it.

It is now that he begins to cry.

He is in fact wailing.

The nurse holding him is slightly troubled, but smiles when the crying starts. She will quietly ask a physician friend that she had an affair with years ago when she had huge boobs and a thin waist.

In a whisper, "Can a baby be born with a hard on?"

Now travel with me in time some more. The Fish is not the oldest and Hotrod is not the youngest. The rest of us have been born and are being born. Our parents are the first generation to adopt the "stop at two" philosophy. They are trading away all the bullshit about what they wish for in a baby and just hoping for health. Yes, the babies are all healthy. They are all okay.

Now time begins to pass in long days and short years, but just before we go, pause a moment and listen to them cry. It's okay. Nothings gone wrong and there isn't any pain. They're just being confronted by everything new outside of the womb. It's a lot to take in all at once.

They don't know anything else to do.

BEFORE THE NAMES

The last moment before it all started just passed.

I guess that means that this is how it started. It might be true. It may as well be true. This was the last of the times that we had before the rest of the times that we would have.

This was before the names.

This is where we were. We had all celebrated eighteenth birthdays that year.

We were in Wisconsin. We lived in a small shit-hole town built around a paper mill. Our parents were happy to live there and we were desperate to leave.

There are lots of these towns. Everyone comes from somewhere. There were five of us, and all we had in common was everything that we had ever done.

Small towns seem like Alcatraz style prisons to the young and island sanctuaries for the old, and we were so goddamn young. There wasn't a real idea as to what would come, we didn't know, mostly didn't care. We wanted something different, we thought that different probably could only mean more or better. We wanted what everyone wants, maybe it can't be articulated. Our version of a normal life, to be a success, a lover, a person worth listening to. To be happy in some way or another with someone or another.

We didn't know then that different usually means more of the same. We didn't know that no matter who you are, you still have a voice and few of our voices are ever very loud. We didn't know how much easier it is to yell than to get someone to listen. We constantly confused the words "best" and "favorite" as we went about figuring ourselves out, out loud. We didn't know that a place is defined by the people you know there. We hadn't learned any of those things yet.

We were aware of drugs and sex, but really, we knew nothing.

This isn't a coming of age story. Those are the stories where young boys are sent by old men to kill and die and love with strangers. Those are the stories of mortality and pointless or perhaps only existential struggle.

Those stories tell us that childhood must end. That one day all of us will die.

This is something different though I don't know how best to call it. It might be that we just come of age later in the West now, a tale of extended adolescence. Maybe a maturity tale more than anything else, the realization that whether or not you live or die your life might be for nothing anyway.

That between the realization of mortality and the end of one's life you need to do something in spite of it all. That if you're only aware of mortality that you've missed the point of being alive.

You can call it whatever you like.

Now is when the names come.

Jani was sitting to my right. Jani, so soft, so pretty and never had a boyfriend. She would never let me be her boyfriend. We always teased her that she was a virgin and even though she insisted that she wasn't, I never believed her. Wild was sitting across from me next to Bonk. He was holding her hand and she was leaning against him. They looked like every high school romance where they count the months from freshman year to forever. Hotrod finished our pentagram, handsome and devilish.

I hadn't had the break yet and the Pilot Fish was still on his way.

He would tell me that he had been far, far back in time then. That he had things to take care of before arrival. I guess this is the only time before him that I can relate, and that makes it the best place to start.

The Adventures of Hotrod and Pilot Fish

We were playing Spades just having learned it from some friends of ours that had gotten out of a chemical dependency treatment center.

We were trying to make it into a drinking game. It wasn't going very well. We should have stuck to Presidents and Assholes. That was a game that we all knew well.

You've heard our names now, we are all introduced.

Our parents did the best that they could, and what they did was fine. This isn't going to be one of those stories about how someone was given life by someone and then that someone hurt them all the time. There was good and bad there like everywhere.

We were laughing and drinking, not mentioning anything. Not even dreaming.

Jani had come back from a yearlong foreign exchange six months ago. She had been in Denmark and liked it there. Since then a distance had come between us. There were things that she could talk about that we couldn't. There were things that she couldn't talk to anyone about given the nature of our small town.

It was the first time that had happened with us. It wouldn't be the last. Maybe she was the most adult or just the most experienced of us.

We had just started to create our own stories. We were too caught up in writing them to be able to tell them. Clumsy with ourselves like lovers that want to hold and kiss so much, but just aren't sure how.

I had tried to do the exchange program too, but I lost out in the selection process. I got the consolation prize instead. Six weeks exchange in Germany. It was nice and sad and old. I lived with a host family in Bavaria. All the students got a three day trip to Munich. There is a huge clock there that has been keeping time for a long while.

The other excursion we had was to Dachau. I stood in front of the ovens that people had burned up other people in. I was sharing the view, our modern understanding of horror with some Persians.

We were looking at the ovens together and I said something in German, I thought I asked what they thought of it, but maybe it didn't come out that way. Maybe they didn't speak German very well either. The woman, she was sweet with kind eyes, she said, "Baha'i" and pointed to herself. I didn't know what that meant then, thought it was a word in German that I hadn't heard before. There are a lot of words in German that I don't know.

I had tried to talk to Jani about Europe. I wanted us to have that in common and maybe it would help her with the distances that came up now and again. It was to no avail, there is such a difference between those that have only visited a place and those that have lived there. The things that are so interesting to the visitor are just normal to the resident. Whatever they are, they have lost the power to amaze.

It was hearts to me and all I had was the two. I played it knowing that you can't win them all. That sometimes you just have to play what your dealt even if you know the outcome isn't going to be in your favor. Every game has rules and skill and luck.

Hotrod and Bonk were arguing about music. They had been having the same argument about talent and who sold out and who didn't and lyrics versus melody for years. It didn't matter then, it can't matter now.

It's the specifics that really matter, that can actually say something. They're so hard to manage.

We were leaving.

Not all of us together, not necessarily even at the same time, but we were all going. It was the feast before the Diaspora, and we were getting the most out of it that we could.

See us for what we were.

We were just like you.

Scared, optimistic, idealistic, proud, vulnerable, unsure, smart, searching, lost.

The perceptions of youth are always flawed. It takes the

conflicts of time to grind those lenses to reasonable levels of perception.

Suddenly, I realize that no one has been keeping score. The books have all been shuffled together into one pile and there is no way to count them out.

It's too late to figure out whose winning. We'll still play it out. It's practice now. We'll make the best of it.

I would have had to play that two of hearts either way.

In the end, it's just a reason to drink. I pull hard on my beer and suddenly get overwhelmed by foam, spitting and coughing up all over the table, while Jani and Wild laugh and laugh and laugh. I was the only one that could get those two to get along.

We were drinking Schlitz or some other shit, maybe PBR. I spit out the extra foam and had another pull.

I'm embarrassed long enough to color up and them I'm laughing too, fuck it I wasn't bottle fed, what can you do?

I knew a lot of jokes then, we all did. Mostly they were racist, blond, or sexist. I can't remember them so well anymore.

Hotrod and I were moving to a housing project in Minneapolis. It was all that we could afford, and we looked at it like an adventure. There was so much glamour in our eyes, the feelings unclear because they lacked the experience to be defined. Hotrod and I had been accepted at the University of Minnesota.

I had no idea what I was going to do with my life, but I figured I'd just write it down along the way. Hotrod was going to get rich.

We each had our dreams. Really, we were all a few steps away from our futures, and everyone is when they are where we were.

We felt ourselves the best that our small town had to offer, and, like a conquering army, we prepared to move with the explicit ignorance that there could be any casualties in the conquest.

Bonk and Wild Child were off to Madison in a few weeks.

Jani was going to Chicago, having decided that Los Angeles involved too much driving. She was accepted at Northwestern, and was going to major in European studies and Music. She would use her Danish. She was going to learn classical guitar and write beautiful songs about how things were or could be.

Most of us were artists in a way. Wild was a figure skater and a dancer. Hotrod was a guitarist like Jani. Bonk could draw and paint. I wrote poems.

I didn't know that I was a writer then. I just liked the way words could rhyme and say something simultaneously. I was amazed the first time that I ever wrote something that was both beautiful and meaningful.

The Pilot Fish was an audience of one to a cacophony of untrained voices.

We were listening to Pearl Jam, Nirvana, Rage Against the Machine, Korn, the Beastie Boys, Red Hot Chili Peppers, and Soundgarden.

We were the tail end of the demographic that watched MTV for the music videos.

We'd already signed the yearbooks. All that was taken care of and we had said good-bye to high school. None of us believed that bullshit about those being the best years of our lives. That the best times could already be behind us was impossible and could only be another lie in a long list of lies.

Wild was so proud of her blond hair. She kept it long and rich and cut off the split ends once a month. She was unfazed by blond jokes, by boys, by girls. By anyone. I didn't want to be her boyfriend, she was with Bonk. I just wanted to sleep with her. It wasn't anything extraordinary.

The only ones that had already been touched by the other side of life were the girls. Once the boobs show up, the world changes and vulnerabilities and powers that hadn't been imagined become real.

It's harder being a girl.

The Adventures of Hotrod and Pilot Fish

It's all coming, I promise you. You'll see it all from the tub and the fights, and the madness and those few moments of peace that are realized only retrospectively after it's too late. It will all be here soon, I promise you, but for now, please just look at us. See us for what we were, some kids hanging out in a basement that belonged to one of our parents, drinking beer that we had shoplifted from a convenience store.

I'll get to New York and what happened there. What it was like for me before and after and during. I'll get to the Pear and the ones that I will love for my whole life.

I'm going to get to everything. The things that could be measured only in moments and the things that take years to measure and more time than that to really understand.

I'm going to get to the end too, the ends of each of us and my end.

Believe me, for on this I will not lie.

For me this is over.

None of the future cruelties or tragedies were evident. There wasn't anything to be said of our hearts except that we were as naïve as we were innocent. I think that we were prepared for the world that our parents had chosen for us.

Had we only gone there instead.

The seeds were planted even then, but this crop would take time to mature, and each of us would meet that harvest individually. There was so much vitality in that basement, maybe too much. I don't think any of us wanted to die, but maybe none of us really knew how to live. Was it born from contempt, just taking so much for granted? We were never going to grow old, and we were never going to fear.

I take a towel and wipe up the foam from the table. Jani helps me with some napkins. The cards are fucked with beer foam, so we dry a few out and throw a few away and keep playing.

Now the math demands a certain number of irresolvable positions in the game, but we don't care. When one comes up we flip a coin: the book goes to one team and the other

Tom Nelson

team has to drink.
>It's a game within a game.
>It's fair.
>This was us, how we were before the names.

FRESHMAN YEAR

I was at the end of a long line of optimistic fucks. Most of us were eighteen. The ones that were older weren't optimistic. They wore grim and resigned looks of determination on their faces. There were several of them, and you could tell that they just wanted to get it over with.

We were divided into two lines. Optimistic fucks go there, disenchanted bastards over there. At the end of the line was an academic bureaucrat who told you some bullshit about how you weren't a number but a student. This was followed by some romanticized garbage about welcoming you to the rest of your life and then she took your picture and gave you a student identification card. On the card was a number. She was the only one that ever used my name. After that, all I was ever asked for was the number on the card.

It took me years to forget that number, and when I did I finally felt emancipated from the university.

This was freshmen orientation at the University of Minnesota. I was in CLA, which stands for the college of liberal arts. We were to study humanities and get a well-rounded liberal arts education that would serve us well through life.

The college experience at a large state school eschews the clique culture of high school for the super clique.

We were now identified as frat boys and sorority girls, business students and humanities students and engineering students. The question of introduction was "what's your major?" and we all looked down on each other no matter the answer. We were described as athletic scholarships, academic scholarships and financial aid. We were divided by anticipated career paths and clarity of goals.

I didn't give any of us much of a chance.

Most of us were just simple straightforward kids freshly graduated from the self-esteem factories of the American high school system. The plan was to have a few sexual partners during freshmen year and then marry your college sweetheart before joining the workforce and following the great line of desperate consumption and deluded complacency that most Americans call a normal life.

I couldn't really blame them. After all, most people only do what they are expected to. The future worker bee's comprised the largest and quietest group on campus.

We had our intellectual rebels as well and I spent some time in this super clique myself.

Most of them were kids who were determined to replicate their hippi parents' college experience of protest and revolution. They wanted to march around with bull horns and occupy buildings. The only real problem was that my generation didn't have a solidifying conflict like the Vietnam War and attendant draft to solidify the movement.

They had to make do with a mish mash of causes and generalized arguments about the invisible hand of systemic social injustice.

Opposite the super clique was the campus hobby group and there were a million of those devoted to everything from chess to intramural basketball.

I didn't join any of them.

That isn't meant to imply that I wasn't taking advantage of the academic atmosphere. I was learning a wide variety of things in particular on the weekends.

I never would have guessed that you could get that fucked up on cough syrup for one thing. The best thing about that first year of college was that you could meet people who had some idea of where things were and how to get them.

It was amazing after living in such a small town to be able to score LSD and psychedelic mushrooms without making a fucking project out of it.

The best part of the college experience had to be the parties. We were finally free to go out without worrying about coming home.

It was refreshing to see the slut shaming of high school give way to the slut adulation of freshman girls making out with each other surrounded by boys trying to hide their blushes and boners as they slurped cheap, shitty keg beer.

Don't get me wrong, the parties were fun.

A lot of my classmates seemed to be in college simply because it was preferable to the military or the workforce. They varied from undecided degree programs to monthly major changes. I made some very good friends out of this group.

Every college class is a repetition of the sexual revolution and mine was no different. Ours was a mix of hedonism and feminism. They clustered together in cafes chatting about movies and music, books and photography. They talked about sex and used words like "fellatio" and "poly-amorous" to describe their sexual freedom.

The first time I heard people talking like that, I thought it was about a Shakespeare play I hadn't read. I asked Hotrod if there ever had been a hero named Fellatio who was renowned for his sexual prowess, but he told me that I was thinking of Rostand's Cyrano.

Most of these students were OK except for a few really pretentious bastards.

I was learning some other things that were so counter intuitive that it took a while to wrap my head around it. I never thought that disdain and cynicism could actually be a huge security blanket protecting people from thinking, but I saw that shit first hand and more than once. That fucked me up.

Most days though weren't that serious.

The academy was a Roman circus and you just had to get to class and home again. There was a new protest every week.

Tom Nelson

The animal rights people would lock themselves in cages and chain themselves to buildings and yell about how cruel research was and the cops would come and cut the locks off and arrest them. The outreach Bible beaters would show up and yell horrible things at the girls and promise all of us hell and eternal damnation.

I didn't get wrapped up too much in anyone's causes or crusades. I'm just not that guy. Most of my energy was spent trying to stay awake through my classes and score something worthwhile for the weekend.

The protest culture was represented in the lecture hall as well with at least one person per class on a hell bent crusade to save us all from the conventional life that we were surely doomed to fall into if not for their crucial intervention.

At times that asshole was me.

I had some good professors and some shitty ones. It's funny how you get told that college will somehow teach you to think critically and develop your own mind, and then you get stuck in a required class where some jerk off with a Ph.D. tells you that you should write and subscribe to his theory of whatever and if you weren't pissed off enough about that then he has the cheek to demand you buy his book to take the goddamn course.

I watched with wonder at slaving and sexing grad students. Prostitution would seem to be built into the academic ladder just as effectively as the corporate one.

I opined once that the corporations probably get the better-looking girls, but I was told that it varied from school to school.

Minnesota just isn't a very pretty place.

I had a cute lady from England who between complaints of diabetes asked us to write an essay regarding the ethical conditions of friendship. Hotrod wanted to have me write about how a true friend will chat up the fat one so that his buddy can score the hot one, but I just said I'd get around to it.

She had us read *The Velveteen Rabbit*. I think she thought

it was cute, some kind of inner child nurturing. I didn't mind. I had just found a decent crystal connection and I would sit in class and listen to people discuss it while the whole world spun.

She gave me a C. The first of several that I would receive over the course of my college career. She wrote on the paper that my final essay lacked depth and insight.

I agreed with her.

I would have given each of us an F, but it wasn't my decision. That was one of the really funny things about college. A lot of it isn't your decision, but the whole time you're there they tell you that everything *is* your decision. Later, when I worked with college graduates in the corporate world the illusions of choice would start to make a lot more sense to me, but when I first saw it I didn't get it.

I had a really cool professor from Scotland. He taught philosophy of language. His accent was so thick that I could hardly understand a fucking word he said, but he motivated me to read some of the stuff.

It was interesting. I didn't think you could get so much out of how people communicate. It made me sad that we use so little of the language we have.

He was the first teacher I had ever had who said that some things just can't be understood. Some geniuses are at times impenetrable or maybe just human and even though they are really smart they can't always find the words to express what's on their mind either. There's nothing to be done about it.

He actually motivated me to read some of the stuff and not just because I couldn't understand him when he lectured, but his passion for the esoteric kind of got into me.

Hotrod was the first to see that a liberal education was an easy way to end up with a CDL, so he dropped out and started working with computers. He'd give me shit that CLA stood for Can't Land A Job, and he had a point. He would go on to out earn every single person I met at the university.

There were only two other things of real note that happened freshman year. The first was the psychotic break although it feels impolite to call it that.

It happened that winter just after Christmas break. I was candyflipped on four rolls and five hits and was looking into the mirror when the mirror shivered in a way that let me see through it instead of at it.

The Fish was on the other side of the mirror looking back at me. He was dressed in a weird robe and when I asked about that he told me that where he was in time was 3,000 years ago. Apparently, that's what people wore when and where he was. Then he told me that he had always been with me, on the other side of the mirror. I wasn't alarmed at all. It felt normal, and I believed him intuitively.

The other was when I saw into the void for the first time.

That happened while out on a binge out with Hotrod.

I met Hotrod at a student dormitory that night. The dormitory is the one exception to the super clique system in that it is a direct extension of high school except that it's easier to fuck your classmates.

Hotrod had just done that.

It was the first nice spring weekend. Hotrod's ambition was to complete a hat trick and he was hoping the future guilt generation would provide him with the action.

I had downed a bottle of Robitussin and taken two tabs of some decent blotter.

He had it all mapped out in his head, "one is done, the game is afoot!"

We went to a house party and I knew I was in trouble. Cough syrup plus LSD just makes me useless. I was drinking a lot of shitty beer, but it wasn't helping. Things were starting to get confusing at that point. Hotrod told me he got number two done in the bathroom, and I thought he was talking about taking a shit.

Then we were on to a frat party where Hotrod knew some guys. I was too fucked up to really do anything. I hid out in the backyard while Hotrod sailed on to his personal record. No one found me, and I was happy about that.

It was then that I saw it, I mean there had been hints before, but I really saw it then.

The void was there before me and it was mesmerizing. It was beautiful and horrible. It looked like it went on and on and on to forever. I stared into it for a long time, and then I could feel it staring back into me. It was like I had been staring at an eye not knowing where it was looking and then it looked directly at me. I could feel it reach into me as I looked into it. It was a complete connection that become stronger the longer it lasted. I could feel myself start to slip into it, and then instinctively I pulled back away from it.

I felt an intense fear come over me like I had broken something impossible to repair.

I sat there feeling completely timeless, not sure about what had just happened, almost sober in a sense that I didn't have a body that could be intoxicated. Then I came back to my senses and was overwhelmed by nausea.

I started throwing up and puked until it came out blood.

PROBABLY

Given a few of the conditions of this new style of life, the pretensions of the higher mind, and the economic struggle of working and borrowing through one's own pointless education, it became necessary to discover immediate and effective solutions to the existential problems at hand. Their names were LSD, crystallized methamphetamines, and Goofers.

Focusing on the latter, Goofers were a somewhat wonderful example of the work from home organic chemist. Synthesized mescaline mixed with crystallized LSD and a little speed. All of this magic was sweetly compressed into a tiny green tablet of variable shape. I guess in the dialog of the later '90s, we would have called it teal, but the color could vary between batches. The third option of the drugs that had made our short list carried some economic benefits as well. We were high enough up the chain to get them for three bucks a pop as compared to the street value of five or six.

The at-home chemist has many entrepreneurial opportunities before him, and it's a terrible shame so much creativity and education is thrown away in the pharmaceutical and food science industries. Fortunately, there are always a few mavericks out there who want to chase black-market dollars rather than take on the full load of corporate or academic prostitution.

God bless.

I was learning valuable lessons in the university in particular in the importance of social networking. In small-town Wisconsin, a quarter of an ounce of weed was $50 and often a few hours of work or more to obtain; in my new life, an ounce was $70 and only a phone call away.

Social networking is the heart of the drug trade.

By the start of my sophomore year I was really starting to enjoy the whole higher education thing. It was true what they said in those recruiting lectures. Higher education really does open doors that would otherwise stay closed, and it promotes diversity. I was able to go from petty drug dealers to pros in a matter of months. That was enriching to say the least. There is a lot to be said for the intoxication of upward mobility or at least the upward mobility of intoxicants.

Goofers were my preferred fix for most Saturday nights. They weren't as demanding as LSD and didn't carry the inherent sexual or psychological risks of meth. This was the best way to throw away four to six hours of a day that was going to pass anyway.

The other benefit was that they mixed well with alcohol and could handle girls. Once sufficiently addled, it was time to charge off to the house parties. All of them filled with the chance to sleep with a girl of impeccable taste and excessive amounts of perfume and lipstick.

In a word: heaven.

The only downside to all of this was the impact on one's budget.

The real question at this stage was nutritional. These beautiful and awful little pills were no fun on an empty stomach, and the malnourished can hardly get their money's worth from the five dollar infinite pour. Not to mention the question of performance, in the event that one procures an overly done-up princess for the evening.

On a note of honesty, I was never any good at scoring girls. If it had been up to me I would have just sunk the entire party budget into crystal. It was the insistence of Hotrod who was more driven by sex than drugs that I get out and rock and roll.

I would have been happy most nights to just stay home burning glass.

Forget about all that though because I am starving.

The average human being requires 2,000 calories of nourishment in a 24-hour period. This should be a balance of fruits and vegetables and doesn't suffer from the addition of meat.

The average drug addict needs about the same, although through the magic of chemistry he or she can often get by on much less. Being young also contributes to this paradox of activity and energy balance. Nonetheless, every so often one needs to refuel. Typically, this is best done before scoring because most of the drugs I enjoyed often served the dual purpose of appetite and common sense suppressants.

The only problem was I got weak and shaky sometimes. I was already at oddly comfortable terms with the shaking, but I wasn't going to let myself get all the way to a full-fledged collapse.

That would have been embarrassing.

It all made sense according to one of my philosophy classes. There is no absolute truth. Nothing ever can be really truly true. The French proved it, although how you thoroughly prove that there is no absolute truth always seemed a little contradictory to me. Although if that could be done, it would be the French that would do it.

It turns out we have at best relative or approximate truths. I was able to logically discount eighteen years of antidrug advertising with a "c'est-la-vie-style" shrug. The fact I had never been a believer of anything anyway made the arguments all the easier to make.

I had figured out college.

Grade inflation was common in the humanities and the fact that you could do almost nothing and still get a C disincentivized all the effort required to get an A while simultaneously keeping me off academic probation and keeping my financial aid status intact. Moderate attendance and minimal effort was always good for a B and could snag the occasional A from a sufficiently apathetic professor.

I took a lot of reading classes which made attendance even more optional. There was a path of least resistance to get through higher education and like water on a hill I had naturally found it.

The only thing that sucked was German.

All the foreign language courses were big on attendance. All the humanities degrees required a foreign language for graduation. Not only did you have to take the fucking classes, but you were expected to pass an exam at the end of the sequence to graduate. Having to go to campus was really detracting from my college experience. If it wasn't for German I would have only hung out on campus on the weekends.

The financial aid checks made Christmas come at the beginning of every semester, but that moneys spent and I'm broke as fuck now.

This brings us up to speed, and welcome to the McDonald's drive-through. We are in the third car back. Its Hotrod's cars as my economic conditions limit me to public transport.

Necessity aside, this whole process could be a headache so you wanted to get it right on the first run. You wouldn't think it, but going to a different place for lunch each day and dinner every night can start to get old.

Our method of foraging required us to range much like a predator on the Serengeti so that we didn't deplete any one region.

In a way it was just the basic design of an apex predator. One covers the maximum amount of territory in order to capitalize on the prey population. I may be romanticizing it a bit, but if I couldn't mix in some ecology with our new philosophy, I was surely failing the cross-disciplinary benefits of a liberal education.

The Pilot Fish called us the scavengers of the service industry.

He had a point, but like the replies section at the end of an academic paper we were comfortable with one dissenting vote.

We felt we didn't deserve so harsh a moniker. The gutter punks digging through the dumpsters were the true scavengers. We were merely thieves. We were confidence men.

We employed guile.

Operations succeed and fail on the consistent application of protocol:

Rule number one: Thou shalt not humiliate the basic service employee. His job alone is humiliation which is our only true advantage over the food monopolizing corporations. Were he to care about his job, then the con is up. Managers are fair game because by the time you've been escalated to them the success rate approaches zero, so you may as well earn your academy award in the category of righteous indignation.

Rule number two: Thou shalt not go after locally owned and operated establishments. This is necessary for two reasons. The first reason is they are our spiritual brothers in the struggle against corporate culinary dominance. The second reason is they have a small number of staff and tend to remember you. Being remembered can be an awful burden.

Rule number three: Never order promotional items. Those corporate marketing whores are determined to track those to the last in order to gauge market impact. They cross those numbers with the raw amount of advertising dollars and penetration by region. Crossing swords with them is a guaranteed loss of venture.

Rule number four: Location is everything. In order to avoid detection and risk future operations, one needs to choose a place busy enough to prevent future endangerments in the case of an unsuccessful run. Also, the larger and busier locales inspire more cynicism in the employees and promote high turnover among the corporate slave workforce.

Rule number five: Present evidence, but do not show it. Like any other venture in the capitalist market, it takes money to make money. You need some acting here to really make it work.

As Americans, we have been trained from birth to be consumers. We are naturally built for this kind of work. The only other thing is tone, just remember tone is everything.

Tone is everything!

Let's move to the heart of the caper. Now really for our own pride, let's understand this. We are not thieves in some brutal or thuggish fashion. We're not out to hurt anyone. No, we are swashbucklers of a higher order. We employ glibness of wit. We make use of well-practiced execution. We have both dedication and discipline to our craft. We're the modern equivalent of ropers and grifters. We're heroes in the gilded age of super-sized and extra fries.

At the end of every shift a fast food restaurant throws away a certain amount of food, we felt that we were only detracting from that. In a way we are performing a service reducing the amount of waste that our consumerist society produces.

We freeload out of a sense of duty to the great god of customer service, not out of some base drive for personal gain. Besides insurance and loss-prevention guys need us. Those are hardworking people with families to feed. Without us, they would be out of a job and probably forced to do this alongside ourselves.

Frankly, we don't need the competition. Those guys who used to work on the inside know everything, and we find that advantage unfair.

We are actors.

We are artists!

Hotrod is driving, I am riding shotgun, and the Pilot Fish is off time traveling. He thinks only the sick and old should be supported. The rest need to hustle their own gold.

We are now two cars back. The receipt is procured. Hotrod performs a mild rehearsal in preparation for the caper. The first step in the drama, as in any drama, is to establish mood for the audience.

The professor I had for a film appreciation class keyed me in to this. He was mad about mood. He thought mood was everything. He called it the true distinguishing critical criterion separating the great works from the mediocre.

"How can I help you?" squeaks the disenfranchised slave of the franchise.

NOISES OFF!

"Aah, yeah, we got a little problem here. We were just here doing a lunch run for the office and our order had an error in it." Hotrod just started his first office job and is our local expert on the atmosphere of office culture.

"Sure, just pull up and we'll get it sorted out." You can hear in his voice he's already given in.

We pull up to the window. There is a huge line behind us. That is proof that God is on our side.

"Yeah, we got shorted a few double cheeseburgers." Then Hotrod flashes a receipt from a few days ago filled with worthless information.

This is an excellent execution of rule number five. Also, though you can't hear it because you're reading, Hotrod's tone is perfect. Just a touch of "I hate to waste your time" combined with "I know it's not your fault, but serve me, you little error-creating worm."

He is playing the role of customer to perfection.

It's priceless.

The poor fucker comes out with our food and even gives us a thank you on our way, "Sorry, it won't happen again."

We'll accept no such guarantee! On the contrary, sir, it will happen again.

"Dude, we scored!"

"Hell yes."

We each eat a couple of cheeseburgers, and I swallow down two goofers. I pause for a moment, just one; if I didn't do so many drugs, I probably could afford to eat out at the fast food chains.

Probably.

JANI'S FATHER

Jani called me with a rush in her voice I didn't recognize. "Fish, can you meet me back home tonight?" When we said "home," it still meant our parent's place. We were in the semi residential status in our new cities that comes with being a student.

"Sure."

I didn't ask her why or what was going on, only when and where to meet. Then she hung up.

I get in my car and start the four hour drive over.

I pull into a gas station not far from her mother's house and wait for her.

The overpowered metal halide lights overhanging the parking lot make everything clinical washing all the color out of everything except for the garishness of advertisements and the undefeatable gray of the concrete.

I smoke and wait. After fifteen minutes or so she pulls in next to me and gets out.

We meet underneath the washed-out light. Her face is blank, white, controlled. I walk towards her faster than she walks towards me. I give her a hug and a kiss on the cheek. She tells me her father had been drinking a liter and a half of vodka a day leading up to the collapse. One of the neighbors found him. He was in the hallway of the apartment building trying to get his key in the lock when the seizures started.

That was a week ago.

There was still something in her voice, but nothing was in her eyes.

I follow her out to her mom's house. Her mom and I have always gotten along well.

When we get in to the house, Jani's mom offers me a sandwich. She never keeps alcohol in the house. I feel a little guilty for having my flask with me. There are a few other people there. No one's surprised by the news. Everyone has the look of inevitability written on their faces.

It's a stoic and sad and tired kind of reservation that I can't feel. The person that caused it never hurt me or disappointed me enough for me to participate in it. I never played a part in the losses that lay quietly around the house and in the back of everyone's minds. They had in many ways already survived him. His dying was anticlimactic as if the last act had already ended and we were just waiting to read an unrevealing epilogue.

No one wanted to talk about why we were all here. Jani turned on the radio and then after a little while shut it off. The noise had been discordant and comforting and then it was gone. We were left with silences that could only be filled with politeness.

"You sure you don't want anything more to eat?"

"I don't want to trouble you."

"It's no trouble."

"No, thank you."

"Coffee then?"

"Yes, please that would be great."

Jani gets up to make it cutting her mother off on the way to the kitchen.

We all know what's coming, and when the day passes without incident, we're not sure to be relieved or disappointed.

Jani's mom gets an update from the hospital. He is still in a coma and is expected to go soon. There are signs of death, but nothing too immediate. Some people leave the house to start a vigil, and others say that they'll meet at the hospital tomorrow. They invite Jani, but she shakes her head. Once they're gone, we watch some television in silence and then go to bed. We sleep together without lust or desire, only emotional fatigue and reservation. I try to hold her and she pushes me off.

I try to leave and she tells me to stay.

I've wanted nothing more than to sleep with her, and I have to smile that I am finally getting my wish.

The next morning we get up early. Jani tells me some of the details, and I nod my head. I don't want to know the medical end of it.

Her mom's gone to the hospital, so we have the place to ourselves.

She makes coffee and we talk with nothing to talk about.

She starts getting ready to leave without making any kind of push to do so. Not intentionally delaying anything, just being deliberate and thorough. She brushes her hair in front of me, measuring out each stroke slowly until she is satisfied. For the last stroke, she puts a little perfume on the brush and the smell washes over me in a mild wave.

I doubt that wild horses could have dragged her there until she was ready.

Her mom calls in the early afternoon. The signs and symptoms are clear. It's probably just a matter of hours.

Jani hangs up the phone and looks at me: "The divorce was one thing, and the relapses, those were each an individual journey. Then he quit trying to quit and that was something else entirely."

She says it without any protecting irony or cynicism. She says it looking evenly into me and through me without any pity or the request of pity. I take a step towards her to give her a hug and she takes a step away from me.

I stop.

We make eye contact for a moment and then she turns away from me and goes to the bathroom.

When she comes out of the bathroom she hugs me from

behind, her hair falling over my face, wrapping me in traces of perfume, beauty, pain, and silence. She kisses me on the cheek.

"I need to lie down for a moment, to be alone. I need to be ready for this." She says it staccato and brittle. The words slap at the future that never was and scream at the past that didn't have to be. The rush moves through her sentences touching each word with a small fire that quickly fades out like the intonation pattern of a foreign language. I can feel the edge inside her, but I can't tell if she is standing on it.

"I'll wait here."

She goes to her room and after thirty minutes comes back.

"I shouldn't have bothered to brush my hair."

"You look beautiful."

"Thanks," she smiles at me unforced, "thanks for coming."

"I didn't have anywhere I needed to be."

She squeezes my arm about to say something and then doesn't.

"I'll drive."

She nods at me and grabs her bag.

Hospitals and the rooms inside them have an inherent consistency in design. You could be in any hospital anywhere and see the same thing, the same lights, and the same floors. Chairs filled with the same people with the same looks on their faces.

The room faces west, and we watch the sun set during the course of our vigil. We alternate our gaze from the lengthening shadows of the dying day on the floor to the longer and longer apneas of the dying man. He was somewhere between deep, deep sleep and death. He had been a strong and large man, not just in youth but even up to a few years ago, before the inertia of the booze had overtaken what once had been a shining vitality. I didn't really know what kind of drunk he had been. Jani didn't like to talk about it. I think it was more from embarrassment than anything else. She had been disappointed in him for a long time.

It would take more than ten years before I would hear her say in casual conversation to someone her father had been an alcoholic.

He hadn't been the violent type. I knew that from having gotten drunk with him a few times. He was mainly straight vodka with a chaser of sentimentality. Every few drinks I'd have a cigarette and he'd have a small outburst about something too far gone to be helped. I think in the end he was poisoned by regret as much as by the liquor.

There were too many of us in the room, maybe ten or twelve. I was standing next to Jani. Most of the people here were friends of her mother. There were two guys there who were friends he had lost along the way. They had said this was coming for some time, and they reminisced about him when he was younger in an honorable and pleasant and sad way. They were there to watch him die, to witness a long ago predicted inevitability that they had done their part to try and prevent.

I was the only one from our circle. I don't know why she didn't invite any of the others.

She was holding my hand, neither loosely nor tightly, just resting her fingers inside mine. She was staring straight ahead and wouldn't meet my eyes. She was waiting with an iron patience and stoicism.

I was looking at him.

We stood like that for a few hours and it was quite peaceful, quiet with only a few whispers, small motions to get some coffee or switch the chairs around.

Then he roused out of the coma for one brutal and beautiful moment of life and death conjoined, staring wildly about as his mouth fought valiantly and futilely working out a sentence that had no sound.

We made eye contact for a split second. The void was all the way through him. It was all he was and all he had left, and then he lay down for good.

The Fish felt it before any of the rest of us, letting go of Jani's hand and putting his arm around her.

Then someone started crying and the flash fire of grief and finality spread across the room. Jani leaned into me and I looked at her, but she was only blinking, very fast and hard for a few moments, and then she shook me off.

She looked at me then, and I saw the wall fall for just a moment and the ghosts and void were there. Then the Fish squeezed her around the shoulders once more and let her go.

By the time the Fish had let go of her, the wall had been rebuilt.

Her mother wasn't one to stand on ceremony. He was cremated the next day. I guess she had made most of the arrangements in advance. None of it was a surprise for her; if anything, it was just a wish for what may have been rather than what was.

There was a small ceremony. It had the same people from the hospital room, maybe a few more. Not many more. Jani told the others in our group about it after the fact. She didn't make it sound like anything, and Hotrod was the only other person I ever told.

I had to drink very carefully at the wake. I didn't want to upset anyone.

Once that was over Jani's mom drover her to the airport and I started back to the Twin Cities.

The drive back was quiet and easy.

I don't know why I was so convinced she would call, but I felt it with an absolute surety. I cut some limes while the Fish contemplated another dinner of hydrated noodles. The first drink was 25/75, and I drank that one quickly more tart that alcohol with a gentle warming to contrast the ice.

I was happy I had the limes.

They aren't so necessary with vodka, but really make a difference with gin. The second drink increased the ratio and I drank it slowly. The third was closer to 40/60. I drank the third one faster than the second.

The limes were perfectly fresh, dark green and cold. When the knife cut into them, you could feel the acid in the juice as it squirted out onto your hands.

It was during the fourth drink, the perfect 50/50 split when the phone rang. I lit a cigarette and let it ring twice more and then picked it up.

"Jani."

"Yeah."

Her voice is the washed out light of metal halide bulbs burning infinite into concrete.

"How was the flight?"

"It was fine. Everything's fine."

"I'm sorry, Jani. I know …" But I don't know. I don't know anything.

Then the rush rushed out of her voice as she started to cry, the sobs breaking out of her like a burst dam.

ROAD TRIP

Summer was coming to a close, and I needed a road trip before I went back to the drudgery of the academy. It was the first summer that I hadn't gone home, and hustling shitty odd jobs in the city had left me restless.

Bonk was a mess on the phone but happy to hear I was coming. Wild was at work. I hadn't been to Madison since high school and had never partied down there. Bonk told me he had decent connections and could set us up for the weekend, but I insisted on treating.

Now a road trip can be accomplished in a lot of different ways.

Sometimes entire families will take to the freeways and byways of the Great Asylum we call home, armed with cameras, diapers, snacks, tents, and flashlights sans booze and drugs and smokes. They will camp out in beautiful, pristine parks and walk scenic routes and nature trails while talking about the sound of silence and the clarity of the water in the streams.

Crazy but true.

I'll never understand it, but what can you do? I do agree with them on one point though.

Preparation is everything.

You don't want to get to somewhere far away just in time to realize you have shot your last picture of your last roll of film and the kids haven't even seen Old Faithful yet.

I diligently brainstormed and wrote a list. Then I procured and stored the items on my list. I had just scored a handful of white crosses for free off a guy that was kicking speed.

The Adventures of Hotrod and Pilot Fish

I have a full tank of gas, a bottle of twelve-year-old scotch, a ten strip of double-dipped Black Pyramid LSD, one and a half grams of cocaine, and two six-packs of imported beer. The beer is for the drive, and to swallow the speeders down with.

Done.

Tonight's entertainment will be LSD, but I'd rather be over prepared than under.

Driving on the freeway when spun is really an experience. It's like a fucking video game and weaving through traffic at 85 to 115 is too good for words when you have enough amphetamine in you to extinguish all common sense and fear.

After a blur of tress and cars and two near death experiences I pull into Madison and start getting lost.

I've gone through the first six-pack but can't really feel anything close to a buzz through the speed. Madison is one of those towns people love because they are small and safe but at the same time seem like cities. It's a university village, and there is a surplus of youth and idealism.

It's also a warren of one way streets.

I stop for directions then drive for a while until I am lost again and then stop for directions.

If that doesn't make me fantastic husband material I fucking give up.

It takes me almost an hour to figure out how to get to the mall that Bonk and Wild both work in. I end up closer to Wild's restaurant than the arcade Bonk works in so I decide to start with her. She sees me before I see her and waves me over.

"What's a good thing to order?"

"Nothing here, I get off in an hour and then we can go somewhere."

"OK."

I swing over to the arcade Bonk works in and let him know I'm here. He has to work later than Wild does, so we make plans to rendezvous back at their apartment.

Then I swing back over to Wild.

It's kind of silly to talk about going out to dinner when you are spun on speed, but I figure I need to force something down so I don't end up with some awful energy deficit and get on TV for jumping off a bridge or some shit.

Wild and I walk out arm in arm and go back to their flat. While she is taking a shower, I mix up a Scotch on the rocks.

One thing that's never bothered me about women is the time they take to get ready. I love how a girl can take a half hour in the bathroom and look the same to everyone else in the world but herself. I love how a girl can fix her hair when nothing's broken except to be beautiful in a different way.

The smells of soap and then perfume coming out into the living room in the apartment compliment the scotch perfectly.

On the other hand, I have to give Wild some shit now and again.

"The Queen of England just called saying you're so fashionably late that you're out of style."

"Fuck you."

Goddamn I am a witty motherfucker.

She comes out with a towel wrapped around her head and goes into the room she and Bonk share. I hear her pick through a few outfits and then go back into the bathroom.

"You know how much I hate chain restaurants. Let's do something local."

"Okay, but not around here. Let's go downtown."

"You need to do the driving from now on. I am pretty much fucked."

"Ok."

She finds a place that is neither wonderful nor terrible on State Street. I force down some soup and some pieces of bread. I can't taste anything and Wild is looking at me knowing I am fucked out of my head, but not commenting on it.

"I brought some coke and ten hits of double dip. I figure we'll get cracking once Bonk finishes up."

"Okay."

I ask her a couple of questions and everything ends in an "okay" or a "sure," so I figure something is wrong. I'm a little amazed I can pick up anything at all through the chemical fog, and the fact it only took a couple hours makes me proud.

And people worry about whether or not I can handle my shit.

There is something to be said for wanting to sleep with a girl for a long time. On the whole it's a pretty frustrating experience but you do develop an intuition for moods.

"What's up, Wild?"

"Are you still in love with Jani?"

"Sure, kind of, I guess so. Why?"

"I'm still in love with Bonk and it's killing me."

"Why? What's going on?"

"I think he cheated on me. Sometimes I'm over it and sometimes I know I'll never get over it."

"Do you have proof?"

"No, not really."

"Have you confronted him about it?"

"I've tried. Look I'm not sure what's going on or how I feel about it, let's talk about something else. How does it feel to be halfway done with college?"

"Well I don't know if I'd say I'm half done."

"Come on, four year degree, you've done two years, that's halfway right?"

Wild was right about that. It had been two years.

Fucking hell, time flies. I was going to be a junior in college in the fall. That's the time when people start to finalize their decisions about the future if they haven't already.

I hadn't given it a thought.

"I guess the math's right. I haven't even declared a major."

"You should probably do that."

"I don't know what the hell I am doing in college, to be honest. All I've really done is partied and read some books."

"Isn't that what it's about?"

"Maybe, I can't shake the feeling that there's more to it though."

We smile across the table at each other in open acknowledgement that we have no idea what's going to happen in the rest of our lives.

"Well fuck it then, let's party."

I force down three mouthfuls more of her burger and swallow some water then we get up to leave. I pick up the tab and we head to the car.

"Let's go do some of that coke."

"We should save at least a few lines for Bonk."

"We will."

We head back to her place and I cut a few rails on an Ani Franco jewel case. One of the problems with trying to save cocaine for someone is that once you start using it conserving it becomes impossible, so I make us each a drink to buy some time. I look at the clock. He's going to be at least an hour. I hope he makes it.

"Let's finish these before we hit that."

"Sure."

Bonk walks in the door an hour and ten minutes later just as I am cutting up the last few rails.

"Just in time, my friend."

"Thanks."

"You're going to have to do those or I will."

He soaks them up, happy it's there. I watch him do it sad that it's gone.

I also give him three tabs of LSD. Wild drops three and I drop four. We've never been the type to take just one hit.

"It will be a very nice shower."

"Thanks."

I look at Wild with feelings of lust that my body would have zero chance of fulfilling in my current state.

Then the ceiling starts bouncing up and down. I think it's the ceiling doing that. I stare down at the floor. The fucking floor must be doing that to the ceiling.

STUPID FLOOR!

Wait, maybe it's something underneath the floor.

Have you thought about that? Is the earth itself doing it? If I look outside the window right now am I going to see the ground bouncing up against the sky? Is gravity a lie? Is it all bullshit, or is it all truth, but our brains are just too primitive to understand it so it just seems like bullshit.

It's all gotta be bullshit.

No, it can't be.

I know.

I am in love with everything in the entire world.

That's gotta be it!

That's it.

I am in love with everything and everything else is bullshit.

Bonk gets out of the shower and I can tell that he is only moments behind me on the cosmic journey.

We hang around the house for a few hours waiting for the mall to close, and then we sneak into the arcade Bonk works at.

We have officially hit light speed.

Bonk sets me up with a bunch of free plays on Time Crisis, and I blast bad guys while hallucinating like hell. It's nice. In fact, it's a great fucking time. The only problem I'm having is that I keep shooting at things that aren't there.

We finish peaking and ride the acid down for a while before deciding to go back to the house around three in the morning.

Once we get there, I mix up some drinks while Wild throws on an anime video. I love to break acid trips with booze, and I need something to take the edge off my nerves. This stuff is a little dirty and I'm hoping the booze kicks in quickly. I feel like I am made up of thinly spun wire, and some of it has been stretched to the point of invisibility.

The movie is one that we've all seen before, so there's no real problem with talking over it or whispering or being so fucked that you can't even follow the plot of a film you've seen a hundred times.

Bonk and Wild are whispering. He keeps pawing at her stomach and boobs, and she keeps pushing his hand away.

How he can fuck on this cocktail is beyond me, I couldn't get it up right now if I my life depended on it.

I watch animated ninjas get cut up ten at a time by a lone master swordsman. I love the over the top gratuitous violence of animated manga.

Then things get fun.

I see Wild get up and start moving. Her arms pinwheel in a scream of how we come together, her legs whisper how we fall apart as she makes her way away from Bonk. The void is full in her eyes. Bonk looks like a confused idiot who wanted to say one thing for some reason and ended up saying something else entirely.

Wild hits the hallway already in a jog, and I hear the door slam.

I'm guessing that the infidelity rumor has somehow been confirmed, but I am too fucked up to take any intuition of mine as credible.

Bonk is staring at me and his eyes are saying bail me out.

I am on five pills of speed, four hits of acid, and ten lines of coke and probably drunk as fuck though to be honest I still can't feel the booze.

And people worry about whether or not I can handle my shit.

The Pilot Fish exits the apartment. He divines the route that a distraught girl is most likely to run when she is flipping out. Then he multiplies that route by drugs. It takes a few tries and then sees her about 300 yards away walking with her head down. Her hands are at her sides balled into fists. The Fish starts sneaking up on her and would have gone unnoticed but she flips her hair over her shoulder and sees us out of the corner of her eye.

She snaps around towards us then. Her hair flies up and

the street light crashes through the blond wave in a thousand shimmering rainbows around two blue eyes that look like ocean pools flecked with gold.

It's the most beautiful thing I have ever seen.

I stare at her overwhelmed. I am Actaeon in awe of Diana, and it is worth dying for.

She takes off at a sprint.

Game on and we rush her. It takes a few moments and then some before the Fish catches her. We come together without any real grace. We hit the deck in a mess of blond hair and concrete and LSD. We roll around for second. She is biting me hard on my shoulder and flailing. There are words in the air between us that don't make any sense.

I squeeze her hard and after a while she stops struggling. I let go of her carefully keeping her in easy grabbing distance. She stands away from me and stares into my eyes. Until now I didn't know how hard she had been crying

"I'm OK now."

"I know that's not true."

"It doesn't have to be, I just have to be OK."

"OK."

Then she hugs hard against me once.

"He was my fucking first. I fucking loved him."

There is no love for anyone left anywhere in the whole wide world.

Then she lets go of me and starts walking back towards the apartment. I don't say anything, I just follow her home.

And people wonder if I can handle my shit.

We get back into the apartment.

Bonk is there looking lost in his own place. He takes a step towards Wild in some effort to comfort, console or control and she looks at him with eyes cut from glacial ice. "Get the fuck away from me."

He folds under her gaze and retreats to the bedroom.

She sits on the couch and waves me to the other end. She looks at me and then looks away. It's time for me to say something, but I can't.

I can use beautiful words and I can use words beautifully, but I can't find any of them. I can't think of anything worth saying. All I can do is light a cigarette and ride the chemical waves crashing inside my body.

Hours later I watch her finally fall asleep on the edge of the couch wrapped around the cushion with a comforter pulled to her lips.

I AM HOTROD

I am tall, dark, and handsome. I have Serbo-Croatian ancestry, and as you may know, the Balkans are home to the most beautiful people in the world. Clinton wouldn't be dropping bombs over there if he had ever seen *one* of the girls, I promise you. He'd be learning a new language and telling Hillary he had some diplomacy to attend to. You could go there and see what it's like, or I could give you a taste right now.

I am Hotrod, aka the Anal Sniper.

I have a brand new Mitsubishi Eclipse. I have money. I have a nice apartment furnished to my own taste and my taste is good. I have a brand-name wallet that cost more than the money you have in yours. There is a certain type of woman who finds this irresistible. By a certain type I mean all of them.

AND HE'S NOTCHED THE BELT AGAIN!

These bitches have sex with me because they want to embrace what I have earned, which is why I fuck them in the ass. It's the only way for them to learn. They deserve it. I'm doing this to help them. It's quite easy, though it does require a bit of spit. All you have to do is get the angle right and then you are IN!

After making cash assfucking is what I do best. I look at it like a service: you were a bored girl leading a boring life and then you met Hotrod.

Hotrod changed you.

He changed you for the better. Now you know what it's like to feel a cock rubbing against your kidneys.

Anal sex has to be the last legal and selfish pleasure

left to men. If I ever meet a woman who likes it, I will have to marry her or quit it completely. I hear those Bible beater chicks call it saddle backing and do it to preserve their virginity, but do they like it?

I can't fucking stand fundamentalist Christians, but I sure would like to try one. I think that just made my personal conquest list, can I saddle back a Bible bitch?

Wish me luck!

Don't get me wrong, I like girls. I'm just not into this poet bullshit that the Pilot Fish subscribes to. I don't buy any of this nonsense about brains or character. Ugly girls have just as much and more of that and you don't see them getting picked up. You don't see a line of guys spending money on them. No, you see the fucking opposite. I am into tits that are still high and asses that are tight. The rest can come later. Someone else can wait for that shit.

I feel sorry for the Fish. I feel sorry for his dick. Most underused organ in the human experience. He could donate his cock for transplant and motherfuckers would think it was store bought, that's how new it would be. You're already too late for his liver though. If his liver and his dick switched roles for a day the whole city would get raped. Homeless dudes under the overpass would get raped and not know what the fuck happened. That's how bad that would be. All booze and no pussy makes for a dull boy. I need to get that kid laid.

It's no wonder he votes libertarian. If it weren't for the gun, he'd have no penis at all.

My cock, on the other hand, deserves some description. I am eight inches, soft. I am your personal porno fantasy. It aint just to look at either, I rock up like the crack those worthless junkies are smoking on Franklin Avenue. I will be thirteen inches inside you and I am wide, broad abeam, to borrow a nautical term. I have the kind of dick that makes you think twice and then the pupils get all dilated. International pussy tastes just as sweet so for you Europeans, that's 20.32 cm soft and 33.02 cm hard.

You got that?

I ain't weighed it yet, but when I do, I'll tell you–and in kilos.

Now it's only fair to talk politics, seeing as I brought the Fish's up. Me, I don't give a fuck about politics, and voting is how adults write to Santa. Fuck the Democrats, fuck the Republicans, Nader, get fucked, and fuck Ken Starr. I'm not green, and I am no fucking hippie, but Clinton, my man, we need to talk.

The only problem you have is that you tend to come off like a used-car salesman, but damn you got some game with the suburb mothers or "older bitches" as I call them. But please, explain this to me, why the chubby Polack? Come on brother, you are the President. All the idiot soccer moms are talking about you like the second coming of Kennedy, that motherfucker had MONROE. That's a name that deserves to have every letter capitalized, fucking hot ass bitch, damn! On top of that, he was married to Jackie O. If I had one political fantasy in my life, it would be having those girls double up on me.

This is your legacy, Bill.

This is why you were smoking weed in Oxford while my dad was dodging bullets in Vietnam, and you're sticking it to some overweight secretary, fuck me, and then you say you're not even sticking it! REALLY! For shame! Listen, I know you had some success down in Arkansas, and that's cool, but you're in D.C. now. My man, you're in the motherfucking capital! In D.C. I'm thinking that rubbing yourself to orgasm on some girl's dress and dildoing her with a cigar isn't how it's done. That's not high style brother. That's not East Coast at all.

USE YOUR COCK!

Please, listen to Brother Hotrod. You can trust me on this one.

Don't get defensive! I get it. I understand you want to defend yourself. I understand that it's all bullshit and theatre. Brother, believe me, I get it. Some of your loudest accusers in

Congress are probably banging their secretaries between hearings. It's all about who gets caught and who slides through.

Bill, I get it.

No one is happy when they get caught with their paw in the honey jar, but you need to chill your girl out. Please, check that bitch. If I see another interview of her saying your penis is in the middle of a right wing conspiracy I'm going to throw up on the television.

Look Bill, I sympathize, I know why you did it. I wouldn't fuck her with your dick either, and it's obvious that you've had this figured out for some time. I'm guessing that your little girl was the product of some nice scotch mixed with bongo beats, maybe a few tokes—right? I mean I know you inhaled if you were going down on that.

I get it, but now you need to step up your game.

You can do it!

It's breaking my heart to have you go down as the only President in the history of the country to half ass infidelity. You already told one awesome lie; now it's time to look the American people in the face and say that you fucked that Polack like the Russians had launched the missiles.

It's time to pull a 360 on the media and the conservatives and just take what's been obvious for some time and slam it DOWN! I'm not saying put out a sex tape, I'm not saying it's time for Presidential Porno, I'm not. Well, it's something we could talk about.

Call me, I know you're secret service dudes can get my number for you.

Anyway, enough about politics. Just listen to me, no props in the pink, you'll thank me for it once you've tried it.

You went wrong, bro, and that's OK: just own it, be proud of it, use it. Describe it! Half the bitches that voted for you are applying to intern at the White House now that they know what comes with the job. They all get wet when you talk anyway, give them something to get wet about.

It's ok to go a little wrong now and again. I voted for you

The Adventures of Hotrod and Pilot Fish

baby and I got your back.

Now when I go wrong, well you got some idea of how I do things. I get to cheating on a girl and before you know it, both bitches are sore and hating on me and wanting more.

On the other hand, if you want to talk sex and politics, you need to cross the aisle. The liberals may treat their wedding vows like campaign trail promises, but it's the conservatives that really get down.

If you ever hear about some hard-core shit like sex clubs and gallons of oil spread over plastic and those thick leather masks, my money says it's a Republican doing it. I'm guessing you have to really, really *believe* it's wrong to enjoy getting completely kinked.

A lot of Democrats swing, but it's that minority of Republicans who really get their fucking freak on.

I'm not really a kink. I'll do whatever, and if a bitch wants to dump some wax on me before giving it up, I'm game. She wants to bring a friend to bed that's fine, but I'm fucking her too. I look at myself as a sexual mercenary, and let me tell you, there is a shortage of fuckers like me out there. This is a good thing; there's not a lot of room at the top. This is a one-Hotrod town, and I am that Hotrod you heard about.

I'm a sexual optimist. Say a bitch has thick tuberous arms that go all jiggly when she runs, well, I just look at another part of her. I'll *walk* that bitch. Say a girl is fat. Well then, she has to have some knockers to go with that ass, right? I mean, if there is an old lady out there with a fat ass and no tits, well then I'll just have to drink until she starts to look good or someone better looking comes into the bar. I am an equal opportunity kind of motherfucker, you know what I'm saying? I do what I do best under the anthem of democracy. Oh, and it's not like I care, but I make those bitches come.

WHY ARE YOU STILL CALLING ME!

While we are on the topic of optimism and equality, let it be understood Hotrod is no racist, the only color I see is pink, and if there's some brown, black, white, red, or whatever around it, so fucking what, that's just some lace on the dress. I'm spitting on it and hitting it and walking away from it.

Oh, and by the way, fuck condoms.

Fuck fucking condoms!

I don't know who got the idea sex had something to do with balloons, but they sure fucked up. Clowns in circuses blow up balloons for kids. Balloons are for entertainment and being made into fucked up looking animals.

You know what I'm saying?

Sex is an adult thing and must be dealt with appropriately. Except for hookers, wear a condom with the hookers. I didn't for a while, and I started having HIV anxiety attacks and shit. Those didn't stop for months.

You don't need that.

Now when I go on the prowl, when I am driving the square of love from Franklin and Park to Chicago and Lake, I tend to stop off and buy some rubbers. I hate them, but you need to make some sacrifices in life.

Look, one more thing, the Fish isn't a hero. Half this shit never even happened and he embellishes like fuck, and if he is a hero, then we are living in the new fucking middle ages and nobody needs that.

Another thing about the Fish, don't take him out when you are looking to score. All this bullshit about love, love, love and poetry, poetry, poetry. The only girls who are digging that bullshit are too ugly or crazy to score a self-disciplined man with some cash flow. Believe me, when it comes to women, the spiritual is definitely playing second fiddle to the material. All this spiritual finding yourself bullshit comes after the hubby's been kidded, castrated and the steady allowance is locked down.

Fucking romantics never get laid. That's why they are so mooney all the time and complaining about "true love" and other nonsense. True love is what you get when the bitch doesn't ask for your number and lets herself out in the morning.

The Adventures of Hotrod and Pilot Fish

No other definition will do.

Another thing and this is totally on the side, always get the bitch's house and cell phone number. You don't want her calling you from a number you don't know and end up having to talk to her when you're obviously with someone else.

That never ends well, just ask my main man Brother Bill C.

You may need to use clues on the phone to remember who she is. This way you can screen her out when you're on the make, and you'll know who to ring up if you strike out and have to settle for a booty call, and you know what I mean when I say booty. One more thing, player: if you got a bitch at the crib, don't leave your cell phone out where she can get her hands on it. If you got a new girl on the side, don't put her real name into the phone, call her the name of some buddy of yours. Bitches are sneaky and they will go through your shit, so protect yourself.

Don't be that guy who spends all his time fighting with bitches instead of fucking them.

Oh, pussy alert! Some bitches just walked in! Take your coat off slowly baby I wanna see how far out your tits push your shirt.

Oh fuck girl, put it back on. Go back outside and take your friends with you, OUCH! You can stalk the snow pig 365 in this city, but you don't have too! Those are bottom of the glass girls that you really only want to ignore as long as you can before your cock forces you to talk to them.

Talking to girls is easy, but listening to girl chatter is a fucking chore! You have to learn to filter out the bullshit and whining while staying alert for key words or tones that show where she's headed. You want to be there before she is. Women like to be anticipated, but they hate being second guessed, so choose your moves carefully.

All bullshit aside all the bullshit that they say about communication aint bullshit.

Every bitch on earth is a virgin until she meets me. Even

the whores on Lake Street get all squiggly and giggly when I lay it down.

I get a little worn out with the feminist shit, but that doesn't stop me from fucking feminists. I've certainly fucked more feminists than Bible beaters, though I am looking to change that.

But the politics does get a little tiring. I mean I get it, if a dude shows you his cock at a bus stop, that's fucked up and he should have his ass beat, but when I buy you a drink in a bar, I don't give a fuck about your star sign or whether or not you want to live in a geodesic dome in the mountains. When I tell you that it sounds interesting, or I am a Taurus or I love the same shows you love, you need to understand.

I AM LYING!

You don't dress like this every day and I don't talk like this every day. We're just on stage and I am on script just like you're in costume.

Later you will tell your girlfriends as you stand because your bottom is still a little sore that you "feel" lied to. There's no feeling about it, it's a fact. Also, if I invite you over to my place to watch a movie with me, I don't give a fuck about the movie. I chose that movie because it is the current most successful cinematic sex doorway. That's all.

Bitch, you have no idea how many times I watched Titanic.

I will watch Lifetime with you, and we can talk about how hard it is to be a woman and a lawyer at the same time, and how rich and complicated the multilayered competitive-cooperative relationships between women are, and if you could turn up the volume so I can hear it better, the conversation will be easier, believe me.

I'm not all bad.

I'll go down on you, girl, and you won't even have to ask me. I'll stare into the void between your legs in reverie and wonder and silence.

I'll never criticize it, I promise.

The Adventures of Hotrod and Pilot Fish

I love pussy and I hate drugs. I need booze, bitches, and smokes. Baby, my engine is always on and if you like the way it purrs, wait until you hear it ROAR! If there's anything in the world sweeter than pussy, I don't want to know about it.

Then, once all the required and pointless chit-chat is over, you know what I am going to do. Let me tell you what I am going to do: I am going to fuck you in the style you prefer before I flip you over and ass fuck you.

Don't give me that look.

Fair is fair after all.

Oh, fuck, the Fish just walked in. I wonder what fucking drug he's on this time. He looks glazed. He's way into the variety there, sometimes I wish he would just settle down and be a junky or a hippie or whatever. Instead, all he says is, "I'm fucked," and then who knows what's going to happen, he could get all weepy and huggy if it's the E or really fucking aggressive and nasty if it's the meth, or straight sleepy if it's those prescription painkillers again. Well, there's booze to drink and I have to score and he's just going to be talking and talking and talking.

My fucking wife is trying to call me again. Can't that bitch understand that I need my space?

Let's have a look at the bar.

Today I am wearing a pink shirt. My hair is styled and is holding well. I have a pair of $300 designer jeans on, and I am an Atkins man with occasional exercise, if you know what I mean. I am wearing a few pieces of jewelry, silver and white gold. Everything goes together well, mildly metrosexual, with a few visible tattoos to counterbalance that shit.

I am totally pulling it off.

I scan the bar before the last hero of the twentieth century comes over here and conversates my dick to the size of an acorn with his bullshit philosophy and romantic jabber.

Things are looking decent. There are a few worth talking to. Now I've got to perambulate, catch the eye, and get a vibe. Just about every woman between the ages of fifteen and

Tom Nelson

fifty is worth fucking once.
      None are worth seeing again.

THE BROTHEL

Hotrod had decided that I needed to get laid.

His first suggestion was to get wasted and drive Franklin to Chicago then Chicago to Lake and back round again until we found a hooker. I had nixed that idea in one of the few acts of good sense I had that year.

Undeterred by my recalcitrance, he had discovered a brothel that had what he called both class and hot girls. He left it at that, and when I tried to question him further he launched into a lecture about the emancipating nature of prostitution.

I think he was feeling sorry for me.

He knew my sexual history thoroughly as he had witnessed all of it firsthand. I had lost my virginity to a sophomore during my senior year of high school that Hotrod had clued me onto. The experience had been sufficiently clumsy and embarrassing to both of us to completely extinguish the crush she had on me. My freshman year of college had involved two forays into romance. A one night stand that existed somewhere deep inside an alcohol fog that I really couldn't piece together very clearly. I remember going to a party with Hotrod and leaving with a girl that seemed nice. I can remember being a bit brackish with her the next morning mainly because the hang over I had was nearly life threatening. After that there had been a short relationship that had started with the theory that I was just depressed and had ended abruptly when my persisting love for Jani had been confirmed.

That journey of discovery lasted all of three months and five days.

She was a nice girl and in retrospect I take the blame for the relationship failing. I should have been clear with the impossibility of it from the beginning, but loneliness makes a selfish coward of all of us at least once in a while. Looking back on that and her tolerance of my chemical adventures I think that she must have really liked me.

I had just started my third year of college and freshman year felt very far away for how little time had actually passed.

Summer was waning into autumn and while the days were still nice the nights already carried the promise of frost. I looked at the new crop of college freshman girls like an alien invasion that was better managed through flight than confrontation. I didn't share any of the enthusiasm of my fellow upper classmen at all on that point. The girls in my classes seemed way too sober for me and they often insisted on talking about a future that I felt comfortable discussing only in vague terms.

I hadn't been kissed since the third month and fourth day of two years ago.

I was pretty OK with it, but it bothered Hotrod in a serious way. Hotrod labored under the illusion that men and women are always in a state of competition over who controls who and what. My pining over Jani without having fucked her meant that she had power over me. I was in his eyes both a cuckold and a castrate. He had asked me point blank if I jerked off to thoughts of her and when I said yes he almost went into apoplectic shock.

"That bitch house broke you without ever even being home."

"You could call her a bitch again."

That conversation had led us into our current discussion.

Hotrod was extolling the benefits of brothels to me as we slowly sipped Long Islands.

In the spirit of brevity I have paraphrased his position thusly:

Patronizing brothels has inherent advantages over working the streets. The biggest is that you don't have to go out and buy some crack after you pick up a girl. That is always a headache, and it adds some additional risk exposure to the whole project.

Brothels also carry legitimate security which makes the experience with the girls much more relaxing. Brothel girls don't have the same concerns that a lot of the girls on the streets have. Plus, it's weird to have sex with a girl who's really nervous that you might try to kill her.

That takes away from the intimacy of it.

I kind of did a double take on that one. I had never heard Hotrod use the word "intimacy" before.

He continues on using a balanced approach to the argument. We now move to the replies section of the thesis.

The cost is really the only downside of the brothel. Girls on the street have the best price point if you're purely insisting on a pussy to dollar ratio. Brothels tend to be non-negotiable and you end up paying a higher cost due to the more extensive overhead involved in the operation.

While he was rambling on I was thinking of Jani. I had held her for a little while when we had slept together and I was thinking over how she had felt. So skinny and soft, but then so strong when she had pushed me away.

I had a feeling that more bad things were coming when Hotrod pulled me out of my thoughts with what I thought was a rude question.

"Are you high on anything?"

"Dude, I'm high on life."

"Oh fuck you, anyway, don't get too wasted. I don't want you to make a mess of yourself."

I don't know that I've ever been too wasted, but seeing as he was paying for most of this anyway, I figured I'd just let him drive as far as the liquor consumption went. I had swallowed a speeder earlier in the day, but that was just for work.

Honestly, I felt fine.

Hotrod concludes with:

Fortunately, you have a well-heeled friend that manages these expenses for you.

Thus cutting short any of the potentially damning elements in the replies section of his argument.

I'm sold.

He then motions to me that it's time to roll.

"I've got to work early tomorrow and want to get my fuck on without making a late night out of it."

"OK, let's put theory into practice."

I don't't have a good reason to go with him, but I don't have a good reason not to either, and he was so determined to help me with what he was sure was wrong with me that I thought, fuck it, best to let him be a friend.

We get in his car and he drives us to a neighborhood on the North side of downtown that I'm not familiar with.

It's a nondescript massage parlor stuffed between a gay bar and a vacuum repair store.

Hotrod tells me that's the secret to its success, no one thinks the guys around here are straight. The cops see all the male traffic and just drive on in disgust.

I guess location really is everything.

We walk in and I have this moment where I think we're going to be asked a code word or Hotrod is going to do some secret hand shake with the thug that provides security, but it's nothing like that. Hotrod has been here way too many times for any bullshit like that.

He nods to the proprietor and the proprietor calls out the girls.

Hotrod and I look them over. I choose a tall, full hipped blond with lots of curves and crazy nails.

She is the opposite of Jani.

Hotrod picks one and then pays for both of us up front and in cash. I wonder for a moment where all this entrepreneurship will go if we ever become a cashless society.

This isn't the kind of place that takes cards.

The Adventures of Hotrod and Pilot Fish

We go our separate ways at this point. My girl leads me by the hand down a hallway to a shower. I haven't held a girls hand since my tumultuous freshman romance.

She's giving me the tour like we're about to move in together.

She tells me, "I know you're friend but not you. Have you ever come here before?"

"No. This is my first time here."

I try to imply in my answer that I have experience in brothels. I can't tell from her expression if she's buying it.

The Fish has always felt brothels beat walking the streets at least for the sake of the girl's safety, but even with all the time travel he was never a patron. He doesn't have any experience to loan me on this one.

She motions me towards the shower and I get undressed and get in. The warm water combines nicely with what's left of my buzz.

There isn't a towel, so I ask for one and she brings it to me. She has a really nice figure and nice eyes. She's wearing a tennis dress that ends mid-thigh and manages to cover everything in a glorious array of hints.

I dry off and put my clothes back on. I walk across the hall and open the door. She is lying on her side facing me completely nude. For a moment I am quite taken aback, and then I pull myself together. I look at her.

She's beautiful.

I take my clothes off again and lie down next to her.

"The only rule is that you don't kiss me on the lips."

With that answer she rather nicely lets me know that my complete lack of experience in this situation is accepted and understood.

"Can I kiss you on the neck or the …" and I fumble for a moment for the right word, I don't want to say tits because that seems kind of vulgar, chest seems kind of juvenile, areola a little clinical or even pretentious, and she bails me out.

"Of course."

I do that for a while.

She has incredible boobs that are the perfect combination of firm and soft. I lick the edges of her nipples slowly. I rest my head for a moment between her breasts and feel wrapped up with the warmth of her. I want to go down on her, but I think that would probably be a breach of the hooker-John terms of use agreement.

I understand that I can't turn her on in any real sense, but it still feels very nice to kiss a girls chest again.

Then there is a small moment of confusion because there really isn't a good foreplay strategy for these situations, but she's a true professional and takes over gracefully guiding me through the steps without pushing or dragging me. She gets a condom and some lubricant. She uses her mouth to get me to the right place and I am just fine with her being on top of me.

We go like that for a while.

I like the way she smells.

I would really, really like her to kiss me. I would really like that.

"Did you come?"

"Yes."

"OK, let's get another condom then. I don't want any accidents to happen."

"OK."

While she's pulling the old one off and putting the new one on she asks if I would like to be on top for the second round.

"Yes."

That goes nicely and I accidentally kiss her on the lips once, and she brushes it off without a warning. She gently moves her arms against me and whispers.

"You're squeezing me really hard, can you let go a little?"

"Sure, sorry." I move to let go of her.

"You can hold me, just not so tightly."

"OK, sorry."

"It's OK."

I relax without letting go and feel the soft pressure of her boobs pushed against my skin. I dream for a moment that this could be every night or every morning, like the half sense of sleep you have while waiting for the snooze to alarm. Then I work up a little bit and finish off again.

She takes that condom off and throws it away.

"How are we doing on time?"

"About five minutes or so."

I sit up and rub my hands across her back until she tells me it's time to go.

After we get dressed she looks at me, "You're with someone aren't you?"

"I'm not with her."

JANI'S VISIT

There wasn't any rush in her voice at all, just a gentle, beautiful resonance that made each mundane syllable magical in the cascade of blood in my ears.

"Fish, you up for a visit?"

"Definitely, what are we celebrating?"

"I'm graduating early. All I have left are some papers, and I can do that from home. I need to get out of this city. I don't want to come back until commencement."

"This is perfect. The Fish Bowl is thoroughly cozy and completely free of charge. Minneapolis isn't much like Chicago, but we still have bars."

"You still drinking a lot?"

"You'll enjoy the parks. It's quiet as well. There's even a museum somewhere."

"Okay, thanks. I'll take the bus. I'll see you Friday."

"Cool, I'll be waiting."

She had taken classes right through the summers. She had stuck with both the music and European studies degrees. She was writing lyrics and melodies now and some of it was forced and some of it was beautiful.

I got a hold of Hotrod and let him know to keep Friday night open.

I went about hustling some money to spend on her. I was still kind of stuck in the economic problem of using too much of my money on using. I had a paycheck coming the next Monday from one of the temp jobs that I had landed. It looked like I would have no choice but to kite some checks and risk some overdraft fees.

The Adventures of Hotrod and Pilot Fish

I spent the week getting wasted as frugally as possible.

Friday morning found me getting up tired after a sleepless Thursday night. I spend the day downtown by the bus station saying no to panhandlers waiting for Hotrod to finish work. We meet up with about an hour to kill.

"Let's get a drink."

"Splendid idea."

Hotrod was disappointed that his cure hadn't worked on me, but at the end of the day we were all friends even if men and women were locked in some dreadful never ending all-consuming competition.

We kill two beers and then head back to the station. The bus from Chicago pulls in and I look along the windows for some sign of her. I see her as soon as she stands up from her seat and follow her all the way until she's standing in front of us.

"Oh, you brought Hotrod!"

"Yeah, it's getting to the point that I can't leave the house without him."

She gives him a hug and then we hold each other, and the Pilot Fish kisses her on the cheek, lightly. There is the same perfume brushed through her hair, mixed with that communal smell of the bus and the worn-out way you feel when you've sat too long. I wanted to pick her up and carry her home.

"You're lookin' good, girl."

"You are too."

"One of us is lying."

"The bars close in four hours. Let's get our roll on."

"No rush, Hotrod."

It's like old times. A dash of high school nostalgia combined with the freedom of adulthood. It feels fantastic.

In our time apart I have only fallen more in love with her.

We play pool and we haven't gotten any better in the time spent away from each other. We make our own atmosphere at each of the places we go to.

The vodka, the jokes, the sound of her laughter.

It's like stepping back into the comfort of past times and into the optimistic future of love simultaneously. What has been seems to flow seamlessly into what could be like a river with a gentle current.

We make a full night of it and end up closing down downtown. We say goodbye to Hotrod and get a cab back to my place. It's a little slippy getting upstairs and into the apartment, but there aren't any accidents.

Once the Fish closes the door, Jani holds him, and the unscripted because it was the dream I always woke up early from begins.

It was the first time and as soon as it started I knew somehow that it was the last time.

I was holding her, the booze was thin in my blood, and I could taste the lime from the vodka tonics on her breath. The smoke in her hair smelled fresh and warm, and the perfume hadn't faded yet.

I nibbled her shoulder and kissed her slowly from there to her neck, and then held her for a moment.

We had no rush, no sense of immediacy at all.

I took my clothes off slowly, and then helped her do the same, each piece of fabric opening up more skin, each movement and moment expanding desire.

It had been three Augusts since that night playing cards in the basement, and a lot and nothing had happened in that time.

We weren't kids anymore.

It went on for some time, a couple of hours of wandering back and forth.

We gave each other all that we could, her on top of me, and me on top of her. The sweat and saliva on her breasts, the brown nipples against the white skin, her dyed black hair falling all over me, stuck to her in some places, and in some places free.

I said her name and then said nothing.

It was reunion and dissolution. We were saying hello again for the first time in a long time. We made the most of it, and after a few cries we were at rest.

She curled into me, and I slept with her in my arms.

I didn't feel her wake up, didn't notice anything at all, until I felt her missing in some way that only an animal would. I was coming to slowly when I heard the glass break and the scream.

The scream was some kind of sound that you couldn't imagine being made by a human being, like all the air in a deep well rushing out through a whistle of steel and crystal and pain and hate.

That kind of got the Fish swimming again. He jumped up and ran to the bathroom. What he saw amazed him.

It was Jani, but not the Jani we'd ever known. It was a wild and crazy Jani. A Jani of rage and mystery. She was punching the mirror, tears all over her, stark naked, sweat and blood running in lines from the impacts of her fists. The mirror cracked every time that she hit it. With each hit it multiplied her.

Jani is all over the mirror.

Jani is all over the floor.

Everywhere I look I see her.

In some places just a streak of black and some just a streak of red, and she keeps on hitting it. Jani is facing us from twenty places at once. Jani in a fury such as the Fish had never seen. With all of her I saw the void. The void multiplied as the glass was divided. It reflected up and between us in the blood and light. Then many of the Janis disappeared, the pieces too shattered and too small to hold any of her and then washed out in blood, drowned on little slivers of silver.

She stared at me, wild and free and broken and trapped. She smiled at me, her teeth reflecting the light like a scar across her face.

"Careful, its sharp."

I had no idea what to do with her, so I put my arms

around her not sure how she would respond. She started to laugh until the laughter transformed into hysteria and finally, after some minutes, fatigue.

I tried to do the right thing.

The Fish picked her up. She wasn't the type who would go to a hospital, and no one called the cops in my neighborhood. The Fish carried her back to bed. Then he got some gauze and cotton balls. Some of the cuts would scar and some would not. The Fish used antiseptic on all of them and applied pressure to the deeper ones. It took a while for the blood to stop running. Some of the cuts were more resistant than others. She had cuts on her feet from the glass on the floor. He cleaned them and covered them up. He kissed her on the middle toe of her right foot.

There wasn't any blood there.

Then he went back to the bathroom and swept up all the glass and wiped up all the blood.

The last thing he did was wash her blood from his hands. It had dried in some places. In others it was thickening and turning black. He scrubbed it all off.

He pulled two beers from the fridge. The clock said 4:17 AM.

He opened a beer for her. She had to hold it with both hands. She was no longer crying hard, just sniffling a little bit.

She started by telling us that she had never reported the rape. After he had raped her she had just taken a long shower and wished for it to never happen to anyone again.

I was the first male that she had let touch her since.

She was as surprised with how she felt about everything as I was.

The Fish touched her face gently with the wash cloth while she talked. There was still some blood there.

I didn't have anything to say, so I just listened to her.

I had no reply to make, so I just listened to her.

Everything was white and red, black and white, pink and amber. I was drowning in the colors of her. I was enslaved by her pain and enraptured by her persona. I loved her with everything I had, somehow never knowing until that moment how fragile and strong she was.

She was completely present and totally unavailable.

I knew then in flash that I would never have her, and that no one ever really could. She saw it in my face, understood, smiled as a small tear, the last one she would shed that night, slid down her left cheek.

"Fish, thank you."

"It's nothing."

"So, how have you been?" She asked with a laugh that shivered.

I put two cigarettes in my mouth and lit both of them and then I handed one to her.

"I'm fine, I'm surviving."

"You still write?"

"Yeah."

"About me?"

"Yeah."

"Please don't tell them what I look like. Please, can you do that for me?"

"Yes, I can do that."

"Will you write about this?"

"Yes."

"OK."

"Will you tell me who he is?"

"So you can hurt him?"

"Yes."

"No."

"OK."

We quit talking. The beers restored a little bit of the buzz that had been fading away in sleep. The Fish sat next to her and held her carefully all the while wondering who she really was, what else wasn't known.

She went on slowly choosing her words carefully sometimes and stumbling over them other times.

She had met him at a party, and he had seemed so nice. He walked her back to her apartment. He told jokes that were funny and he was clever. He paid for the drinks, and it had been so fun that she had more that she normally would. She had let him into her apartment, and they had kissed. She had planned to talk about books and play her guitar for him. That was as far as she had wanted that night to go, but he had taken the opening of the door as yes and after some struggle it became clear that he wasn't taking no.

I think her making love to me that night was finding a way to remember the dead without having to live in death. It wasn't over though. The Fish could feel it clearly inside her, it may have helped but it wasn't anywhere near close to over.

She looked at me and said that when she tried to talk to some people about it that they had just told her she was drunk.

When she told me that she looked into my eyes and the void was full between us.

She stayed a week and by the time she left, all she had on her hands were a few Band-Aids amid a sea of scabs.

Amber, black, and red like some spider web gone wrong, starting from her knuckles and streaming up toward her wrists.

I held her at the bus station. It was just the two of us. We kissed once.

I let it linger praying it could last forever.

THE AUDITION

Winter had passed into spring without anything more than a long bout of seasonal depression. I found myself at the end of my third year of college reading the results of my end of sequence exams in German.

Pass, Fail, Pass, Fail.

I figured that shit should average out, but when I called and asked I was told that any individually failed element fucked the whole thing.

I had more than enough credits to finish my degree, but passing the test was required to graduate. Based on my experience there I was thinking my road in higher education had come to a dead end.

I looked things over and said fuck it.

It was now time to enter the workforce.

I applied at a bunch of places, and got a few interviews. When it came to describing my education I used phrases like "in lieu of" and "vis-à-vis" which I figured sounded erudite. I thought my interview polish would make up for my lack of credentials. I lied about graduating on my resume, I figured with a degree in Philosophy no one would bother to check.

Not a single motherfucker had offered me a job.

My using had accelerated after I realized that the same temp bullshit I had done as a student was here to stay.

You would think with the amount of meth I was doing my place would be spotless, the sheets pressed and all the rest of that bullshit, but it was exactly the opposite. You could smell rotting food all through the apartment from dishes that needed to have the dust blown off them to even start washing.

The whole process of coming down had become so unpleasant that I had to resort to a cocktail of pharmaceuticals to soften the landing.

Introducing benzodiazepines into my life had emancipated me from memory which I found fantastic, but not knowing why I was where I was wasn't without an awkward moment or two.

In the last month I had awoken to find myself in a park, a movie theatre and my closet.

Of those the park definitely offered the best rest.

Anyway, I had told Hotrod about my difficulties competing in the softest labor market in 25 years and he had offered advice that I found completely unconstructive.

"Quit poisoning yourself with speed."

After I had explained to him that I had sorted out all the issues with the ice by adding pharmies to my patterns of use, he had come round to a more helpful perspective.

It was then that Hotrod introduced me to Sam.

Sam was a sweet girl with nice knockers, and a surprisingly shapely waist. Hotrod said that her boobs were 100% natural. He also told me that she was a size four, and I nodded like I knew what the fuck that meant.

She supplemented her stripping income with work in pornography. Nothing too serious, soft core lesbian clips and some strip shows. She'd appeared in some phone sex ads as well.

In the commercials she would rub the telephone cord up and down between her boobs.

That was her thing, like I said she had amazing tits.

She was completely comfortable with Hotrod's marriage and seemed to have a pretty relaxed attitude towards life in general. More importantly though she was all about getting us into the industry.

You see, we were to become porno stars.

The only thing she told me about it was that the work didn't pay anything like most people thought.

To which I said, "it's gotta beat temping."

Today was the big day and I was kind of nervous.

I'd been told that you wanted to research the industry of your prospective employers before going to the interview. I only had dial up which made it a little difficult to get much of a survey done.

To make up for the slow download speed I had started walking the sixteen blocks to Sexworld and jerking off in the porno booths they had there. I'd pan handle for singles on my way through downtown and then dump them one by one into the porno machine.

My favorite porn stars are Leanna Fox and Chasey Lain and I spent most of my quarters trying to find videos featuring one or the other of them. I loved Leanna because she had the devil in her smile and it convinced me to always live in the passion of the moment, and I loved Chasey because there was a dusky sadness in her eyes that had convinced me that we were kindred spirits. I had a dream that after we nailed this gig and then the next one and then became stars and then went to California with huge swollen cocks and then I would star in a threesome with Chasey and Leanna and MY LIFE WOULD BE COMPLETE!

Then I could throw myself off an overpass and let the cars run over me in bliss.

If I couldn't find a film with one of my two angels in it I would survey the 80 some channels they had in the booths with a critical eye, looking for strokes, techniques, what seemed to work and what didn't. I was almost college educated and had taken an aesthetics class, so I figured I could critique this work as well as anyone.

Threesomes always seemed to be out of balance, but I blamed the directors for those errors. Threesome from the 70's though deserved their own category of artistic critique, it seemed like every one of those ended in a double penetration or a multiple cocks in one pussy penetration and that shit seemed almost more Freudian than erotic. It took a minute to process that shit. I watched a 70s threesome where the guy on top in the anal position of the double penetration pulled out and came over the entire mess below him and the guy in the vagina penetration position just kept ramming along in the bath of his buddy's cum. Given Hotrod's predilection I knew where I would be in a scene like that.

Still that would be more pussy than I'd gotten in the last year and no one said this business was easy.

Lesbian material was usually solid, I was surprised to discover how erotically charged a catfight clip could be. Even just some nude non-competitive wrestling got me a little crazy.

In in my final preparation, I made myself watch an entire gay male porn scene from start to multiple finishes.

That had taken a little getting used to, but after a while it's just two people fucking.

I wanted to be prepared for anything that could be thrown at me.

I was now ready.

I took a long shower and looked over my naked body. I have a junkie six pack which I'm alternately proud and embarrassed about. Meth does keep you skinny, but whatever, thin is in and they say the camera adds fifteen pounds.

I had come to the conclusion that pornography was one of the few public venues that celebrated a purely feminine type of physicality and looking over my body I was happy to play a supporting role to someone else's beauty. I just hoped I could be as functional to they were beautiful, that would be good enough for me.

I couldn't decide about shaving. I really don't know how to judge my own look especially my face.

Should I be clean shaven vis-a-vis the boy angel, or could I lean on the stubble in lieu of muscles in an effort to present some form of hyper masculinity? I couldn't decide and then just thought it was too much work to change anything. I didn't want to do it and then miss a spot or cut myself.

First impressions are very important when you go to an interview.

I put some clothes on and looked at myself in the mirror. I figured I looked fine, but really I don't spend enough time in front of the mirror to trust my opinion.

Hotrod and Sam showed up and I buzzed them in. Sam was wearing a tight red leather top that was everything you could ask for with her figure. Hotrod was in jeans and a tee shirt.

Hotrod had shaved and I thought, fuck.

He looked at me and said, "You've lost some weight."

"Yeah, I've been hitting the gym."

Then we started off.

I had already started writing our first script. It had a working title of: "I get it when I can" and it was about the exploits of a transient rapist. I had most of the scenes sketched out but I was running into trouble with the dialogue.

We arrived at a light industrial park without any light or industry. Hotrod navigated past a few abandoned warehouses and empty lots to get to what Sam called "the set."

We get out of the car and Sam walked us to the door of one of the grey buildings. It looked as unattended as everything else, but Sam knocked and some dude answered the door.

He let us in and then introduced himself as John. He looked very normal. I would have placed him in his late thirties. He had a pot belly and was wearing jeans and t-shirt that said PLUR on it.

We followed him in.

"The bathroom is over there," he kind of waved in one direction towards a door, "that's where the mirrors are." Then he walks us to a section that had been walled off on one side. There was some stage lighting and a divan there. I thought for a moment of one of my many shit temp jobs. This place would have been perfect for cubicles.

That was it, the "tour", as the guy called it, was over.

This was followed by the interview.

"We primarily do interracial content mainly black on blonde and same sex material." He gave what I could only guess was a professional nod towards Sam, "That's where our market is right now, but we plan to do a variety of content besides that down the line. Right now we're mainly direct to video, but we plan on getting a web presence here soon as that seems to be where everything is headed. So, who wants to go first?"

I volunteered.

I was told in my speech class at the university that you should always go first.

Sam and Hotrod left our little room to let us have some privacy. He asked me some questions, "Are you Bi-Sexual, or at least able to pull yourself through it?"

"I've never tried it, but I have familiarized myself with the process."

I thought that was a great interview answer, but the dude just gave me a weird look.

"OK. We're really trying to push some of the limits of male bisexuality as well as doing some more traditional content."

I wanted to ask him who the fuck "we" was in this abandoned warehouse with one divan and one camera, but I didn't want to get off on the wrong foot with my potential boss. I'd been fired from a temp job once for insubordination and was trying to keep everything professional.

"Now we have to do a screen and light test and see what we're working with."

"Sure, what's that about?" I was really wondering if I was going to get to fuck a girl. That shows how much I knew about where I was.

He gave me a sympathetic look, "You see a lot of guys have no problem with getting it up in the comfort of their own home, but when you put some pressure on them, some real stage and set lights, then things can get more difficult. You wouldn't believe some of the videos that have been given to me over the years, and then the audition is just a flop."

I wasn't really looking for any details on that shit, so I just said "sure."

Then he had me undress and kneel on the divan facing where the camera would have been if we were actually doing a movie. Then he shined a 3,000 watt bulb on my cock. I could feel it warm me when it hit, and I thought about the crystal in my jeans under the divan.

If that shit melts, I will burn this fucking place to the ground.

Forget about the speed!
This is you're moment!
Showtime!

I cleared my head and looked down at it. It looked like it didn't really know what to do. It was kind of soft and pinkish. It looked lazy. I think some girls would even have called it cute, but I wasn't feeling very cute.

I started to practice some self-arousal as I suddenly realized it wasn't going to get hard on its own. I focused on the last films I had watched in the porno booth, but I kept thinking of this chick that had given me some singles when I was panhandling.

She wasn't hot, just sweet and nice and naïve.

That's not working!

I knew it could get big enough for the purpose of the work. I'd paid special attention to a few dudes in the films and made comparisons and I knew I had what it took.

I thought of the girls I had been with. I pictured each moment that I could remember. I thought if how much fun it was to get the shirt off a girl for the first time.

I thought of Jani, but then dumped that as it felt kind of vulgar to use that memory.

Fuck I'm losing it!

I thought of all the beautiful girls that I had ever seen. I thought of this hot blonde girl I saw at the bus stop a few times a week. I thought of hot girls that had fucked me off.

FAIL!

Ok fantasy time! Who are the hottest girls in the world! I tried to imagine Maui Taylor and Gina Gershon in a sexfight.

I pictured them lip locked, titty to titty.

I tried to focus on that.

Believe me, I was doing everything I could.

I was pulling out all the stops.

This was not the John Holmes moment that I had been anticipating at all. I massaged it and I was gentle with it. I even pulled on it and got a little rough with it.

I got rougher with it.

Nothing was happening.

Finally I said, "Look man, I've been doing a hell of a lot of meth lately and I think I'm just shot. I'll have to come back another time. I'm just not up to snuff you know, what with all the drugs and booze. I'm sorry to waste your time like this. I'd like to thank you for the opportunity."

I didn't want to close the interview on a negative note.

He just stared at me and nodded.

I've noticed that every time you tell someone that hasn't done crystal that you do they usually just kind of blink at you.

I was a little bit ashamed about the whole thing, but when you're beat you're beat. I put my clothes back on and went into the bathroom and put a few lines up my nose. The shit wasn't melted at all, just a little soft.

I felt much better then.

I looked at myself in the mirror and thought that surely this was the face of hot, rough sex.

Or not.

Oh well, not everything you try ends in a success. I took stock of my employment situation. I had finished my last temp agency assignment pretty well, so I figured I could call them again when I finally ran out of money and sobered up. I wasn't going to have a crisis because I had a bad interview. I'd had plenty of those this spring already, and I figured at least I didn't have to lie about not having a degree in this one.

If I got anything out of my philosophy classes it's a measured perspective towards life little setbacks.

I leaned against the wall of the bathroom as the chemistry hit me. This was some of the best shit that I had ever scored and I was just lovin' it. I was trapped in the contradictory effort of trying to conserve it and use it all up at the same time.

I walked out and saw Hotrod on the divan. He was standing tall as hell. Sam had her shirt off and was kind of rubbing her boobs like there was a phone line in between them. Once in a while with her would've been amazing, really just once for a while would have been enough for me. I didn't want to stare, so I just glanced back across the whole thing before dipping out to smoke.

Cigarettes on a crystal high is one of the greatest experiences this life offers. I smoke about half a pack back to back to back before Hotrod and Sam come out of the building.

Hotrod looks pissed as hell.

I wait until we get in the car before saying anything.

"So what happened dude, I couldn't do anything under that light. It was like blinding the fuck out of me."

"Oh, the light was rough, but I got through it. No, those MOTHERFUCKERS just want me for faggot shit."

"Faggot shit?"

Sam leaned over the back of the car seat and looked at me. It was the first time that I had ever looked into her eyes. They were grey and soft, and a little tired looking. She kind of smiled and frowned at the same time, "It's because he's white."

I lit another cigarette and just laughed and laughed and laughed and after a while they joined me.

SCHADENFREUDE

Hotrod found me at my local watering hole rather to my surprise as I had quit answering my phone to avoid collection calls.

I had been spending a lot of time at the bar. I had stopped using cocaine, ecstasy, LSD, goofers, and methamphetamines along with the attendant pharmaceuticals in an effort to condense my workforce participation down to the lowest absolute limit of sustainability.

There had been some withdrawal and that had sucked, but I figured it was worth the pain if it delayed me even a day from sitting down in another cubicle.

In an attempt to broaden my strategy for minimalism I had stopped paying some bills as well which had lead rather naturally to my current phone avoidance policy. I was debating getting rid of my phone altogether, but that discussion was still in committee as I did need it to maintain a toehold in the world of temporary employment.

The upside of this was a generally stable heart rate, but the fact that I often didn't get a buzz until my fifteenth vodka tonic was starting to impact my budget almost as bad as the goddamn drugs had.

I wasn't about to quit drinking.

"Don't you answer your phone anymore?"

Hotrod looked awful. It was probably the only time that I ever remember looking better than him. His clothes looked like shit, like they had been washed and dried on him. He had dark circles under his eyes and long deep scratch marks on his neck that had covered over with scabs. Some of the scratches ran from throat to shoulder and were a full fingernail wide. You had to admire the determination that went into the work. He had a shiner and the vain fucker had applied foundation to it in an effort to cover it up.

Seeing him like this immediately brightened my day.

"It's tough to get foundation to really shade well from purple to yellow isn't it?"

"Oh, fuck you."

He sat down with his drink and stared into it. I looked at his hands and could tell that the violence had been one sided which could only mean one thing.

"Face it asshole, you're just not marriage material."

"I know, I know."

"And she had such high hopes for domestication."

"Some of that was fine."

"Did you try to leave her for Sam?"

Hotrod was one of those fucking people that couldn't end a relationship unless he was starting a new one.

Marriage in a perverse sense was the perfect institution for Hotrod as it provided him with the ultimately secure point from which to launch romantic conquests.

"No, I broke it off with her a few weeks after the audition. Bitch was getting too attached."

I got up and grabbed a round for us. Number sixteen is my new favorite. I start to feel relaxed inside my skin and my mind becomes free of pain inside the clear buzz of hard alcohol.

I sat back down and pushed his drink across the table to him.

Hotrod couldn't speak. He would start to say something and then just drink his beer instead or light a cigarette.

"The infidelity finally broke her?"

"Yeah. I thought she had come to terms with it, but I was wrong."

I pursued my line of inquiry, "Oh Jesus, you fucked her sister."

"She doesn't have a sister."

"Thank God!" He had done that once with two sisters who had an unhealthy dose of sibling rivalry.

That family used his name like a curse word.

I decided to switch tracks, "Was it the matron of honor at the wedding?"

I thought of her because all the other bridesmaids had been to the benefit of the bride. Not that Hotrod was above any of them, but I thought it wisest to start with the most tempting. I had initially ruled her out due to her being married, but then realized my romantic naiveté was getting the better of my otherwise sharp detective skills.

Hotrod nodded at me with pride and humility intertwined.

Then he looked back down at his drink in shame.

I leaned back against the wall of the booth and lit a cigarette. I gave him a full once over.

"She's stronger than she looks."

"Yeah, she was pretty wound up."

"I don't mean to pry, am I safe in assuming you did that too?"

"Oh yeah, even more. I went ass to mouth on the bitch she got a Sanchez sucking me off. Girls a fucking freak."

It was now my turn to stare into my drink.

"I deserved that."

I was smoking Camel shorts again and the acrid harshness of the unfiltered smoke mixing with the acid in the limes and alcohol from the vodka is as close to nirvana as a sinner like me is going to get.

I could watch the whole city burn with a smile on my face.

"Well, you may as well fill in the rest," I resigned myself to the story. I knew it was going to be good, or at least terrible.

"So, we had our little thing and I hadn't heard from her, so I was thinking it was just a one timer."

"So far, so good."

"Right, so a few days later the bladder infection kicks in and she drinks more than she should, and ends up feeling guilty about the whole thing. You know how bitches are."

"Yeah, the wine really brings out the guilt and shame in them."

"Wifey and I are down at the Parrot having a beer when her cel rings. I don't know who is on the other end, but I can tell from the expression on her face that it's bad news."

"Well yeah, it could have been a bad day for stocks."

"Will you let me fucking finish? Wifey talks for about five minutes just getting madder and madder the whole time. Then she calls me an asshole and throws her drink in my face, and the whole time, I'm thinking it's because of Sam, so when I tell her I quit fucking her I get one of those "I *KNEW* you were fucking her!" screams and then she storms out."

Classic Hotrod.

Hotrod was powerless against his prick, and while we found that lack of self-control a weakness our general attitude was more sympathetic than critical.

He is our best friend after all.

The fucking guy should be in some sex junkie support group, but if he was he'd just try to bed his sponsor.

Hotrod had never been faithful to any girl ever, so the developments in his marriage were unsurprising and represented little more than an extension of well ingrained habits.

How the individual girls responded to the cheating was almost always more interesting than the cheating itself. This varied from the few tough souls that had bounced at the first transgression all the way to some extreme cases. The worst one to me had been a girl who insisted on smelling Hotrod's dick each night to confirm his fidelity. That had led to a few awkward moments and some intense fights. Beating the hell out of him for his transgressions was rather pedestrian on that scale, but we had to give Wifey the gold in damage done.

"So, what happened next?"

We were moving through time slowly having arrived at

Wednesday in our story with still some distance to cover getting from then to now which was Saturday.

"I gave her some time to settle down while I got drunk. Then I drove home."

"And?"

"I get into the apartment and go to the bathroom, and I'm taking a piss and look over my shoulder a bit and I see that there's something in the tub. Once I'm done pissing I look into the tub and what do you think I find there?"

"A horses head?"

"Haha."

I could see the pain, but the alcohol had drowned my compassion.

"Not that, just all my shit. Everything, my CDs, my fucking guitar, my amp, all my clothes, fucking brand new laptop, soaking there, waiting for me. The sick bitch had stirred all of it together with a broom."

"I don't get it, were they dirty?"

"Oh, you got jokes! The guitar is fucked, you know me, my shit is dry clean only man, that's thousands fucked right there. That amp wasn't even a year old."

I was doing my best to sympathize through my laughter.

"So, I went to the living room, and I pushed her stereo receiver through her television. I'd just assumed she wasn't home, but I was wrong about that. That got the bitch out of bed. She comes out and starts screaming at me. I didn't say a damn thing. I just started to take apart her glass menagerie."

I compressed more than two hundred Tennessee Williams references down to one question, "Was she a trinket girl?"

I honestly had no idea what the girl was like.

Hotrod lived in a carefully constructed world in which the victims of his crimes were quarantined away from the conspirators. I had stood up in his wedding because it had an open bar. That and the irony had been too sweet to pass up. I'd done my part as a friend and advised him once against marrying at 21 and then kept my peace.

I'd seen his wife only a handful of times since.

"Well, not so much anymore. She attacked me when I started the stampede of the crystal elephants," he gestured towards the marks on his throat, "the bitch tried to choke me to death and tear my head off at the same time. I shoved her off and she punched me in the face. Then the cops showed up and she let them in."

"I was wondering when they'd get there."

"Oh yeah, so the cops come through the door and see me holding this giant candle made to look like the Eiffel Tower."

"The police apprehended you with a large candle sculpted in the shape of the Eiffel Tower?"

"Yeah, it was made so that it burned through the center and glowed from the inside."

"That's really nice. Where do you get something like that?"

"Oh Jesus Christ, anyway, they thought that I was using it as a weapon, stabbing her with it, so the cop gets his taser out and tells me to drop it or else. Of course I complied. I threw it down as hard as I could and broke the fucker."

"Really it's kind of a Sampson and Delilah ending don't you think?"

"Look, I know your enjoying this; can you just not enjoy it so much?"

"No."

"OK. Well, that set her off and she attacked me in front of the cops. They had to pull her off me."

"Did they take you to jail?"

"No, one of the cops was a musician and when he saw the guitar in the tub, he took pity on me. He told me to cab it to a hotel on account of me being too drunk to drive. He said if I go back there, then I go to jail. Dude, it was a 1962 Fender Stratocaster!"

Hotrod had an affliction with the material.

"That was nice of him." I'm not a big fan of cops, but you

have to respect someone sympathetic to the loss of art and the tools of expression.

"So, I've been in a hotel room for the last three days. It's too expensive to keep this up …"

Ahh, the moment arrives.

I'd already said yes as soon as I'd seen that his hands were clean. Hotrod was our best friend after all and a friend in need is a friend indeed, but it still felt good to make him ask.

"… I don't suppose that you could put me up for a little while?"

Now pause, look mildly surprised, make him pay for it just a little bit more, "I don't know. I suppose I *could* take you in for a little bit."

Oh, the Fish Bowl was a fair but small domicile. He could sleep on the couch with just one small caveat to keep things from getting messy.

"No ass fucking bitches while you live with me. They can take you to their place. I don't want to walk in on any of that shit."

"Absolutely."

"Ok, future rounds are on you. I'm taking your rent in trade."

One advantage of high earners falling down is that they can get up quickly. I figured a couple months and I'd be free of him, and he'd keep me drunk in the meantime. My ambition to emancipate myself from the work force could take another step forward with some off the books income.

Hell, I may even pay one of those bills I keep getting called about.

Hotrod came back with some drinks. He looked relieved.

"So, what's the next move?"

"Well, I've got an attorney. We don't have a house or kids, so there isn't anything big to fight over."

"Even less now than what you started with from the sounds of it."

"Ok that was funny. I'll give you that one. I might have to cut her a check for the damages to her stuff. It depends on how things add up, and how much fucking stress the bitch wants to put me through. I doubt anything on my side is recoverable."

"Well, here's to a clean exit."

We toasted that.

Hotrod went to the bathroom to apply some more make up.

While he was doing that the Pilot Fish took me back in time, but not very far. Just 21 months to when Hotrod and I first met his future wife.

Hotrod had just landed his first IT job and was making real money for the first time in his life. We were walking down Nicollet and Hotrod was hitting on every pretty girl he saw. He looked sharp and confident in his new clothes. She was just anyone except that she came along for a drink where someone else had said no.

It was just like any other night.

The Fish walked me over the next few months and we listened to Hotrod tell us in a bathroom of a bar while I threw up in the sink, "Damn, this girl is amazing. I think she's the one."

He showed me the ring he'd bought for her and all I could say was, "Yeah dude she seems really nice."

But what had been in his eyes were streetlights and sky scrapers, something new and more than our small town.

The intoxication of success, and the knowledge that doors were opening and things were becoming available that hadn't been before. The Fish recognized it and had tried to caution (to no avail) that it's something ephemeral though in its throes we can't seem to know it so.

From then to now and how nothing is a surprise just a thing to laugh at in some ways and mourn in others.

As soon as Hotrod sits down from the bathroom his phone starts ringing. He looks down at it and then looks away.

"Who's that?"

"It's the bitch I gave the Sanchez to. She wants to hook up again. Now that she knows I'm single she won't stop calling."

PRIVATELY SAVING JANI

Hotrod's moving in with me was fantastic from a financial perspective. He cut my rent in half and reduced my booze budget by 95%. My new financial stability allowed me to relax my determination to live a drug free lifestyle into a seek nothing do everything mentality with a baseline of Hotrod picking up the tab.

I had gotten ahead enough on bills to safely answer the phone.

It took him about four months to get ahead enough to get his own place again. I helped move him in, and then returned to my feast and famine life of temp assignments and minimum work force participation in a state of general equilibrium.

All in all it wasn't too bad though sharing a studio with another guy is a bit cramped. If I'd had a romantic life to interrupt there may have been some resentment, but lacking that and with a steady anesthesia of alcohol it hadn't been that bad at all.

Truth be told I could only really remember it in spots anyway.

Relative calm is all that I have ever asked for and it's interrupted by the phone.

"Hello, welcome to the fish bowl."

"Hey."

There's a pause and I know what the rush in her voice means now.

"I really fucked up this time. I'm in real trouble."

"What kind of trouble." I can tell that her drug use has escalated. I can hear the void all the way through her. Like static on a line that interrupts only the most important words of each sentence the void reverberates between us.

"I need some money. They have me at their house. I can't call my mom. You're the only one that would understand. They're going to hurt me."

I can tell that they already have, so the rest is just details.

"They're really dangerous believe me. I'm so sorry."

I get the amount and the address.

I take a survey of my weapons. I have a .45 ACP pistol that made the move with me from Wisconsin, and a medieval mace of sorts that I welded on the sligh in a general elective welding class at the U. of M.

It's the only real memento I have from college and looking at it now all I can think is that I must have been really fucking high when I made it.

I have nowhere near the amount of money they are asking for, but I withdraw everything I have.

I get a hold of Hotrod. He won't come along. He encourages me to call the police, but doesn't argue about it too much. He will give me 600 dollars, which is what friends are for.

Then I'm roaring down the road thinking about the directions.

The sun is starting to set when I get to Chicago. It only takes me an hour to find the address. I park a block away and get out and walk around for a while until I can feel the road recede and my senses come back to normal.

It hasn't started yet and I already want it to be over.

I walk up to the door of the house. I knock twice and a guy answers the door.

"Whatcha want?"

"I'm here for my friend."

"Got the money?"

The Adventures of Hotrod and Pilot Fish

"Let me see her first."

He moves to let me into the entryway. He is bigger than me and is kind of standing over me in an aggressive manner. He looks pretty tough and I can guess that he is the kind to do nasty things to people, in particular when it comes to money. He has a gun stuffed in his belt. So do I, but mine is concealed while his is on display.

They have her laid out on a couch. She's been beaten, though not badly. She looks pretty drugged up. She's wearing a beige slip covered in stains, no shoes, no socks. There's a guy sitting next to her. I don't like the way that he is looking at her. He has his hand on her stomach.

He looks up at me and says, "You're not gonna make this bitch *earn* it back, are you?"

She stirs at the sounds of his voice and sees me through a blackened eye and smiles at me with filthy teeth. "You came?"

Her voice is a hollow that echoes the void.

The dude on the couch moves his hand up and starts to massage one of her breasts slowly as he tries to stare me down. He wants to show me how powerful he is. How people get trampled after they fall down. He wants to make it personal, but he's wrong about that.

It's been personal from the start.

I nod at him and then tell the doorman, "I'll go get the money."

The door slams shut after me.

I go down to the car and open the trunk. Sitting side by side is the pouch with the money in it and the stainless steel club. The club is quite overdone. You can see my childhood love of Tolkien coming through in some weird tweaked out kind of way. It looks like something an orc chieftain would carry with lots of extra points and edges on it. The underlying welds though are thick seams of hardened steel, ugly and overdone, and very strong.

I remember how hot that steel was when it melted and it's nothing compared to how I feel inside.

Pilot Fish, what the fuck!

He comes up before me like a manifesting apparition.

I don't need a mirror anymore to see him.

I face the Fish in his fullness with just a shimmer between us like the beginning of a mirage. I can see from his clothing that he was time traveling in Elizabethan England.

"I was wondering when you'd call."

"I'm sorry to interrupt."

"Don't apologize, an interruption is all that it has ever been."

"Were you having a good time there?"

"Nothing short of splendid! You know, the original Shakespeare is amazing. To see an actor give the soliloquy of Marc Antony for the first ever is really something amazing. I especially loved the raw pleasure the groundlings took from the battle scenes. The commoner of that time had a greater imagination than the artists of today. The only thing lacking was the feminine touch of the female parts done so by male players. Who would've guessed that modernity had anything to offer the stage?"

"What should I do?"

"First, you must remember that nothing has changed. All of it is still a stage. Then you should do the right thing. You should always do that."

"I was going to plead the second on this one."

"We may yet. Oh, I like the look of that! What is it?"

"I made it in the welding class I took at the U."

"Does it have a name?"

"No."

"Well, the first thing is that that you should name it. It strikes me as a flange. It is now christened the Flange of Power. Not as elegant as say Excalibur, but it's a fair name nonetheless. What's that?"

"Ransom money, I guess."

"There will be no ransom here, though you are right about it being money. More properly, a ruse to help us to our end. Who steals our purse steals trash."

"Twelfth Night?"

"Othello. Now, are you committed to this, to doing what is right?"

"I think so."

"It has to be more than that. We can't be heroes without accountability. That is an ancient law."

I did it.

I said it.

I meant it.

"Yes."

The Pilot Fish stretches across the shimmer and kisses me full on the lips as Damien kissed the young Upton Sinclair, "Then let it be the cry of havoc. You still understand little of love, but you're learning. Today's lesson is that there is a love in holding fast and a love in letting go."

And we have changed places like becoming one's reflection.

The Fish grabs the money pouch and the Flange of Power. He slams the trunk closed. He walks up to the house and knocks. He is holding the pouch out, some bills are visible.

The same guy opens the door and the money provides a simple misdirection.

"You know I'm gonna count ..."

"Speak hands for me!"

Such has been the decline of our public schools that the man evinces no knowledge of the Great Bard of Avon at all. It's just a sad state of affairs all the way around when you think about it, but that's a subject for another day's pondering.

The Fish swings the flange up in a smooth arc right into the poor bastard's ball sack.

The blood gushes vertically so high that it splashes his chin. He tries to bend in half clutching his scrotum as he crumples to the floor. He is still reaching towards the money with one hand and cupping his balls with the other.

"The maiden is for valor and not for cost. There shall be

no tax on love!" Then the Fish bears down with all his strength in an overhand strike to the head that splits skin to bone and bone to brain.

What others call the strength of a psychotic episode I call the power of love.

The Fish stops and surveys the entryway. There is no motion, and no one seems aware of him. How that entrance failed to draw any real attention is a severe disappointment. If you don't have the audience at the first scene how can you keep them to the last?

Heroes shall not go slinking about! He slams the door shut behind him and gives his battle cry, "FLARGONNNNN-NIIISSSSSS!!!"

Then he charges into the living room.

The guy sitting next to Jani still has is hand on her breast. He is squeezing it while looking at her face. His lips move but we can't hear what he's saying.

He looks up at us and his hand stops.

"The hallowed roads did open before him, and what stood at the end of the wood was Avalon, and how he wept at the sight of what he'd sought so long that it became the substance of a dream!" The Fish does a spinning back fist move with the flange. It hits the man's face so hard that his eye explodes in a loud liquefied GUSH! The ocular fluid mixed with blood is like a volcano erupting from the crater that had been the eye socket.

"MY EYE, EYE, EYE EEEEE!"

We can hear him now.

"Ah, Polyphemus, we meet in the quick and there can be but one judgment, for of the tribes of giants some were themselves noble and well descended, but the Cyclops were always beasts."

There, he is completely blinded now and missing more than that.

"Oedipus, you poor thing, lay you down now to rest."

Motion from stage left and the Pilot Fish spins as Theseus did when first hearing the roar of the Minotaur. "Ahh Ariadne, where is thy blessed thread?"

A dapper chap stumbles into the room. It looks like he was interrupted in his toiletries. He has his dick in one hand and is desperately trying to get it stuffed back into his boxers. He has a pistol in his other hand. He starts to point it towards the Fish. The Fish thinks to himself, "Tis a good thing I prepared so well for the Glasgow games, and indeed won a kiss from the Third Duchess of York for my performance in the throwing of axes." Then he lets fly the Flange of Power which lodges deep in the belly of the fellow causing him to drop his weapon and begin screaming.

"Avast, yeh bastard!" the Fish shouts as he leaps towards the moaning man. "It was the Blue Jackets of Drake that fought off the Armada, and a bloody test that was when it came to the cusp!"

He tears the flange free ripping out the man's guts in the process.

"God save the Queen!"

The man looks down and tries to push his intestines back in, but the genie won't fit back into the bottle.

The Pilot Fish kicks his gun under the couch, oh to go back to that long ago time and faraway place when the elegance of the light saber overcame the vulgarity of the blaster!

The Fish dashes down the hallway to the kitchen.

In the kitchen someone is busy stuffing a lot of white powder into a bag.

"Salt Miners!" the Fish screams bewildered as he bashes the Flange of Power into the miner's head several times. The miner flops around the kitchen before coming to rest on the floor.

The Fish swims back into the living room and then stalks up the stairs. There is a single hallway with three doors, "Veni, vidi, vichi!" he boots the first door so hard it buckles off the hinges.

"Here's Johnny!"

Two men are inside at the far end of the room next to a window. They seem engaged in some complicated transaction involving salt and currency. They both look at the Fish mouths agape.

"I don't know about you, but I believe this whole thing should help the lad find some closure on a love that's lingered on a bit, wouldn't you agree?"

"Jesus Fuck!" one man shouts and leaps out the window while the other stares at the Fish in shock. The Fish advances and feints twice with the Flange of Power in preparation for the braining.

The man falls to his knees begging for mercy. "Dude, I'm just a custy!"

"You know that this salt is nothing but poison, you poor deranged piker!"

"SALT!?!"

The Fish knew this condition well. On long Aegean journeys while transporting goods for the great King Priam, Charon ferry him across and curse the line of Menelaus, he had been on voyages where weak souls that couldn't handle a few days without water began drinking from the sea. Such madness had befallen them that they rushed to the Siren's call and were feasted upon by them. Others had thrown themselves to Charybidis. This one before him would surely and speedily do the same. "A pity, but I fear you are past the point of salvation."

There was nothing to be done for this poor fucker, and he was harmless enough to leave alive.

The Pilot Fish goes to door number two. It opens revealing two girls trying to hide. One is in the closet, and the other beneath the bed. Neither of them are doing a good job of it.

"Please don't kill me!" The closet girl screams.

"Nay, maiden, I have but pre-empted your own knight with my arrival. You are free and should you care to wait for your beloved, you may, otherwise, I have set open the gates. The salt miners are all dead or surely shall be ere this day finds sunset."

She faints and falls out of the closet, as during the speech the Fish has been using the Flange of Power as Henry the Fifth had used a long sword at Agincourt, waving it about for inspirational effect. It has splashed no small matter of dross upon her and she like any maiden pure of heart was ill conditioned to the sight of blood. "My deepest apologies, my dear, *dramatis personae!*"

The Pilot Fish solemnly bows to them after the fashion preferred by Catherine the Great.

Now there was a woman that could throw a feast!

The Fish turned to make his exit and discovered what could only have been one of the surprises of door number three bursting through door number two.

Standing before us is a male of medium height and fair build. All in all rather fetching but for a certain coldness about the eyes. His appearance suffers a further detraction due to the addition of a Mac-11 to his otherwise reasonable wardrobe choices. He seems determined to spray the Fish with bullets.

The Fish swings the Flange of Power at the gun knocking it out of his hand. The Fish rushes into him as the gun falls. We clinch for a second and then the man brings his fist sharply up to the Fish's chin.

For a moment there is numbness there.

Then the Fish swings the Flange of Power down onto the man's knee. Such a cracking has nay been heard since the Turks brought the cannon to the great and last Christian-Roman stronghold of Constantinople!

Curses on those that no longer call it Tsargrad!

He's hopping on one leg holding his knee and we swing laterally baseball style at his head.

"IT COULD GO ALL THE WAY!"

The Fish kicks the decapitated head hard across the hall as he leaves the room.

The Fish had fought at Alesia and later at Pharsalus. Such a man had never lived that even dying for him was the greatest honor, and one can't help but learn from such genius or be forever damned, even if he was a bit full of himself. Never ignore your flank. Such is the wisdom of the first and greatest of the Julian Emperors.

Damn you Brutus!

The Fish flippers open door number three. He is rewarded. There is a skinny little man holding a gun in shaking, terrified hands.

The Fish roars at him like the great white whale sounded through the water as he rammed the Pequod.

The man drops the gun. It hits his foot and discharges. He collapses holding his bleeding foot. He stares in terror and speaks, "Are you insane?" he is already blanched from the flesh wound.

"Nay, though there are many that would call another's courage madness to cull the pain of their own cowardice." He then swings down with great strength towards the braincase.

But the Fish, as all great heroes, in particular those that know the discipline of Odysseus, was not without mercy. He stops the blow short by three inches.

There is a pause as the idea of alive becomes a fact. The huddled coward looks up at us tremulously.

"Have you pissed yourself?" then the Fish is bellowing with great belly laughs as the poor half man turns about in a pathetic dance of fear, pain and disgrace, clutching his foot and trying to hide his shame.

"Had you courage enough to fight then I would have slaughtered you like the Moors when they met the Hammer of Martel, but you, you are a worm tongue and fit only for the work of scullery maids! I will let you live in the event that should you become a man, you may find me, and on the field of honor, we can settle what differences we may have. Should such a day come, your challenge will be welcomed!"

Then with that barrel laugh that was his signature, for the Fish could court and drink and tell yarns as well as he could smash and cut and burn, he made his exit. There was nothing else upstairs and nothing left downstairs.

There was no basement, which the Fish found disappointing. It's hard to live without a cellar, one needs a place for the wines and stouts and cheeses that great feasts require. On the other hand, all in all this is a very poor place for feasting.

Very poor indeed.

He checks in on Jani. She is half conscious. She looks at the Fish, and says, "Wow, they really shouldn't have invited you!" Then she flops off the couch onto the floor.

The Fish goes back into the kitchen, pushes aside the body of the fallen salt miner and proceeds to carefully wash and dry the Flange of Power. He can feel now that everything is done how little strength we have left.

It lasted long enough and thank God what's left can finish the job.

There is a lot of salt here, so he just washes it down the sink along with the blood, bits of bone, and whatever else.

As he washes the Flange of Power, he sings to himself. He selects a modern tune by a chap from Surrey.

"I want to be your SLEDGEHAMMER!" His voice is still there, but it isn't carrying as far as before.

Then he breaks song for a moment, and carefully dries the flange. He smiles with a little pride. Those welds held up very well.

Then he goes to the bathroom and cleans up the clothes, and face trying to get all the blood out that can be. Like Robin of Loxley, it's always best to leave the king's men guessing.

For one moment we wish we had brought gloves, but we're not particularly afraid of getting caught. Whereas the vast carelessness of the Buchanan's was bought and paid for the vast carelessness of the American underclass derives itself from opposite principles. Laws and the rule of law are for middle class people, the poor and the rich live without them.

The Fish goes back to the living room. He grabs the money we brought and goes over to Jani. She is still on the floor. He sits her up as gently as he can. He grabs her purse. Her earrings are gone, her slip fits her like a shroud.

There is hardly anything here at all.

She is so far away from normal.

The Fish dumps her purse. Three syringes, a tampon and some lipstick fall out of it along with a notebook. There are songs in it, the notes and words lining out a beauty that the Fish can't interpret. There is nothing here that we can understand.

He puts everything back into her purse.

Then he turns his attention to her.

He looks her over carefully, running his hands over her arms and face. The Pilot Fish touches her feeling the slender thread of life in her that is simultaneously vibrant and impossible. She must have gone fast and hard. You can still find her somehow hidden underneath the layers of dirt, neglect and addiction. What is left of her is really all that she has ever been, and whether she will choose death or resurrection is a decision beyond our influence.

The Fish sees the hole that death has been going into pushing life out of her. He closes it with his hand. He doesn't want to look at it. He takes a few deep breaths to combat the fatigue.

I know holding her that love is the worst thing that can happen to anyone. I know that time will eventually dull my feelings and I know that even as I heal from it that I will be diminished by its passing.

She comes up for air only once, just a little breath. She opens her eyes and I see the void all the way through her staring back into me from her eyes.

"Oh, Fish, look what you've done." Then she fades out.

We don't have much energy left. I gather our things. I pick her up and carry her out to the car. I lay her down in the backseat. I make her comfortable. I brush the hair out of her eyes and across her forehead.

I get an hour out of town before I have to pull over to sleep. After a couple hours I wake up and drive us the rest of the way home.

TAG TEAM

Jani stayed with me a few weeks until she looked well enough for her mom to see her. She'd put on a little weight and her teeth were white again. We'd replenished her wardrobe from a few thrift shops and she looked close enough to normal to fake it.

I'd tried to make love to her after she started feeling better and she hadn't let me.

I felt I was entitled to that at the very least, but I wasn't going to force the issue. That had turned into a long late night conversation and she cried a lot and kept saying a lot of "I'm sorry" and "Thank you" but all I wanted to hear was "I love you back" and "I'll stay."

It fucked me up because shit felt so simple to me and so impossible to her, but I think after we talked some of the things the Fish had been telling me started to make more sense.

I didn't like any of it though.

When her mother got to my apartment to get her, she asked me, "Is this everything?"

I said, "Yes."

I hugged them both and carried Jani's one bag out to the car and put it in the trunk then I hugged Jani once more trying to feel how she wanted me to feel and not how I couldn't help but feel.

The whole thing has left me cold.

The Fish tells me even that is a good thing. Just having feelings about it is probably a sign of emotional recovery.

In a silly way I feel betrayed by all the fantasy literature of my youth. The Fish criticizes most of those texts as making better guides for swordplay than love. He says when it comes to romance that they have it exactly backwards. He tells me that the sacrifices and battles come after the relationship has been going on for a while not before. The relationship is never a price or reward for sacrifice unless you wish it warped from the beginning.

But I'd take it warped if it would just begin.

I'd take Jani any way that she would have me.

He tells me that there are no hero endings outside of the stories and it's more my fault than anyone's for reading so much into those.

He tells me it's a long way back to earth.

We wrote a poem about her called "Wild Disregard and Reckless Abandon" and after working on it until it was perfect I set it on fire.

I held the paper until it burned away in my fingers bringing up blisters as I smiled and cried.

I called Hotrod and told him I was going to start drinking now and he'd get to me when he got to me.

I headed down to the local pub.

I started with three shots of different liquors and two beers.

I raise my glass to the void. I toast that every ecstasy be dissipated. I toast that every ambition be disappointed. I toast that every dream be bankrupt.

The idiot box whose one eye can only see the Great Asylum was whining about hanging chads in Florida.

There were excellent arguments on both sides of the massive mobocracy's decision.

The citizens of the United States of America had been asked to choose between someone who wanted them to drive less and spend more on what they already had because if they didn't something bad might happen someday, and someone who couldn't formulate a complete sentence.

The Adventures of Hotrod and Pilot Fish

It was a tough call, but if I can say anything about my fellow citizens it's that they love their cars.

The fact that the loser of the Electoral College had won the popular vote contributed fantastically to competing claims of legitimacy and illegitimacy. Everyone had a fair bitch to make and it went on and on and on beyond the election to the constitution, to the future of the country to the future of the free world. Everyone had the chance to whine about what was going on, who was counting what and where. Intent and action were being debated along with systemic racism and overt fraud. Everyone had brought a slide for the slippery slope of their choice.

Pundits sacrifice babies for this kind of shit.

I thought that it was mainly a vindication for Hillary Clinton. She'd been talking about a right wing conspiracy focused on her husband's penis for years and hadn't been taken very seriously. Seeing Jews for Pat Buchanan stepping out in such strong numbers to help swing the State of Florida convinced me that she'd been right all along.

Hill, who knew?

I felt the real culprit was karma. The Democrats had stolen the 1960 presidential election and it looked like the wheel had turned and the Republicans were going to get 2000.

Fair is fair and karma is a bitch.

I'd voted for the man mainly because I liked his father. His dad had a strong grasp of subject-verb agreement, and had done a unilateral nuclear arms reduction. I was thinking we'd get more of the same just with stilted rhetoric instead.

My vote hadn't had any impact on the electoral allotment of the State of Minnesota and I was doing my best to try not to feel like I had a stake in any of it.

The fate of the nation was hanging on a chad in the Supreme Court of Florida and all Hotrod could think about was pussy.

I could see that in his eyes as soon as he waked into the bar. The boy just didn't give a fuck about politics.

"Jani gone?"
"Yeah, her mom came and got her."
"You miss her?"
"Yes."
"Let's get a bitch."
"Let's get drunk first."
"How'd you burn your hand?"
"I touched something hot."

Hotrod goes up to grab a pitcher of whatever's on special today.

I have a comfortable buzz, the kind you could go to work on, but it's not enough.

We live by begging the question of living.

We toss back another five or six drinks. It's obvious now that we have the heavy, strong buzz that can cause miracles to spontaneously occur. Hotrod gets some shots.

"I wasn't sure if you'd left any of these up there."

We toast and slam them back.

"Let's roll."
"One more drink."
"Sure."

One means two and shots need regular drinks for chasers and mixing is what I do because no one wants to be alone.

Then just like that I'm putting out a cigarette and we're on the street.

"Dude, you need to take a left and head towards Lake."
"No, man. A lot of girls are hanging out down here now."
"Really?"
"Oh, yeah."
"Shit, and here I was thinking I was up with the news."

This kind of pisses me off because this is my neighborhood. You'd think I'd be up on this shit. It didn't seem to me like there were any more girls than normal walking the block, but I've been so faded lately and my mind has really been on other shit what with Jani and all.

I guess I just haven't been paying that much attention.

"What do you think of her?"

"Man, we ain't even started looking yet and you're out to get us a busted heffer."

"How about that one?"

"Not tonight."

"Since when were you picky?"

"I can't believe I'm hearing this, I've always been picky."

It takes a few runs before I see a girl that I consider suitable. Hotrod only sees pink so he always lets me pick the girls. The lads a right fucking gentleman.

"That bitch right there, the one in the white."

"Jesus Christ, finally."

She's an attractive female whose race can only be described as Urban American. She's in her late twenties with a fair gait and strong, nice legs.

She's got curves for years.

"We're going to have to get some coke too."

"Ok, man, take it easy."

We stop about half a block ahead of her. It's best to only have one person do the approach.

"Go after it Cowboy."

"I'll be back in a minute."

Hotrod gets out and starts the long half block plus discussion time. I sit back and light a cigarette. The fresh air adds some clarity to my intoxication. I have a high energy drunk going, and those are rare and nice. I wish I had a joint with me. I've had enough booze that it would really put me over the edge, but not so much that I'd be in critical condition.

They come back. Hotrod opens the door for her like a true gentleman.

"So, who are you guys?"

We give our real names every time because we don't give a fuck. We're not going to run for higher office. We can't be blackmailed because we're not ashamed.

We make some small talk about living in the neighborhood. She doesn't give a fuck about our names. All she's doing is trying to feel us out to the point where she's decided we're not a couple of sociopaths that are going to kill her.

We're obviously white and sometimes you get a race feel out as well during the initial negotiations. There are two races in the sex trade of the Great Asylum, White and Non-White and there is only race in the serial killer of whore's category and that would be the color of us.

We've never hurt any of the girls that we've picked up. We don't want to hurt anyone, we just want to party.

"Just one thing girl, do you have a pipe cause I don't."

"You two are cool."

"Damn right we are." says Hotrod.

She gets in the back seat, a true sign of trust.

We stop off on the corner of Franklin and Clinton and buy some rock. Some of that is for her and some of that is for me, but we make it clear that none of it is in her fee.

Like I said baby we just want to party.

After the buy Hotrod drives north to a shitty little hotel that he's used in the past.

"You can rent by the hour here, they're discreet."

Hotrod would be the ultimate underworld tour guide of this northern town.

"Nice."

We park on the street and stroll in. In a twin world we are the three musketeers on our way to rescue a dignitary or captured piece of the crown, but in this world we are three people engaged in the business of giving and taking.

"One hour or two?"

"Two."

Money changes hands with a perfect sense of amorality. That's the nice thing about money, money doesn't give a fuck and the presence of money tends to make the feeling contagious.

"Room 18." He hands me the key.

"Thanks."

The Fish swims the stairs and the long hallway. The key fits and clicks, and we're into our little sanctuary.

The room is simple. One bed, one desk, one chair, one bathroom. No balcony, parking lot view out of the one window. We came for the bed not the view and Hotrod isn't wasting time when time is money.

Hotrod asks our girl, "You want to get high first?"

"Yeah, sure. You gonna hit it?"

"Not me, that's all you two."

She takes a hit and then kisses me blowing the smoke slowly into my lungs. The only altruism that cocaine ever inspired was based on greed. I take my hit and hold it for a few moments before kissing her back. She matches my breath perfectly taking in everything that I can give her. Our tongues touch and we taste each other alike like getting high.

I know how to get the hookers to kiss me now.

She takes her clothes off with the ease of someone that's been in the profession a while. I'm always surprised at the lack of accessorizing involved in the prostitution racket. These street girls are not courtesans. They all dress and undress like women raised by single dads, no frills, nothing cute. I often wonder how they look when they aren't working. Do they do their nails when they can take a few days off, do they carry a cute little purse? Do they put on some frilly underwear?

"You first?"

"No, he's first."

"Thanks."

I slip out of my clothes and into a condom. It's thick and black and looks a little ridiculous. I sit down on the bed and she starts to give me a blowjob through the condom. Hotrod is running his fingers through her hair, he mouths, "in the ass," to me and I nod.

"You always use your own condoms?"

She comes up for air, "Yeah baby, you gotta be safe,"

"I hear that. I'm a big proponent of personal responsibility."

She winks at me and gets back to work.

I guess every business has some overhead.

I'm not really into blowjobs, never have been, but under a cocaine high everything feels good even through an industrial strength balloon.

Coke is the ultimate sexual intensifier. Every mundane touch is pleasant, every caress is magical. The smallest friction between us makes fire.

That being true this could still take all night, and we only got two hours.

"OK, baby. That's enough."

I roll her onto her back on the bed and with a little assistance from her, slip it in. It's been awhile since I've been with a girl, so it takes me a little time to get into rhythm. I stay on top of her until I start to get tired, and then we roll over.

I stare up at her breasts which are nearly perfect and they go up and down and up and down synchronized to the rhythm of our bodies. Her nipples are light brown and just a shade darker than her skin and I reach up and hold one lightly as she stares down at me for a moment and then looks away.

The only thing that detracts from it all is the noise she's making. It's a strange kind of snorting when she breathes like a coke fiend who relapsed after a rhinoplasty.

It's not very alluring, but I'm too fucked up to do anything about it but smile. She puts her back into it and rocks on me pretty hard, hard enough to get it done even with the fucking ultra-thick condom, booze and coke.

You gotta give the girl credit, she's a true professional.

Coke, booze orgasm. My brain is full of only good sweet things.

Goddam, this feeling could last forever.

Jani, jani, JaNi, JANI.

I close my eyes and remember every detail of her waving me goodbye. The little fly away hairs that escaped her bangs, the little bruises too faded for her mom to see that my memory filled in. Her smile saddened by her eyes and her eyes brightened by her smile. I know that everything horrible in this world is deserved.

The good things can only be stolen.

Hotrod has been intermittently watching her and me and not watching her and me. There's not a lot a lot of space so your options are limited to either looking at the couple having sex on the bed or obviously not looking at the couple having sex on the bed.

Fortunately for us, years of heavy drinking have trained us to ignore the elephant in the room.

She picks up her pipe and lights the last rock. It's decent sized and she finishes it off before kissing me and filling me out with smoke.

She tells me, "This is what those guys in Washington need. If they had this shit we wouldn't have all this fighting going on."

"Couldn't agree more, but Marion Barry already did all the rock in D.C. The town is dry."

"Whose Mary Ann Barry?" she asks me.

I empty the slivers and shards out of the baggie into the pipe. I hit it and lean into her with a kiss in response.

She holds it and I move my head down kissing one of her nipples running my tongue across it tasting the mix of our sweat left on her skin as she blows the smoke down across my neck and the back of my head.

I hug her for a moment feeling the warmth of her breasts against my face. We're just fine here on the edge of our skins, here we're perfect. It's when you get inside that the sickness and the sadness begins.

I look over and see Hotrod staring into the void between her legs. We are synchronized by a greater instrument and change places in a nude dance of the ludicrous my greased, and sheathed in black latex dick leading the way like the drooping prow of ship slowly sinking through the air.

His eyes are screaming, "IN THE ASS" as she gets out another condom.

She takes one look at his dick and says, "Damn." Then she pushes a large pink condom on over it.

When I see that I have to smile.

She starts to give him the condom blow job, but he cuts that way short. Hotrod has fantastic time management skills and never needed any encouragement getting a hard on. He starts her up doggy style, which puts him behind her from the start, right where he wants to be. To borrow an analogy from the dying American pastime, he is batting cleanup.

He is playing for position.

He slaps her ass a few times with his dick and then starts working her hard. His dick is too big for the pink balloon and it's stretched to the max.

It reminds me of the fact that I need to get rid of this black balloon. I slip into the bathroom and give them a little bit of privacy more for my sake than theirs. I take the condom off and throw it in the garbage. I smoke a cigarette and give them twenty minutes or so before I come back into the room. Hotrod is finalizing negotiations when I walk back into the room and sit down on the chair.

"How about a little in the booty."

"Ahhh, come on man I thought we were cool."

"We are cool, now how much more you need."

I grab Hotrod's wallet out of his jeans, as I can already see where this is going.

"Come on, a little extra for that ass."

He hasn't let up at all, still working her hard. She thinks it over and between snorts they come to an amount.

It's not clear to me what exactly happens during these moments. The girl might just be acting reluctant because it gets more money offered, or maybe it's because all of the control in the room rests on our good graces. Maybe saying yes and getting some extra cash is the only way to at least tell yourself you're still in control of the situation.

They decide forty more dollars for some booty sex. I'm not really in the mood for a second try at her, so I'm quietly relieved that Hotrod doesn't push for me. We don't have that much time left on the room anyway. I throw the twenties at the head of the bed where she can see them. She looks them over and nods.

Hotrod sees the green light and hits the gas. He spits on her ass and rubs it with his finger. Between that and the lubrication from her and the condom the stage is set. The condom splits after a couple thrusts and it's off and gone without any objections from anyone.

Hotrod then hammers home with little concern.

Ours can be a messy business.

Her snorting intensifies.

Hotrod can't even hear her as he stares past the back of her head into the void.

I switch gears and sit in the one chair in the room and obviously watch them.

I think back to the first time I ever got a beer buzz. I remember thinking that I wanted to feel like that every second for the rest of my life, that there was no other way that I ever wanted to feel again.

Time passed and I got laid.

Time passed and I tried cocaine.

All time does is make a liar out of you as it tells you the truth.

Jani flits in and out of my mind. I remember one of the things the Fish told me about the arrivals and departures of love as he was trying to console me.

He said that falling in love with someone is easy. It's so easy you hardly need them there to really fall in love with them. You can fall in love with them while waiting for them to appear. You can fall in love in the silences of assumed agreements and you never need any part of falling in love explained to you.

Falling out of love is the opposite of that. When you fall out of love with someone you want to share every moment of it with them. You want everything explained and you want the intentions and even the definitions of the words themselves explained.

And that's the part you really have to go through alone.

He went on some more about obsession and maturity, but I tuned him out.

I know that I'll love her forever and we'll both change and the love will change and everything will change. On and on and on until one day we'll see each other again and we'll be free of each other and happy to know each other and life is just life again like the way the world was before the wind of what could have been blew through.

I guess the road ends in nostalgia, but I don't want that. Nostalgia is too cheap a memorial my feelings. Nostalgia is the thing that *I* want the opposite of.

I want the fabric of time to tear and those pieces cast away.

But we have no such power over time and the longing just has to be endured until it runs its course.

I get that part and I don't like it because it hurts, but the pain doesn't prevent the course from being run.

Run, run, run.

SNORT!

I can't say that this part looks like much fun.

For one moment we make eye contact and the void is full between us, sister to brother in the game of fading sparks.

Then with one last thrust Hotrod stretches up finishing off.

"Thanks baby, you were great."

She doesn't respond. She just pulls away from him. She sits carefully on the edge of the bed. I light up three cigarettes and hand two out. I sit next to her. All we are wearing are six socks. Mine have a multi colored red and black pattern, hers are little white booties and Hotrods are black.

"You got you some funky-ass socks."

"That's because the Fish floats in European style footwear."

"No shit."
"No shit."
We get dressed and bounce.

CLEAN SHEETS

Loves wears more than anything else, it wears, and it waxes, from tiny things it waxes and it wanes from great things, at last it wanes.

It takes its own time though that's for sure. The worst thing besides the heart ache was the crack cocaine addiction that I had incidentally picked up along the way.

That came as a huge and really annoying surprise.

I'd used a lot of meth and never found it habit forming, just amazing in a shattered glass and cracked concrete kind of way. Coming down from meth was certainly wretched, honestly the only thing worse in pure awfulness was acid, but it had never lingered. I'd used coke and smoked coke in the past as well and it had mirrored the meth experience until this last round with it.

To wake up feeling normal except for some underlying insistent desire to get some more rock really pissed me off.

Everything that caught light in milky white. Everything that had some dull waxy translucence. It could be anything at all and it looked like heaven to me. My brain wanted it in my mouth, my lungs, my blood.

I'd walk down the littered sidewalks of Minneapolis in cascades of desire and disappointment.

I didn't have a reason to resist it. I knew where to get more and I had money.

I didn't.

I couldn't tell you why.

At least I got to go through it alone.

Hotrod had been booted out of the urgent care for getting too many HIV tests too close together. The doctor told him, "You need help that we don't offer here."

The doctor also said, "Use a fucking condom for Christ's sake."

That was the official and final diagnosis of the best of the medical community that Hotrod's insurance could afford.

This discussion triggered a severe panic attack as Hotrod took the doctors assessment as confirmation that he was too riddled with sexually transmitted diseases for modern medicine to save.

He had fucked off to Wisconsin to await death in the comfort and familiarity of his childhood home.

This was probably a blessing as we could sometimes bring out the worst in each other and I was having kind of a vulnerable moment.

At least my recovery got me out of the apartment.

I became a tourist of serene places.

I'd take the bus over to Como Park in St. Paul and sit in the Japanese Garden. I'd sit in silence and sunlight in the peaceful whisper of running water and endure the alternating current of anxiety and addiction.

That was a strange oscillation.

People would approach me slowly and then walk past me quickly much like encountering a wounded animal in the wild and I'd smile at them as I pictured them covered in blood.

I'd walk from the Cathedral in St. Paul to the Capitol slipping back and forth between romantic anguish and psychological withdrawal.

Those feelings were pretty intense for about a week and then started to fade. It took a few more weeks and at the end of the month I came close to relapsing, but didn't.

That one was a real test and I started feeling better after that. I understood the relapse pattern and I looked forward to the six month mark much like a fighter scheduled with a challenging opponent.

Addiction sat in my mind like a chipped tooth that was

gradually getting worn smooth, but could still cut me if I wasn't careful.

Jani on the other hand was bleeding out of me.

I poured whiskey into the wound. I'd call her at all hours of the day and night.

That never went well.

Then I'd sober up and call her and apologize for what I could remember saying and she'd remind me of what I couldn't remember and I'd apologize for that too. Then I'd fight about that too.

Those calls never ended well.

There wasn't anything revelatory or insightful in what was said. All I was doing was punching my way out of a clinch. That wasn't without its therapeutic elements, but it followed its own law of diminishing returns.

I realized in my hangovers that I am a punitive and bitter human being. I wanted an equalization of pain and I took pleasure in inflicting it. During the act I felt fantastic, powerful and righteous. In my hangovers I felt horrible, weak and guilty.

That oscillation dovetailed nicely with my broader psychological experience.

Time ticked away, so long during the during of it and so short in the reviewing of it.

My dick hurt from masturbation.

I jerked off repeatedly to the one time we'd made love. Just nostalgia hand fucking myself into a stupor of self-pity and shame.

I'd listen to PJ Harvey and pull away. I'd turn the music up and down some vodka tonics and lie in my bed and jerk off to the memory of her.

I remembered AP Modern Literature back in high school. By a miracle of enrollment and alphabet I sat right behind her in that one class of all the classes we took together. I'd ask her to wear a swishy-swashy skirt to school and sometimes she would. I'd stare into those pleats, the ever shifting line of black and red and skin, so thankful that she'd wear that for me like a private dancer flashing the poor house with the pleats of the skirt dancing around the top of her thighs while I was dying from desire inside.

And I'd think of that skirt and just want to scream and die and cry all at once.

YOU'RE NOT RID OF ME!

Tears and come and vodka is my cocktail of choice. They say liquor won't solve all your problems, but its worth a shot.

Christ I'm making puns, I need to die.

I knew when I did it that it was the most pathetic form of nostalgia imaginable, but I couldn't help myself. I'd think of her boobs, her nipples and the taste of her skin. I'd think of her stomach across and down to the top of her hip and how tight the skin was and how soft it was to kiss her there.

The biggest thing that I wept for and remembered and longed for was the willingness of her.

Sometimes that was more than I could take and I'd quit wanking and think of the impossibility of her. Of her holding me, wanting me, talking to me through touch.

My dick would go soft and I'd stare away into nostalgia.

I'd never washed the sheets since she'd been there and I'd lie to myself that I could still smell her there somewhere underneath the layers of dried sweat and slobber and come.

Then I'd think of the eventual resistance in her eyes and I'd put a straw in the bottle and pick up the phone.

Once I was out of the darkest part of that night I felt bad about my behavior and took some steps to correct it.

I started telling myself before I picked up the phone that this conversation was going to be how I wanted her to remember me. I made it a point to call her when I was sober.

It wasn't a panacea, but it helped.

I took refuge in mindless entertainment.

I got a TV and learned the names of the characters in the inane situational comedies. OK these six fuckheads live in

New York, but it's not the other six fuck heads that live in New York, this one is a love drama masquerading as comedy this one is a comedy focused on awkward love …

I began to anticipate new episodes and kept the plot points clear in my mind. I'd emotionally participate in their struggles in active ignorance of my own.

And time continued to pass.

I became a connoisseur of interruption.

Once I had been an introspective person who enjoyed the individual journey of consciousness, and now I wanted nothing more than to become inert.

A creature of instinct without the burden of intentionality.

I started to become a good employee. Besides the obvious benefit of reduced anxiety about money I found that eight hours of mind numbing labor did wonders for romantic and chemical depression.

Establishing a solid work ethic isn't very hard. The core of it is just not giving a fuck about yourself.

This represented a reversal of my temporary employee experience where the agency began to recommend me for jobs instead of ducking my desperate for money phone calls. I ended up landing a nice gig at a hospital that was within walking distance of my apartment. The work wasn't terrible. It was a temp to perm and I hadn't done one of those before.

Permanent employment was an idea I'd never taken seriously.

I had a supervisor that was pleasantly mad and I didn't mind her. She'd ask me frivolous questions about what I did on the weekend or what I did for fun. I would mouth banal falsehoods that passed me off as a normal person.

I got buzzed one day sure that it was Hotrod back to start the show over and almost got shocked out of my skin.

"Fish Bowl."

"Hey, it's Wild."

That didn't seem possible, but when I walk down to

the entryway of the building there she is with three bags and nothing else.

"He did it again, so I left him."

Her makeup was run on her face, but really she looked fine to me. She looked really good. I said, "Ok."

I picked up two of her bags and walked her up to the apartment.

She'd cried pretty much the whole bus ride up to the Twin Cities.

Apparently, she'd called me about twenty times and left me several messages, but it's not like I've got a fucking secretary.

In a way Wild and I found each other at the perfect time. We were completely worn out with love. We had no romantic tension because we knew how horrible it was to love someone.

We had no sexual tension because we both felt sex was meaningless without love and we both knew where that got you.

Intimacy is the first sip that poisons the well and our lips were sealed.

We were completely free.

Just being friends with a girl is amazing. I felt like I had won one over on the other half of the race. I wrote a short story about it called, "It's not in my penis this time," but no one would take it. The writing was fine once you got past the fact that there wasn't anything compelling about it.

Wild and I would watch movies together. She'd have popcorn and I'd have candy. Both of us mildly drunk and side by side without a need to touch each other or be funny or interesting. We wouldn't talk about the movies or analyze them or bother each other trying to sound like film critics.

We'd just watch the movie and when it was over one of us would say, "That was nice."

That was it.

That review covered: Sophie's Choice, Leaving Las Vegas

and Requiem for a Dream.

Other times we wouldn't say anything, just light a cigarette or take another sip of whatever we were sharing for the night.

We got a Super Nintendo and played Super Metroid and Mega Man X and Super Contra and Castlevania IV. We didn't have to beat the games, just play side by side until we were done.

She started watching the stupid television shows with me and we would talk about them like they mattered. We'd root for one of the characters or hope that another character found love.

It was nothing short of fantastic.

Wild's moving in also got me front row seats to the film, "My Bad Behavior Redux" as Bonk began to put her through what I had just put Jani through.

I found it all a bit cheeky considering that he had cheated on her, but he found some very creative ways to make the infidelity either immaterial to the greater argument at hand or her fault.

Watching someone else perform the same stupid pattern of behavior that you have is an opportunity for humility.

I didn't pass on it.

I thought I had been noble and determined to save the greatest love the world had ever known when I got trashed and called Jani at 3 AM to yell at her for not loving me.

When Bonk did exactly the same thing to Wild all I got was really fucking annoyed.

The whole process was surprisingly therapeutic.

Wild would apologize as the phone began to ring and I would say, "No, no worries. It's just him again. It's just something you have to go through."

I would say, "It's OK, answer it. He's only going to keep calling until you do."

I would say, "I deserve this as much as you do."

After going through that a few times my conversations

with Jani really improved. I thanked her for talking to me, for picking up the phone when she knew I was going to be a monster. I thanked her for all of that cold sober and she started to cry.

That conversation was good for us and kind of represented a turning point in our relationship.

Wild moving in also introduced me to the world of living with a girl. That really helped me understand why so many people get divorced.

The charm of feminity wears off faster than the chrome on a shitty BMX.

I'd look at her tits desperately trying to jump out of her t-shirt. I'd look at her ass stuffed into her tight jeans. I'd look at her fucking bras and panties hanging on the heat register and her jeans on a hangar on the door. I'd look at her fucking make-up and hair products all over my dirty bathroom and just sigh.

All in all things were fine though.

We only had a couple of intimate moments and they were always centered on grief and were never more physical than snot filled hugs.

Sometimes I'd cry and sometimes she'd cry and sometime we'd both cry.

She had one serious melt down over the whole thing and soaked my shirt with tears. It was one of those deep sob fests filled with the questions that can't be answered and I could see that she was finally getting into some things that she had only touched on the surface before.

Infidelity is a special combination of betrayal and rejection. It took her a while to deal with those elements individually as well as what they totaled up to.

It took her a while to subtract herself out of all of what that meant without diminishing herself in the process. It took her awhile to let it just be Bonk.

That was the worst part for her and it took a while to get through it.

After that we had a few mini meltdowns here and there

and with time the time between them grew,

I think for her the idea that she knew she was making a good decision helped with the pain. No matter how awful the whole process was it was for the best.

We passed through the winter in a state of half hibernation and healing. She bought herself a pair of used ice skates and found an outdoor rink where she went a few times a week. She said it really helped with her peace of mind and was a way better work out then going to gym. I went a couple times and watched her do flips, axels, lutzes and loops pretending that I could tell the difference between them while I pleasantly froze.

We celebrated the millennial New Year by watching the ball drop and drinking champagne in the apartment.

Once spring hit she started to bug me to go out and explore the city with her, but I couldn't catch her enthusiasm. We were on the same road, but I was miles behind her.

I'd tried to take her to some of my meditative places and she'd gotten bored with them pretty quickly.

Fortunately for me Hotrod had recently come to two conclusions. One: he was not about to die a horrible though deserved death from sexually transmitted infections. Two: His family drove him nuts.

He showed back up literally in the nick of time.

I gave Wild a trustworthy tour guide. He told her straight out that sex was always available and then took her dancing.

She was looking at community colleges and bus routes and new apartments. She found work as a waitress and started saving up to get a spot of her own. She found thrift shops and fun places to hang out. She wasn't ready for a relationship yet, but she was definitely ready for boys again.

I never charged her a dime for rent more in the spirit of speeding her course than any real sense of altruism.

By the time Hotrod and I were moving Wild into her new apartment I started to really feel better. Jani and I hadn't talked in a couple weeks and it finally felt OK. It felt OK to talk and it felt OK to not talk. We'd gotten to the point that when we talked there wasn't any sadness in the silences or resentment corrupting the meaning of what we said to each other.

Wild had found a decent one bedroom in a decent part of town and between her three bags and some furniture we got for her it wasn't much to get her moved in.

She deep cleaned the whole apartment before she left. The last thing she did was wash all my sheets, they were still warm from the dryer when I laid down that night.

All I could smell was Tide.

CARPET CRAWLER

After Wild moved out my life went back to the dull wild ride of living between work assignments. I'd work and party, and then when the assignment ended I'd sober up. While waiting for work I'd squeeze my pennies and do my best to make sure I could pass a drug test. Then work would come, I'd pass the drug test and start partying again.

I'd had a crush on a girl at one job, but instead of sleeping with me she conned me in to taking care of her two cats for a few weeks while she did some travelling.

Not that I minded the cats, I'm definitely a cat person, I'm just not responsible enough to take care of them and I really wanted to sleep with her. When she got back into town and set up in a new place she came and got them back. I kept hoping to get another assignment with her, but she was the kind of girl companies kept at the end of assignments and I was the kind of boy that companies didn't keep at the end of assignments.

If the drought between assignments got too long my chances of passing a drug test usually got worse, and if things got tight enough I'd reach out to some local charity resources for some help. No one was going to cover my rent, but there were a few food shelves in my part of the city that could really help cut your grocery costs with some donated bread or canned goods.

Sometimes some organization could squeeze some white guilt out of the suburbanite fucks that pitied us in the urban core and there would be some nice shit at the shelf.

That's how I met Carpet Crawler. We both walked into the food shelf at the same time and looked at four hamburger steaks and two full trays of chicken thighs along with two loaves of day old French bread.

He looked at me and said, "Shit, it's like the first of the month. Let's grab it all and cook it out in the park."

"I'll grab the steaks."

We split up, me with the steaks and him with the chicken and met back in the park after twenty minutes or so prepared for our little cook out.

While I got the grill going Carpet Crawler brought me up to speed on his life. He had been doing the young and homeless thing on the west coast before making his way north where he connected with a Minnesota welfare program that gave him and his girl a rent subsidy to get them off the streets. He planned on meeting the state minimum rent requirement through selling drugs.

I always admired the gutter punks and travelers that worked their way through the Twin Cities as resilient and interesting people that had the balls to do something I couldn't, and Carpet Crawler was no exception. He had some nice stories about getting beat up by some cops in Chicago and making it to LA just in time for the summer and laying on the beach panhandling for months at a time.

There's a pulsing homeless current in the Great Asylum that could be studied in the same fashion as migrating wildebeests in the Serengeti.

We waved over everyone that walked by for a plate and one dude was nice enough to pass a joint with us while we ate.

I had brought some instant mashed potatoes and a flask filled with Kessler Whiskey. I always liked a whiskey drunk with BBQ.

I was passing the flask back and forth with Carpet Crawler when we got on the topic of smoking coke. It was one of those typical round about conversation that a lot of people have about drugs. The kind of bullshit where you kind of feel each other out with those silly guarded questions to establish a comfort zone and then move into the things that you actually like to do.

The little taste I'd had with Snort had left a tickle in the back of my throat that wouldn't quite go away, so when Crawler suggested we smoke some coke some time I said yes, we just need to find the time.

We exchanged numbers. He told me that it was the first time in five years that he had actually owned a home phone. We finished the cook out and I forgot about it for three weeks because I had an assignment again.

I rang him up when I ran out of work.

"Yeah it's me."

"You on?"

"Sure."

"Where do you want to go to score?"

"The dealer I get from lives in your building, lets hang out there."

"Cool."

I knew the dealer he was talking about, but like the hookers that lived in my building I'd never taken any business there. I kept that shit or at least the knowledge of where I lived and what I did separate.

I met Crawler on the street and we went up to the apartment. I cleaned off the table while he went upstairs to get some shit.

Carpet Crawler came down and pulled an eight ball of rock out of his pocket and a pipe out of his shoe. It was a cheap glass tube stuffed with steel wool. The glass was run through with black.

The first eight ball takes its time. We have some water and a few beers, there is some bullshit on TV and we talk about what's been happening on the block. Somewhere around the last gram or so we start to run into a problem.

Our problem stems from the unfortunate confluence of the physical properties of crack cocaine and my shitty housekeeping.

When you break a crack rock up to smoke some pieces

We are in a rather disgusting pattern as we torch three pieces of litter for every piece of candy. The magnifying glass and flash light haven't yielded the results I was hoping for, but we soldier on as best we can. I'm thankful that my mouth is so numb because I can't imagine what I taste like.

Isn't that shit supposed to clump for fucks sake!

We finally look at each other and realize that everything is gone and we are broke as fuck. All we have left are those little plastic baggies which we each lick clean.

I give Crawler a beer and we make small talk around the fact that we have no more money to get high with.

After he finishes the beer he gets up to go. I can tell that he is going right back upstairs to try and get a front and sell what he can for the night so that he can smoke some more. I'm just hoping that if I die of a heart attack that I do it before I come all the way down.

I walk Carpet Crawler to the door, and lock it after him.

Then I lay there sipping beer that I can't taste running all over the world in ups and downs and back arounds until I finally start to come off of it in the real rather than fiending for more sense.

I don't know how, but eventually I sleep.

The next day I wake up to an emergency fill call from the temp agency for which I am unbelievably grateful and completely unprepared to take on. I have a pretty straight relationship with my main recruiter guy and he tells me no time for a drug test we got work to do.

Walking to the bus stop I realize that everything that catches light on the sidewalk glitters enough to make me think of getting high. Physical addiction is horrible and the pain of it drives you to relapse, psychological addiction is the opposite of that, the little gnawing hunger in your mind that makes you a traitor to yourself.

The only silver lining to this nightmare is the work itself.

My new assignment is staring at books on a conveyor

belt. They are all pulp fiction detective and romance novels. The covers alternate between variations of some big busted girl in a dress and some dude in a trench coat. I had a funny idea that I would read them on my breaks, but ten pages of the first one I chose at random sorted that out.

Theoretically, I am checking them for defects, but today is pure survival mode.

When I get home my nerves are completely shot, but I am over the worst of it. I grab a beer out of the fridge and sit down with it and smoke a cigarette. I have five smokes left and my account is so negative that when I get paid in a week there won't be much left over.

I see I have some messages on my machine. I listen to them in the vain hope that some girl that I have given my number to will actually call me back.

Instead it's a couple bill collectors and Carpet Crawler. He wants to know when I'll be up for hanging out again.

I hold down the delete key until everything is erased and gone away.

WILD CHILD IN THE CITY

It's nice to have a place of my own, finally!

I've got my furniture figured out and while it's not much all of it is mine. My bed, my dresser, my kitchen, my alarm clock, my schedule, my bills, my place.

The whole living with a dude thing is fucking bullshit and totally not worth it. I've seen enough girls go from having daddy pay for everything to having their husband pay for everything. Cradle to grave in the pocket of a man and I'm saying FUCK THAT!

I was on that path because I didn't know any better, but I'm getting it figured out now.

It's got its difficult moments, but the whole never having to explain yourself to some judgmental, staring fucking dude part is really winning me over.

I'm going to play with the boys for a little while if you don't mind. My game, my terms, my rules.

No honey, you can't have my number, but it's been fun.

First things first, no more redneck dick for me, that's for sure. Now don't get me wrong, some of it was sweet and strong and long and could go on and on, but I am a young girl with ambitions and the world even if it's just this city is big enough to do some exploring in. Say it with me girls, don't want no, don't want no, don't want no REDNECK DICK!

That's right.

Now, what's a young girl with a great body and good hair

day to do? I don't care what the Fish says; Minneapolis is the greatest city in the world. It could be the capital of the planet for all I care, and now that Bonk is history it's time to start enjoying it.

My job isn't perfect, but it's good enough for now.

Serving is just like stripping except that you have to keep your clothes on, and charming dudes for tips is only demeaning if they're wallets are light.

Two rolls suits me perfectly. It's the right amount to go with some drum and bass and it lasts just long enough to close the place.

Dancing is easy when you have a body like mine, put on one of those super tight T-shirts or tit shirts as I call them, and then add short skirts and just slip around. Don't shake it too hard, let it move on its own and it will. You gotta work it, but you don't have to hurt it, just push it, push it, then reverse it.

I like the dreadlocks and the copper skin. I like the shaved head and B-boy style. I like the hard muscles underneath the clothes. I like the look and I like the cologne. I don't care about the game you talk just don't come off too fucking stupid.

I don't go for any one style, but I only go for stylish. Whatever you wear you just gotta pull it off. Baby, all you gotta do is prove it to me.

I like men that get it. Men have to meet some standards too. I'm the center of attention, sure, but you can't be some slouchy piece of shit. You have to compliment me and you have to complement me.

I don't smash it on the rink so you can slouch it on the couch.

I work hard to look this good and you better respect and reciprocate that baby. Otherwise you're just going to be a spectator in the show of me. Sex is the only exercise I enjoy, but I'm not partnering up with just anyone. I'm in it to enjoy it and not just be enjoyed.

It's tough being a single girl alone in a world of aggressive cock. I want to use some of it, but I don't want to get used by any of it.

Trust is the punch line of a bad joke and no one is the only one that can cheat on you if you're not with any one. I'm done playing favorites with boys. I'm not going to be "the one" for anyone, from here on out everything I do is going to be just for fun.

Just for me, no strings and no promises, no expectations or worries.

It's amazing what a girl can get away with just because she's hot as hell. I got into a club last Saturday night for free and when the line to the bathroom was too long I just pissed on the floor. Did I get thrown out?

No.

Why?

Because the bouncer wanted to fuck me as soon as he set his eyes on me. I batted mine at him and opened my purse and he just waved me in as I shook my ass.

That's fucking class right there.

Can you imagine that for all the fucking Revlon ads and bullshit on TV and in the magazines that some girls go their entire life without ever once feeling beautiful?

And I'm talking about the pretty girls that should know better.

Not me, I am wise to that game. Not going to get caught up in any bullshit, not going to have any of those drama problems, easy come and easy go. That's what I say. Just get your head down there because you gotta make me come before you get some!

That's the spirit!

I went to a high class club with Hotrod last night. He paid for everything and told me that I would get a man in no time at all, and he wasn't kidding.

Kevin is a nice boy.

I wish he would stop calling though.

There is a thing or two to learn from Hotrod.

He's not my type, but he is fun to go out with. Last night two different girls got jealous when we danced together and of course he had already had his fun with both of them. They should know better. There was nothing to do but slut out on him on the dance floor. Why not? If you're going to act like that then you may as well have someone hotter than you ruin your night.

Too funny!

Oh, this is one of my favorites. I am going to bump on this boy, grind on him for five or ten minutes to get him good and hard, and then I am going to walk away. I love that look in their eyes when they realize that all that tension isn't getting any release from me.

I'll watch them out of the corner of my eye and see if they go to the bathroom to jerk off.

If they do that, I win.

It's the same when I make out with another girl in front of them. It's a great show, but if my body's the stage then I'm the one that calls the curtain.

That game can go so many ways. Right after I moved out of the Fish's place I had a thing with this girl named Brandi. It started with a little kiss just for fun and I realized that she wasn't just admiring how pretty I am.

She fucking wanted me.

I played around with her for a while, I'd never done anything with a girl before and I'm open minded. I've dreamed about having sex with other girls, dreamed about their hair being soft and their bodies being beautiful.

We took a shower together once and she hugged me from behind and massaged it, the outer part, and a little inside and all the right places in and around, the map that the boys can't read.

When I came she looked victorious.

But God, what a clingy bitch. Getting rid of her was a fucking head ache. I can see why Hotrod is always telling lies and giving out fake numbers and blocking bitches on his phone. They just don't get it. It's not about that! Besides that girl was so selfish in bed it was just unbearable.

Great in the shower and awful in the sack.

The shower was the high point of that relationship.

Oh my God, I went to a gay bar the other day. It was downtown under the sky scrapers and all the lights. I had never seen men do that kind of stuff before. I watched two guys going at it. It was crazy! One of them was really aggressive with the other one, but he didn't seem to mind at all. I didn't know what to think of it.

It was kind of hot though.

God, Bonk and I never went out. All we fucking did was lay around and get high and watch movies and play video games. I can't believe I threw away those years doing that. That's what you get for thinking you've found forever at fifteen.

Maybe I could find some switch hitters and have a two on one. I don't know, I think one of them always has butt sex with you if you do that. I don't know if I want that, but it would be cool to watch them stroke and kind of wrestle with each other. I don't know.

I have to think about that one.

The fucking drugs that you can get for free! It's amazing. I got this dude over in Dinkytown. I just visit him and he gets me high. I don't kiss him. I only call him when I want to get stoned. Every time he sees me, he just glows and gives me whatever I want. He stares at me with these big doe brown eyes like he's the happiest guy in the world just for being around me.

I may have to visit him tomorrow.

Black cock, white cock, yellow cock!

I hug up on a girl and we give the boys a little show. I rub my tits against hers and we kiss a little bit. I always kiss with my eyes closed. It's a damn shame because I would love to see the looks on the guy's faces.

You can't pay for this kind of fun. You can only have it if

you're willing to take it.

It's only eleven. There's plenty of time, but I should start thinking things over. That's one of the most important things for a girl to know. If you're not the one choosing then you are the one losing.

I love watching guys compete for me. One second they're men and the next second they're boys out on the playground.

It's so cute!

They act so tough with each other. That one over there is trying to pretend dignity, he's all stand offish, but it's just an act. I can see in his eyes how much he wants me and how much he hates the other guys.

Sorry buddy, no fairytales here. You're going to have to earn me.

The lecture hall is the same as the night club except instead of dancing they are trying to sound clever.

After class they ask you out for coffee and want to talk to you if only to show off how smart they are and how you should listen to them.

Slacker geniuses with their hardons hidden under the table just waiting for you to be the one that finally understands them.

Fuck that.

Boys are just desperate to impress. That's the trap though because once they've got you impressed all it turns into is another way to be your boss. Then it's all about trying to control you and tell you what to do by telling you why you should do it.

Not this girl.

Not anymore, not now, not ever again.

Well, this guy wants to buy me a drink. He seems fine. After a drink or two I'll dance with him. If that feels okay then we'll see where it goes from there.

I'm so glad its Friday. I hate going through the morning after bullshit when you have to throw the guy out and get ready for class at the same time.

Oh they're playing my song and all the boys want to dance with me.

I think we've found our winner. I can feel him naked underneath his clothes and he feels fine and strong. Damn, this boy fits like a nice pair of jeans.

I've had it with love.

GAINFULLY EMPLOYED

I had been warned. That was for certain.

I had heeded the warnings. I'd listened.

It wasn't like I hadn't pursued alternatives.

I had tried to sell drugs for a living, but that had proven unsustainable. Being your own best customer is a business model that only works in government. I guess it just goes to show you why business and pleasure are typically segregated. Still, you can't blame a guy for trying.

I had done day labor and temp work.

I had been a mover and a packer of trucks. I had sat in offices. I had answered phones and validated parking tickets.

I even completed one of those job training programs for poor people and became a certified nursing assistant. I'd worked on a hospice floor at a hospital. I watched a lot of people die there and I learned something about death and life.

I had to quit that one though. It got to be too much.

I had prayed daily that all the Y2K shit in the news would come true and we would have a massive financial meltdown that would make us all equal again, but I had been disappointed.

The citizens of the Great Asylum live a frustrated dream of apocalypse.

I had been released back into the wild at the end of the probationary period of several promising career opportunities.

I had been told, "this just isn't working out," and "we

just don't see you as a long term fit here," and "we are no longer in need of your services."

I had begged, borrowed and stolen.

Depending on one's perspective I had sunk or risen to the level I naturally belonged at. That location had a name: the You Slave for US! temporary employment agency.

We had come together like destiny.

You Slave for US! is a big believer in second chances. Their applications didn't bother to include a section for references, and they weren't rude enough to ask for a resume. They felt that the past was a territory best left unexplored, and they put little stock in the slanderous opinions of previous employers.

At You Slave for US! I worked with people whose legal status was questionable as well as people actively participating in the legal system.

There was only one downside to the otherwise refreshing atmosphere of near absolute forgiveness. They didn't pay the kind of rates that people getting it right the first time through life would suffer.

Even the process of getting paid involved costs.

They gave everyone these ATM payroll cards that were connected to individual accounts that your weekly wages were deposited into. It cost three bucks a month to have the card. If you had questions you had to call some fucking automated assistance line and if you had to talk to real person it was a buck. If you didn't use it for a while the card would expire and you'd have to spend another three bucks to activate it, or if enough time had gone by you'd have to buy a new one. That was ten bucks. It was the same if you lost one, and with the way I drink you'd think I collected the fucking things.

It was the banking cartel version of the company store, and I hope I get to share a room in hell with whoever came up with it.

As a holder of a legitimate social security card and the good fortune of never having been arrested for any of the felonies I'd committed I would occasionally land gigs that fell outside of You Slave for US's wheelhouse.

One of them had been at a customer service call center for a telephone company. I had picked that one up just after my heart ache and depression had really settled in. I was so numb that I became the perfect drone and repeated their call center scripts with precision. People would yell at me about money and I would respond in a near-Buddhist perfection of someone beyond the grubby hold of possessions or wealth.

I had finished the assignment with flying colors and wished them Godspeed as they shipped the operation off to India. Before leaving the country they gave the agency a five star review of my performance.

There's a first time for everything.

That had led to the medical records secretary and coding position at the "Theirview Health Maintenance Organization Insurance SubDivision" where I had been offered a temp to permanent position based on performance.

It paid over ten dollars an hour and I'd rarely pulled that in and never for very long.

My job was to take confidential medical information and break it into three categories according to a chart. There were things that the government had to pay for, things that the patient had to pay for, and things that Theirview refused to pay for. The insurance offered by Theirview read so nicely that too many sick people had signed up for it and it was too expensive for any healthy person to buy.

My present employment provided a resolution to that dilemma. There were days when I was sure ethically, at least on a scale of harms, that I would've better benefited society by staying in the drug trade.

The job wasn't particularly difficult as long as you followed the golden rule of doubt equals denial of claim.

You had to overcome some internal resistance to get that down, but being unemployed for long periods of time has a way of wearing out all those moral reflexes.

The Adventures of Hotrod and Pilot Fish

The other thing that I had to do was organize medical charts for staff to carry along with the patients to certain tests that Theirview was absolutely not going to pay for. The final irony was that this insurance was the only employer based option available to the employees of Theirview.

I was trained by an overworked woman whose command of English seemed constricted to the use of adjectives and adverbs.

As a poet warrior who could compose quatrains, sonnets, free verse, iambic pentameter and could pursue and complete a haiku, this was at times a strain for the Fish, but he hated everything to do with my job so he often time traveled while I was at work.

My supervisor was neither fat nor thin, ugly nor fair, old nor young. The simple fact that you couldn't even dislike her completely fucked me up. It's always easier with people if they fall into simple classifications like the patients whose claims we denied or passed on to the government.

Her ordinariness was so complete it became enigmatic, and my depression was so complete I just did what she asked me to do.

We worked in an office that was located underground in the basement of the building next to the pharmacy. All of our light was artificial. My boss told me that in the winter you could go weeks without ever seeing the sun.

When she told me that I looked at her and smiled.

It had been three and a half months, and then the day came. A skinny fake and baked male and a nearly translucent round female came to visit me.

"We are from Human Resources." They said in a terrifying unison in such a way that you knew the department was capitalized.

The Fish had come with me to work that day, and he started and stared at these strange creatures. He regretfully realized that he had left his sword at home. He examined his options. He could bull-rush one of them while dodging the other. With a little luck, he would make it to the combination copier-fax machine in the back. Next to the machine was an old fashioned hat rack. With that and his back to the wall, he could keep them at bay for some time, certainly long enough to hatch a plan for escape. He stood up and edged slightly between the door and the hallway to the copier.

"What can I do for you?" I asked. But I already knew. When the human resources jackals arrive, it means that they are either going to fuck you off or worse, offer you a job. I suppressed the desire to run screaming out of the building, after all, it was this or the book factory, or back to selling drugs.

I was sure that they were going to cut me loose anyway, so I figured lets ride it out and maybe try to file an unemployment claim.

"Could you come to our office we'd like to talk to you about the conditions of your employment?"

"Certainly." I replied silently praying for my dismissal.

I went over to my boss's office to give her the bad news. "Lilly, I have to go to human resources, should be back soon."

"Super large, slick, heavy, slippery files, coding becomes increasingly and unerringly ..."

Alarming on the first day of work, yes, but the Fish now understood it as a natural phenomenon. I left her between nouns, and followed the HR people out into the hallway of the tunnel level that connected two buildings that I had never been in as we were able to go directly underground to our office from the parking lot.

The Fish noticed how the vermin fanned out on either side of him. He was not nervous. He prepared himself for the DOUBLE SWITCH tactic should they turn on him simultaneously in a coordinated attack.

We abandoned hope when we got to the elevator and instead pled with the divine. The Fish prayed first to God, then to St. Christopher, Jude the Apostle, St. George, St. Dwynwen, then to Jesus Christ and then the Holy Spirit. After that it was on to Athena and then to Isis and Mars and Horus, which

The Adventures of Hotrod and Pilot Fish

seemed like double duty, but hey desperate times. He was going to offer something to Sargon of Akad, but the elevator slammed open on the fourth floor interrupting his plea.

We marched down another hallway to a stairwell that connected this building to yet another. Then into a skyway, after three hundred meters, another elevator and then a left, down a hallway carpeted the color of blood into a waiting room without any windows.

The Parthenon had been exhausted, the Ogdoad had been covered, Allah had been sequestered, and now the Fish was deep into the Rig Veda, but this is slow going as the Sanskrit is hard to pronounce even in the mind.

"Could you wait here please?" They said it together and then motioned each with the opposite arm to a couch. The couch was littered with maternity magazines.

"Perhaps they were Siamese twins and though no longer conjoined, they share the same *mind*." Thought the Fish. He had seen such phenomenon explored in a few films, but had never taken any of it as credible.

They walked past us into what I could only assume was their office. They shut the door behind them.

The Pilot Fish took a seat and stared at the bloated female shapes on the covers. As a hero the Fish held nothing but the deepest regard for pregnant women. He hated dogs along a similar logic. The great and eternal holy host would be commanded by a man born of a virgin woman. In this army the Fish expected to ride lance in hand against the forces of the jackal spawn.

Our plan was to sit out the rapture.

The Fish engrossed himself in an article regarding the hassles of pre-term labor. Pregnancy clearly is a mysterious and magical process; the body itself, the host, can rebel and misapply the forces of nature. The Fish mused, would there one day be a pre-term labor female inside the Fish Bowl?

Oh, but the life of the hero is a solitary one.

The male opened the door and motioned to me, "We're

ready, could you come in please? Would you care for some coffee or tea?"

The female's voice matched his in everything but pitch and echoed out into the anteroom.

We hadn't lived this long by saying yes to every cup of tea offered us by enemies.

"No thanks." I said as I sat down across from them.

They shared a gigantic desk.

"Well, we'd like to start by saying that You Slave for US! recommended you very highly and you have certainly kept them from being a liar!"

I took that as a cue to laugh and brayed at them like a donkey.

The Pilot Fish cased the room for something long, preferably with a point on the end.

"We have decided to ask you, would you care to stay on here, on a permanent basis. We are prepared to count the time you've been with us already against the standard six month probation and would offer a slight raise."

"Uh, yes that sounds good."

I think this was my depression talking more than anything else. I had gotten used to the place and the stress of unemployment and new assignments was more than I was willing to take on in my already weakened condition.

"We'd also like to tell you about the retirement plan possibilities that Theirview Health Maintenance Organization Insurance SubDivision offers its employees."

"Retirement?"

"Yes, we have company contributed options for both 401a and 403b plans, as well as a 401k plan." The duo in unison pulled out two folders from the desk that they shared. The left arm of the female had a folder marked 401a and the right arm of the male had a folder marked 403b.

"You have thought about retirement?" they said in chilling unison.

We had thought about it.

The Adventures of Hotrod and Pilot Fish

Our retirement plan was to die in battle.

"A little bit, but honestly not with a lot of specificity."

Specificity was a word that I had recently learned from my overworded and overworked boss in the medical records department. I was trying to use it in as many sentences as I could.

The Pilot Fish scanned the forms intently. Was there some ancient numerology at work? 40*1, well that wasn't going anywhere. 4*0, again a dead end. 4+0+1, but then if one needs the prime of five, why the superfluous 0? I had picked that word up as well from my boss, but using it had been last month's project. Like I said, she was a wealth of adjectives. The Fish applied the same approach to the 403b and came up with 120.

Interesting product, but what does it mean!

If the forty was divided by the one, 40/1, again, pointless, and dividing four by zero gave only an undefined result. Could this be another one of man's futile efforts at understanding infinity? Perhaps, the A and B play a special role, but what form of gematria employs variables? Was there significance in the exclusive use of lower case? The Fish ran single substitution cyphers on the numbers across several alphabets searching for significant words, but nothing consequential came up.

Was this the algebraic numerology known only to the fabled witches of the Islands of the Ever East?

If only the Fish had a ship and a crew and a fair wind.

Only possibilities, and again, it could just be trickery on the part of the human resources harpies. We had been warned about before, in other jobs, by other temporary employees.

"I will take the 4—0—3" my eyes darted between them, the lady and the tiger, the third door, "b".

"Excellent choice. How much of a percent would you wish to contribute at this stage?"

"Zero." I said.

"Of course." They replied.

Now I knew I was being lied to.

"From your work in medical records you are also aware of our excellent employee health plan."

"Why yes I am."

"Well, then we'll conclude this with a few forms, and we'll have you set up as a permanent employee."

"Thank you." I said.

They both looked down at some papers on the great desk and every instinct inside the Fish shouted, NOW, strike NOW, while they are distracted, but alas all that was on the table was a stapler, and it was one of those little shitty ones, if it had been a big swing stapler there may have been a chance.

"Sign here, please. It's a permanent employee non-disclosure agreement regarding the medical information that you will be viewing, as well as ever disclosing or insinuating anything about the inner or outer workings of "Theirview Health Maintenance Organization Insurance SubDivision," its associated clinics, limited and strategic partners. It's quite different from the temporary employment non-disclosure agreement that you signed when you started in that this form is pink, the other one as you no doubt recall was blue."

The Fish signed the pink piece of paper with a flourish and walked out the door without turning his back to them. They both waved, opposite arms in the air in a slow half circle motion.

"Welcome to the family." The synchronous echo followed the Fish down the hallway all the way to the elevator.

I made my way back to the office,

I gave Lilly the news, "Hey Lilly, they made me legit."

"Larger, largest, pushed onto the smaller and smallest 'till the billowing..." her head slid slowly down her chest.

Strange on your first day of work, certainly, but once your used to it you'd miss it if it didn't happen. I chose to interpret it as congratulatory.

I sat down at my desk and began filing the long list of things that Theirview was refusing to cover for some poor fucker. It really is a shame I failed in the drug trade.

After work I went home and cut up 70 dollars' worth of payroll cards.

THE FUNERAL

Bonk stands by the casket looking at his brother's body. He's absolutely alone and I feel terrible for him. I wish that I could reach him in a way that would make him feel better, but there's no way to do that. All I can do is stand by letting him know that he isn't alone in this even though he is.

Bonk and I were never very close and I knew his brother only vaguely. We connected to each other only through the stronger relationships that we had with the friends we held in common. I have to be here because of all those things, but my being here doesn't do anything. I fill in a space that would only be noticed if it was empty.

That being said, I can still do something. I walk up to him and give him a hug.

"Thanks for coming."

"It's nothing, I'm so sorry."

"Thanks."

We look at each other and we've already run out of words. He turns away from me towards the casket and I leave him to his silence.

I look over the rest of us that came.

Wildchild is still beautiful and wears somber to her advantage. She and Bonk haven't let their failed relationship interfere with their grief and I am happy for both of them for that.

She looks me over in a casual calculation yielding a familiar result.

She wins in the competition that I have spent my life trying to avoid. I can't respect her because she wants so hard to play the game and she can't respect me because all I want to do is quit.

It doesn't have to be this way, but this is how it is.

Can I just concede? Will someone accept my surrender? Can I just give up? If I did would I be left alone?

The Fish steps in between us. He holds my hand in one of his and one of hers in the other of his then he puts his arms up and around both of our shoulders as a silent entreat to play nice before he walks up to Bonk and puts his arm around him.

The Fish has told me all about her antics up in Minneapolis. Wild plays with her sexuality in the sense that it creates another erotic dimension with men. Her sexuality has multiple facets through which a man can desire her. Her sexuality is a circus mirror scintillating before one great eye.

I am the opposite of that.

I want to be left alone, can you please leave me untouched, I didn't get dressed for you, please don't stare, my expression is my own, don't tell me to smile, you have no right to my feelings so please leave me unhugged, and if you're stronger than me I entreat you to leave me uncompelled.

Is that too much to ask?

This funeral makes me think of my father's funeral. I wrote a song about it, kind of, but it didn't turn out right. Not every song does.

Woolf was right about feelings, they can only be fully realized as memories. In their moment, intense feelings only make you laugh at something horrible or scream something unintelligible.

My feelings are the foundation of my art and there's nothing worse than working with a feeling too new. It can't be distilled or denied. There you are feeling so much and not able to move it or touch it at all. It just sits there and weighs you down, killing you, crushing you, wearing you out by wanting out in its stubborn immobility.

There isn't a universal velocity, some feelings move into memory quickly and others linger.

It's been years since he died.

I guess I'm over it.

I guess I'm not.

Grief and recovery, you get as far as you are and you go as slow as you go.

This is where I am now, but this now is just part of a greater present and this place is just another place in the sense of a greater path. I heal and hurt and hurt and heal and walk and walk.

It's one step at a time and the road is long.

The Fish is standing next to Hotrod in front of the casket. They look perfect together. Two things nicely damaged alone and together better reflect each other's wounds.

That's not fair, that's only one half of what they are.

The Pilot Fish is discreet with a silver flask and a rented suit. Looking at him, I can tell he's been drinking since he got up. He's all about the difference between drinking and drunk. Hotrod is looking good as usual, stylish even at a funeral.

I walk over to the Fish and lean against him as he puts his arm around me.

He looks me over blind to everything my eyes have said to me and deaf to everything I've ever said to myself. Of all the men that I've had and the loves that I've felt this is the only one that I regret.

We really could have been something.

It is what it is. We don't get to choose these things. It's a damn shame made worse by the fact that neither of us can compromise in matters of the heart.

Can you understand me when I say that I just wanted to be friends?

He makes such a fine friend.

He smells like a combination of dry clean only, cigarettes and booze. I can feel him in that suit and he is still strong, still the same.

"Hey Jani, how you holding up?"

But you knew that already, didn't you?

The Adventures of Hotrod and Pilot Fish

Hi.

Welcome to the show of me, talking or not talking, dreaming or singing. My mind wanders. You're the next hitchhiker I've picked up for a ride.

I have been clean for seven months and I won't be going back to Chicago. My mother worries about me. She thinks coming to a funeral is going to push me over the edge and I'll be back to using again. I tried to explain to her that I don't want to die anymore, that the part of me that did is dead. That I'm fine, but she has a hard time believing me. I'm moving to New York for graduate school in a few months, and she is terrified that I will start dying again.

I'm going to get my M.F.A. at New York University.

The Fish is going to help me move in. It will be the first time for both of us to see New York.

I look away from the Fish, "Numb, I guess."

"I've still got a way to go."

He looks like he wants to destroy something beautiful. Male emotion is just a broken bridge between two disparate seas. The Fish slips his flask into my hand. It feels cool, almost not real.

I take a smooth and long swallow of the vodka as usual.

There is no cold to be warmed against, there is nothing left to feel guilty for unless you feel guilty for the whole world and all that's in it.

"I'm ok, I guess, how about you?"

"Yeah, I guess, about the same."

"Can I have another?"

"Sure, it's an open bar."

I wait until I can feel the warmth from the first pull get all the way down to my toes before I take another sip, this one smaller. I swallow hard and think of something else until it settles. I hand it back to him.

"It's not fair," God I sound stupid saying it, "It's been too long since I saw him last. I don't feel like I belong here."

"It's important that you came."

"I didn't want to, but I knew I couldn't forgive myself if I didn't."

"I feel the same way. I thought we'd have more time."

But there isn't any time left and there's nothing to be done about it except witness it, experience it, endure it. It's beyond our reach to rectify and throwing a solid dose of helplessness into the mix doesn't help.

We talked about Chicago, once, and I thanked him and we've never talked about it again. It's not something either of us wants to dwell on. It has a strong sense of unreality about it, and honestly I was so messed up at the time I don't have any clear memories of what happened there.

I'm grateful and sad, and guilty about it at the same time.

I remember the events leading up to it. I remember sliding down the spiral staircase. I remember pawning my guitar for drugs.

I still can't believe I did that.

Rock bottom is the topic people prefer to talk about. Climbing back up to normal is usually left out of the conversation. No one talks about how hard it is to say, "Yep, I'm normal today. Normal is good, normal is enough."

What a sad lie. Normal was never enough, I always wanted something more than normal.

No one talks about that, you just bottom out and then you become a fucking housewife with perfect teeth and two kids married to a man who pays the bills and looks after you.

What a joke.

No one talks about how much fun it is to go to the dentist after three years of neglect from using.

They just ask you why you don't smile more.

No one talks about the depression and that you as a rational animal have now experienced things beyond the ken. I have had my highest highs and lowest lows already, and that leaves little to look forward to. If there was a pill to make me ignorant of my own life I would swallow it without hesitation.

The Fish pulls on the flask and offers it to me once more, but I don't think that I can handle another drink of warm vodka quite yet.

I wave it off.

The viewing is over and we take our places in the pews.

First, the priest speaks and then the parents share a few words with us.

Bonk closes with the eulogy that the Fish wrote for him. It's mainly about how we always assume that the time is there until one day we wake up and discover that it's already over.

The Fish is a fine writer.

I have a confession: I am beautiful. You could get lost in the maybe of my eyes. If you try to quote me on that I'll deny it. I'll never tell you a secret again.

Being beautiful isn't what's hard, its being a woman that's hard.

Men get to live under the illusion that they are what they're body does, and women live under the reality of it and the unfairness of it wears me out. It wears me out that someone else's illusion takes precedence over my reality. It wears me out that my reality just gets swept under the rug of some collective idealism.

I'm the one that has to live that reality, don't I get a vote?

Other women wear me out with the way they look at me. With the way they ask me questions so they can rub the answers in my face: Don't have a man then you need one, got a man, when you getting married, No kids, you should have one. Got a baby, when you having another.

You get to play dress up for a day and wife for the rest of your life.

And the pot of gold at the end of the rainbow is filled with these words: virtuous, stable, smiling, kind, wise, loving, nurturing, energetic, selfless, perfect. But they'll still measure the space between your thighs even if you've had two kids and sacrificed away your everything.

They call me the opposite of all those things now, carefully so that I don't crack to pieces in front of them, but they say them just the same. They want to encourage my conformity instead of bullying it, but the end goal hasn't changed.

But.

I won't.

I tell them.

Call me what you will.

I'm saying.

No.

It's the same way when I try to talk about being raped which is why I don't talk about being raped. I don't tell anyone about it because the questions wear me out. Our culture frames the debate before I get to speak. The answers to those questions map a path back to me and away from the person that raped me. The questions start at the rape and end at me. The answers are about what I did to deserve it.

I DON'T KNOW THOSE ANSWERS!

I don't know what I did to deserve it. That's the question I get wrong. And I've asked myself that question many, many times. That's the irony in the injustice. I never raped anyone, but I know what it feels like to get blamed for rape.

Oh, and I know what it's like to be raped, but that's the place we're trying to get away from, right?

I told you my mind wanders.

I wear the Color Purple and I've drank from the Bell Jar, and I've walked unescorted in the dark To the Lighthouse, and I basked in the glory of that radiant illumination.

I've been naked and free and refused that province to the isolation of boys and I understand that men will always be more interested in women than women in men.

Women let their sons go but our fathers never stop looking after their daughters.

The service has ended and I look at the Fish with my eyes holding the question, "Why hasn't anyone said anything at all about his being a suicide?"

The Fish smiles sadly and just nods away the fact that this is how people are, and the rest of it is how we wish to remember people as we wanted them to be rather than how they were.

But for the Fish and I who only wish to remember things exactly as they were. We need the stock pure so that we can distort it with our art. Our eyes rolled back in our heads looking over the fields of our experience for the feelings that have matured enough to be fully experienced and then transformed and pushed out into the present for others to pick up, rinse off and repeat with.

My cousin and aunt and uncle are on their way to get me. My mom's at work. The whole family looks out for the fallen angel.

Don't get me wrong, I am grateful and I love them.

My cousin is a beautiful girl. She takes very good care of herself. She eats carefully and is quietly obsessed with her bowels. I like her nails. They have fades and shades and whirls and tails. She is a good girl and she has never played with fire.

My aunt wants me to be fat and happy and cute and friendly and she takes me for what I am. There's a me in her that never happened, and we keep that as our secret.

Sometimes she'll squeeze my hand and it says everything. She simultaneously celebrates and laments my great self-destruction. She does it without being jealous or self-righteous about it and I love her and thank her for it. My uncle looks at me while looking like my father. There's too much there and sometimes as we go through this I feel confused as if I'm angry at him for the resemblance of someone else's sins.

My mother runs in my blood and tongue.

My father is where I am stopped in time.

And here passes another one of those things that we call days.

I told you my mind wanders.

It wanders around trying to find a better place to be, but

all it has is me. When it gets to be too much I go for a run, and I run until it stops wanting to leave.

    Sometimes that can take a while.

FLYING FISH

It's very important to me that we are clear on this point. There have been some long sighs on the phone and some serious bullshit in some people's attitudes about this whole thing, so I need you to understand me clearly when I tell you that this whole thing was the Fish's fault.

He is 100% to blame.

What I did wasn't at all what Bonk's brother did, and I tried to explain that to everyone. No one believed me though, they gave me some oohs and ahhs and some condescending bullshit about how much pain I must be in.

That gets fucking annoying.

That gets old real fucking quick.

It wasn't supposed to hurt at all and it was only going to be a onetime thing for the fun of it.

It was supposed to be a grand adventure.

It just didn't work out that way.

After the funeral I went home and kind of fell into a rut. I would get up, go to work, go home and go to bed. That was all the energy I had. A waste of a summer if you ask me, but doing that was really taking all I had.

The Fish wanted to get me outside. He told me that he had made a special flying potion that only the Fish knew how to make. I took the potion and jumped off the roof of my apartment building. He wasn't lying about the flying part. I did fly, about fifty feet, but mainly straight down and really quite fast. It turned out that it hadn't been much of a flying potion at all.

It was gin.

That's hardly a suicide attempt, now is it?

It's really more of a piece of aeronautic witchcraft gone wrong. I should have known that motherfucker didn't know what he was talking about when I asked about the broom.

"Don't you need a broom to fly?"

"Not with this stuff."

I should have known right then and there the motherfucker was up to no good.

But to call it a suicide attempt is just bullshit.

It was if you're willing to take a broader perspective a simple hazard in the pursuit of some magic. Spells devoted to flight and fire invulnerability carry with them special risks if they fail.

That's hardly a reason to sew your cape into a pillowcase; it's just a fact that needs to be reflected in your preparations.

I ended up in the hospital with a broken leg, dislocated shoulder, and severe concussion.

More precisely, some girl walking by my building listening to "When Doves Cry" on her iAUDIO nearly tripped over me. We made eye contact and I was feeling the lyrics over the melody. Her eyes moved over me stopping at the point where my left fibula was shoved out through my jeans. She called 911 and left the scene, I don't think she wanted to be a part of whatever had happened there.

God bless her, I have no idea who she is.

While I was in the hospital I was visited by several doctors and nurses. One of them told me that I had a blood alcohol level of .41 when they found me. They told me that I was almost dead from booze, and I said, "Well, if you drink enough gin that's basically bound to happen."

One of them was a psychiatrist and he told me that after I was medically stable that I would be transferred to a psychiatric floor. He informed me that I was on a psychiatric hold, and I was not allowed to leave on my own.

I felt pretty stable then and there. Honestly, I hadn't noticed the concussion at all.

A few weeks later some poor fucker with a name tag that said "Mike" under his photo wheeled me from my airy and open orthopedic recovery floor over to a locked psychiatric unit. I asked him, "Don't you have a last name?"

"Yeah."

"Why isn't it on your name tag?"

"They don't want to let the patients know our last names, for our safety."

"When you say patients, you mean the crazy ones right?"

"I never said that."

"Why are they locking me up now?"

He said, "I don't know, maybe you're getting around too good on that leg."

Dude had a point.

The psychiatric floor was actually pretty cozy. There were a bunch of lazy psychology grads that played games with us. None of them were particularly heroic. When I told them about the Pilot Fish and the true nature of heroism as it was changing with the new millennium and the coming age all they would do was nod at me and then scribble something down on a notepad.

I figured even if they weren't heroes at least they were taking notes on it.

I also got to see that psychiatrist some more and he told me some crazy ass shit.

We didn't meet often because he was so busy with his other patients, but he was able to cover a lot of ground in a short amount of time.

The fifth time we spoke:

"Have you had any thoughts of suicide or self harm lately?"

"No."

"I'm going to increase your anti-depressants, keep you on the Antabuse and get another lithium level."

"OK, any idea when you'll let me go. I only work down the tunnel in the other building, maybe I could get a work pass?"

"At this stage we had better keep you here."

I really didn't want to go back to work. I was just concerned that my insurance claim would get processed and denied before I could get to it. I didn't want to get stuck with a bill for all this bullshit.

I could best describe my psychiatrist as one of those middle aged bastards who thinks that fifty is the new forty and golf is the new tennis. He was basically a Freudian with a chemistry degree.

We had some challenging discussions about identity:

"So the Fish gave you the flying potion?"

"Yes, but it was a trick, it was only gin."

"Is the Fish here now?"

"Of course he is. Vigilance is a requirement of heroism. You can't be a hero if you are sleeping all the time."

I snapped my fingers for emphasis after I said that and he raised his eyebrows at me in response.

"And who is the Fish?"

"I am the Fish and the Fish is me."

"But he is different from you."

"His ways are sometimes strange to me."

"Is he always with you?"

"Not always, sometimes he stays in the Fish Bowl, he doesn't like my job you know, so he usually stays home when I go to work. That or he travels in time."

"He can travel in time?"

"Yes."

This was often a stopping point in our conversations as my doctor wasn't familiar with time travel at all. He had a hard time getting his head around it. Then he would charge off on a different line of inquiry.

"Due to the circumstances of your suicide attempt would you consider the Fish to be your nemesis?"

"You mean like the Ratched to my McMurphy?"

He never appreciated my metaphors. After we hashed that out he would go on and approach the same question from a different angle.

"Would you say that the Fish is your alter ego?"

"I think the Fish's ego has been altered, he certainly seems to have altered mine."

"Wouldn't you be the alter ego?"

"You mean like Batman to Bruce Wayne?"

I watched him scribble: schizoaffective on his notepad. That was a word I didn't know, but it sounded serious.

"I seem to be getting sicker the longer I stay here. Any chance I can get that work leave?"

"I don't think at this point you're stable enough for employment."

"Doctor, is there a cure?"

"There is no cure," he said gravely, "but there are treatment options."

"Well, if it's anything like gin I'll have to decline."

"No, nothing like gin. We have antipsychotic medications that will help you."

"Are you going to scan my brain?"

"We're going to do whatever it takes to make you well."

He'd threatened me with ECT which would have been tragic considering all the fish that have been electrocuted over time, but I knew my insurance didn't cover that bullshit.

I admired his optimism, but I didn't really dig his determination. I think from his perspective his concern was not only profitable, but ethically and clinically justifiable.

I was partly to blame for the clinically justifiable element of the argument. My experience in public school had generated a significant medical file that further legitimized my treatment as an adult.

Somewhere during childhood my natural positive spontaneity had been reclassified as negative impulsivity. From a young age I had been deemed "abnormal" and had caught a truck load of child psychiatric diagnoses from attention deficit disorder to oppositional defiance disorder.

In their defense, I've always had a hard time sitting still or doing what I'm told.

Those were the meds are what got me started me in the drug trade. I was selling my ADD pills and whatever else for five bucks a hit from the age of twelve or so on. Methylphenidate was my gateway drug into drug dealing. Not that I was particularly good at that either.

All in all I preferred my psych nurse Karen's evaluation, "You are a drunken dreamer who is wasting his life."

Though she may have cut the alliteration short and just called me a drunk.

She makes a good point and she understands something of heroism as she is a recovering alcoholic who volunteers at one of those places that the uninsured detox and rehab at. She helps poor fuckers put their lives back together. She also works with prostitutes though I was never able to confirm if we had any clients in common. I told her about my anxiety over my medical claim and she said, "That's the first thing you've said since you got here that actually makes sense."

I liked Karen.

Now the Pilot Fish thought this whole thing was nothing but complete bullshit. He felt that it was also a disservice to society. As far as the Fish was concerned, locking up heroes instead of giving them capes and the freedom of the night to stalk the evil doers of the city was to make one complicit with their crimes.

The medications had no noticeable affect on him, as he told Karen and me, "it would take two Delilahs with huge shears to cut my beard and I'd still be running shit."

He told Karen that he made me the flying potion because I had been through too much pain and was disengaging from life instead of reveling in it. The only cure in his mind was a form of airborne shock therapy if you will.

He spent most of our medical incarceration time traveling, his third journey:

The Pilot Fish, armed with a spoon had been tunneling for three weeks before he realized that what he really needed was a bigger spoon. The tunnel itself was intact though only a few meters long and with a larger spoon he could start making real progress. From pacing the exercise yard while gradually distributing the collected dirt he had determined that the tunnel would have to be 18 meters in length minimum and accommodating the grade and slope maybe more like 23.

Once the tunnel was finished the plan was simple. Sneak out at the dead of night and from there it would be easy to make the escape to the beach. It was a long swim to Italy, so a raft of some form would have to be fashioned. After the escape and a few months to learn Italian he would return to Paris, retrieve his intended and revenge himself on the guilty betraying bastards who put him in here. Now though it was simple, keep that prying warden from discovering his plan, and get a bigger spoon.

Personally, I was complete with the Fish as far the idea of escape was determined, but the fates had something else in store for me other than underground construction.

Hotrod visited me every week and told me silly stories about pushing his cock into this bitch and that bitch. Then he gave me a carton of cigarettes for the week and had this way of hugging me, right in front of the psychiatric technicians where I would pick his pocket and pull out a little speed or something. One time we worked out a half liter of vodka in a big fat coke bottle, but the fuckers wouldn't let me have more than one glass at a time.

That turned out to be a bad idea as the Antabuse interaction was complete hell. They are not kidding about how fucking miserable that whole thing is. It was always better to get some meth or cocaine or whatever and just run with that.

Hotrod told me that Wild wouldn't see me here and I understood.

He'd let Jani know and she called me here and there during visiting hours and it was very nice to hear her voice no matter what she was talking about.

Family and friends have their own way of interacting with you once you've been deemed mad and I can't complain about any of mine. My parents got over once to see me and stayed for a week or so, and I played brave and I took all the calls that came in for me.

That part of the experience wasn't that bad at all. The only thing that sucked was the condescending grief and oohs and ahhs that I mentioned earlier. And as annoying as that could get it was always well intended.

I have to say there are some really fucking crazy people on those psych floors. Take this orderly or as they were called on the psych floors: Psychiatric Technician.

Anyway, this fuck, I think his name was Jonathan. He would make coffee. He would make shitty hospital coffee and he would make quality roast coffee that he would bring in from home. Any young girl with the charcoal stains fresh on her lips, or the wild eye of a woman expecting to get hit could have some of the quality roast as long as they would talk to him about their problems. He would take some notes on what they talked about and then say nonsense like, "You are making progress." The whole time staring down their shirt and slobbering all over them.

The only diagnostic criteria for the coffee treatment were good looks.

The Pilot Fish hated this son of a bitch. The Fish would stand by the nursing station and shout, "All hoarders will be executed!" and "He who is the coffee king is not the king of coffee!" and "Covetousness and lust are punished on Earth and in Heaven!" and on and on and on.

If you acted up you got some warnings and then they'd tie you to a board. We got tied up a few times mainly for the above. We couldn't really fight back too much on account of the leg, and I silently prayed I'd meet some of those guys after my release.

I thought to myself that if you are trying to have sex with a patient on a psychiatric care floor you had better be one.

The rest of the techs were fine, after all it's just a job with decent benefits. Really, Karen was the only person worth talking to as far as I was concerned.

When I was walking pretty well with a crutch and my shoulder had healed I started hitting on her. I figured if Johnathan was doing it why not me?

She usually froze me out though.

She was pretty and sweet, but I didn't let myself think about that shit too much. I didn't want to get caught jerking off in my bed.

That would've been too embarrassing.

One morning she came into my room with a box and said, "It's time to get ready for your discharge."

I said, "You're joking? I thought they were going to keep me locked up in here forever."

"No one's money lasts forever and you're not dangerous enough to transfer to long term care."

"It's a shame I'm not wealthy."

"Were you expecting something more climactic?"

"My plan was to throw the coffee machine through the window and make my escape."

"That would be tragic and romantic and ridiculous, you'd like that."

"Add a dash of comedy with the landing in the courtyard and it would be perfect."

"It's none of those things, in fact I'd say it's the opposite of those thing. It's indifference that's discharging you. I'm just filling out the forms against my better judgment."

I looked at her wanting to hug her and run away from her all at once.

ONE DAY IN NEW YORK CITY

The leaves were just starting to change. Spring in Minneapolis is two weeks of mud, but our autumns beautifully linger. The encroachment of death and dormancy is wonderfully colored here like an Aztec army announcing its advance with waving gold and burgundy banners.

I'd been discharged from the hospital just in time for the season of sunset and mulled wine. The Fish was sleeping off a mild hangover nicely and soundly in the Fish Bowl when he was disturbed by the awful ringing device that he kept beside his bed for emergencies.

"Hello?"

"My God, you actually picked up the phone."

"Who the hell is this?"

"It's your fucking mother, Jesus Christ, the day has finally come when you don't even recognize the voice of your own mother. I thought we'd raised you right."

"Jesus Ma, I'm sorry. What's going on?"

"I never thought I'd ever say this to anyone, but you need to turn on your TV."

"What, yeah sure, what channel?"

"It won't matter. Listen, we'll talk later, I gotta make some more calls."

"Yeah Ma, thanks." She had already hung up.

It took a second for the silence on the line to sink in. The only other thing that my mother had ever told me to watch on TV was Princess Diana's funeral.

The Pilot Fish turned on the television. He stared at what was happening there and felt unreality course over him. There was something happening, but what he was looking at couldn't be what was actually happening. It was a moment of shock like all the movies that you ever watched and knew couldn't be true were suddenly happening right in front of you. The Pilot Fish picked up the phone and called Jani. There was nothing there, and we should have known right then and there that it would be a few days before we could get a call through to New York. I called Hotrod.

"You see this?"

"See what?" Hotrod sounded like I felt.

"Something terrible has happened in New York City. It looks like an airplane has crashed into one of the Twin Towers."

"What? Do they know what caused it?"

"Not really, it looks like some kind of horrible accident. I don't fucking know what to make of it."

I lit a cigarette and turned the volume up enough so that Hotrod could hear it through the phone, but no one was thinking or saying anything other than shock.

"JESUS FUCKING CHRIST, THE OTHER ONE JUST GOT HIT!"

"WHAT?"

"The other tower just got hit by a fucking plane! Oh, fuck, fuck, fuck, fuck."

"I'm on my way."

The Pilot Fish sat in front of the television and stared in a sense of vacuum at the scene. Our theory of mechanical malfunction had just evaporated and all we could think of was Oklahoma City, but in a way that didn't make sense.

There were two columns that looked so strong, so straight, just slit on the side, some small piece of them, midway laid open. Battleship gray, utilitarian like the Arizona stood on end, just as wounded but twinned. Standing in what could only be called a beautiful fall day in New York City, held together still by the steel and dreams of those that made them.

The cut seemed so small and thin compared to the massive linearity of the tower itself. It didn't seem like anything that large could bleed so much fire and smoke from such a small hole.

We buzzed in Hotrod.

"I tried calling Jani on the way over. No luck."

"Yeah, the whole city is locked up. I need to talk to her, maybe she was there." I didn't think about it then, how stupid and pointless that statement was. If she had been there then nothing was there, if she hadn't then it didn't matter except to say. "I love you. That I thank God you're still alive, I love you, did your friends ..."

There is nowhere to go but hope in these situations, or you just lose yourself in a rage of inadequacy. It's the worst and most hard won variant of patience knowing that nothing can be done, but waiting while everything is happening too far away for you to do anything about it. Being impotent in the face of such horrible information is absolutely maddening.

"We're never going to get through. She was temping up town wasn't she?"

"Yeah, last she said. It's been a minute."

"Don't think about it."

"No, there's no way. I hope not at least."

"Yeah, me to."

Then there was just quiet. There was nothing to say for some time. Each of us in turn walked to the fridge and got a beer, sat back on the couch, lit cigarettes.

"They just need to get some fire crews up there and then things will be fine."

"You remember, some fucking terrorists set a bomb off in the basement of one of them few years ago, that was in the foundation and it still stood."

"Yeah, I remember. Did they ever catch those guys?"

"I think so, I can't remember."

The Adventures of Hotrod and Pilot Fish

"Are those people fucking jumping?"

"Oh sweet Jesus."

Then one of the towers slid down over itself collapsing like a house of concrete and steel cards. The grave overtook the living pushing into the heavens a column of smoke that mimicked and mocked the original tower. The ash and dust rose higher than any architect had ever dreamed to build pushing towards forever into the sky.

"Mother of God."

Hands grabbed cigarettes. The feeling was completely new and absolutely hollow. The language had the words but our culture couldn't express them. This was something that we didn't know how to feel. It was like watching a loved one that was assumed to last forever waste away overnight. It was like receiving an act of total cruelty from someone who you trusted with your life.

We're Americans and we're too young to have a sense for this. This is the first that the future will be measured against, and we have no idea what to do or how to react.

It didn't take long for the replays to start. The media had no answers and no tools for interpretation so it just replayed everything hoping in vain that the words would somehow come. The tower fell again and again and again tearing a piece out of me each time.

I was holding onto the armrest of the couch remembering it. I had been there just a few months ago cursing and complaining as I hauled Jani's loveseat up to her little apartment. I remember standing on the roof of her building drinking a beer and looking across the lower east side to their simple elegance. I'd walked in their shadows surrounded by people busier and richer than me running off to work or home to their families. The poor that cleaned the floors, the middle class that built and maintained it, the rich that inhabited its upper levels.

All of them now equalized and dropped into the eternal void.

All stopped in this horrific morning.

Before everyone tried to rationalize it. Before the dialogue about ground zero as though we could borrow from the fears of the cold war to make sense of the new war. Before any of this bullshit had been capitalized on. Before the fat man hijacked the soundtrack to sell his own propaganda. Before the power mongers turned the tragedy into political currency.

We sat there and watched.

Before the shock turned into rage, and before the politicians found a way to use it. Before my government began to systematically destroy the ideals of the founding fathers and the contemporary citizens with their programs of aggression. Before our staunchest allies began to question their resolve to our causes.

Before the secret jails and torture.

Before any of the bullshit, the fucking nonsense of trying so hard to make sense of it turned into poison. The faggots brought this on us, the decline of social values, and whatever else the worthless rich evangelists could come up with to support their own agenda of hate and separation and control.

Before God had anything to do with it.

Before the finger pointing about the goddamn intelligence failures, the great line, how did that go: it's not a failure of us except for the failure of our imaginations. Before the terror sex, before the broadening of the victimization, before the oversharing got started.

While the Palestinians were celebrating in the streets of their open air prison that Goliath can bleed from a stone.

Before the whores on the right side of the aisle started waving the flag. Before the PNAC got wet with the knowledge that now the war for the world could be declared. Before the empty rhetoric and the deck of cards. Before war bridged the partisan divide.

Before the god damn polls.

Before the greatest military to ever advance freedom became the mercenary tool of mercenary politicians. Before one of the largest and most generous displays of global sympathy and support was ground into bitterness and distrust. Before the world really began to hate us not for what we could do, but for what we were doing.

Before we changed their minds.

Before the fucks who can never believe anything but what they themselves invent began to pollute the memories of the fallen with their insane theories of causality. Before the stupid movies and the nonsensical debates. Before the insanity that a bureaucracy that can't hide a blow job from the press somehow orchestrated the single greatest assault on American civilians ever.

Before the re-telling of our government as all powerful.

Before the constant replays of our idiot in chief promising us that everything against us would be set on fire or chased into holes and then smoked out of said holes to die before our righteous soldiers. Before the bluster and bravado better reserved for the playground became national policy. Before the bait and switch.

While people were jumping to their deaths terrified of being burned alive.

Before the worthless TSA started searching old women and Al Gore to make sure that we were safe from them. Before we became rows of ducks in flip flops waiting to board a plane. Before travelers from the world over got to be greeted by armed soldiers as they entered the land of the free. Before people started getting the lie about some balance between freedom and security when all the politicians were after was more control.

While the President was reading a children's story.

Before the fucking we deserve this for being rich and fat, we deserve this for being insular or for being the pioneers of globalization. Before we got the whole story, equally told and elucidated that we had this coming for being too much and not enough of everything and nothing all rolled up into one.

Before the fucking exposes.

Before first rate actresses were reading second rate but heartfelt poetry on late night TV, before the posters of the heroes that survived graced billboards (and under the dust of their faces were the ashes of their brothers), before the endless and hopelessly repetitive and eventually irritating dialogue of those that weren't there trying to cash in on the tragedy of those that were.

Before the ghouls and grave robbers.

Before those poor Sikhs and others that looked like what fools thought our enemies looked like were run down and murdered. Before the dark and turbaned that came to America in search of a dream that no one really believes can happen anywhere but here got singled out for harm. Before they got killed, and beaten and scared, by people that were too ignorant to know who our enemies are, or what an American really is.

Before the blood lust.

Before the phone calls to the city finally got through to find out that the few that I knew there and I mean few, were still alive and OK. Their friends were too. Almost all of them. Friends of friends that would find days and months of funerals and not knowing who was dead or alive or where. Before the realizations of the forever missing came into focus.

Before the call for unreasonable war.

Before it could get pre-empted for whatever and however anyone could use it to pre-empt what was nothing more than a cruel ambition waiting for an opportunity. Before we were told to support the poor that make up our military by politicians who have never supported either. Before all the grief of a great spirit could be manipulated by the most mean and low of scum.

While the fires raged.

Before any motherfucker could try to use what should never have been used at all by anyone. What only should have been mourned by everyone. What should have only been left to those that laid flowers next to the names of the ones they loved. Before the fucking pimps started to show up on the block that should have been left sacred. Before the god damn theories and before the WMD's and falsities were passed off as congressional testimony. Before no one read the report and voted for war anyway even though they didn't mean to.

While the prodigal son of our disastrous and aggressive foreign policy of intervention was coming home at last.

Before the fear whores sold their product and before the libraries became suspect. Before the home of the free became the land of Homeland Security. Before the child murderers of Waco got newer and flashier badges to go with the same guns and tanks and lust of power.

Before my country changed.

I sat there with my best friend and watched waiting, hoping, and praying against the fall of the second tower.

INTERLUDE

There is nothing like the nothingness of the western deserts of the United States, and we are come here again. It is here that I feel the best when I think about birth and death and time.

The process of life seems much more immediate out here. There is so little of it in the desert. I watch a few cactuses stubbornly holding onto water and the tracks of little rats that must be able to metabolize silicon. Here most things struggle against the sun, it's too much for them to fight with each other. All things stand here in worship to a cruel and magnanimous god that gives only the barest means for survival combined with the maximum of attention.

The scorpions are the exception to that. They have love and war here.

The desert though is really no crueler or kinder than the rain forest. It has an advantage too, as there are no hungry cats or huge lizards. For me, it's the huge river lizards that are the scariest.

The worst we have here are a few poisonous snakes, but they like the scorpions don't eat people. We easily avoid each other, me by being clumsy and large, and them by being small and cautious. Once in a while there is an accident and I get too close to one. It tells me so by rattling at me. I pause and wait, and a little while after the rattling has stopped I continue on my clumsy walk. As anyone on television can tell you, communication is the key to a successful relationship.

The scorpions can be more stubborn. They will try to

stand you down on occasion.

Right now it is hotter than the hinges of hell, but I have prepared myself well with water and cigarettes. I'm struggling with my lighter. It makes me smile, fighting for fire in a place that is so hot already.

Hotrod doesn't like the heat very much. He has barely come with me, and I guess when I look around, when I see him and me and the Fish, I guess we are all only barely here. This place where I was born is better fit for shades than the living. Our very size seems an affront to what life can be naturally supported here. Creatures of our dimensions are meant only to pass through. We're not fit to stay. Or in my case to leave and return and leave and return.

God, it's hot.

Its high noon and our shadows cast themselves in perfect silhouette.

I hold the feeling of thirst for a moment before quenching it.

On the other side of the mountains the heat is driving the clouds up. The mountains are so high that it takes a lot of work to get the clouds over them. There are no showers here only storms.

Aquarius is coming.

The heat brings clarity before it manufacturers the mirage.

This place has known mirages like no other. Political mirages that wrapped the whole valley and eventually the world in grand illusion.

My government tested nuclear bombs in the 50's and 60's just south of here. We were told that nothing that happened there could come and affect us over here. We were just too far away to worry about it. We were told that being downwind of nuclear tests didn't carry any risks.

The official line was that the massive pink clouds floating over the mountains were harmless.

And we believed them.

Of course all the great lies are told by politicians. They have to lie. No one really wants the truth. Besides all that the truth is a very hard product to sell. It's not necessarily pretty or convenient. The truth is simultaneously stubborn and elusive.

It's a tough product to work with.

Lies by their very nature are flexible and easy. They can shape themselves to fit any tongue. They can be constantly repurposed to achieve an evolving end. You can get a lot more mileage out of a lie, and if you believe your own lies enough you may even believe that they've taken you somewhere.

At the very least you will be where they have taken you.

The truth on the other hand does very little for you. It doesn't care what you think of it. It doesn't go anywhere, and you do all the work of getting to it.

If you do manage to get to a truth, it doesn't even have the civility to thank you for your trouble. It doesn't even have the decency to announce your arrival.

I find the search for truth to be the most tiring of all of my travels. It is the hardest journey and in many ways the least rewarding. I've been long on that road and can't see the end or even be sure I've gotten anywhere.

I'm no more sure of anything.

One of my mom's friends, a woman her age who saw me when I was just a little baby, when the Pilot Fish was just a minnow with skinny little fins, has breast cancer. It turns out that the radiation from all those nuclear bombs can harm you after all. She is not the only one. The down winders as they are called number in the tens of thousands. The conditions vary just like the bombs did. Some are winning the battle against cancer, some have been cancer free for seven or more years, and some have died. They had a class action lawsuit. The whole project was conducted and concluded quietly. They each received around 50 grand.

That's not that much money.

I've asked a lot of women all manner of questions. A

lot of the time they just tell me no. Hotrod tells me that it's because I don't dress well, that I need to do my hair. That I shouldn't ask, but simply show. The Fish tells me that my courtship ritual lacks a certain élan. They're probably both right, but whenever I ask a girl if she would take breast cancer for $50,000 and the assurance that our bombs would be able to kill a huge number of people they always say no.

It doesn't matter how well I've done my hair, or if my clothes are new.

Here in the desert is the secret that no one wants to know, the one that's obvious except that recognition of its obviousness would force us as a people to see how much we have left behind. Here is the immutable and stubborn truth that exposes our collective lie.

You can't see it here, but this is where we started to trade liberty for security.

You can't hear it here but this is where the chaotic strides of free men were first disciplined to march to militarisms drum.

We have done it to ourselves, and so gradually that only by traveling in time and looking over our history can it become clear.

We've done it with the best of intentions.

No one wants to say that our democracy lies in perilous wait. That power and empire stand at the ready to undermine individuality and liberty.

No one wants to say that we have lied to each other and ourselves, and that we gradually have changed to fit the task. No one wants to be told that they became the part when they thought they were auditioning for a different role.

We are all complicit and we are all to blame.

We are all down winders now.

All we had to do was go south beyond those mountains to the largest surviving group of aborigines and talk to them about empire and genocide, but we don't feel they have anything to teach us.

It's just a sad fact about people. If a lot of people don't want to know something they will choose to ignore it rather than confront it. This is one of the lessons of Auschwitz and the wall in Palestine.

It's the cornerstone of our great tragic comedy.

I've been laughing and crying over it for thirty years. That's not very long, but I don't expect it to let up. The more you know the longer it will go. As near as I can tell I'm just getting started.

The Pilot Fish throws out his arms, his shadow runs across the sand and dust, and proclaims, "All those bombs have outlived their protective duty, and now stand as the foundation of pawns in the new Great Game for the World!" The words echo back to us running between the mountainsides becoming weaker with each reverberation until they fade into a solitary sound unrecognizable as words.

Then it disappears entirely.

He drops his arms to his side and makes a wish against empires and the human compulsion to create them. Then he smiles as he thinks about how things come together and fall apart and then come together and then fall apart.

We wonder for a moment if we're not yet all the way together or if we've already started to fall apart.

There's a point on that line that's identical from either end.

It's so quiet here like walking past the bramble that sheltered Romulus and Remus. You wouldn't think anything could come from here, and yet this is where it all began. The bone filled fields of Flanders signaled a changing of the guard and Hiroshima declared it. Korea and Vietnam fed it. Now, the course of my country has all the feeling of a car crash that you can see coming, but can only stare dumbly at, as the inevitable rushes towards you.

Here though in the crucible where its might was forged there are no monuments to its greatness, its sacrifices, and all the death it's done.

Here there is nothing.

Here is the here that unifies the beginning and end of it. This is the point that starts and ends the circle. The rest of it, well, the rest of it is the rest of it.

We are somewhere in the great middle of that journey round the way. Where we are in that course I can't say, the middle has great summers punctuated by floods, and many of those are meaningless in the ebb and flow of time. The middle denies its origins screaming like Caesar that it was born full and whole and the middle says that there can be no Armageddon. The middle lies about how it all started and how it will end, but I won't lie to you. I don't know where we are in the middle, but I can tell you the beginning and the end is real. They are made of stone and they are waiting for us.

Hotrod and I are surrounded by those rocks.

These old and heavy stones aren't as beautiful as their cousins over in Moab, but some are quite similar. There are even a few arches. You see there was a boulder there once, but the wind eroded out all the sandstone leaving the granite and basalt left in whatever shape it was in when the whole molten mess was thrust through to the surface.

The wind will get the rest of it to, in time.

The stones whisper to us. They taunt us with time. They threaten with their silence. They promise that we will fade before they do, and then they will fade, and so on with all things. They take our feeble sense of permanence and our desire for more than a single stalk of tallow and throw it to the sun.

They tell us that we are their revenge.

The Fish has done so much time traveling that the stones are a comfort to him. He holds out his hand to them. He tries to tell me what is so hard to know, that time is neither enemy nor friend. That Diogenes was right. That though our culture values artifice over truth, we are not determined by it. That though our culture perpetuates a flawed morality that we are not bound by it.

He reminds me that the iron in our blood was born in the explosions of ancient stars, and all we can fear is the now of our lives when everything in our lives is eternal except the movement that makes us alive.

He tells me to let go the moment and fear not forever.

But I can't.

I hold fast the present terrified I'll disappear with its passing.

As one day I know I will.

It should feel strange to us that we can run the mightiest of kingdoms through our fingers after only a thousand years, but we don't feel that. All we feel is sand, and though we may say ashes to ashes and dust to dust, we don't believe it.

We don't believe in it.

Maybe we wouldn't know how to live if we really did. It might be a truth too great for us, but it is a truth that these stones know very well. Most of the time that I come here it has been all they have to say.

The Fish and I look at each other holding still in the mirage.

We travel back in time to just two years ago.

We revel again in that great celebration of time.

A thousand years ended that day in the West. There were festivals, dreams, new ideas and old fears. There was religious talk of apocalypse and futuristic dialogue of what could be done in the next thousand years. Champagne bottles blew up in an ecstasy of the passage of time and nostalgia and optimism battled for space in the mass mind.

There was a great shout out to time, but the refrain was whispered back.

A thousand years ends every day.

Our history doesn't deserve celebratory markers or special dates. Our history should be looked at differently and less discreetly. Our history is just one season of love and lust and loss of reason.

Our history is just one war that we fight over and over

The Adventures of Hotrod and Pilot Fish

again without learning from it and without a desire for peace.

The Fish chides me for my pessimism and reminds me that I only speak from the absolute narrowness of my own experience. He says it better maybe he's even right. We've made fantastic progress he says, progress on every front even our own human hazards. It's just that the progress hasn't occurred evenly. In some spaces we fly and in others we crawl and we each have to navigate the great labyrinth from the nothing that we're born with to the something that we die with.

Our irony is that our success grows the maze.

Our madness is that the maze should have some other point than being walked.

The Fish says it couldn't be any other way.

He says that there is no escape from history. It scars us even in a state of willful ignorance. It follows us even as we add to it as we flee it.

That being said we aren't a slave to it either. We are as much a part of our history as it is a part of us, and while we can't choose the conditions that we are born to we have our part to play from that point forward, and by the time we die history may very well be going in a way impossible to imagine from when we were born.

All it is, all it can be, is what happened before we came along anyway.

It's within our power to make sure it stays that way.

It's also our duty.

We can contribute to those glorious moments of change, transition, or transcendence. We can add time to our history in meaningful ways and make the future a greater stranger to the past rather than a perpetuation of it. We can choose to preserve the best things along the way. The present moves through us and that is a very important thing.

It is the most important thing.

It may be the only thing,

This though, this now, is none of those things.

This is not a glorious moment.

This is a pause, an intermission, an interlude.
This is the quiet that isn't noticed.
This is the moment lost.
This is the truth bumped into unrecognized.
This is the whispered refrain.
And the now of this now is almost ended

We've found some time for reflection in the mirage. Let's put our arms out and up and feel that heat. Let the sweat run, and feel the fatigue that can be found in taking a single step when you're already worn out from standing still.

Now, arms down and drop to your knees.

We'll pray now, and we're not known for prayer.

We pray that though we are made from clay and will one day go to dust that our ideas and ideals can outlive us. That as a people they can be carried on and somehow as people we can keep learning and becoming better as a whole. That instead of lies and enslaving institutions, we can preserve our liberty in the individual mind living the individual life and facing the power of ideas alone.

We pray that those ideas will be shared.

We pray for a vigilance to do good in the world.

We pray for a wisdom to manage that vigilance.

We pray for an end to our self destruction and our cruelty.

We pray for an introspective life and a clear morality.

Now my friend, my brother, my sister, my lover, my confidant, my enemy, now it's time to leave. We have seen the desert in the dawn and now we've been burned by the sun at its mightiest. We'll come back here once more. The sun will be setting and the evening is very beautiful here.

It will be cooler then.

FRANKY AND ZOE

Hotrod and I were conserving funds so we met in the alley next to the recycle bin behind my building for pre-saucing. We give a hoot and it kept us out of the wind. It was February of 2002 and we were caught between a lingering recession, a war already underway in Afghanistan and the begging for a new war with Iraq.

It was cold as fuck out.

Times were not good. The attacks had taken the dot com crash from bad to worse and Hotrod was riding unemployment. As my drinking was directly connected to Hotrod's prosperity I'd dropped from the top shelf to the rail to the alley behind my building drinking a Natty Ice next to the recycling bins.

I tried to think of all of it as character building, if you could maintain going through this shit surely you were meant for something special in this world.

It was hardly the fall of Icarus, at least we still had a decent buzz on, but going from cheeseburgers to steaks is easy and going from steaks to cheeseburgers tastes like a can of near beer with a shot of vodka poured into it.

At least the press was having a good time. They cover war so well in this country and there were lots of explosions to watch and lots of heartwarming stories about saving people and stopping evil. The war was getting fantastic ratings and the new drum beating for a second war with Iraq had the danger of feeling like an over anticipated sequel that couldn't live up to the original.

The dialog about the stolen election had disappeared,

and it should have been a sign to all of us that the first thing to drop out of the news was questioning the legitimacy of our leaders.

"Man, I'm fucking freezing."

"Shut up and finish your beer."

"You need to get a nice job again."

"Fuck you."

There was madness on each side of the hour and the day.

I had finally gotten my medical claim from my psychological incarceration approved. It didn't pay all of it off, but I had been able to come up with an arrangement after the insurance payment to give them 75 dollars a month for the rest of my life. I had made some jokes about killing myself again to get out of the bill and not gotten a chuckle.

Insurance adjusters are a tough crowd.

We finished off the last two cans and tossed them into the recycling.

"Did they extend your unemployment?"

"Yeah, but the deposit was late, so we gottta write checks tonight."

"Cool."

We made it down to a local that had a long shitty happy hour and half price pitchers. We grabbed happy hour cocktails and a pitcher and found a booth.

Hotrod went to the bar for another round of cocktails as we finished the first round in about three swallows. At the bar I could see him chatting up a black couple. The woman was in her late thirties. The guy was somewhat older than that. It's always hard to tell real ages between races. The girl was flirting with Hotrod, so I figured it was just an invitation to freak. The dialogue was short, and then Hotrod returned with a smile and the unfortunate and rather thematic question "You want to get high tonight?"

"Sure."

I've become predictable.

Hotrod was solidly drug free so I knew sex had to be

involved.

The beer was soon split into four glasses and our new friends joined us.   Introductions were made.

Franky and Zoe meet Hotrod and Pilot Fish.

On the television the first set of lies were being put together to sell the war in Iraq to the American people. The talking heads and pundits were trying very hard to express a link between Saddam Hussein and Al Qaeda. There was a lot of theorizing and talk about unholy alliances made in secret. The mixing of secular and theocratic motivations was a bit mind numbing, but no one seemed bothered. This line of reasoning was saturated with talk of weapons of mass destruction. On and on and on with the WMD's and on some more.

I didn't find any of the arguments compelling, but I'm not really in the TV watching crowd and like I said, this stuff was getting great ratings. It's not something I can easily explain.

We ordered some food and a few more rounds.

Once the poison won out we took to the street. We didn't have far to walk before getting to a shit concrete highrise with some name that might sound nice in conversation.

The front door was jammed shut with the lock broken in, so we had to take the service entrance, which was conveniently jammed open. It reeked of urine and was littered with broken glass and condoms.

"Damn, them hookers upstairs are starting to do shit safe!" Franky said with a laugh.

We walked up three flights of stairs underneath flickering fluorescent lights.

Our journey ended in a one room apartment. The walls were white wash on cinder blocks, "Is that a Louisville slugger or an Eastman?" asked the Fish about the bat next to the sink.

"That's an Eastman motherfucker." Said Franky.

"Nice." Not the Flange of Power, but totally adequate.

Then the pleasantries are dropped and business begins.

"You want to get high, huh?"

"Sure."

"And you, we know what you want."

Hotrod nodded at Zoe.

Franky pulled out a small bag filled with crack.

I hadn't done that shit since my time with the Carpet Crawler, and while I felt that I was over the addiction, it hadn't been anything I was planning on doing anytime soon. I looked over at Hotrod and saw in his eyes that this was also unexpected. I could also see that it was irrelevant to his getting laid tonight, and just like that the conversation had already passed the point where asking about a nickel of hay would have been appropriate.

"Yeah, sure, what's it going to cost?"

"These two be fifties and this one be a twenty."

"How pure?"

"Shit, this was for personal. I just cooked this shit up this morning."

"OK."

Zoe whispered something to Hotrod and he nodded.

This was shaping up nicely. Hotrod and I were the Jack Spratt and his wife of vice, and as Franky shoved some steel wool into a glass tube I couldn't decide honestly if the option to trade places ever came up if we would.

I'd recently sworn whoring off anyway. I had a date coming up with a girl that occasionally ventured into my subterranean domain in search of medical charts. She was an RN, and just far enough out of my league that when I asked her out I'd just expected a casual no and we could have gone on about our business without thinking anything more of it.

She'd said yes and in my surprise all I could get out was a time and place. Her name tag said Prickly Pear.

The Fish had applauded my courage and given his approval.

Now we have to pay for what is going to happen anyway, and these people don't take checks.

We emptied everything out of our wallets. That didn't

quite make it, but Franky was willing to negotiate. Watches and jewelry joined the pile. Hotrod had a nice watch and mine wasn't worthless. For jewelry, earrings and rings.

"Those are white gold."

"Bullshit."

"You can look at them yourself."

"Maybe." Was all Franky said after a short inspection.

"We covered drinks and wings at the bar too." Hotrod threw in.

Franky made an analysis of the whole thing and then added, "leave the wallets in the pile."

That didn't bother me too much, but I don't carry a designer wallet. Hotrod painfully nodded.

The bed held what could only be described as a seizure on a bad episode of COPS. Two watches, an association of jewelry as well as an assortment of American dollars ranging from some twenties all the way down to several ones.

"Deal."

A rough calculation placed Zoe at about a twenty-five dollar whore, but fuck it she was smoking too.

That didn't make Zoe the cheapest piece of ass on Franklin Avenue by a long shot. Hotrod had once picked up a worn out little junkie for 8.50 in quarters. He'd been on his way to the Laundromat and wearing dirty underwear for the week wasn't actually that bad.

Franky hands me the virgin pipe and I offer the first hit to Zoe like a pure fucking gentleman.

"Na baby, you start it."

I hit the pipe.

"Shit, you look like you've done this before."

"It's been awhile."

I kiss her blowing the smoke into her lungs. One thing I'll say about crack, it's a lot nicer to share a hit than a needle. She does the same thing back to me. Franky is just watching to make sure I don't fiend the fuck out.

"What's it taste like?" asks Hotrod asks me.

"It tastes like getting high."

Franky hadn't been kidding this was some very good stuff. It's head and shoulders better than what I had with the Carpet Crawler, and what little survival instinct I have tries to remind me how dangerous this shit can be.

"I don't like smoking with people that don't know how to use this shit. You cool, but you never know with some motherfuckers."

"You've got to be smart about it. Everything in moderation."

"No joke."

The rest of the shit vanishes as fast as you'd expect, at the speed that only cocaine and government money can disappear at.

The waves of euphoria and death ride in alternating cycles through my mind. I wonder for a moment at how lucky I've been.

Zoe looks at Hotrod, "You ready sugar?"

Hotrod has also become predictable.

They walk into the bathroom giving Franky and me a little privacy. I can briefly hear Hotrod start to talk Zoe off of the importance of condoms and I feel too good to take a side in the debate.

Franky and I fill in the silence with typical American conversation.

"So, where you from?"

"Oh, a few places. Lived in 'Sconi for awhile, Michigan, Utah…" Franky cuts me off before I can get through the whole list.

"What part of Michigan?"

"Oh, some shitty little prison town. It was west of Detroit about an hour and a half called Jackson."

"No shit." Franky pulls out a cigarette paraffin with some white powder in it, and starts rolling a mentholated cigarette with a rail on each side of the tobacco. His fingers are surprisingly dexterous.

"Don't say anything."

"I won't."

We hear some moaning and motion from the bathroom. The clumsy steps and sounds make me think of High School kids hug dancing at the prom.

"I used to live in Jackson."

"No shit, when?"

"When was you there?"

"I was there when the Bad Boys won their rings."

"Me too, damn you for real."

"Hell yeah, Isaiah, Rodman, Laimbeer, Dumars, good shit. I think I liked it more when they beat Chicago then the Lakers."

"Hell yeah, I'm a Detroit kid, born and raised. Shit, Jackson is where I started selling drugs. My uncle and couple cousins was locked up there, and we moved over."

"Funny that's where I started selling drugs too."

"What did you sell?"

"Ritalin. What about you?"

"Just weed back then."

"Small world."

"You know it."

"It was good fucking money too before we got caught up."

"It happens."

He lights the cocaine cigarette and passes it to me.

I pulled on the almost shorty, the cocaine pushing everything out of my mind and replacing it with a chemical glow. I pass it back to Franky who hits it twice.

"You think we're going to have another war in Iraq?"

"Yeah, I don't see anything stopping it."

"Me neither. Damn shame."

"It is."

He handed the cocaine cigarette back to me, "That's all you dog."

"Thanks."

I finished it slowly feeling my life turn over like the paper fleeing the flame, all the way down through my body until my feet go numb and fall through the floor while behind the bathroom door Hotrod hit Zoe raw.

THE FIRST TIME WITH THE PEAR

It's the seventh date. You could say that we have been seeing each other. We haven't had sex yet, only kissed. The kisses were shy at first but linger now. Her lips move across me like velvet and I drink like all I can do is drown.

You could say that we've been taking our time.

Hospital staffing is round the clock and the Pear is a new grad, so she gets a medley of evening and night shifts. This produces strange dating opportunities. I've dipped into my P.T.O. here and there to meet her for breakfast when she finishes graveyard shifts.

She's working PM's this weekend so we've met for breakfast. It is ten in the morning and we're at the C.C Club. I am drinking her Bloody Mary now that I've finished mine. She is drinking tea. She won't let me take a bite out of her steak. She has recently confided that most of her patients this weekend are morbidly obese. She says that it's inspired her to grow a pot. I honestly hate fat people, but whenever I say anything in that direction she hushes me. She thinks that I need to become more tolerant and caring.

"They are not fat. They are fluffy." She says it light and laughing, but clearly closing the discussion.

She can feel a certain intolerance in me and she tries subtly to correct it or re-direct it and I'm trying to be compliant about it.

We finish the steaks and I order another Bloody Mary. She refills her tea. We go to play some pool.

The vodka in the Bloody is perfect and I'm both loose and cool on the edge of a perfect buzz that can't be maintained, but only enjoyed.

The Pear is not an American, but is on her way to becoming one. She is from Kazakhstan, but she isn't Kazak. She is a mix of Russian, Roma and Soviet. In her far away central Asian country they only play straight pool and Soviet pool. Soviet pool is a thoroughly impossible game played with white balls the size of ostrich eggs. Fortunately, it is unavailable in the CC Club, so we are playing straight pool. This involves scoring and strategies that are unfamiliar to me. Fortunately, she is such a stronger player than I am that it doesn't really matter. I try to shoot in at least a few while she runs up eight to twelve points a turn. She explains the foul and racking rules to me, and I do the best I can.

It's a little frustrating on a pay table, but she has a little notepad in her oversized purse that she writes the score on. We only play to fifty anyway.

After I see her hit a two rail cross bank I realize that she has been playing down to me, and I don't like that. I don't have that kind of mercy or pity or whatever it is that makes people do that.

I never have.

I play harder and can modify the outcome in my favor by a few points. That doesn't change anything about winning or losing, but I tell myself that now she has to play her best to beat me. It's a matter of pride and besides I need to get something out of all those nights that I can't really remember that were spent playing pool and darts in bars.

"You gotta bring your A game."

She smiles at me and then runs the table.

The Pilot Fish is laughing at me, but he isn't being critical. He has let go of Jani, and I guess I have too. We knew that we would fall in love again, but how that would happen wasn't really thought about. We don't have any strict criteria for the romantic. It's a space I've always wanted to leave unclear, the more mapped out it is the more you guarantee disappointment, and we don't need any more venues for obsession or perfectionism to pollute.

This is the next way that I am falling in love and it's quite different than the last time. You can't compare them, you just appreciate how beautiful they are and that you're getting another chance at it.

I choose Willpower by The Replacements on the juke box.

I take a long look at the Pear. She is racking up the balls looking and doing everything carefully and with attention. Her hair has fallen over her shoulders and is running across her face and down long enough to touch her arms. It's a black waterfall framing and covering everything that I desire. The gypsy in her is only evident in her hair, eyes and height. She looks up at me and smiles.

"Do you like the song?'

"It's OK."

I tell her about the Replacements and how Minneapolis was a scene that no one saw once upon a time. She appreciates my metaphors without really caring for the song. I try to push a little on the idea that this place was the place that made other places happen, but it's a fool's errand and she really doesn't give a fuck.

Now is now.

I get us refills.

I want this to be simple, but really I have no idea what I am doing.

We're still in that awkward beginning where I feel like we need a full list of activities to so that we can be distracted from each other while spending time together. I have a full list of topics to keep us talking without ever having to talk to other. She works at three today and I have an itinerary in my mind that should push us to 2:30 giving her just enough time to jump in her car and get to work.

I hand her a new tea and say, "After this game would you

like to go get some coffee?"

She looks at the tea and laughs like I made a joke and just like that my itinerary is fucked.

"How about a walk?"

"Yes."

We finish up and walk out into a wonderful spring day. There's been enough rain to wash the mud off the roads and the snow has been gone long enough now so that you don't think about it. The winter of discontent seems to have ended and love mixes so well with sunshine. We hold hands unconsciously, and that feels so natural and nice.

I understand why so many romances follow the equinoxes.

We walk around and take in the fresh green and new growth. I realize after a few blocks that it's the longest silence we've shared and my pressure to perform kicks in to try and ruin it. I swallow back something that was only going to be anything to break what I want now to sustain.

The Pear looks at me almost expecting me to say something, but we just hold eye contact and I smile at her.

There's been a stillness in me since we started being affectionate that I don't find a weakness or a danger. It's a source of strength that I haven't known before, and I am not really sure what to do with it.

She has it all the way through her and I wonder if I am stealing or borrowing it from her. I tried to talk to her about it, but the idea of it got muddled in the words.

The Fish told me that she was like the Muses of ancient times that could produce passion or stillness at will.

We get off the street and walk through Mueller Park when the Pear breaks the silence, "What was your last time with a girl like?"

These are the kind of questions that bring the downsides of whoring into sharper focus. The honest answer would be: about 140 bucks and two fifty rocks of crack cocaine which we shared. Hotrod had been nice enough to pay for it all, and the hotel had been discreet about it.

It wasn't a long term relationship and it hadn't exactly been a one night stand.

I'm not particularly dishonest, but I do believe in comedic or at least dramatic timing and this isn't a good moment for either.

I've told her some things and not others. I figure we'll get to everything if she keeps seeing me. I think over the last couple years and I don't see much that I really want to talk about. It's hard to talk about past loves without nostalgia or regret or a second guess. Really, it's hard to talk about anything in the past when one is in the midst of a beginning. Beginnings are so fragile. The ghosts of lost years can easily destroy them.

The only one I loved was Jani, and the few other girls I've been with don't seem to be enough to answer her question with.

"Her name is Jani. She's a musician." I think that's honest enough. I don't want to get into it.

"Were you in love?"

"Yes."

"Do you stay in touch?" There is a subtle shift in tone with the question. The kind of question that is supposed to sound nonchalant and innocent, but instead comes off clearly pretending to the opposite of what it really is.

"We're still friends, but we haven't talked in a while. She lives in New York City." I think about it for a moment, how long it's been since I've seen her. We talked pretty often after the attack, but it's been about eight months since then. The last couple times I called she was either just about to finish something or just about to start something, and was covered in the business of New York City life.

Part of my poetry has gradually gone away and I can't feel anything.

I couldn't tell you when it left except that just now I've noticed it gone.

"Did she get hurt in the attack?"

"No, she was far away from that."

"It's good that you can stay friends with her."

Then the conversation moves along to other things. We talk about work and I am polite and sensitive to the position of the over eaters and under exercisers. I can feel that Bloody Mary buzz rolling through me in a nice relaxed way. It's right at that point where I wish that I had had one more, but I know its better that I didn't.

Sometimes when you start drinking at ten in the morning it can get ugly.

I pull her into a kiss underneath some shade in a discrete section of the park and she submits for a few moments before pushing me away.

"Why don't you get an American girl?"

"The American girls are all fat. Besides that, they are all Minnesotans. They will balance their checkbook while you're making love to them. Then they want to see your checkbook. If things aren't perfectly reconciled then they can't come and they start asking all sorts of banking questions, and you know how the Pilot Fish feels about banks."

"What?? That's nonsense and besides all that they are beautiful. You could get a girl from the countryside. They aren't like that. They have great pots, perfect soft tummies. You'd have something in common with them. You should get a western girl."

I run my fingers through her hair.

"Don't touch me! It's only the hair. I should cut it off and sell it. Then you would leave me and all this bullshit about romance would be exposed."

"You could get a lot of money for your hair."

She is being such a Prickly Pear!

I don't mind, it's another part of falling in love. It's a process and I know I am on the way now. This is just one of those spaces between these things. Sometimes her being prickly just makes me feel the more needed, and I don't know if she has ever needed anything.

She pulls me in for a kiss this time, "No more drugs, OK."

"OK, no more drugs."

The moment cared for, the moment marked, the moment remembered, the moment passed.

Then we leave the park and walk back to her car. The sun is hiding behind some clouds. We haven't said anything else and we don't ask each other about where we're headed. That stillness and strength is running all the way through me in some slow and beautiful way. She pulls into the alley behind my building and we start holding hands in the hallway. I let us in, ladies first, and shut and lock the door behind me.

The Pilot Fish runs his fingers up her arm stopping at her short sleeve. He turns her around and out of her top in one smooth motion ending with our lips on her neck.

It's our first time, and we're safe about it.

Just before it starts, she whispers in the Pilot Fish's ear, "It's smart to wear one of those because I have AIDS."

I freeze for a moment and then start laughing. We laugh then giggle then kiss then hold each other, finding the paths in love, the ways of love, and the touches of love.

It went on and on into the afternoon. It went on all over the room. At times it trembled and shook. We took little breaks and as we wore ourselves out against each other, the breaks got longer and the tenderness deeper. Making love to her was like finding yourself. Lightning crashed and gentle waves kissed the shore.

The sun came out from behind the clouds.

TWO STEPS FORWARD ONE STEP BACK

We are all raised racist in some way and to some extent in the multicultural maelstrom of the Great Asylum. Just the process of growing up in an all-white town that viciously hated the few surviving local aborigines for getting an extra fishing season as compensation for surviving first genocide and second colonization spoke volumes to me as a kid.

The beginning of my generation was born when segregation was still on the books and the end of my generation thinks of segregation as black and white clips of white cops turning fire hoses onto crowds of black protesters.

All of my generation was raised by people who lived through segregation.

And none of us are happy with the timing of it. We all wish that it was further away from us, and we are all desperate to say that it is all finally over. That we have collectively as a society put all of this behind us.

None of which is true, we are just further along moving at the speed of glaciers in the experience of time passed too slow amidst too much human cost to celebrate its progress.

That doesn't mean that great progress hasn't been made.

It just means that we can't really celebrate it too much yet with so much work yet to be done.

We want to celebrate it desperately and this desire to

accelerate the passage of time towards an idealistic end has spawned its own awkwardness. Just as our parents will be remembered for their part in ending formal exclusionism as well as their embrace of tokenism, we'll have our own milestones and setbacks along the way.

It's a dangerous job to judge our own progress.

That task mainly falls to later generations who will also have their growing pains and unintended consequences of fine intentions and on and on and on. The apple doesn't fall that far from the tree.

We'd be better off just admitting that we all started out saying nigger and now we don't anymore. We weren't cowed into silence by the political correctness cops. We don't say it anymore because it's rude and hurtful. We don't say it anymore because Richard Pryor was right when he said it was a descriptor of personal wretchedness.

We do still think it though sometimes, you're not wrong about that.

On that note, I'd also like to personally apologize to the Williams sisters, I rooted against you for all the wrong reasons, and you broke down some serious barriers, you two kind of went into one of the last great white spaces and you kicked some serous ass. You made a lot of us who thought we were past it uncomfortable and it showed. Bravo Venus and Serena. Serena in particular, you are the athlete of our generation.

Not Jordan, not Rice, not Lemieux, not Calzaghe, not Maddux.

Serena.

Sister, you'll never get the credit you deserve.

The Fish has helped me get a handle on it, not so much because he is immune to any of it, but because he has seen so much of it in his travels through time.

He's seen enough of it all over the world and all through history that he's not an American about it which gives some distance and makes the conversation feel less accusatory.

He took me over our history from as many angles as we could from the whole villages of natives dying of smallpox and measles to the brutality of the plantations to sitting in an auditorium listening to Boooker T hash out the Atlanta Compromise to the demonstrations in full color that got made into those black and white films.

That helped.

Racism may be a feature of multi-cultural societies just as classism may be an inevitable feature of societies themselves, but if there is any end to it or approach to minimizing it, it's in acknowledgement and compassion, not just looking past someone's skin color, which is less relevant than anyone believes, but in acknowledging that it can impact the outcome of one's lives and dreams.

It's important to understand that to do otherwise can further marginalize someone's dreams and experiences.

The fact of that frustrates our cultural intuition. Our idealism as Americans, of living in a meritocracy is very important to us and it's hard to acknowledge that it doesn't hold for everyone and worse than that, it fails to hold specifically for different groups of people, disproportionately.

We would completely prefer an evenly distributed unfairness to this.

Balancing all of that against the fact that most of our destiny is individually driven creates more opportunities for miscommunication and misunderstanding than anything else.

Our self-determination is our most important attribute, but our self-determination doesn't determine everything about ourselves.

Not yet anyway and probably never will.

We need to do all those things and more without becoming a generation of race cops too, but it's a tough tight rope to walk, and silencing debate is easier than opening it.

That and we need to turn our criminal justice system into something other than a shitty employer processing poverty applications for slave labor because of drug charges, but I digress.

You really don't want me to start on that one, once I get started on that one I can go on and on and on.

My generation is also the bridge between a primarily black-white United States and a much more multi-cultural black-white-brown-yellow United States, which has happened too quickly in some ways for us to hold in focus.

We all want a "To Kill a Mockingbird" frame of reference, but it's just not true anymore. It's quite unfair to stuff anyone else into that historical narrative and there is enough shit to sort out in there as it stands.

We're much more comfortable looking at things in black and white than rainbow, and that challenge will be passed on to the next generation. That challenge will also be diversified as the country continues to change which in some ways can only be refreshing even if the process seems a little scary.

The Fish tried to show me through travelling in time that the great white backdrop of America throws things into sharp relief even as it camouflages other things, so that I can come closer to understanding something that I can't experience.

It's very hard to understand something you can't experience, but looking at it that way helped.

The Fish and I are mild futurists and we hold out hope for the next generation to keep the progress going and maybe they'll be faster at it than we were. Or maybe there is a discrete end to it all and they'll get us to it, or at least get is closer to it.

They probably won't solve it, but we hope for everyone's sake that they get us closer.

I pray that we pass on any positive momentum that we may have.

We temper that optimism with the knowledge that this will probably be a battle for every generation to come. We just hope the challenge of it gets smaller over time and the individual costs and consequences less.

All of which is academic until one of your close friends from childhood starts dating outside of her race.

And voila, you're transported back to those black and white clips with the fire hoses.

I didn't see that one coming.

Of course Hotrod dated outside of white all the time and it had never bothered me. I did as well though to a much less degree than Hotrod mainly due to just sucking at dating in general.

All this line of inquiry did was muddle the mixture with some misogyny.

I wasn't sure if the race thing even played that much of a role in her selection process. I figured that Wild wanted to be with tough guys or at least tough looking guys. In the late 90's and early 2000's masculinity was trapped between Ice Cube and the Backstreet Boys. Black had become the color of tough and hard.

You had the choice of being a J-Crew clone that got fifteen year old chicks wet with your dance moves and gelled up hair, or a gangsta who had to pull his pants up before a scrap. Metrosexuality or sagged jeans. You're damned if you do and damned if you don't.

We really needed a James Dean in 2002.

I didn't criticize Wild for her choices for several reasons, the main one being that it wasn't any of my fucking business, but she could still sense my discomfort on some level.

The Pear was first and foremost on my mind anyway. When you're in love with someone you kind of lose your world. I asked her about racism in the United States and she said it was hardly an example of American Exceptionalism.

It was made a little more ridiculous in that this bothered me more than watching her go off the rails with the drugs and partying while she was getting Bonk out of her system. She had pretty much righted the ship, was killing it at school, and found a nice boy, and now I've got something to say about her life choices.

That's hardly fair now is it?

Wild had started talking black which did get a little annoying, though I'm just as guilty of it as she is. White people have been stealing black slang for a very long time. She did call him "Beaux" though and that does annoy the fuck out of me. That's just something I'm not even trying to get over.

She'd do that and I'd say, "Boo hoo?" and screw my eyes up like I was crying.

God, I'm fucking funny.

Wild invited us all out to hang and Hotrod and I said yes. I took a rain check for the Pear due to her work schedule and Wild half believed me. We all met at Brother's downtown, and I suppressed some more super funny jokes.

Wild gave me a hug and then Hotrod one.

"We're in the back over there."

We follow her over to the table and meet Kevin.

He gets up and shakes my hand and Hotrods and then Wild kisses him, and I feel uncomfortable about it for a moment. Then the moment passes.

I get to the bar for a pitcher and shots and come back. They all want to dance and I come along for a song.

I watch Wild and Kevin, they actually make a fine couple. Neither of them can dance very well, but they do OK. I'm by far the worst dancer and Hotrod is already taking over the floor.

We get back and finish our drinks.

"I'll go get us another round."

"I'll help." Says Kevin.

"Sure."

At the bar we kill some time with conversation while waiting to get served:

"So, you met Wild at school?"

"Yeah, we had a Sociology class together."

"That's cool."

"We're going to transfer to the U next year. Just saving money this way."

He's wearing a polo sweater and doesn't sag his pants.

"Are you from Minneapolis?"

"No, I was born and raised in Edina."

"Edina?"

"Yeah, I went to Edina High, don't tell me you went to Wayzata."

"No, I moved here after high school."

"Oh, that's right Wild told me you guys went to high school together."

Jesus Christ, with all the Chicago refugees you could ask for shooting up the north side of the city Wild has found herself a fucking Oreo. He's probably gotten as much shit from blacks about talking white as Wild has gotten from whites about talking black. I am sure that they will fall in love and have 2.1 cookies and cream kidlets and a dog and mortgage in the suburbs.

God bless America.

Kevin picks up the round and we go back to the table. They all get up to dance again and I sit this one out.

The Fish pushed me backwards through time to a drive taken in the Wisconsin countryside. I had just gotten my license. Wild Child must have been thirteen or fourteen. She was a little sister to me and I was a crush to her. She was the little girl in the neighborhood that talked to everyone, and had never been afraid.

Wild would make me stop the car, so that she could get out and pick flowers and wreathe them through her hair. The whole car would smell like fresh flowers run through with cigarette smoke.

That's how she got her name.

She wore wild flowers.

She's all grown up now, and watching her dance and make out with her boyfriend on the dance floor is just further evidence to the immobility of the feelings attached to our memories.

Hotrod swings by with a girl whose ethnicity would best be described as "urban" and lets me know he's out for the evening and I wish him well.

After the song ends Wild and Kevin come back. I let them know Hotrod is out and Wild gives Kevin an "I told you so." kind of look.

"The rumors are true, huh?"

"Yeah, the kid is one of kind."

They sit down and we make small talk for a little bit before deciding to call it a night. We walk out together and they offer to drop me off at home, but I say no. It's cold and shitty and I feel like walking.

"It was nice meeting you."

"Definitely, be safe."

"You too."

Its progress, it's the illumination of the better parts of our natures. It's just slow, and it's easily derailed by the carelessness or maliciousness of individuals.

THE GREAT ESCAPE

Time travels slower here. That's one of the things that I've learned about hospitals. They are the living proof of psychological time dilation. The Pear grabs my hand and squeezes it. Her eyes reassure me that everything is going to be fine and that we will get through this thing together.

Which is nice, but I only know how to go through things alone.

After a little more time the psych nurse comes out and tells us that we can have a short visit.

Bonk has been committed to a different hospital in a different city and I still have a moment of anxiety that I'll be recognized as a former patient. That's so ridiculous and probably proof that they should just lock me up in the room next to his, but what can you do? At the end of the day I just really don't like these places.

We go in and find him sitting on a couch staring into the void.

His mother had called me and asked me to help. The Pilot Fish said yes immediately and so here we are.

We moved out all of his stuff yesterday. My car is filled up, and her van is packed as well. The landlord was very understanding.

According to the nurse Bonk was found walking around downtown Madison naked calling out Wild's name. He was on some wonderful mix of ecstasy and LSD. It must have been some good stuff and a lot of it, after he had been grabbed and put in a hospital gown he continued to hallucinate for another forty hours.

He was weak from malnutrition and blood loss. He'd been donating plasma and then using laundry detergent to remove the dye they put on your fingers to keep track of how often you donate. Clever fellow. He had hit every plasma and blood drive in the city to fuel his binge.

Apparently, he had come pretty easy. The cops didn't have to shoot him or beat him or tase him. They told him that Wild was with them and safe, then he got in the back of the car.

A rarity of a peace officer, most of the ones in Minneapolis shoot to kill when it comes to the mentally ill.

Once he got to the hospital they tied him to a bed and let him ride it out. There wasn't much to give him at that point besides some drugs to calm him down.

The Pear looks at me and smiles in the only way that isn't rude or out of place.

I've kept my word about staying clean. I drink once in a while and almost always with the Pear and rarely with Hotrod. The clarity of sobriety is both beautiful and horrific.

The world is much more comfortable muffled under some booze or dope.

I look at Bonk in his hospital gown and confused stare and know that it should be me laying there.

The Pear knows all of my history and can read my mind now, she touches my arm once and leaves it at that. She doesn't say anything and I am grateful.

I feel guilty and then I feel stupid, and then I feel guilty again. It could have been any of us. It could have been all of us. It didn't have to be any of us. Why some get lucky or unlucky has so little to do with anything but fate or chance. We were all making the same choices. We carried the same risks. We lost in different ways.

He's on a lot of medications. I can see that from the first glance. One kind of chemistry is being used to try and undo and repair the damage of another kind of chemistry, and all of it without a clear understanding of why it works. Doctor's and users alike just put something in to see what comes out.

The behaviorist model has come to life in the laboratory. It doesn't work very well, and there are some things that just can't be fixed.

"So, how are you doing buddy?" That sounds so fucking fake coming out of my mouth that I want to vomit all over myself. I just don't know what to say when it's so obvious that the person in front of me isn't really the person that I grew up with.

"What's the terror threat level?"

One moment, in with a breath and hold, hold, hold, exhale.

"It's low. You're safe here."

"Green, green, aquamarine, we're all safe in the submarine."

He looks at me and we share the void between us like a gaze of quantum gravity.

"How is Wild?"

She told me that this was too much for her and wouldn't come. I understand. I guess in a way I don't care. She has a lot of future to deal with and doesn't want to get dragged down by the past. I could call her a shitty friend if I wanted to have a fight with her, but I don't.

I don't hold it against her.

"I need to escape and find her."

"You don't need to do that. I'll take care of her."

He gives me a hard look and then nods his approval.

"They lied to me."

"I know."

The nurse motions to us, and we get up and leave him there.

His mother is in the hospital lobby and her face is screaming at me that I did all the same drugs that he did, so why am I okay and with this wonderful girl while her son lives in hallucinations.

"Thanks for coming."

"It's not a problem."

I motion towards a little café across the street. "Let's grab a coffee and get this figured out."

"Okay."

We sit down and she explains to me that the hearing was yesterday. He's been granted a conditional release. He's damaged but not a threat to himself or others. The drugs are gone, and only the damage of their passing remains. She shows us a PET scan of his brain.

It looks like the surface of the moon.

It's nothing but craters connected with lines of scar tissue.

I want to tell her about my own time in the hospital and the problems that I had there, but I realize that it's a waste of words. So much of life has to do with what we can share with others, but the line between the survivors and the casualties can't ever be crossed.

"He was using pretty heavily."

"Yes, he was. So, what can I do?"

Her eyes say that the best thing would've been to keep him from using in the first place and for me not to have used either, for our friendship to have been focused on video games or chasing girls, or getting a great education, a career and a normal life. Then she says one of the worst things I've ever heard in my life.

"I've lost both my sons."

The Pear reaches over the table and puts both of her hands over one of hers.

She looks at the Pear and for a moment I think that she will break apart completely, and then through a few breaths and a focused control beyond my understanding she comes back.

She's tough in the way that long winters and unreliable men can make you tough.

Then she tells us about the power of attorney agreement and the supplemental security disability income. She has found a place for him to live and with the direct deposit from the government and the automatic withdrawal for rent he at least will be able to live and eat. She has gotten a psychologist up there to take him on. She really has done a lot of work. She looks very tired, and I want to tell her in some way that there isn't much left to do, but I can't find the right words.

She says that she wants him to have his own place and get better.

"It's important for him to be as independent as possible."

"I agree."

"It's a psychotic break, and he's not expected to have a full recovery, but he can get better. Just no one knows how much better, it could be a lot better."

The Pear lets go of her hand and we go back into the hospital. Once everything is sorted out we go our separate ways.

"Tomorrow at eight o'clock?"

"Yes. Thanks again for coming down on such short notice."

"It's not a problem."

The Pear and I check into a hotel for the night. The Pear goes online to check her plane ticket. She has to go back to her home country for some green card bullshit. She understands it better than I do. Since the terrorist attacks it has gotten much harder for decent hard working people to come into my country. That is unless they walk across the southern border.

I actually have some vacation saved up myself. Being sober and with the Pear has stabilized all sorts of things in my life, and a lot of those little boxes on the pay stub have numbers in them now instead of zeros.

I am going to New York to see Jani. I told the Pear about it and she said yes. She wasn't jealous or upset at all. She told me to have a good time and to stay clean.

Once the Pear is done we brush our teeth together in front of the mirror. The hotel has a Jack and Jill set up and it's quite cute. Then we go to bed. We don't make love, we just touch. I have one moment when I become overwhelmed with it all and she gets on top of me and hugs me until it passes. We fall asleep mostly holding each other, and we sleep well together for it being a new place and all of that.

The next morning we have our continental breakfast and our coffee and juice. The Pear is trying to get me to be healthier and drink juice every morning. She thinks I smoke too much, but since she smokes too it's hard for her to make an argument about it.

Then we go back to the hospital and meet Bonk's mother.

She looks worn out, but she is ready. We go upstairs and she goes through all the paperwork with the nurse.

"Okay Bonk. It's time to go."

"Can I ride with you?"

I look at his mother and she nods at me.

"Yeah, you're coming with us."

"I knew that you would help me escape."

"Sure."

My car is so filled with shit that the Pear can barely squeeze into the back. Bonk sits shotgun and I start us off. He's so medicated that he falls asleep after fifteen or so minutes.

I ask the Pear, "Do you think that he will get better?"

"Some of the neurology will slowly heal over time. He'll stabilize a little more once the medications are figured out. I think that he will improve, but no he will never get better."

I figured she was right.

"I wonder if he'll find some way to at least have a normal life."

"I wonder if anyone ever anywhere will or ever has."

She reaches from the back seat and rubs her hand on my neck for a little while.

We lose Bonk's mom somewhere on the WIS 29 and US 51 interchange and pull into town without her. The Pear reads me the address for his new place and we only get lost once finding it. His mom is already there.

I look at him and wonder about all those moments that

passed while one of my best friends from childhood was losing his mind.

He has finally come out of his stupor and we move him in. His mom goes to the store for some groceries and cleaning supplies. When she gets back the Pear helps her get the kitchen organized while I assemble the bed and book shelf.

Bonk is really tired.

The Pear takes all of his medications and begins to organize them. He has one of those boxes that have each day in a separate container. She puts the box on the kitchen table on a calendar so that it will be easier for him to manage. She pulls a pen out of her bag and marks off the days through today so that when tomorrow starts he will know where in time he is.

He sits on the couch and stares around himself in wonder.

All of the essentials have been unpacked and organized and everything else is in the house. Bonk's mom kind of motions us out onto the porch.

"I can't thank you enough."

"It was the least we could do."

We hug each other. I can tell that she is finished, but wants the last moments of today to be just him and her. I go inside and say goodbye to Bonk.

"Where am I?"

"You're home."

"What's the terror threat level?"

"It's low."

"Green, green, green, aquamarine and ..."

The Pear is standing by the car waiting for me. She's lit her first cigarette of the day and I follow suit with my fifteenth or so.

I drive her around the little town and she takes a look at it. We stop at one of those small countryside bars that could be anywhere where the population is thin and the winter is long. She gets a kick out of the fish and deer that have been mounted on the walls. The bartender and the patrons have never met anyone from her country before and they are insular and curious at the same time. There's a moment of cold war tension from one of them because she is from the former Soviet Union, but it comes to nothing. I don't get angry about it and she is patient with them.

We eat some hamburgers, and I have only two beers. Then we take a little walk around the town. I show her the house that I lived in before I moved out and then my parents moved out. It's been a long time since I was here and feeling that makes me feel disoriented in a way I can't explain. Where I come from here is a time that has moved on.

Time may pass slower in small towns, but it still passes and I have no family here anymore, no allegiance to this place in this now which feels so conflicted with all my desperate desires to flee it combined with all the experiences here that made me who I am.

The prodigal son came home to find emptiness and the rebellion meaningless.

Then we get back into the car and start the drive back to Minneapolis. The Pear flies out tomorrow afternoon and we don't want to get in too late. If we make good time we'll hit the city right after the rush hour is over.

She relaxes and looks out the window at the trees.

"There isn't much here."

"That's why we left."

REQUIEM

The Pilot Fish has been back in New York since yesterday. I told Jani that I was arriving today. I wanted some time to myself, to look around and see how things were the same and how they were different.

March feels like summer in New York and winter in Minneapolis.

The killings hadn't started yet. The torture hadn't started yet. The detentions and deportations and extraordinary renditions hadn't started yet when I was last in New York.

I asked a girl in a café for directions to ground zero and she had no idea where it was. She was a little embarrassed about it, she told me she moved here after it had happened.

New York City turns over and over and over like no other place in my country.

I walked and asked and walked and asked until I got to it. There was a barrier surrounding the site and I walked up to that. Now that the towers have been destroyed you couldn't walk to them. I wanted to. I wanted to slip and struggle around on that concrete. I wanted to taste the ash. To lean down between two great and shattered grey concrete slabs and think and feel and cry. There were things that could only be said there, ideas best expressed between me and the Pilot Fish and god and country and ash and memory, but you couldn't do that. There was a barrier.

You would get into trouble if you did that.

So, I stood at the barrier and looked and thought and felt. I was trying to find some sense of ruinenlust in the wreckage, but all I felt was a kind of pallid emptiness, it was all too new with war and I knew that the city would never let this have the time and weather needed to wear it down into those kind of feelings.

I wasn't the only one there though I wanted to be. I imagine that's what everyone in New York City feels every day. One of the other people there made eye contact with me, and I could tell that he was going to talk to me.

"Can you believe it?"

"No, I still can't."

"They won't let anybody down there, they say it's too dangerous, but I know the real reason."

"Really?"

"Yeah, the government has over a 100 million in gold buried down there. They have to take it out secretly, so no one can go down there."

"Really?"

He said, "Yes, yes, yes."

I had nothing to say and could think of nothing to add. I nodded at him, and then I wandered away along the barricade.

I passed a placard with the builder's plan for the new project. There would be a smaller tower and then a larger one. The larger one would be the tallest building in the world. It looked like a huge uncircumcised penis. In the hooded head of the penis was a giant fan that would use wind energy to help power the building. The penis was going to be built right where my interlocutor said all the gold was buried. It would overlook everything, and all that ash and death would be gone. The huge uncut cock was going to be called the "Freedom Tower."

I wondered if that meant the tower was going to hold the freedoms that had been taken away from us. It was big, and I figured it could hold a lot.

I looked at the future one last time and then back to the past. The guy was still there. He had found someone else to talk to about the gold.

Then I find a pay phone, still 25 cents in New York and

call Jani.

"Hey sister, I just got in."

"You sound tired."

"I am."

"Are you at the airport?"

"No, I took the train in. I figured we'd meet somewhere."

"Two hours and your already New York."

"Just a few parts, you're the local."

"Ok, do you remember the bar on Rivington that we drank at after you helped me move?"

"Yeah, I could get back there."

"Perfect. How about an hour?"

"Sure."

It takes me a while to get over there, but I'm not in any rush. I get there first and get a beer to wait with. I light a cigarette and look at the hipsters and cool kids. I'm in a philosophical mood after seeing ground zero and have no animosity or criticism in me. I can feel Jani without seeing her when she enters the bar.

"Hey Fish."

"Hey Jani."

We hug each other and she feels healthy and beautiful and strong. We look at each other for maybe the first time in our lives as just friends.

She looks into my eyes and smiles, "You're in love."

"Yes I am."

"Is she nice?"

"She's wonderful."

"You deserve someone wonderful."

"No, I don't. But it's very nice."

We get a round and sit next to each other at the bar. She uses new slangs like "bridge and tunnel" and talks about the authenticity and price of life on Manhattan. She's really where she belongs.

"You hungry?"

"Always am, take me some place interesting. It's on me.

The credit card bill comes after the vacation."

She laughs and we finish up our drinks.

We walk south for about half an hour to a Dominican place that she promises me I'll love.

I complain about the TSA and the flight and she agrees. I give her the full story about Bonk and she just shakes her head sadly, "Poor guy and all of us had some heavy trips. I'll make sure to visit him when I go through there again."

"Please do, it would mean a lot to him."

I look into her eyes looking for the void, but it's not there anymore. It has been replaced by something else, something beautiful.

We steer clear of politics, neither of us are happy about what's going on, and neither of us can do anything more than bitch, so we leave it alone.

"So, what's going on with you?"

"Part time waitress, full time student, full time musician."

"On a label?"

"You got a publishing deal?"

I smile at her. "Touché."

I feel it then for one moment, that ghost from the past that can poison the present. It wanders around inside me looking for something to haunt, but I won't let it. After a while it fades away.

"Why are you smiling like that?"

"It's enough that I am, isn't it?"

She touches the top of my hand.

"I'm glad you came."

"I am too."

"I wasn't sure ..."

"... You are now though."

"Yeah, I am."

"Good. That's good."

The waiter breaks our stare filling up our water glasses and I order a glass of red wine.

"So, I am playing out three nights a week now. I even have a few fans, not just friends." She takes the last bite of her plantains.

"That's great. I'd really like to see you. You aren't playing tonight by any chance?"

"No, not tonight, but I am tomorrow night."

"Cool, that should be fun."

She writes out her address and gives me her keys, "I have to be at work in half an hour. We'll talk more tonight."

"The waitress gig?"

"No, I have a catering thing at a hotel tonight, somebody rich is getting married."

"Have fun, I'll see you later."

She gives me a kiss on the cheek and leaves. I order another glass of wine and let my mind and feelings wander.

Then we're off. The Pilot Fish leads the way swimming around the city of Gotham for a few hours soaking in all the grotesque and beautiful that you can find in one day before happy hour hits and we find a few bars, slowly drinking and working our way closer to the Hells Kitchen address that Jani calls home.

Then we buy some bottles of beer and go in to her flat. It's what you would expect, small, and messy. We see the casual evidence of a boy that stays over every so often and wish him luck.

It feels fine.

The Fish guesses that the keys I am now holding are generally with the transient male. She doesn't want us to meet.

That's probably fair, and I don't blame her for that.

Maybe next year.

The Fish flops on the couch and flippers on the television, finds a baseball game and sips away. The alcohol supply is almost low enough to make anther sortie necessary when Jani unlocks the door and comes in.

"I lifted two bottles of wine from the reception. Not a bad value." She hands them to me and finds a cork screw. I read the labels, Chianti. Not my favorite, but I haven't the class or education to judge if it's a good one or not. I put one in the refrigerator and uncork the other while she changes into comfort clothes.

"I don't have any wine glasses. Just pull some coffee cups out of the cupboard."

"On it."

Then she comes out of the bathroom rubbing some make up off her face with a napkin. I hand her a coffee cup.

"Thanks." She says as she sits down next to me on the couch.

We toast and drink.

"So, is it serious?"

"Damn it Fish, I thought everything was cleaned up!" she laughs.

"You cleaned up fine, I'm just asking if it's serious."

"His name is Steve. He's okay. He's a musician too, you can't really expect much from musicians."

"It's the same with writers."

We laugh, and then it happens, just a moment between us, it feels really good. I squeeze her hand and she squeezes mine back. An absolution of all the things that were and all the things that came to be.

The wine gets finished and I fall out on the couch. She wakes up before me, and makes some coffee. I know New York well enough to skip the touristy bullshit. We take a walk through Central Park. She brings her guitar along.

I read her a poem and she can tell what's parts are about her and what parts aren't. She plays me a song that she wrote about me, and I like it. It's strange and kind of flattering to hear yourself set to music. Not just the lyrics but the way someone else feels the sound of you.

The day goes away without any wish to hold it fast or push it along.

Then we are off to the open mic for tonight. The bar is small and shitty. In New York this can and often does mean trendy and cool. It's a bipolar culture well mixed with ideas that don't work, fantasies that can't be realized, and calculations that we follow against our conscience. I don't have the radar that Hotrod has. He could tell me if this place had already had its moment or was blossoming into the scene. Jani may still be coming to play here then. She might be famous and people will talk about how she started here.

I'll have to come back to find out.

Jani gets called after about an hour.

She begins and the critic in me awakes. This is Indigo Girls, this is Ani DiFranco, this is Tori Amos, this is Jim Morrison, this is this and that is that. And something new, this is her.

The real her.

My God has she gotten better at voice and guitar.

I promised her that I would never write about how she looked. I won't break that promise here. I'll use words that you could use, that anyone could use for someone who they love and that they've let go of. She was metal and magic and minerals and glass, and she was more than all of that, and then the moment passed.

It's not to mourn, just to feel. People leave each other incomplete all the time. Few desires are equally shared and love can transform into friendship without loss. Sometimes you have to get there and back again to find where home really is.

I have nothing to complain about and I am in love with the Pear while watching my great love of so many years playing away getting along in her own life. People move on from each other and bring along what they can or don't have a choice about. You grow, you heal, you scar. Sometimes you just have to let go and watch the show. It's not perfect, but it's fair.

I'm thankful that this is the ending we're getting.

The Pilot Fish was listening too, but he didn't hear the influences, and for him it was not to mourn, not even elegy. He heard the rape and breaking glass. He heard his battle cry. He heard the girl, just old enough to wear a bra, running, laughing down the dock, just a little bit ahead of us, jumping into a cold spring fed, in the middle of nowhere Wisconsin lake. Taking a moment before surfacing to fix her top, imperfect teeth in a perfect smile, so young and healthy, and so close and far away from the woman she is today.

Jani finishes her last song to more than polite applause. We drink a few beers and watch some of the other acts. Then we leave. I ask the cab driver to make a detour back to the grave.

There were two beams of light pointed up towards heaven in each of the places that had been the towers.

They looked like they went on to forever.

WHERE'S MY SHIT BITCH

The Pear had gotten all her green card stuff figured out and was going to be flying back in a few days. The security put in place to keep us safe from terrorists had made it really hard for her to get back to the States to take care of Americans in the hospital. She had a lot of determination though and was making it work.

You would think that I would have gotten loose right after she left, but I had been a good boy. We talked on the phone over scratchy long distance lines and I wanted to be present for that. Now that everything had been figured out, I felt I deserved a treat.

I dialed up Hotrod, "I am still a free man. You got any plans tonight?"

"No. We'll have to at least get a drink and see some tits."

"Strip club it is then."

"Let's break it up and get some drinks first."

"Meet in thirty?"

"At the usual place."

I have a pitcher waiting for us when Hotrod walks in.

The financial stability that has come into my life with a steady job and the Pear has shifted the economic balance of our friendship so that I can pick up the occasional tab. We drink just enough to be drunk without losing one's edge and then start off to the temple of naked solitude.

We like strip clubs mainly because they balance splendor and desperation so well. If you believe that you must suffer to be beautiful or that the beautiful deserve to suffer alone then you are in the right place.

When I was single I'd dream the romantic dream that one of these attractive exhibitionists would spontaneously fall in love with a heavy drinking introverted writer. I thought there must be a desperate artist on one of these stages looking for someone to worship her in verse.

That never happened, but a lot of my blackouts are overrun with beauty.

You would think that the thousands of dollars and hundreds of hours spent in strip clubs would have dulled the romantic optimism, but loneliness mixed with booze and beautiful bare boobs can kill off any amount of common sense.

That and Hotrod didn't help. He was the only person I'd ever met that could pull girls right out of the club and into bed. He'd actually been picked up before he paid his cover on one occasion. It was inspiring and depressing at the same time.

We were picky when it came to strip clubs. We tended to avoid the chains filled with single mothers shaking their hips to whatever song was their favorite at the time of their original conceptions. We stayed away from those joints where there is a protective layer of glass between you and the girl.

That's just bullshit.

We preferred the places that had single moms with long drug histories, whose make up hid bruises and the stage lights were low enough to make anything possible and everything illusion. We liked the darkness and the whispers that come with it. We liked new school racket, two bills to get laid, and score something along the way. No point in walking the streets if you can walk the stage.

We liked the places where the money made the contact rules.

The great city of Minneapolis has little to offer in this direction. You don't want a lap dance from some "Minnesota Nice" bitch.

That's the opposite of erotic.

It's better to find the places where the girls are illegal and don't speak English well or are from harder cities with more life and desperation.

There's only one place downtown that comes close to satisfying our taste. They check us for weapons and let us in.

We don't mind being the only whites in a sea of brown, yellow and black.

We came prepared with a stack of singles for the stage and a roll of twenties for the dances.

Some girls dance to hip hop and some to rock. We are patient with the process. I am a picky son of a bitch in general and if this is my last time to get loose for a while, then I don't want anything, but the best, and she's come out to "What's Luv." And she had me at the sarong and the Victoria's top.

"Come get me when you're done."

"Ok, baby."

Damn, sweat just thin enough to notice. She glistens and glows and smells like something that I'm never, ever going to get. She's got an accent that I don't give a fuck about and everything about her pushes against you in a way that pulls you around.

"You are amazing."

"Thanks sugar."

After that Hotrod and I get down to excess in general. I get dances from girls that look the opposite of the Pear. A few full figured sisters that could grind booty and have rich black skin covered in gold glitter and perfume. It rubs off the girls bit by bit and sticks to you. The perfume permeates your clothes with the contact. You smell like heaven and sparkle like the stars when they're done with you.

Then we switch to mixers and Latinas.

"Not bad, Hotrod, not bad."

"You're telling me. I would fuck that bitch from here to hell."

"But Hotrod that could be any of these."

"True, but there's always some more than others."

With only a half hour to close, in a sense of peace and alcohol, the trouble begins when a well shaped white girl adds an additional element to the equation.

"You want to get high?"

"No, but my friend might."

It's a good thing Hotrod didn't use because everyone looked at him and figured he did and no one looked at me and thought I did. I guess if the wave doesn't collapse there is an alternative universe with Hotrod doing life in the joint for drugs and me dying of AIDS.

I'm just drunk enough and the Pear is just far enough away that I'll say yes.

"How about you?"

"Yes, what do you have?"

"Glass."

"Anything else?"

"No."

"OK" It was already late and I didn't want to start a binge. All I wanted was a little lift. It was stupid, but most of why I scored that night was to say that for all the Pear was she hadn't taken away my will. Not all of it. That I could control everything in love or alone.

My logic LEAPS!

The Fish thought I was a fucking idiot, but he can't run the show all the time.

"Yeah."

She comes back to our table and hands me what should be fifty dollars' worth of glass. I slip off to the bathroom to get the party started and open the bindle to find nothing.

This pisses me off.

It pisses me off for several reasons. One: I don't like getting fucked by anyone under any set of circumstances. There was a reason for keeping a hand gun in the Fish Bowl. Two: I wasn't even that interested in getting high, and now I had to do something nasty about it. Three: The Pear would obviously be disappointed in me for breaking my promise. Four: I had this feeling that she had fucked me over because she figured I was white and wouldn't do anything about it. Five: Being clean had actually been fine with me.

The Fish said that this was a sign, just drop it, finish the drinks and get on home. Forget about it because it's not worth responding to.

But I can't do that.

I briefed Hotrod on the situation, and went looking for her.

She wasn't hard to find, and the look in her eyes told me that she had thought I had planned on getting high after I left.

"Where's my shit bitch?"

"What?"

"Listen bitch, you fucked me bitch. Now try to understand what a terrible mistake you've made. I know where you work bitch, and I'll leave you in a fucking dumpster, and whose gonna give a fuck about you bitch."

I didn't raise my voice. I just said it into her ear just louder than the music looking like I was asking for one last dance.

For the record, I don't think I'm capable of doing that to her, but she definitely believed that I was.

"You understand me, bitch."

"Please stop calling me that."

"Get my shit."

"I'll get it for real, I promise. I'll give it to you."

There was something in her eyes that I'd seen before, but couldn't place.

"No bitch, you give it to Hotrod and if he gives me the nod then all is cool and if he gives me a shrug, well then you are fucked."

She walks quickly away from me towards the dressing rooms.

After a few minutes she comes out and goes to Hotrod. Hotrod gives me the nod. Then it's last call. One more round and then we're out on the street drunk and smelling of ten different perfumes.

I tasted it in the car. It was ok, good enough to stop being angry about it.

We'd thrown all our singles on the stage, so I rolled up a twenty and snorted all of it up quickly. The burn was right and I felt the rush quickly.

"What did you say to her, when she handed me that stuff she looked terrified."

"I told her that I was going to leave her in a dumpster if she didn't come through."

"Jesus Christ brother."

Things were picking up quickly.

God, it's been a long time.

God, its heaven.

God, its hell.

God, I wish I hadn't taken it.

God, I'm glad I did.

Oh Jesus fuck me Christ.

Sometimes this shit can take you right to the edge pretty quickly.

The Pear came back a few days later. Her green card stuff was sorted and it looked like she was solidly on track for permanent residency. She told me that being home was both good and bad, but it was going to be a while before she did the trip again.

A few weeks later we got wasted and I had a mini melt down and told her everything.

She was very disappointed in me. She told me that it's not fair to hold good behavior or sobriety on the condition of another person. It's cowardly, and those things have to come from within.

If they don't then they don't have any value.

I couldn't think of anything to say in my defense and just stared at her terrified that she was going to walk out the door forever. I realized then that being honest about things wasn't always enough. Honesty is just facts.

Then she forgave me.

Completely and unconditionally.

I'd never met anyone in my life that could do that.

Before we made love she whispered to me, "Never again or you lose me."

"Never again."

"You wouldn't have really hit her, right?"

"No, but she didn't know that."

A few days later irony kicked me in the face.

I opened the mail and amongst the junk that I typically just threw away there was a missing person flyer. It was the stripper from the club. I showed it to Hotrod later for verification, just to make sure. Could it really be her?

"Yeah dude, that's her."

The photo was old. She must have been in High School or just out of it when it was taken. She'd had some ups and downs since then.

According to the flier she had taken her daughter and ran. It said that she was twenty two and that her daughter was five. She came from a small town in the middle of nowhere just like I did. In the photo she was smiling directly into the camera.

She was beautiful.

I could see why she was in a cash only line of work.

The flyer had in bold red type "Do you know where this person is?"

Yes.

I remembered asking her who the fuck would notice her being gone. I guess I had an answer to that question now. Whoever that was had already noticed.

I was mainly thinking of grandparents and the father of the little girl when I picked up the phone to make the call about where she was when it hit me.

That look on her face.

I know that look.

She'd been hit by men before.
I hung up the phone.

JUST FOR THE NIGHT

She feels like a cliché. All dressed up and nowhere to go but the end of the bar. She is wearing a nice short black skirt and black heels. They both have white stripes and go well together. She always buys brand name. She has a white blouse on that tightens nicely around her boobs without placing any emphasis on her stomach. It really completes the look.

Almost all of her tops are like this.

She has a cute little tummy and can still wear a bikini when she goes to the beach, but she really only feels comfortable with it when she's lying down. When she lies on her back or stomach it flattens out perfectly.

Just flat enough not to hang, just soft enough to want to kiss.

She checks herself carefully in the mirror before going out. She won't risk being called a muffin top.

She's happy with this skirt, which is rare, most of the time she'd rather be in anything else. She's not very tall and she doesn't think that long skirts look good on her.

This one is one inch above the knee and it really works for her. Her stature makes it almost fit like a mini which is a rare example of that working out.

She never realized when she was young and everything fit to advantage how hard it was going to be to put on clothes as she got older.

She has learned now, but still has some resentment over it.

She's dated good guys and bad guys and had her choice from High School into the University and then after she dropped out of college in the workplace and nightclubs as well.

She almost got married once.

They dated for a few years, and lived together for a year. She thought that he was okay to talk to. She thought that he was okay in bed. She thought he had an okay job. She had felt great about all those things in the beginning and then she felt okay about them, and she was ok with that until one day when she wasn't.

They didn't fight about it. They just let it go. They had even helped each other move into new apartments. They don't stay in touch. Once in a while she thinks about him.

It's not nostalgia. She only wishes that it could have been different.

There have been floods and droughts since then.

She works as a legal secretary and she makes enough money to have what she wants and to save and splurge a little. She is thirty-one and she felt the first youth come in a rush and fade with a whisper. She always colored her hair, but now it's for different reasons. She hardly ever plucked her eyebrows until the silver showed up.

Yeah, we're calling it silver.

She took a man once on the hood of his car in weather that was almost too cold except for the heat between them with no time for condoms or questions.

She had been on top and she hadn't though about it until later.

She had taken the news with a grain of salt. She had thought about it for a month or so, and she came to her decision. She had cried before and she cried after. She never told him. She didn't think that it was his decision and she didn't want to talk about it. She hadn't wanted anything more from him than what they had already had.

It had only been for the night.

She doesn't regret it, but only her two closest friends know.

She knows what she wants tonight. In a word what she wants has just come into the bar.

His eyes sweep her in one glance taking in all the necessary parts and lingering a little bit on the state of mind.

Hotrod checks his engine, yes his lights are on and his oil pressure is good. He hasn't been laid in three weeks. In short, he is in a fucking awful drought! His cock has been half hard with readiness for the last week. He has been in the throes of a masturbation temptation for a fortnight, but he won't do it. He never jerks off because it dilutes the sexual power.

He won't give that away to the internet.

Better to go a little mad with lust and anticipation.

One time a long time ago he wanked and then ended up hooking up with a girl that night. His performance, at least on the Hotrod standard, had been a four, fucking pathetic.

Fucking absolutely unacceptable.

He had been twenty, and that was the last time. It was one of those rules that once understood became unbreakably reinforced through the strength of its intrinsic logic.

She has an emptiness inside her that comes and goes and is always awful. Hotrod can fill it for a night and make it go away. He approaches her almost coyly and orders a drink sitting two stools down from her. He pretends to not know what was known from the first impression.

She has a good idea where things are going and plays it patiently.

There is a newspaper between her and Hotrod on the bar. The pages are filled with editorials talking about the benefits of the new domestic security legislation that is being debated.

It's been one year since the attacks in New York.

She had been listening to the song "Zombie" by the Cranberries in her cubicle when suddenly the music stopped and the DJ said that something terrible had happened in New York.

She went on the internet and couldn't understand what

she was seeing.

Then the newspapers and televisions had taken over. The will in Washington towards empire had a place, an opportunity for more than it could have imagined. As she watched the television she began to feel how they wanted her to feel.

She wasn't the only one.

She had never wanted a war specifically. She didn't really have the words for the feeling. She just wanted something to be done. She wanted proof of action from the liars that claimed to protect her. Something big enough to undo or equal what had been done in New York. That was all that she wanted and the television had provided some expert testimony and the Senators in Congress had shown that it was a bi-partisan effort.

She wanted revenge and penalties and retribution, and the politicians promised it.

We had the Brits standing side by side with us, and there were so many nice speeches about solidarity and hands across the water and heads across the sky to the place that empires go to die.

It was about guaranteeing that it couldn't happen again.

It was about making the world a safer place.

That's what was shown to all of us, and in the end she had agreed.

We'd all agreed.

Now there was a call for a second war and the drum was beating and the press was so well trained from the first bit that it felt like a smooth and well-rehearsed performance.

Consent was being manufactured. Consent was being co-opted. Consent was being stolen.

The chicken hawks had come home to roost.

She's angry about where things are now. She can't make sense out of how things came from then to now. She is going to vote for sure in the next election.

She doesn't want another war.

She looks away from the newspaper and watches the

television in the bar. There is an advertisement to buy a video devoted to the expressive sexuality of college age girls being filmed while intoxicated. The girls are all young and beautiful and filled with vitality and booze and the desire to take risks and the ignorance of consequences and exploitation.

She misses those years and is glad that they're over at the same time.

She's never slept with another girl or kissed one to make the boys excited. She's never been in a car wreck or felt fear for her own life. She's never left the country except one time to go to Mexico. She hadn't liked it much. All it had been was American college kids getting drunk and fucking each other. She had already been too old to really feel a part of it. She's only moved a few times and never outside of her native state.

She is sipping a glass of Chardonnay. She knows that if this is going to work right that she must be drinking, but not drunk. She has been taking her time and is now only half way through her second glass. She pretends to look past Hotrod as some people enter the bar and the charade is prima fascia successful. She has a twinge of nervousness because he is very good looking and younger, and while obviously alone, may not stay that way for long.

She pretends to catch his eye by accident and smiles.

He smiles back.

Hotrod thinks to himself, "I am going to fuck the hell out of you." After the shared smile ends Hotrod feels the contract at this point has been signed and sealed. All he has to do is deliver it. He likes to delay feelings of gratification a little bit, and besides all that, he has only just started drinking. He'll drink a few more and then start a little chit chat and then drink a few more. Then when the time is right everything should fall into place.

He sits back and lights a cigarette. He will have to quit these some day. They can affect one's sexual performance not to mention emphysema and lung cancer.

He wonders why he has never been in love before. Is it

possible to even fall in love at this point? He takes a little stock of things as he moves from one round to the next.

Certainly, a life of fucking is pretty fun at least in the short term. There are a few bitches that complain, but what can you do? Bitches are always going to complain about something. Some yell that they never want to see him again. Others demand that he stay in their lives forever and ever. Some believe that there is a necessary connection between sex and intimacy. Some yell that a one night stand is supposed to be the start of a relationship.

What's already over has been called a beginning.

What a joke.

Then there are those that think the booty is some private sacred refuge. Well, he has opened a few eyes there.

It's amazing what you can do to a bitch and still get a call the next day or even a week later. Fucking ridiculous, but that's the way people are. It's funny but the more people you fuck the more you look at them as only things that are to be fucked or not fucked. Hotrod drifts across memory a little bit and wonders about the last time he actually talked with a girl.

That was a very long time ago.

He gets up, orders another drink and goes to the bathroom. He hates condoms but buys one anyway and then takes a leak. He looks over his wares. Everything appears to be in good working order.

Houston can we get a countdown?

He zips up and washes his hands. Gives himself a good look in the mirror, and makes sure that nothing is out of place. Tilt the head back and make sure no boogers are hanging foul in the nose.

Hotrod, you are cleared for launch.

He sits down next to her this time. He slides his beer over. This time they make eye contact and the void flows between them.

"Are you waiting for someone?"

"No, I just came down." She's actually nervous for a moment when she looks into his eyes. There is something there that she doesn't want and then it's gone. Her words stumble for a moment and then the conversation picks up. He's quite charming in kind of a roguish way. They have a few laughs and she sips her way through her third glass of wine to his last two beers.

Hotrod picks up the tab.

It turns out that they were both thinking her place.

He paces foreplay perfectly, lips on shoulders, tongues in mouths, tongue on nipples, and some time spent there and then tongue on pussy and he knows where things need to be kissed so that nothing chafes when he comes in.

He uses the condom for round one and after thirty minutes of work she is COMING so hard that she can't breathe but in gasps. She drags her nails across his back drawing red lines and then blood, and he's having all of it!

Oh FUCK IT!! There it is! It rolls and then there is a second, a THIRD, a string: RING DING DING!!!!

"Oh, God!"

It's not over. There's another one and another, of fuck, OH Fuck, OH FUCK!!

It's something new. It's better than anything old. Her stomach is perfect and everything beneath is just fire and nerves.

The cup runneth over.

She can feel the heat envelop her, another one, and then kind of half of one and she is collapsing, sinking and swimming and feeling and not feeling. The emptiness is gone, turned inside out and pushed away.

She breathes.

He turns her over onto her stomach gently as he pulls off the condom.

She doesn't care what he does now.

FEASTING

Minneapolis, Minnesota, had entered the glacial months, and there is nothing better than being in love on a cold, cold winter night. Everything about outside justifies being inside. Everything about being alone justifies being together.

It's impossible to leave the bed and when we do its hot coffee, hot cocoa, hot tea, Hot Toddies, and little sorties out for supplies doing our best to return from the corner store before our noses have frozen shut.

Then the Pear says that she has nostalgia for Siberia and we need to go out for a walk. She tells me that it's cold enough to count, but that she has seen much worse.

It's the kind of cold that runs through your clothes finding every hole in the fabric or rip in the cloth that autumn would ignore until it gets to the center of your bones where it settles in and then radiates out in shivers and shakes.

As we talk our breath creates a cloud of our conversation with exclamations hanging in the air and sighs made visible as we listen and interrupt each other on our way down the street made barren of pan handlers, hustlers, and hookers by the God forsaken cold.

Our walk lasts just long enough for it to start to hurt.

Then we warm up with snuggles and cocoa before the Pear gets ready for work.

The sun sets so early that we live in half days and double nights.

The Fish walks the Pear to her car and then comes back into the Fish bowl.

The Fish gets his quills and parchment out. He will dedicate a poem to her. He looks hard through the parchment trying to see her. The flashes of inspiration, those delicate bridges between heart and language come out in little bursts and the work begins to take shape.

The theme: Her power was silence and honor, action and love, stasis and fluidity.

We face the impossibility of her:

"My Penelope in complete stillness and upheaval before the loom, weaving and re-weaving me as my colors bleed through the wool, knowing nothing valued except that I know it through you. You are the pool at the base of the mountain. I am wind and flame at the peak. I blow and burn. My dream is dissipation. I want to be extinguished within you."

Trash.

We ball it up and toss it in the garbage.

The Fish fills in and I relax away.

He puts the quill down and rolls up the parchment. He caps the ink bottle. It's just not going to come today and that's fine. That's just one of the parts of poetry, waiting for those moments and running them through when they arrive.

It'll happen again.

They don't always make for a masterpiece, all they are, all that inspiration can be, is just another chance to get it right.

If we can't work, then let's play.

Lock up the parchment and forget about it, enough is always enough and that's enough for today. Our belly is growling, let's feast!

The Fish surveys his surrounds.

He ponders.

What to feast?

More significantly, how to feast?

There ought to be a cultural understanding of feasting in the Great Asylum, but we have lost our understanding of the generosity of the spirit in the excesses of the flesh.

We don't even know the proper ingredients for feasting.

Here, let the Fish walk you through it. The first thing you need is good will, and a soul without acrimony. Then, an end of the jealousy of others' time, add two dashes of humility for the sounds of your own voice and you are almost there.

After the table has been set with that all you need to add is a nice spread of meats and breads and cheeses. There is no centerpiece to the table, there is no center of attention, only a series of plates that must be passed around as you sample from each. No need for a microwave. Everything here is served as close to raw as possible.

A good feast requires ales, stouts, lagers, and fine wines. There should also be glasses of pure spring water, although any water will do so long as it is clean, clear, and cold. The meats must be done with as little preparation as possible. Logs of sausages and shanks of ham. Feasting to be done properly requires one to be constantly cutting and slicing. You have to work your way through a feast. The breads are of the blackest rye, the kinds that are moist and if left out become harder than concrete.

The cheeses must be in blocks. The more they crumble the better they are. Slicing them should be more an exercise of watching them disintegrate under pressure.

A small bowl of raw brown sugar is a fantastic idea though not required.

The hours pass quickly if the feast is done properly. There is the greatest opportunity for the telling of tales and the relating of stories.

There is constant interruption.

As one cuts combinations of meats and cheeses layering them onto dark breads new ideas come and go. Everything is worth mentioning if it had the virtue to cross your mind. Everything is worth feeling so long as the feeling adds beauty to the experience.

Legends are made.

The Pilot Fish has a great laugh that bursts out easily

between sips of cabernet. It rocks along the length of the table, shaking the snow off the windowpanes.

Music is another one of the ingredients of a great feast.

It is best if one has a cordon of minstrels, but these are hard to come by in our barbaric era. All of the great arts, both dark and light, have faded in the scientific illuminations of the last couple centuries.

The Fish yearns for a superstitious age when heroes are better appreciated. He dreams for the times of kings and dragons. Especially the dragons. Of course, with some time traveling both minstrels and serving wenches can be found.

We invite them into the present.

The Pilot Fish has written an entire ode to the feast, and I know it's around here somewhere.

Well, no matter it will show up if it wants to be found.

One of the many ambitions of the Fish is to educate the world on the proper forms of feasting. There are so many that live in ignorance of the celebration of life. Others, worse still, think that the celebration of life requires things and certain special kinds of things at that.

You need bring nothing to our feast, but bring whatever you wish.

The most important thing is that you came.

Of course, no feast is really a feast without guests. Believe me the only barren table is the one you eat at alone. The Pilot Fish has traveled through all of time to find the best company to share the bounty.

We shared wine with great leaders and generals.

Genghis Khan brought his grandson Kublai Khan and they explained to us the ultimate consequences of power and bloodshed. They felt it glorious and I honored them as guests though I can't say I liked all the stories.

Of all the ways to shape history I feel doing it through killing is the worst.

Caesar is indeed fantastic, but like Alexander, it's nothing but bragging and bragging about how this battle was won and how this city was besieged.

Really, it's something you want to do so that you can tell other people in later feasts that you were feasting with this great conqueror, but you wouldn't want to have them over every time.

Philip of Macedon was a great drinker and story teller. He tells us about arguing with Alexander and Aristotle between battles, and how a practiced hand can guide a sword one day and a pen the next. He told us about he wept for the Sacred Band in the aftermath of Chaeronea.

The Fish really enjoyed that discussion.

The great artists and engineers from antiquity to modernity have been in attendance.

Frank Lloyd Wright spilling the sugar out and drawing the plans for a fantastic house with a tree planted in the courtyard that grew out past the roof!

Hemingway and Faulkner had been our guests, but you couldn't have them over at the same time or all the booze would disappear in a hurry and they'd start fighting.

The Bronte sisters had two conversations, one with us and one between themselves.

Da Vinci, he had a genius that hurt in its isolationism. He was always invited though he rarely attended. Frida Kahlo got him to come once and we took all the plates off the table so that they could draw on it.

Copernicus showing us the inspiration behind the telescope and just listening to him describe that feeling when the moon was seen under magnification for the first time by human beings made you feel like a revolutionary and discoverer at the same time.

Galileo Galilei told us about how he took that telescope and changed the course of human knowledge purchasing our enlightenment with his freedom.

He said it hurt, but it was worth it.

Newton is a good crack, really enjoys a stout. He laughs as he tells Einstein across the table about scientific revolutions.

Beethoven directed our minstrels to perform the most beautiful sonata we had ever heard and then asked us in sign language how it sounded.

We'd seated our share of spiritual leaders and philosophers as well.

Siddhartha Gotama spent the feast fasting. Which was weird, but he was so gentle about it that you didn't feel bad enjoying the food while he abstained.

Joshua bar Joseph was really kind, and he drank our wine without irony. When he looked at the "Last Supper" by Da Vinci he smiled like the Mona Lisa.

Al-Amin politely refused the wine, but with a glass of spring water told us about water from all the oases of Arabia. He taught us that all guests come from God.

The Fish and I have done our best to put that into practice.

Socrates walked us around and around with his method while Plato asked us if we feasted in a cave, and if this feast was in fact the Form of all Feasts or a Flicker of the Form of all Feasts.

Aristotle provided us with a strict taxonomy and metaphysical analysis of the feast before digging in.

Kant, Hume and Russell spent the whole feast arguing about how we know things from how we smell a flower to our most strongly held convictions. It looked like those guys could go on forever about that.

Nietzsche pulled the Fish aside and whispered something to him that he won't tell me. I think it was about the dangers of nihilism. Then he told me that he's shown me three corners and it was up to me to find the fourth. Then we reveled in our time.

We had guests whose names weren't in the history books.

The two centurions from the Lightning Legion were great fun. It's more interesting in some ways to listen to the stories of those that simply participate in history rather than create it.

There's no sense of destiny or grandeur then. No arrogance, just the same simple truths and troubles that we carry with us through every age.

We had a group of soldiers all in different uniforms and all the same, and all so young. They told us about walking out of the trenches and across enemy lines to share bread during Christmas.

They told us about the end of the meal and walking back across those enemy lines and climbing back down into the trenches so that the ridiculous and terrible task of killing one another could begin again.

The women that have feasted with the Fish!

Queen Elizabeth the First, the Virgin Queen of England, coyly referring to men and privateers! She could wink at you and make the most masculine of men blush like schoolboys seeing knickers for the first time.

Catherine the Second, now there is a woman to invite to a feast! Crazy beautiful and with great stories, she drinks pure cold vodka and eats pickles after each shot. God, could she tell toasts!

Cleopatra, such stately grace, her walking was a form of levitation, and her eyes held such sadness and desperation.

Sappho, such a poetess, her passion justified every risk you had ever taken in your life and her sadness justified every risk you had ever taken in your life.

Nefertiti, so genteel and beautiful, was telling us about a vision she had of everyone simultaneously looking into the sky and seeing one sun.

Just to hear Eleanor of Aquitaine and Tzu Hsi talking about men and power was about as enlightening a conversation as one could find.

Marie Antoinette was a fantastic dancer and much nicer in person than the historians would have you believe. She was just fine really. She only had the terrible misfortune of being wedded to her age as it was ending.

She told us about the pure shock of waking up to a world that no longer had any room for you in it.

The Pilot Fish closes his eyes and tilts his head to better hear Margaretha Zelle whisper to him about love.

The guests come and go and come and go, all of us completed with the cost of our sin. Sharing the camaraderie and truth borne out by the wine, the Pilot Fish engaged each and every one of them.

Ours was a movable feast that floated along on the current of time. Our feast was the riddle of knowing and not being sure. Our feast was the satiation of spirit that can only be felt in the throes of love.

The Pear will be home soon. The Fish begins to escort his guests back home. We get the place cleaned up so that she won't come home to a mess, and then we have one last cigarette before brushing out the taste of the wine.

It won't be long now.

The Pear's key is in the lock, and she has arrived.

The great feast has concluded and the Fish gets up and hugs the Pear. She has everything to do with being tired and cold at the same time.

While the Fish finishes putting some books away that were still on the table the Pear brushes her hair twenty-five strokes on each side and then brushes her teeth. The Pilot Fish turns back the covers. She washes her face and hands. She is too tired to take a shower.

She comes out of the bathroom and the Fish has drawn all the shades.

"Let's make spoons."

"Yeah, sugar doll."

She smiles for a moment at a joke that we've shared for a while.

She arranges everything to her comfort and lies down. Then the Fish throws his fins around her. He rubs her tired shoulders, and holds her as she warms.

There isn't anything to say.

Sleep flits around the corners of the room, but doesn't come to bed.

Then as tired as we are we make love, briefly, impossibly, sweetly, carelessly.

THE TALE OF THE CLOTHING THIEF

If you had told me about all the fucking laundry you have to do if you want to maintain a nice full time job in an office I would have reconsidered.

I'm not fucking kidding.

All that unemployment required was a wife beater and jeans and you could get a week out of those jeans. Selling drugs or taking advantage of customer service policies didn't have a formal code of attire either though dressing up always helped avert suspicion.

When you lined up for day labor you always wore something you expected to get dirty or torn.

My current employer had a well-defined dress code that someone must have put a lot of time into. The Human Resources handbook referred to it as "business casual" and it always had the quotes on it, which kind of fucked me up. As near as I could tell all it meant was that you got to dress like how your mom wanted you to look in pictures when you were eight. The professional expectation was slacks with small pockets, shirts with collars, shoes without laces.

We had one fucking guy that bought into that whole dress for the next job you're going to have line. He wore a suit to work. He wore that fucking suit to his first day of work and his employee badge had him there in that fucking suit with this fake ass smile on his face.

You know he planned that shit.

I hated that son of a bitch.

The Adventures of Hotrod and Pilot Fish

Jeans were allowed on Fridays.

That was "Casual Fridays" and they always had that in fucking quotes too. They always talked about that in HR like it was a big fucking deal and somehow made up for the fact your weekend got to start eight hours late because of them.

If there was a holiday or something that caused the work week to be shortened someone from human resources would send out an email reminding everyone not to wear jeans on that day.

Every year people got sent home for showing up in jeans the day before Thanksgiving.

If the holiday coincidentally fell on a Friday then jeans were fine.

I'd taken a psychology class that had talked about this stuff, they called it classical conditioning, but the way the class did it you thought that shit only applied to dogs rather than being a blue print for the rest of your fucking life.

If you wore clothes that you weren't supposed to you would get a dress code violation and sent home to change. That counted as a write up and if you got enough of those it could impact your development plan, raise, and eventually end in termination. The edge of the wedge disciplinary policy of the company was based on the logic that anything taken far enough ended in termination.

I wasn't entirely comfortable with all of it.

The Fish made a sign and hung it in our cube, "The Thane of Cawdor lives/Why do you dress me in borrowed robes?", but nobody seemed to get it.

No one gets us.

I didn't particularly like playing dress up for work every day and it pissed me off how much money I had to spend doing laundry. The startup cost of buying these "business casual" garments pissed me off. Going to fucking Old Navy really pissed me off.

I felt sorry for my boss.

As usual, the girls get fucked worse than the boys do.

Women have to put up with a lot more bullshit than men when it comes to dress codes. There were rules on everything from open and closed toe shoes to blouses and bras. The code didn't use the word "slut" but if it had you could bet that would have been in quotes too.

I was told that the idea behind the additional restrictions on women was twofold. One, guys didn't know fuck all about clothes and could only follow a dress code if it was written in Newspeak for the Fashionably Illiterate. This line of reasoning I couldn't really fuck with. Two, if left unchecked, women would show up to the office dressed like harlots.

The idea of wearing club outfits to your cube seemed perfectly balanced between comical and ridiculous to me, but it had happened. I was told about one of the secretaries and "the white pants black thong" combo that contributed to her eventual termination.

There were additional points that the Fish and I would ponder on.

We spent forty hours a week in an upholstered box at the end of a long row of cubes in a basement bathed in artificial light reviewing insurance claims looking for grounds for denial.

It was hard not to chuckle.

I dressed up for this.

At least we could laugh about it.

I wonder if anyone who lost their house because their insurance didn't cover the cost of their illness thought about the time and trouble I took to look sober and dress appropriately.

Ties were optional which was great because the only Windsor I knew was a Canadian whiskey.

I thought about shoe polish. I wondered about black socks versus white socks. I questioned myself about the necessity of a belt.

I kind of had to buy into the bullshit a little bit to make the whole thing work and I didn't like that either.

I didn't like that at all.

I'd never looked more conventional in my life. The look of success is earth and sky tones, lighter covered tops, mediocre and boring combinations that imply stability and presence. I dreamed of the outfit I'd wear on my last day.

That one would be grounds for immediate termination.

There was some room for philosophical inquiry as well.

I'd look at my coworkers and wonder about the relationships between clothing, sensuality and dignity. The first deception from the serpent of Eden was that we were uncovered to our shame.

God has been letting us punish ourselves for that one ever since.

The worst thing though was the fucking laundry.

I can't do laundry sober without losing my mind at the inanity of it all. To even get started usually took around four drinks. That fortified me with the necessary level of calm and determination to get the job done.

On top of that I faced additional challenges.

My building had two washers and two driers in the basement. The washers ate quarters like gluttony wasn't one of the big seven, and the driers heated up like tax accountant conventions.

One washer barely ever worked and the other was a cantankerous piece of shit that was always off balance and shaking about or spitting water all over the fucking place. Whoever wrote "The Terminator" had probably lived in my building.

The spin cycle didn't work on either of the washers, so you'd wring your clothes out one at a time by hand and then throw them into the dryer.

That fucking sucked.

Then a dollar and an hour later the dryer had cut the weight down to a measly eighty pounds. You could waste another dollar on a futile second dry cycle, or you could haul your clothes like Sisyphus's rock up the stairs to the apartment. Once in the flat I'd hang the not quite dripping wet clothes on a makeshift clothes line I had made that stretched from one wall of my studio apartment to the other.

I usually had two beers between trips.

The drunker I got the better it got.

The drunker I got the worse it got.

Wrestling with a spraying washing machine really inspired something Spartan in the Fish. Stripped to the waist covered in soap bubbles swearing in Latin or Greek as the mood inspired, our conflict of Man vs Machine was comedy and honor, art and combat.

The only other risk besides potential injury from the washer was that sometimes the laundry to alcohol ratio got the better of me and I passed out in the midst of my struggles.

I awoke one Wednesday morning in exactly that predicament.

I was at risk of being late to work and wearing wet clothes for the day.

Not for the first time, but just when you think I've learned.

I was in a state of mild confusion, which wasn't uncommon in the morning and rarely seemed to be a problem. I went down to the laundry room and opened the washer only to find my business casual shirts and slacks mixed in with someone else's clothes!

What sort of fuckery is this!

The only logical explanation for this situation was that someone was trying to save money by sneaking their clothes into my washing!

The chiseling bastard!

I was immediately filled with inconsolable rage.

Revenge I decided was best served between spin and dry! Not only would I take back that which had been stolen and so carefully hidden in the mixture, but I would go beyond that and take every garment that had aided in the deception!

No, not every.

The Adventures of Hotrod and Pilot Fish

I left that motherfucker one sock and a pair of boxers.

Consider that my laundry calling card you sneaky, stealing, cunt, bastard, FUCK!

Goddamn, my head hurts.

Then I went upstairs and got my clothes and took them down to wash them.

Such is the inconstancy of man!

I was committed to wearing wet clothes for the day. I just needed to get something clean enough to get out of the house with. I didn't have enough for a full "business casual" outfit for the day. I had forty five minutes to get to work and the washer took forty minutes.

It wasn't looking good.

While I was getting my clothes into the washer and securing the hoses so that they wouldn't blast water all over the place a young man walked into the laundry room and opened the door of the other washer.

"What the hell!"

I turned and looked at him through the fog and haze of last night's binge. He seemed distraught about the contents of the dryer.

"Hey man, was there anyone else besides you down here?"

"Not that I've seen." He was about my size and obviously not hung over, but I still liked my chances. I kind of stared him down psychically blasting him with the truth.

"I DID IT! I WILL DESTROY YOU! FIGHT ME NOW"

No effect.

I didn't want to call him out right away though because that would spoil my subterfuge.

"Some motherfucker just robbed me and all they left me with was a sock and a pair of boxers."

He was holding the boxers in one hand and the sock in the other.

I'm not gonna lie, that did make me smile.

Revenge though is one of those things though that can't

stay satisfied.

I decided to mildly bait him and then respond based on his reaction. Sun Tzu always advised using a ploy on the enemy to judge his strength and I thought it a fine idea to use one here.

I looked into his eyes psychically blasting him with the truth, "Your garments look thick as thieves to me."

Ten POINTS!

The verbal thrust of Shakespearian quality!

I am a fucking genius!

Goddamn IT, my head hurts!

He stared at me and then the washer started shaking and spitting water and I was called to battle. After I had settled it down I noticed that he was still standing there. I gave him another couple of seconds to accuse me, but he just kept looking at me, the dryer and a table we had for sorting clothes. I psychically blasted him one last time, but there wasn't a response.

I went back upstairs to the Fish Bowl to try and sort out a way to not wear wet clothes to work.

I separated my clothes from the stolen items and wondered at the subterfuge of it all.

Some fucking people, I tell ya.

I tried on one of my work shirts to see if its perfect form fitting shape had been altered by the violating contact of someone others clothes. It felt different to me, and that made me even angrier. I was examining it in the vain hope that perhaps the Pear could iron the thing back to its original dimensions when I noticed the label.

That observation created a thought that led to another thought and so on.

And so on.

It only took another minute or two for things to become clear to me.

These clothes weren't really mine.

Ahh fucking hell.

I also realized that it was Saturday and that I had gotten

up with my work alarm on a weekend again.

I hate it when I do that.

I'd often do laundry on Friday nights because no one was around to compete for washer time. They were all out drinking with friends while I was at home drinking alone with my laundry.

Well, this certainly cast things in a different light.

Oh fuck, it's all coming back to me now.

It's all come back.

We're at war again.

The war just started and I got upset about it and drank too much. The Pear did a night shift into a day shift because our one year anniversary is this next weekend and she had to do a shift trade and ...

We've been together a year. I've never been with anyone half that long. It's the fastest and smoothest course of time that I have ever felt in my life, time run along in peace and plenty.

And we're at war, again. Now time running along in stress and strife for so many so far away for so little.

Oh fuck, I'm going to be sick.

I make it to the toilet and empty out everything in my stomach.

Now dry heaves for a while and that disgusting thick saliva.

SPIT!

On the bright side at least I wouldn't be wearing wet clothes to work again.

Now, for the other part of the problem. I didn't really know what to do. Should I sport the false clothes of others and make myself a hypocrite to the verses shown so vividly in my cubicle? Should I wait until late at night and then sneak down to the laundry room like some shame faced child peeping about for the shadow of his father?

Nay!

The Pilot Fish prepared for battle. I figured that the

dude may actually want a piece of us after all when this shenanigan came to light.

If he smacked me I'd oblige him one, after that it's a straight up fight.

The Fish held our head high against our shame. We gathered the clothes together into a great pile, and marched back down the stairs to the laundry room.

I hoped that he would be gone and then I could just throw the clothes on the sorting table and be done with it, but no the dude was still there. He was standing guard over his washer still holding a sock and a pair of boxers.

Who the fuck gets up this early on a Saturday anyway?

He started at the sight of us.

I wanted to say something, but just wasn't sure how to break the ice. I thought about discussing the strangeness of coincidences or even complimenting him for choosing clothes like mine or perhaps even chiding him for buying the name brand version of clothes that I bought the generic version of, but all of it seemed out of place.   The Fish decided simple and direct was best.

"These sir, belong to you!" bellowed the Pilot Fish.

An awkward moment for some, yes.

He took the clothes from us without saying anything, only opening his mouth for a moment and then closing it.

Then the Pilot Fish turned around, marched upstairs, yanked the alarm clock out of the wall and slept.

THE PERSPECTIVE OF THE PEAR

My lover is a fish.

FISH BALL SOUP FOR THE POET'S SOUL

The Pilot Fish lit a cigarette and swam the Fish Bowl. The Pear slumbered. Yesterday's evening shift had worn her right out. Her hips and pot ambitions were static, but I didn't mind the lines. I liked her just how she was and I wasn't afraid of any changes that the future might bring.

Her strength and determination were not obvious and looking at her sleeping I could imagine her being anyone.

The Pilot Fish made coffee quietly and read. The book was "Master and Margarita." The Fish imagined the Pear flying naked over the Minneapolis skyline cackling like hell, scouring the Mississippi River for the Fish. The Fish of course was composing poems for her beneath the muddy surface of the river, only rising to meet her when the last line was cemented in with rhyme.

The Fish smiled to himself and looked over at the Pear. She almost woke up, but decided to rub her nose and fall back asleep instead.

Whenever we read anything about artists we always picture ourselves as the writer.

The Fish for now is in the present. We're trying to hold on to these moments when we can be both alone and together with the Pear.

He was in a bit of a struggle. He had to perform some chores in the Fish Bowl, but he had to do them quietly.

We didn't want to wake her.

He had just finished quietly drying the dishes when he

quietly exited the kitchen kicking the corner of the wall on his way out spreading his little fin on his left flipper out at an angle that said "broken."

A mind divided walks a path of hazard.

He bit his hand until two small lines of red began to run, hopping on one foot, slowly splashing his coffee out onto the hardwood floor with each hop.

Hop, splash, hop, splash, hop, splash.

Slip.

We countered this by gently and quietly throwing ourselves into the breakfast nook in the kitchen. A movement we executed well barring the part where we spilled the rest of our coffee over our stomach and crotch.

Besides that part, we'd done just fine.

The cup had been pretty full and quite fresh.

I know how the lobster feels now and I pity it in its pain. We thought for a moment of our balls being served in soup at a high end Beijing restaurant to cure anhedonia and nihilism.

We set the coffee cup on the on the table, quietly, and waited a few moments for the pain to lessen. It was an interesting cocktail like mixing two drugs you haven't tried before with disastrous result. Our balls were on fire and the toe was screaming at us. Each of those pains receded in their own way.

OK, steady now and up we go. We made our way, dare I say stealthily, past the Pear to the tool box.

Hop, heel, other flipper, hop, heel.

OH, FUCK THAT HURTS! OTHER FOOT, OTHER FOOT!

We took three deep breaths at the tool box that sounded like wordless whispers.

We quietly opened it and pulled out some duct tape and then hop, heel, other flipper, hop, heel, and back into the kitchenette! It was the best place in the Fish Bowl to sit down when being quiet for the Pear. There he grabbed the fin in question yanked out and UP!

THE RIDES NEVER STOP AT FUN TOWN!!

His vision dulled slightly, and he heard the bones line up

with a sharp SNAP!

We needed to take a moment after that.

Then he started to cut the duct tape into strips, quietly. Once around younger brother leaning into older brother until the little piggy was tied snugly though throbbingly into place.

The lights receded and reality returned.

He looked over at his love and life and she still slumbered.

Success!

Then the Fish cleaned up the floor quietly and toweled himself off quietly and refilled his coffee cup.

Our cock and balls looked like underdone salmon that you'd send back to the kitchen.

Then the Fish completed his little household tasks of replacing burned out bulbs, and screwing together squeaky joints. He did it with more attention than before and with the same dedication to quiet.

Once all the work was done, the Fish silently slurped coffee and smoked, waiting for her little body to recover from the physical labor of the previous night.

It was funny to look over at her and think that all the quiet and peace before him was actually a process of rebuilding and re-strengthening. It was shocking to me after all my years of meth use that people actually slept in regular patterns at all. Sleep for me was usually something I woke up from with a sense of surprise and confusion. I was generally just thankful that I was in my bed instead of my closet or on some floor somewhere.

The Fish could travel time back to the first rains that fell on a cooling crust of lava, but he couldn't see a second into the future.

We faced that great unknown equally and together.

The future.

Well, we were pretty free of wealth. This was standard considering that the Fish didn't trust paper money and whenever he had gold he buried it and then made a map of where he buried the gold. Then for security purposes, he buried the map. This fiscal system had inherent problems that unfortunately hadn't become apparent until it was too late.

He didn't like to think about it in great detail preferring instead to desperately rack his brain for where he had buried the damn maps. Next time, he would tattoo it onto his back in Da Vinci script and fashion a special mirror.

He was on his fourth cup of coffee and fifth cigarette when the Pear began to wake. He walked over to her as she slowly sat up. She stretched her arms out and up, her night shirt stretching above her tummy for one moment of skin before settling down again. Her hair was everywhere. She brushed it free of her face and out of her eyes with care. She reached out her hand for the Fish's cigarette, which he gave to her.

"You smoke too much."

"Good morning."

"It's not that good besides if we're going to sleep together. I should be able to wake up comfortably. You need more pillows."

Pillows!

The Pilot Fish could sleep samurai style on a pallet of gnarled pine with only a top knot for his head and Bujin to keep him warm. Enduring discomfort was one of the things that sharpened heroism, kept the Fish thin and hungry and strong.

On the other hand, sleeping with the Pear was fantastic and fulfilling in ways that honing your warrior discipline at rest just wasn't.

He eyed her warily as she slid over on the futon to make room for him. He sat down and she held a fin, leaning into him. She took another drag and then handed him back the cigarette.

He looked over the pillow supply. While completely inconceivable, it was just barely possible that some barely detectable inadequacy existed there.

Like a quantum fluctuation a virtual pillow flashed into existence followed the course of its Feynman diagram and annihilated.

"I will purchase some pillows at the height of the next pay cycle, but they are for the Fish Bowl. You may sleep with them and use them as you wish perhaps even getting cozy on the couch with them, but you may not take them beyond the rim of the Fish Bowl unless of course, we are going camping or something."

She smiled, "I never had running water in my life, and you'll buy me pillows just because a woman complains."

"I ..."

"Shh. I know, baby I know." She took the cigarette back and took two slow drags, her lips like perfect lines, her face still sleepy shifting in expression as she smiled and exhaled from compassion to satisfaction and back again.

The divide that neither of us would ever be able to bridge, would never want to, the difference that made life magical loomed between us. Mountains and landlocked seas, warm winds and alpine breeze.

She looked around the apartment and then at the Fish.

"There has been an accident?"

"If you're referring to the floor it has been secured."

"I see." Said the Pear peering at the floor.

"Do you have to work today?"

"Yes, at three."

That gave the Fish two hours minus travel and shower time to spend with the Pear.

"Could we take a shower together?" I asked that question purely in the sense of time management. As my boss could tell you in the claims denial business my time management skills were second to none. I had already showered, but figured I could use another one after the coffee incident.

"No, baby, I don't want you to watch me wash."

"I wouldn't be bothered."

"There are two of us here."

"OK."

The last hero of the twentieth century put his arm around her.

Twenty immeasurable minutes of silence and calm passed between them. The Fish followed her into the bathroom, held her in front of the mirror feeling our reality in the reflection. He held her from behind and we looked each other over. Our eyes are exactly the same color. I looked at myself and I couldn't see the void at all. In between us was only warmth.

She looked down at the Fishes fins, "Baby, is that the special tape you Americans are so crazy about wrapped around your foot?"

"Why yes, yes it is."

She looked down at it for a moment, "I'll re-wrap it after I get home from work tonight."

She'd rather take me to the ER, but she knows I won't go.

She leaned into me, her hair running across the bottom of my face snaring the occasional fugitive whisker. I can smell the smoke in her hair. I tightened my arms around her and she held her arms across mine hugging herself through me.

"OK, get out, I need to get ready."

"OK."

I left her to her shower and went out to wait for the fresh result. My foot was down to a warm throb that spoke slightly of pain and physical memory. I pulled the shoebox out from its special hiding place.

There was a nice stack of bills. It's amazing how steady work combined with sobriety has such a positive impact on the budget.

If she didn't wear herself out with a double shift I could take her out for dinner. I hated the fact that she worked weekends. Denying people's medical claims was a strictly nine to five Monday through Friday kind of job. Taking care of the people was an all-day every day kind of job.

I pulled some cash out and put the box back into its special hiding place. I wasn't hiding it from her. She cleaned my apartment when I wasn't looking, and knew where everything was.

I was just holding the discipline.

She came out wrapped in a towel and made me go into the kitchen while she selected her clothes out for the day. She would choose everything individually and lay them out on the futon in facsimile of how she would look for the day. She would make changes and then put everything on. Then she would think about it and look in the mirror. This was often followed by additional changes.

I peeked once and she caught me.

Then once she was prepped for the day she called me out from the kitchenette. We walked out of the apartment hand in hand.

While we were walking down the stairs the Pilot Fish pulled me back in time along ancient lineages and genetic memory. The gypsy roots of the Pear, the greatest grandmother, when our languages were spoken by all, but only read by the nobility and the ascetics. Before the sons of Arya had come from the middle Asian plain and set the wars and genes on the course that would one day create me. Back then the Roma and the Arya wandered by the same stars.

And we are back to each other across the mirror in a country unimagined by the ancients who thought the world flat and the edge an endless waterfall patrolled by dragons instead of unknown continents filled with people unaware of the coming genocide.

The Fish pulled me further back to when we had only one language and few words to describe the bitterness and brevity of our existence as we struggled in the savannahs of Africa before beginning the diaspora of man. The diaspora that has a destination in each of us as it becomes us the thoroughfare of the greater journey.

The tribe of man has traveled long and far since Eden.

How the millennia have changed our blood.

How the passage of time has found us again and again the same.

FREEZING

The Fish and I aren't in any rush on this trip. We've driven the speed limit the entire way. The road has been clear and traffic light and we've enjoyed the scene of the naked forest run through with evergreens.

I feel a little lost when we turn off of Highway 17 onto a country road and then the geography awakens a familiarity and nostalgia inside me that tells me how far I have left to go and how this used to be the way home.

It's been a long time since that was true.

The Fish and I put this trip off as long as we could, and we've come alone.

The Pear is working this weekend and we've promised to be back tomorrow night. I spoke to Bonk on the phone yesterday and he's happy that we're coming over. I hope it isn't a surprise when we show up, though I guess it doesn't really matter anyway.

The third snow fall is the one that sticks.

Before I get over to Bonk's though there is something I have to do.

Our little town was either big enough or old enough for three cemeteries. I stop off at the one that Bonk's brother is buried in. All the stones are in neat rows and look identical.

Looking at the row of stones I hope that when I die that they just burn me up and scatter the ashes.

I stop in front of his grave.

It doesn't say suicide on the headstone, only his name for an epitaph and the dates. Alone in a row of people just like him and completely different.

You can do the math and see how young he was, and all those questions of youth cut off too short hang in the melancholy air.

I haven't brought any flowers. I haven't brought much of anything at all. This isn't why I made the trip. It's just something that I have to do along the way.

I kneel there for a moment.

It's December, and the ground is hard beneath my knees.

I pull my flask out and pour him out a sip.

The booze melts its way through the thin layer of snow on the ground.

"Hey, it's been a while."

It's my first drink of the day and I let the whiskey tell me everything it knows.

I don't pray with words. I don't ask for anything because what's gone away can't come back. It's just the feeling of what it is to know someone and miss him, love him, and wish that we'd had more time.

This thing we have, this rich internal psychological experience with ideas and images made continuous through memory and immediate through inspiration bound into this physical being that can know a loving touch.

It's the only miracle that I can really believe in.

It terrifies and saddens me that all of this will one day go dark.

I feel terrible for anyone, whatever their feelings or reasons, for rushing the journey.

I take another swallow from the flask and it runs dry.

I get back in the car and drive around a little bit soaking up the old and familiar. Small towns are stalwart islands resisting the flow of time, and the Fish and I take some comfort from that. They are stubborn in ways that large cities can't be.

The little town has had some changes too. When so much of it has stayed the same the few changes stand out starkly adding a sense of unfamiliarity to the otherwise constant atmosphere.

I guess nothing anywhere ever really stands still.

I stop at a bar downtown. I want to have at least a few drinks to get rid of the road before I go over to Bonk's place.

I look around at the patrons.

Some of my generation never left and with some glances around the bar it looks like others still that had left have chosen to come back. I feel the unspoken question of whether I have come back to stay as well. I have some casual chats with people that remember me from high school.

I'm not the prodigal son.

I'm not looking to stay, just here to see a friend.

It's a strange feeling. I don't belong here anymore, but I don't feel out of place at all. It's like looking through a photo album at old pictures of yourself. It's still you even it seems impossible and in a way it feels peaceful to feel time in a gently progressive way, a slow river that meanders along without any rapids or rush.

I started dreaming here.

I got beat up in that park.

I opened my first savings account at that bank.

I kissed a girls chest for the first time of my life in this small town.

I look outside and I can see it start to snow a little bit.

I order another round and smile.

This is what really happens to people when they grow up. Most people that couldn't get laid in high school end up getting married. Some want kids, some don't, some just have them anyway. Just getting older can be both balm and blessing.

High school with its bullshit social competitions and problems of acceptance and confidence fades away under the pressures of adult life and we find our way to where we belong, or at least to where we end up.

Our youthful ambitions fade, our petty jealousies fade, our fears and insecurities get replaced. We don't set the world on fire; we just find a way to survive in it.

Our challenge as adults is coming to peace with all of it.

The Fish believes in the eternal recurrence. He sees all of this as steps taken within a greater sense of repetition. Our lives are moments in the broader cycle of enthalpy and entropy.

He says that in another fifty billion years or so the universe will turn back in on itself as gravity overwhelms momentum pulling all of the galaxies back to a single point that is all of matter, space and time, holding it for a moment that lasts forever and is simultaneously so short that it never even happens because there is no time left to measure it with before exploding out once again.

We argue over that.

I can't agree with him.

If time flows on uninterrupted towards the future's past then I'm the one that fights against the current swimming back to what's been left behind. If it all repeats then it does so meaninglessly for me because my mortality prevents any participation in future re-occurrences.

I believe that everything only happens once and our morality is dealing with the long term consequences of the actions of fleeting moments.

And the Fish says it would be such a shame if all of this only happened once.

The Fish is right about one thing though.

This place is as close to happiness as any other place.

Amor fati.

I let my feelings loiter for another round before paying up and getting out.

I stop off at a liquor store for provisions before I find my way to Bonk's place. I park outside his house and give it a once over. It looks decently kept up, and I am grateful for that.

I knock on the door.

I have two packs of cigarettes, a freshly filled flask, and a six pack of Heineken.

From what he's said he's sober now and happy to be so. If he asks me for a beer I'll give him one, but I won't offer.

If there is anything left I'll take it with me when I leave.

I figure that he must have missed me knocking so I ring the doorbell a couple of times. The sun is going down and it's starting to get cold.

I can see him coming towards the door now. He moves slowly through the medication.

Bonk has gotten fat, I think that's another side effect of the pills. He stares at me for a second. It takes him a moment to remember the call from yesterday.

"Fish?"

"Yeah, you going to let me in?"

"Sure, yeah, sorry," he opens the door.

The house is a disaster. There are empty pizza boxes and soda bottles strewn about in some kind of flotsam of snacks and late night meals. It smells, but not really bad.

"Man, thanks for coming over man."

"No worries, I thought it would be nice to spend some time together."

"Yeah, dude, I cleaned the place up for you and everything."

There is a spark of the old him and we laugh for a moment, really laugh.

"I brought some beer, I'm a shitty friend."

"No dude, that's cool, I don't drink anyway."

I walk past him and put the beer in the fridge. I get one out and pop off the bottle cap with a cigarette lighter.

"That's a neat trick."

"One of the benefits of higher education."

He smiles at me.

"You always liked your beer. How long will you be here?"

"Just tonight, I'll head out some time tomorrow."

"Cool, want some pizza?"

"Sure."

"Want to play some video games? I got the coolest collection of the old ones that we used to play. I'm going to fucking own you!"

The old rivalry, the competition, it brings back some good feelings.

For the most part he does exactly that. I stop sometimes and pause when he drifts away. When he talks or swears to himself I don't let it bother me.

I think back to when I was in my own mental health incarceration, and wish we could split the difference somehow.

After an hour of video games I can tell that he is wearing down. I think that the pills he's on are heavier than the ones that I was on.

"I piss in the shower, so don't go in the bathroom unless you have to."

"Okay."

"I need a rest, I gotta go. You can play one player or watch a movie."

"Okay."

He moves slowly and I can hear him lay down without bothering to undress. After a few moments I can hear his breathing become steady and he starts to snore. I wonder what kind of dreams he has. Do the meds take those away from you? I guess I dreamed when I was drugged up. I hardly ever remember my dreams anyway.

I look around at the best that social security disability income can buy. It's a notch lower than the working poor, but all in all it's not too bad.

It's enough for a simple life.

I play a few games for nostalgia's sake and then shut it off.

I flip on the TV and watch some news. The wars are turning into problems that no one seems able to solve.

I can't take much of that, so I flip through some channels about celebrities cheating on each other, or making outrageous fashion choices, or doing whatever passes as important in the popular culture.

I don't get angry about it, I just finish my beer.

There isn't any evidence of an ashtray, so I open another bottle and then go out on the porch to smoke. He seems better. I wonder if this is as good as it will get for him. Neurology heals very slowly if at all and without much power of prediction.

I'll keep checking back regardless.

He's unlikely to ever get married, or have a career. It's unlikely now that any of the dreams of youth will ever be realized.

It is what it is and it can't be changed. I just try to accept it as it hurts.

The Fish takes me back in time, not too far away, only seven years or so. All of us hanging out, playing video games and telling each other stories that we had only just lived.

I can feel the vitality and hear the laughter.

Fucking hell, it was the nineties. The whole country was in party mode and everyone was invited. The president was getting great head and we all had jobs and drugs for fucking days.

The girls were so beautiful in that rush of youth and independence.

I remember mixing screwdrivers and we'd each take two tabs of Yellow Felix to go along with the vodka and orange juice. Two hours later it would begin and we'd be out raving and eight hours later at some after party drinking a beer and starting to feel like hell. Worn out with techno and talking about how our creativity was going to change the world.

We were having the time of our lives.

We all took our chances.

The lessons of Ajax the Lesser had been read, but couldn't be understood. They were still theoretical in a way that didn't connect with our experience. We were still finding out how our bodies connected to our brains, finding out how we'd been lied to and when we'd been told the truth, trying to find out how the ideas in our head corresponded to the canvas of life.

Besides that, these negative things just couldn't happen to us. We were too lucky, too young, too beautiful, too strong, and too new to it all, to suffer from these risks. We were the immortals that heeded nothing and endured all without scars until the end of time.

But time had been running out on us all along.

The Fish holds me there suspended in those moments when we were killing ourselves and calling it paradise. It's not worth it now and there is no way to get what is known now to matter somehow to back then. Then the Fish brings me back to the present.

I won't be coming to a school near you to tell the kids about how bad it is to use, but I will tell you this:

I feel terrible for my friend.

I feel very guilty about the fact that I am unharmed.

I feel hatred for myself for being the unfairness of it all.

I can hear Bonk get up and come to the door. My cigarette has gone out. He cracks open the door and looks at me with an unclear gaze.

"Dude, what are you doing?"

"Freezing."

INALIENABLE RIGHTS

The Pilot Fish knew that women had three natural rights that were not expressly defined in the Constitution of the Great Asylum, hadn't been covered by the Supreme Court and didn't apply to men.

A woman can be twenty minutes late to anything except work. Honestly, anything beyond twenty requires an explanation, anything less merits only recognition.

A woman can decide at any point in time that what she is wearing simply will not do and must be changed immediately. This could be as simple as heels to flats or as complicated as tearing apart the entire wardrobe.

A woman can begin to cry at any point in time for any reason or for no reason at all. The Fish had learned to leave the why out of it.

The Pear on the other hand was quite punctual, resolute in the simplicity of her dress and seemed to cry only with cause.

I'm not gonna lie, that sort of fucked us up.

It's been common knowledge from the eleventh century on that a hero must have a code for women. Whether he is a Casanova sleeping with all and sundry or a celibate warrior monk that dies a virgin, you can't be a hero without one.

It's part of the social contract that all heroes sign.

The Fish felt a little lost without one.

Our heroism could be cast into doubt with a single glance our way.

Our heroism could be cast into doubt when she looked away.

We weren't sure quite how to go about things and sought refuge in the mundane tasks of running security, defenses of honor, and opening doors. This was barely filling as the Pear was quite adept at taking care of herself.

There had been one time, kind of, with one dude who was maybe more rude by accident then intention, I mean his intention had been to sleep with her, I think, anyway that motherfucker was just a bitch and backed off as soon as I swung on him.

I may have been overreacting too.

That's what she said anyway.

Like I said it was hard to keep things in a traditional focus.

The Pilot Fish opened the door of the café for the Prickly Pear.

The Pilot Fish was attired in thick sinew and razor sharp wit. His armor, swords, and shield were back at the Fish Bowl. The Prickly Pear was wearing Capri style pants which the Fish hated. She was wearing a frilly green top which the Fish also hated. She was wearing green flats with yellow buckles that the Fish also hated.

She looked wonderful.

She matched perfectly.

Inside her very large bag were a collection of Russian chocolates that her mother had sent her from back home.

While the Fish ordered concoctions off the menu the Pear broke off a piece of chocolate for our favorite barista. After paying for the drinks I carried them over to a table by a window.

The Fish pulled out a chair for the Prickly Pear and seated himself across from her after she sat down. She set the bar of chocolate on the table between us. She broke off a large piece and then broke that into smaller pieces and set them on the foil.

The sun shined through the window reflecting off the foil splashing her face in random flashes of light as what little breeze was in the room shook the wrapper.

The Fish held the coffee in his mouth with the chocolate. Acrid, bitter with the fading taste of a cigarette, all of the awful tastes we loved so much wrapped up with the warmth of almonds and the sweet of the chocolate putting a fine finish on the entire sensation.

Time washed over us and the Fish slip streamed back to the far away and so near. One of our favorites: Pilotius Fishus, former second in command of cavalry to the Prefect of the Lion Legion. He thought about the war, yes, the Germanics make damn good soldiers. Thank Dionysus that was over.

He had mustered himself out after nine years of dutiful service to the Republic become an Empire.

He had taken his salt and his sword and said goodbye.

There is work a plenty to be had in Judea and Samaria, he had told his friend Hotrodius Largus Cockus, and the Fishus had not been lying.

Camped now on a hill overlooking a group of tents, Fishus surveyed the terrain with an eye out for both advantages and vulnerabilities. The daughter of a local magistrate was being held for ransom there, abducted by brigands.

"Oh, even under the fist of Rome and the great administrations, Greek auxiliaries and cohorts galore, banditry still thrives in the Empire."

"It's because of all the trouble in Judea." said Hotrodius.

It was true. The region seemed to have only war for its history and only war for its destiny.

Recently the Judean king had demanded the execution of a philosopher. The philosopher had said that heaven could happen right here on earth if people would just choose not to steal from each other, not to kill each other, to love each other, all strangers as brothers. Pilotius had heard of him and thought him mad, certainly, but hardly a danger. Then the rebellion had started and everything became clear. You couldn't have some son of a bitch like that running around fucking up the war fever.

Well, the chaos of war created lots of opportunity for work.

"Hotrodius, I think this will be a night operation."

"You play to my strengths Fishus."

"Now Hotrodius, the girl must be returned intact. Your fifty gold pieces depend on that."

"Hah." Hotrodius snorted.

Hotrodius claimed prior knowledge of the maiden in question from a previous trip through the kingdom. According to Hotrodius, "she had moves, and if she was a virgin then I am the Emperor of Rome."

This of course wasn't true.

Tiberius was the Emperor of Rome.

"Get some rest, nightfall is still an hour or so away," said Pilotius Fishus.

As Hotrodius stretched out on the desert floor, the Fishus took out his parchment and quill.

"Such were the times that sunsets could stand for more than day's death or sleep's first breath, and darkness not as an end of life but something that could hide and clothe us as we nakedly shared the night."

He said it out loud a few times testing the meter in a few different languages before making a decision and tossing it into the fire.

Perfection is all he ever wanted from a verse, is that so much to ask?

He thought about Epicurus, a genius.

"Oh humanity, each generation inborn with the knowledge of theft and murder while our greatest thinkers struggle to survive in fragments and scraps of parchment passed down the torturous path of scholarly memory!" said the Fish.

Hotrod snorted and rolled over quickly falling back asleep.

Pilotius thought back to his bargain with the chieftain, the slave girl mixed of Arias and Roma blood, the lady in waiting of the captured, "She'll be set free on the return of your daughter and then she'll decide."

The old man had nodded his head slowly. One slave from so many was a small cost, but he couldn't be respected as a leader if he didn't drive a bargain even in the recovery of his fifth albeit favorite daughter.

"It shall be so, but ten less gold. For you forty and Hotrodius fifty, as long as my daughter swears she is intact."

"Done."

Men have always been fools for gold.

The Fish didn't even acknowledge the equated value only shook the man's hand to hold the bargain.

The wind scattered some sparks from the fire. They landed and listlessly burned out in the sand. "What would she say?" Pilotius thought to himself. It was a gamble, but everything important is.

It would only matter if it was from natural desire unsullied by gratitude. There is nothing born inside us that can be called a slave only the conditions of the flesh, not the spirit, can be in bondage.

Except of course the heart which knows only bondage as refuge and liberation as prison.

Another poem?

Perhaps another chapter in the philosophy?

Servitude, love, freedom, natural rights, and our subservience to our own passions. Disparate themes dancing around ideas.

Fishus scribbled a few notes in his native language on a fresh parchment. Just some impressions unclear, but like the Chinese proverb, the palest ink is better than the best memory.

Work for another time, it never ends. Philosophy may not bake any bread, but its continuous interest on intellectual curiosity.

Then he ruffled through his notes watching the language change from Latin to Greek. There's something from Heraclites that relates to this he muttered to himself. He looked but couldn't find it.

Oh well, just because you can't find it doesn't mean it's lost.

After this it would be to Tyre. The roses would be in full bloom and there would be gold enough for some fun. He would present his poems and his philosophical essays at the Symposium. He was still working out his metaphysics in "The Suchness of Sand" and his magnum opus of value theory in "The Ethics of Smashing Cowardly Fuckers by Quill and Brush and Sword While Posing for a Painter Before the Great Canvas of Life, Love and Battle."

He looked over the title. Something was missing, but what?

The sun was going down. He pulled his blade free looking over the ending of the sunshine in its perfectly maintained metal, and thought of the slave girl, long dark curly hair blowing in the desert wind.

The Pear's fingernail slides down my left arm from the elbow to the wrist bringing with it the tingling of all anticipations and the comfort of five hundred mornings woken unburdened by solitude.

"Baby, come back." says the Prickly Pear.

The Fish looks into eyes that match his own and says it. "I know baby."

Then she says it back, truly, and with "too" at the end.

The words held and then faded away with both us acknowledging what had been true for awhile though exactly when for each of us couldn't clearly be articulated or known.

Back in the present, the Fish engages it, "What were we talking about?"

"Work, I'm scheduled for a double shift tonight. I'll be over pretty early, so make sure you aren't so drunk that you won't hear the buzzer."

"Yeah, I'll be fine. I'll call you after the bar closes."

"Okay, that would be nice." She smiles at us.

Then she pauses and looks away.

"I don't want to nag or remind you, but I do want to know that you haven't forgotten."

I pause for a moment and express surprise just long enough to bring some sparks into her eyes and then smile and say, "I haven't forgotten."

"Good."

The Fish was a Renaissance man, but the 1530's had never felt so far away!

We had a fight last week.

It was just an argument mixed in with some emotions clouded over with pride, the need to win, to be right, regardless of the cost or content, mired by some misunderstanding, then protests evolving into shouts.

Patience and passion, they come and go and come and go.

We got over it and made it up.

That night we had some wine and made love with our minds on the future amidst the stings of little left over hurts.

It had not been angry sex or I am sorry sex, or we're still fighting sex.

It wasn't I want you sex or one night stand sex or I am lonely sex.

It was making love.

That leaves a mark.

It was over her cleaning the apartment. She'd organized all my genius clutter in a way that left me feeling violated and territorial. It sounds silly now, but it really pissed me off at the time.

She told me that if she was going to stay over all the time that I'd have to start sharing the space. It took a while, but we figured out a compromise that didn't involve taping a line down the center of the bed.

"Should I grab a movie for tomorrow?"

"Sure, just nothing overly romantic."

"I'll pull something off the list."

We'd made a list that intersected all the movies that

one of us loved and the other hadn't seen.

"Look baby, I've got to go."

"Ok."

I walked her to her car and then I went back to the café and read newspapers for a few hours.

The President wanted a constitutional amendment to prevent the queers from getting married. They still hadn't found any WMD's that didn't match up with our receipts, but no one was giving up the search just yet except the Conservatives in England.

John Kerry had wrapped up Super Tuesday and Ralph Nader was still getting blamed for what happened in 2000. There was some nostalgia that Gore in '04 hadn't kicked off, but most people seemed more concerned with the coming battle rather than licking old wounds.

It didn't look good for anyone, really. At least all the pretentious reasons for the invasion had been exposed as lies.

Now all the killing in Iraq was being done for humanitarian reasons.

All I can say is that it's been a cold spring.

Then I went to the video store oblivious of our list and got something whose only merit was that it caught my eye.

Then I slipped back to the Fish Bowl and did some writing, nothing special, just some lines and a little revision work on a poem that I had written the year before. It didn't want to finish.

I wandered down to the bar around nine more from boredom than need.

The vodka had me warm, but not drunk.

Truth be told, I just haven't felt the need so much lately.

The Pilot Fish was slipping in and out of time. He was weary with the present, so I mainly had the evening to myself. I went home and called the hospital, but didn't get through. I left a message on her cell phone.

She called me back an hour later and we talked about nothing for the length of her break and then wished each other good night.

I slept well and woke up before her shift was over feeling clear and without a hangover. After a while she buzzed and I let her in. She was worn right out.

The Fish and I helped her undress and laid her down on her pillows. There were some murmurs and some kisses and then she fell asleep.

Tomorrow was our two year anniversary. I was taking her some place nice that I couldn't really afford.

I'd made the reservation six weeks ago.

HOTROD HAS A SOUL

Goddamn this summer has SUCKED!

Six bitches in May, and that's really still spring up here. Then nine bitches in June, not bad right? A little spring fever does a Hotrod good.

Then July came with its summer heat and anticipation. The first real beach month in this frozen hell hole. The first bikini month, the first month for why you went back to the gym in January and what happened?

Three bitches. That's what happened.

Why only three bitches in July? July, what do you have against Brother Hotrod? What has Brother Hotrod ever done to you? What happened to the frolicking of summer love? Past Julys were filled with bikinis pulled off in a hurry, nipples licked and shoved back into tops, intense orgasms in the changing rooms at beaches and public pools.

July, you and I, we used to enjoy those hot summer nights more than anyone.

Why? Why? Why?

Why were there no fireworks in July? Now it's almost the end of fucking August and I aint had a bitch yet.

Goddamn it!

The sixty four thousand dollar question and I am ashamed to answer it.

How many times this summer have I flipped it and hit it? How many times have I found my way through prodding and talking and licking and sticking into the stink? How many times has Brother Hotrod found pay dirt? Dare I answer, from when the last flake of snow melted to the fleeting moment of now naught but thrice.

That's it.

Stop that hearse it's driving away with my sex life!

It's shit like this that starts to make a motherfucker have doubts. You begin to question your abilities, then your confidence gets stung and bitches can smell that through the body wash. They can hear that in your voice. You can't spit game with a weak voice. Then the downward spiral begins and you're just a passenger on a sinking ship bailing away in futility.

Your belt is too notched up to slide through a loop and you're wondering if you can chew the leather anymore.

I know. I know.

I should just go to a fucking pro, but honestly that's grown tired. There's a strange and terrible anxiety and familiarity that's started to go on with that. The last couple times I've done that I've started to wonder what we're both doing there.

You start asking why and it loses all its sense.

The thing that's worse than the anxiety though is the boredom. So what, I paid for another bitch, so what? She did her job and I did mine and it doesn't knock the rust off anymore. It's not filling things in the way that it used to, and that's the real problem.

I'm left with the same noise and bullshit after that I had before, and the only thing that's lighter for it is my wallet.

I can't find any quiet in it anymore.

I think I'm done there, not saying never, but at least for now.

Plus hookers won't kiss and kissing on a girl can be a hell of a good time.

The mating ritual, the dance and the displays, that rhythm of speech and motion ending in success or failure. There is something very nice about all of that, and it's always as new as the next girl. There is always something beautiful in the new and the different even if it doesn't last for long.

I just hope this drought gets some rain soon or I will be pulling some bitch off the street.

This is starting to fuck with my self-esteem.

It's not like the hunt holds that much thrill anymore either. People are not that unique or interesting and fucking a girl takes less work than you'd ever believe. I've had it with some bitches where it's just a dance with well-defined steps and expectations. We go through the motions of acknowledging first impressions and attractions and we end with sex and some silly talk about a next time that will never come.

Then you have the ones that need to be just drunk enough to deny accountability, but still sober enough to fully enjoy it. They think that their mom is watching them from somewhere every time they fuck. That can be a fun balance beam to walk, but it can just as easily end with me wandering through some dumb cunts wasted bullshit way too sober for it knowing I've got sloppy drunk chick sex for my trouble.

It's been worth it before not so sure about it now.

The girls almost always have the same concerns at the end of the day. It's either for fun, and that just means that they are guarded against love, or they want something serious, as in love. Either way, they are either looking for love or afraid of love as they grasp at it, flee it, dream it, deny it.

Why they think sex has anything to do with it has always been the ironic source of my pleasure.

Up until now.

Maybe I really am jaded. I hear people use that word and they don't know what it means, but maybe I really am.

I've let some go over the last couple months. I've thrown a few back. I'll admit it. They just haven't seemed interesting enough to fuck. I've been close to closing the deal and then the appeal just dissipates in a cloud of banal conversation.

It's been a cruel summer for sure.

I need something new.

Maybe a change of locale would help.

A break from the standard boring shit that has dominated the season.

That ought to improve my chances. I need a new pond to fish in, a new hunting ground. A change of scenery would do me good. Go to a place I haven't been in a long time. New faces all around, strangers with one another and a chance to dig for that different or new that might turn out to be interesting.

I slide over to Dinkytown and start walking around the college kid clubs.

I'm older than average for this scene, but that's ok. I still look young enough to pull it off. There are enough retreads and professional students out there that I can get by with a few extra years. We're all in a head long rush to avoid the rest of our lives, and as long as the girls mistake me for that guy then I am in business.

I'm drawn by Usher's voice into a place wall to wall with youth and sweat.

Goddamn, this brings back some memories. No wonder people spend the first part of their lives looking towards these years and the rest of their lives looking back on them.

I grind on some young Asian girl for a couple minutes, but she doesn't spark my blood, just a nice dance partner. A few more beers are needed, and fuck you have to wait for your drinks when the place is bumping like this.

I buy them two or three at a time in cans. I learned that trick from the Fish who can only handle places like this if he's wasted.

The next girl I grind on is hot as hell, but dangerously young. Obviously on a fake ID and glassy eyed from E or whatever the young kids are swallowing these days to get high. I can feel that rush of reckless and for a moment I almost succumb to what I know is a bad idea, but then I pull myself together. It's only eleven, let this one swim away.

Thanks sugar, but not tonight.

Then I slip outside for a smoke and some fresh air.

I hit on some girls out in the smoking area, but all they

want to talk about is who is fucking who in the dormitories. I can see that they made the pact to come home together just like they went out. After listening to their chatter for a few minutes I can identify the weakest link in the chain. Last year I may have made that a personal challenge to break her loose and then send her back to a long lecture of "I told you so" and soft pathetic pity, but it doesn't look worth the trouble.

I make nice and leave them alone.

I'm feeling it though. I'm feeling damn good. The summer heat is in the cocktail. I could fuck all three of these bitches back in their dorm and come back here for dessert. My confidence is sky high and I am totally maintaining. Tonight is going to end just fine.

I think the old boy has got his mojo back.

I go back in and work my way on the floor without worrying about any overall agenda. I got this shit on lock down and I don't feel any urgency at all. I grind on one girl here and another girl there. They can feel my sex hot and hard beneath my jeans rubbing into their asses.

I am the pulse of this city.

I am why you go out at night.

I am what makes it all interesting.

Oh yeah.

There she is, the one with the dyed blonde hair with the dark roots coming out about an inch. Goddamn her tits are fucking fantastic and that ass.

Goddamn!

I approach from the side and when the DJ starts bumping Nelly it's like a sign from above.

Green lights everywhere and I start to grind on her and she definitely likes what she is getting.

We work on each other for a few more songs then she turns around looks right into my eyes and I can see Lucifer falling from heaven in her baby blues as she rubs her tits right into my chest.

I try to kiss her right then and there, but she slips me.

The she leans into me and kisses me on the neck with just a flicker of tongue out against the skin tasting my sweat and then back in followed by a little nibble. Fuck me, ten points.

I see how it is. This little bitch wants to play hard to get, that's fine with me. I am hard. I am get.

Buckle up sweetheart this ride hasn't even started yet.

She spins around whipping her hair across my face and I can smell the cK one mixed with sweat. Then to complete the motion and to apologize and tantalize at the same time she grinds her ass hard into me as the song comes to a crescendo.

Well played little sister.

I slide my hands up her sides and she pushes them down right before I get to her tits. She holds them down at her waist and rocks against me before turning around again. She puts her arms up and shakes her shoulders. Her tits are so fucking firm and round I almost lose my shit right then and there.

Do you like to play with fire baby?

I can see in her eyes the anxiety of someone that's enjoying the moment but doesn't know where she's headed. She's flushed and rushed as she leans against me, "Do you smoke, I need some fresh air."

"Of course."

I love social smokers. Baby, today is your naughty day. Today is your day to experiment. Let Hotrod be your guide. Let your hair down! I won't judge you baby, you laugh a little nervous and I smile. It's ok baby. We're all actors in the great masquerade.

It's high time you came out in society.

Outside in the cool air we are overcome with the quiet that would normally pass for noise. I light her cigarette and she coughs a little from the smoke.

That's fine baby, it's a strong cig. Take a breath. One at a time until you start to enjoy it.

Push your boundaries, baby. You need to test the waters of life. You need new experiences, stories and revelations. Why not let the man in black be your guide? Your rebellion against whatever is just starting and I can't wait to be a part of it.

"Thanks." She has stopped coughing and draws lightly on the cigarette.

"Anytime."

From the way that she holds the cig you can tell that she knows it's bad for her. I get the feeling that she is acting. It looks like she pictures herself in the theater doing things that are daring, being beautiful and clever. I'd love to tell her that the real rules aren't written down and that the game is played most for the things off stage, but I don't want to spoil the mood.

"What's your name?" she asks.

And I start lying to her like I've always lied to all the women that I have ever known.

We go back in and dance to a few more songs and do some shots together.

We toss back modesty and then we toss back common sense. I can tell she is right on the edge of being drunk enough to justify anything, but she wants to make sure that she is over that line before making any commitments.

The atmosphere is saturated with sexual anticipation and the DJ is reading my mind as he gives us one great mix after another to dance to between rounds.

Instead of the third shot I lean and whisper, "Do you want to get out of here?"

"Sure, where do you want to go?"

"Some place quieter, maybe slower pace?"

"Sure."

I want to say let's get a hotel and start fucking, but I know this one is a little more bluster than brawn. She's safe to be a slut on the dance floor because she has the crowd to protect her. She's nervous to go into the shadows, but she's excited to as well. Oh my little faun, whatever will you do?

I'm racking my brain for a quiet bar within walking distance when she decides to just take the plunge all on her own,

"We could go to my place. I live pretty close to here."

A bold move that mixes reckless with caution. Well done baby doll, let me escort you to your domicile. If you shut me down at the door of your building I'll hate you until the end of time.

Once we're out on the street I light two cigarettes and hand one to her.

The beats blasting out from the competing clubs melt into a mud of noise mixed in with the sounds of the traffic and the artificial light of the streetlights.

She smiles and takes a drag, this time without coughing.

I smile my approval and I can tell that she was looking for it.

The unspoken is more sublime but can't carry the stress of time.

I start to ask her the nauseating and mundane questions of what she is studying, how she likes the university. What town she lived in before moving to the Cities and blah, blah, blah. All the unimportant and meaningless shit that I learned to talk to college girls about before I dropped out.

She lives in private student housing that screams wealthy parents and we make out in the entrance surely for the benefit of the neighbors.

I'm really starting to like her, she is lively.

She opens the door and invites me up. I had a moment of nervousness that the evening was going to end right there.

This is in the bag!

She leads us to an elevator and then up to the third floor where her apartment is. We walk in and she locks the door before going to a well-stocked liquor cabinet.

"Let me mix up a couple drinks."

"Yes, thanks."

I take a sip of the whiskey and water. She has Johnny Walker, so she can't be all bad. Then she goes to the bathroom to freshen up.

I've always found it funny how girls want to check out

how they look before they take their clothes off. I can hear her mist a little more of that perfume into her hair and once she feels restored from the madness of the club she comes back out.

She looks simply amazing.

I set down my drink and we make out for a while. I put my hands on her this time and she fills in all my spaces. She takes it on the lips and eagerly, all the reluctance she had in the club is gone.

She kisses well.

We go back to our drinks after that.

She looks away from me and seems to be about to say something for the sake of saying anything, but ends up saying nothing.

Silence fills the room.

It's verging on an awkward moment, and I am suddenly terrified that my recent drought has poisoned the well of my confidence.

I am blowing it! Fuck, fuck, fuck! I can feel this whole thing going down.

Stop.

Take a breath, it's only been a moment and nothing bad has happened yet.

Say something you fool!

I put my arm around her and compliment her on some of the less boring furniture choices in her apartment, and she leans into me excited for the chance to talk about something. She goes on about her shitty Ikea trash and her obvious pleasure of having a space of her own even if it is on someone else's dime.

I relax as I listen to her talk. I realize in a way that for whatever our experience has been in life up to now that we are both novices with each other. That adds a little comfort to go with my growing confidence. It's as much me as it is her.

Oh my little princess, you aren't too adept at bringing boys home to your bed. That's ok sugar. Brother Hotrod absolves you of all awkwardness.

We're almost done with our drinks and the mood has been restored.

"You want to have one more cig before calling it a night?"

She nods and puts on some jazz before opening the door out onto the balcony of her student apartment.

Goddamn this girl is an actress.

She makes some allusions to sophistication that do little more than betray her age and inexperience and I smile with indulgence and generosity. She's not that funny, but it doesn't really bother me. She's trying just hard enough to make sure I smile and I smile just enough to keep her from trying any harder.

Then we put our drinks down and make out some more. Once she feels warmed up to that I steer her towards her bedroom.

I get her top off and linger there for some time on her nipples, a soft pink that compliments skin too white for sunlight. I move my lips over her from the outside of the areola to the center and she moans and leans against me as she perks up.

Then the rest of the clothes come off and I can see the sun coming out from the clouds.

There is a little stiffness in her as I lay her down, but with some subtle dominance, just a tiny bit of consistent pressure and we're soon on track.

I'm taking my time and working with my tongue. This girl's body is fucking smoking! Her stomach, the space from where her ribs end and her hips begin, goddamn! I kiss her there for some time before moving to the well shaved stripe that marks X on the treasure map.

That's when I sense it.

She's freezing up underneath me.

I look up and into her eyes and she has saucers of terror for pupils. Her arms are rigid at her sides.

"You ok?"

She whispers yes while saying no.

I move my hand up her arm rubbing it a little to loosen her up, but all that does it make her more tense.

"Take it easy sister."

"It's just that I've never taken anyone home from a club before."

Now this isn't the kind of thing that's ever really stopped me before, but this time is does. I'm harder than the Rock of Gibraltar and I know I can still make this happen.

I could gentle off of her a little bit. Give her some time and with some extra work probably still convince her, just a little tender coercion, and then push in. I could still get it done without too much of anything but a night that started out nice and ended maybe not so well.

I could do that and she would probably just lie there and take it without surrendering a yes or risking a fight on no.

I've manufactured consent before.

I could do that and the bitch might still call me someday for more.

I know that because it's happened before.

I know all of those things and more and I don't.

I do kiss her tits once more because they're too goddamn nice to walk away from without that, but then I just put my arm across her middle without touching anything private.

She's staring straight up at the ceiling.

"I'm sorry."

"Don't be. It's ok"

"It's embarrassing. I don't know what I'm doing."

"None of us know what we're doing, you're fine."

She looks at me, smiles at that remark. Her smile lights up her eyes and relaxes her body. Her breaths go from shallow to deep and with each one she becomes less stressed. She rolls onto her side and looks at me.

"It's been a tough summer. I just thought I hadn't been out in a while."

"I can relate to that."

She laughs at that, unforced and genuine and I do as well. While we're laughing I can feel us connect in a way that we couldn't on the dance floor.

"I'm not ready."

"I know."

She slides over and we hold each other for a few more minutes and I feel something that I can honestly say I have never felt before.

It's the opposite of the rush. It's a quiet that kills the noise inside me without fighting it. It just overwhelms and subsumes it until it's all gone like waves washing out a fire on a beach.

I hold onto that for a few moments until I can feel that peace run all the way through my body and then I get up and put my clothes on.

She puts on a pair of clean panties and a bathrobe.

We go out into the living room and she tops off what's left of my drink, and I take my time with it. I kiss her once more on the mouth and she holds against me in a lingering way that forgives tonight without prejudicing tomorrow.

I get her number and I decide not to decide right then and there how it's going to end. I think I'll leave this one up to fate and see what happens. She smiles at me as she opens the door for me to go.

"Thank you."

THE FIFTH OF NOVEMBER

Autumn had hung out in Minnesota long enough to keep us from freezing to death as we trudged to the polls to cast our apathetic votes between Tweedle Rich and Tweedle Richer.

Now that the election was over winter was settling in nicely. All of the trees were naked and all of the windows in the city were closed. Snow fell with nowhere to go. The frost had already hardened the ground and we all sat in a state of political and meteorological depression waiting for the ice age to begin.

I looked down at my newspaper and shook my head.

I'd read enough about politics for one day.

There were some whispers of voter fraud but nothing like the first time the cronies had won. There were complaints about how some voting machines in Ohio were designed, and there were questions about how some of the votes were counted. There wasn't anything like the hanging chad debacle of the last election. This time around it just sounded like whining instead of a legitimate argument.

It made for great ink and op eds and monologues though, and in a way it's just another public display of grief. In ancient times the wealthy of Egypt would pay peasant women to march in funerals beating their breasts to make it look like the deceased was loved.

In modern America we turn on our news outlet of choice for commiseration.

All the people that had voted for Tweedle Richer because he could beat Tweedle Rich, I might have that twisted, had woken up with a terrible hang over, and could do nothing but vomit all over the airwaves and newspapers.

The general populace on the other hand didn't seem to give a fuck. Not one bit and not at all. The electorate had vindicated all of it. The great mass had signed off on the wars and the frauds and the lies, or at least said that it preferred it to the offered alternatives.

I blamed both the left and the right for the negative outcome.

I lit a cigarette and looked at the paper.

I need to quit doing this to myself.

I spend way too much time raising my blood pressure in the solitude of reading political commentary. I keep myself up at night and wear out my days with pointless fatigue as I fret over the world being such a mess.

I need to accept that I am a meaningless note in the great noise of a mobocrisy powered by media and cash attempting to gather votes for policies and problems in a super tribal social reality beyond the scope of understanding of all the players involved.

Not only am I a citizen of the Great Asylum, I am a patient as well.

Take a deep breath. Don't you find that a deep breath helps to keep you calm?

My medical history: I was committed at birth with the diagnosis of an unquiet mind. My care plan is getting used to the idea that this is all that there is, and that this is how it is.

My treatment goal is to be a good boy and to be well behaved about it.

What I should do is wear my fucking hospital gown in public and walk around the streets in a fucking rage exhorting everyone and all towards self awareness holding a burned out lantern aloft in search of an honest man!

Ahh Diogenes!

I am sorry.

The Adventures of Hotrod and Pilot Fish

I am a coward.

Well, if I don't have the balls to do it right then I should just get better at chewing my cud and getting on with whatever athletic season is currently relevant. I should become a fan of all teams and just root, Root, ROOT for a TIE!

I exhaled smoke and closed my eyes.

This is the best that I can do.

The cigarettes weren't doing much to calm me, and my head was starting to hurt and spin from it all. Caffeine, nicotine and politics combine for a certain swooning effect as my emotions turned my political inclinations into a frenzy of disconnected angry thoughts.

My internal voice of introspection begins to try and calm me through placing everything into a broader perspective. It whispers sweet political nothings to me, "It's just one election and it's just a bad time in a country that has already had many elections and many good and bad times" and on and on and on it goes trying to wear down my impotence and rage.

My hand drifted over the paper in my complete powerlessness to change anything and I had to smile for a moment at the idea that I certainly didn't understand it all or very well for all my pride to the contrary.

My ignorance is not bliss.

Stop!

Don't read another line, not one more word.

No.

There, isn't that better.

No.

No, it's not any better.

My hangover is throbbing and there is only one cure.

It's the hair of the dog that I need.

I throw myself into the briar patch of editorials. There's one about the TSA strip searching kids to keep the skies safe from terrorists and passengers safe from racial profiling.

The end of rationality had to have been a while ago, but I doubt anyone could really tell you the moment that it passed.

I think it went out with a sigh instead of a shout.

There's another piece about how exposing CIA operative Valerie Plame for petty political revenge on her husband was treason.

I agreed with the author, but it seemed a little late by now to start talking about treason. The G.reat W.hore Bush had gone beyond treason and gotten into the kind of crimes that we struggle in naming and only indict the losers of wars for.

Winning the war and co-opting the only countries that could possibly try you guarantees you immunity from prosecution for crimes against humanity.

The "Project for a New American Century" had spelled it all out, and we were just passengers on a ship bitching about fish for dinner again.

Then with all the lies about our preemptive necessity exposed and the complete pointlessness and incredible costs of our wars with little discernable gain entered into the public record the electorate stood up and vindicated all of it.

This is what democracy looks like.

I dived right into some screed about DOMA, it looked to me like the crisis in marriage that the social conservatives were so concerned was going to destroy Western Civilization had found an unlikely ally, but it was hard to find that tone in any of the sentences I was getting through, it seemed like the only thing lately trying to save marriage was getting the blame for the end of it and that was just more than I could take.

The next editorial was about justifying torture by first not calling it torture and then saying that they deserved it anyway. It felt to me like a state of unreality that these kinds of ideas could be considered debatable and it felt beyond reason that those against torture could be losing the debate.

I added several dollops of shame to the soup of impotence and rage.

The last editorial was focused on how we, the citizenry,

should support the troops regardless of our opinion of the war. I agreed with him completely. I thought a fine place to start would be to stop sending them off to war, but he didn't mention anything like that. He didn't even talk about the leave cancellations and extended active duty rotations. The dude seemed to think if we all wore ribbons a lot of the problems would sort themselves out.

I finished the editorials and charged right into the international news section of the paper.

The case against Saddam Hussein was underway. That looked like it was going to be as long as the O.J. Simpson trial but without the surprise ending.

I need something stronger than a cigarette to go with my coffee.

I was feeling nostalgia and elegy as I wondered about it all. I was feeling time like a weight instead of an adventure. I was feeling the *duration* of it, how much longer things last than our inspirations or impulses. The effects that outlive our ideas and the unintended consequences of our idealism that might well be the black plague of the twenty first century.

It goes on and on and on and I'm worn all the way through with it.

Our shock at the terrorist attacks of September eleventh had passed, and we had captured a dictator and put him on trial for suppressing a local ethnic group more than twenty years ago.

There was no mention of the attack on the twin towers in the indictment against Saddam Hussein. There were no charges based on possessing weapons of mass destruction or intending evil deeds with such weapons. None of that had come to light at all and the rest of that bullshit that was now being swept under the rug to make way for newer not yet discredited bullshit.

The crime: Saddam Hussein had ordered the destruction of a village in 1982.

The victims: The Kurdish ethnic group living in northern Iraq.

The response: The United States primary action that year was to improve relations with Iraq and remove Iraq from the "State Sponsors of Terrorism" list. This allowed us to sell Iraq "dual use" equipment, the first use being secondary and civilian, the second use being primary and military. This narrow and immediate real politik foreign policy helped Iraq in its war with Iran.

We didn't consider the use of mustard gas on civilians a terrorist act in 1982.

How could we, a thorough investigation would have revealed our complicity.

It could have interfered with our long term vision for the region at large.

If that doesn't bring a smile to your face I don't know what will.

If that doesn't have you laughing then I don't have what it takes to make you laugh.

The point of it all, the why for what we were doing where we were doing it, the dialog, and the sales pitch all moved and moved and moved while we stayed and stayed and stayed and killed and killed and killed and died and died and died.

The neo conservative liars shifted the target every time it became the focus of the debate and we always had a new reason for being where we were, for being in a state of undeclared war, for killing people in a foreign land, for risking our soldiers.

I tried to picture what the defense attorneys for our precluded guilty would do.

I imagined a new legal strategy whereby the defense demonstrates that the defendant is the victim of foreign policy decisions in the new Great Game for the World that in a complicated systems of power balancing and ambitions combined with resource scarcity that this particular despot had just failed to be sufficiently maneuverable.

It's not the end of the world, it's just the end of him.

It would be a new Brandies Brief showing that banana republic tyrants can't be held accountable for crimes against humanity as they are only pawns of a larger game that they are compelled to play.

The press would have a field day covering the trial with headlines like, "Don't shoot the dictator until he's finished his chores!" or "Leave the oil out of it!" and maybe with enough creativity and passion the jury could be swayed to spare the petty monster.

On the other hand, political ironies aside, the man was a murderous fuck and deserved to die.

The fact that we were complicit in it clouded the moral coffee on the side of the prosecution but not the guilt of the defendant.

I just wish that our international interventionism could somehow be seated in the dock alongside Saddam Hussein, but there isn't a court in the world with the power to put our interventionism on trial.

I wanted an end of our interventionism.

I wanted our soldiers home from Afghanistan where the American financed bullets to end communism's spread were being repurposed to kill champions of democracy.

Jesus fucking Christ is this really happening?

I wanted us to stop and think about more than right now and look at countries as something more than right now.

I wanted to rebel against the inevitability, against the current of power and the winners of power. I wanted my own Major Kong moment riding a huge missile called "The End of Interventionism and Partisanship" into a joint session of Congress during a State of the Union Address. I wanted my own Guy Fawkes moment that got them all and wiped the slate clean so that we had to start it all over from scratch.

But most of all and what made me the angriest. I wanted to know why we had vindicated it.

I thought back to the small town I came from and the

end of my high school years.

It's been a long time since before the names.

I've done a lot of thinking since that time and I know a bit more and I am certain of much less.

Time for another cigarette.

Breathe in.

Breathe out.

Close your eyes and breathe in and breathe out.

Don't you find a deep breath helps make you calm?

But all I am doing is blowing on the flames.

I opened my eyes and looked towards the door of the café just as it opened. Some cats I knew in the neighborhood came in bringing a rush of the outside cold and mary jane perfume with them.

"Fish, we about to start a game. You be our fourth?"

"Yeah, get my mind off of this shit." I balled the paper up and walked it over to the trash. I waved them over to my table.

Playing cards with junkies and loonies is a nice break from politics. It was rapidly becoming my alternative to keeping up on current events.

Instead of making my head spin with the problems of civilization and the world and how ineffectual we all are in this mess we call humanity I could play cards with junkies and half way house crazies that viewed lucidity as the carefully traveled border of a much broader psychological experience.

It was nice to be around people so new to sobriety. These junkies had a childish sense of discovery in the mundane combined with a world weariness of human awfulness that I couldn't help but find refreshing after my political soirees.

The atmosphere of the café was urban renewal without the ethical conundrum of gentrification.

Spades was the most popular game as most of the café's patrons found some comfort in carrying the pastime of the prison into civilian life.

The three to my fourth today was one recovering addict, one actively working prostitute and a schizophrenic who had psychologically stabilized about a month ago.

"You been reading politics instead of the funnies again haven't you?" the schizophrenic asked me.

"Is there any difference?"

"You always look kind of tired and crazy after you've been thinking too much."

"Ain't that about a bitch."

"Ain't it though."

He laughed as I shuffled up the cards and pushed them over to the hooker to cut.

My country was fighting two wars simultaneously without a declaration for either. My country had built an extraterritorial prison on occupied foreign soil and claimed that it was beyond the bounds of all law. The location was used to torture human beings presumed guilty and denied due process.

The dialog of justification was euphemism and technicality. Ambiguous phrases like "enhanced interrogation" and "extraordinary rendition" had replaced simple words like torture and kidnapping, but it was only the words that had changed.

Our national character was being prostituted into lawyer speak and politician babble. Our principles had become the voice of an abusive spouse claiming there wasn't harm because the victim won't testify.

How did all of this come to pass and how could it be worth it?

I was never afraid enough to find comfort in barefoot walks through the airport. I was never afraid enough to find comfort in Orange alerts and illegal detentions. I was never afraid enough to find comfort in another person's pain. I was never afraid enough to justify the Patriot Act or the DHS.

The hooker cut the deck into three thin piles and stacked them one on top of another before pushing them back to me, "kick me some juice baby."

Tom Nelson

> I winked at her as I dealt the cards.
> For luck.

THE COLOR OF ILLUSION

This is what we have to talk about before going to the Korn show.

The Pear pulls an unopened pregnancy test out of her bag and I immediately feel a dropping sense of dread. I'm not ready for this and I know she isn't the dramatic type. She wouldn't have bought it unless she was already pretty sure.

She takes it into the bathroom and after a few minutes she comes back out.

"I wanted you to be here when I took this one." That says everything to me, but I don't reply.

"Blue means I am."

I nod. She hands me the box and I read it while we wait for the result to come in.

It takes a couple minutes.

The box says that red is a negative result and blue is a positive result. I try to picture a doctor telling someone that they tested negative for pregnancy, and it just sounds very strange to me.

The Pear says, "There it is, it's blue."

I confirm that it is indeed blue.

They really aren't that hard to read.

It's just that it's hard to read them.

Its nerve wracking like adding up all the points on a test and then checking the bad grade at the top hoping that there is some error in arithmetic that can save you.

I think of those stupid fucking commercials that never

showed if the people were pregnant or not. They'd just look at the test and smile with relief.

I can only imagine my face as it must look right now in one of those commercials.

A full thirty seconds of faces like mine would make for some funny shit.

It's actually kind of a pretty blue, the kind that actors and models want to have for their eyes. The kind of blue that newborn babies sometimes have that shades its way into more mundane colors over the first year of life.

A perfect blue.

"This is the second month that I've missed. I wanted to be sure before I spent the money on a test."

I ponder on the significance of the word "missed" while I watch the Pear reach into her bag and pull out another pregnancy test that I guess must have been the first one she took.

It is also blue.

The results of the two tests match.

The box for the test claims that it is 98.5% accurate. I do some quick math. Two positive results on a test that is 98.5 percent accurate is: 98.5%*98.5%=97.02%.

I think I see a way out of this!

With a decrease in probability based on an increase in measurement, all we have to do is take pregnancy tests until the pregnancy becomes statistically improbable.

The Fish tells me that won't work.

The Pilot Fish is happy as hell and I am terrified.

The Pear and I are tying to figure this out.

I try to gauge how she feels about it while she tries to gauge how I feel about it.

We kind of probe each other back and forth without ever really asking or saying anything. It's like playing poker with neither of us sure of our cards, but both feeling compelled to bet.

I can feel that starting to transform into a fight, so I stop it and just say it out loud.

"Have you thought about an abortion?"

There I said it.

That settles things down.

"I won't have an abortion."

There she said it.

That livens things up.

Here we go:

"I can't take on the responsibility of being a father. I don't have the money to afford this."

"Everyone feels that way in the beginning and no one can afford it."

She pauses for a moment and stares into my eyes.

"They just make do."

I look away from her but breaking her gaze doesn't cut her off.

"We could to."

The Fish is thinking that the first thing we're going to need to do is get a bigger Fish Bowl.

He is asking himself where he buried the damn gold.

"I love you."

"I love you."

"You'd be a fine father."

"I don't know about that, but you'd make a great mom."

"I know about that."

"Ok it's just a lot to take on right now. Let's go to the concert and have some fun. I don't want to think about it anymore tonight, ok."

"Ok."

The line to the concert is pretty long by the time we get there. We are about ten minutes early and we didn't really talk much during the drive. I had a terrible shiver in the car, but it passed.

For as much as I don't want to think about it I can think of nothing else.

I really don't want this.

There is a moment when we are only a few spots back

from getting into the auditorium when I suddenly feel the complete opposite of how I felt when I saw the blue line on the pregnancy test.

I feel like saying fuck it, let's get married, let the chips fall where they may. We'll get a starter ring, and I will buy a better ring when we get a little ahead. We're both working, and we don't need a house. We can start in a flat, and I'll quit drinking and work some overtime. I could have put my arm around her and let her know that she wasn't alone in this. That we were in it together for all of it no matter what all of it might mean.

The Fish surged in me and I almost did just that, but I didn't and then the moment passed.

As we get weapon checked I can hear the opening act starting. It's Limp Bizkit and they are already into their second or third song by the time we get to the general admission section. We watch them from the edge of the mosh pit.

Well, what happened at Woodstock '99 makes sense now.

The Pilot Fish tells me that even though the Pear is only a tiny bit pregnant that she shouldn't be getting banged up in the mosh pit. I pick her up and hold her on my shoulders for a few songs. Then I set her down and memorize her location before going in and thrashing about in the pit for a while. I come back feeling more worn out than I expected.

Then Korn comes out and the stage rush nearly knocks us off our feet.

We fight our way back against the swell of people until we get to where there is room to stand. The Pear is on my shoulders again and I can barely see the band over the crowd.

I look around at the other fans. It takes me back in time to 1994 when I heard "Blind" for the first time. That was the zenith of the summer of wrath. Spring had been Pantera, Summer was Korn and Fall was Megadeth.

Music kept the time of our adolescent histories and provided the discordant tune of our youthful rebellions.

We thought we were such bad asses and the disdain we had for popular anything was so intense that we were as defined by what we despised as we were by what we so passionately endorsed.

We'd come back from a metal concert with bloodied hands and bruises that didn't even really fill in purple until a day or two later.

"Are you ready?!"

Were we?

Was I?

I don't think that any of us were.

I can feel it coming home to me as I see everyone around me trying to get some of that back, but it could only have been ours for that moment, and it was supposed to go away.

That's the way that life is.

All that we are and all that we do is made of sand and we build our sand castles magnificent in defiance of the tide, but the tide always comes in. That doesn't make our lives meaningless or our actions futile. It just means that we are constrained by elements beyond our ability to control. The enigma of humanity isn't hidden in our transience. Our enigma is our determination to build the sand castle anyway.

Fucking hell, look at us, we're grown.

The Pear and I have the same favorite Korn song. It's "Did My Time" and it takes them a while to play it. We wait for it together and I am too worn out to go back into the pit. When they finally play it we sway back and forth as we sing along as loud as we can.

The set goes on for a while longer, and we get an encore. Then the show ends and the lights go up. I buy the Pear a standard black concert tee and we make our way home.

We're kind of sleepy now and whatever I did in the mosh pit took something out of me that I needed gone. We talk about the show and both of our voices are a little cracked from shouting and screaming so much. Our ears are worn out with the overload of sound.

We make love that night like we haven't before, tired and worn and knowing each other very well.

Then we fall asleep half holding each other.

The next morning starts out well and before I know it we're in a fight.

"I don't want to have a baby."

"That's FINE. You're not the one that IS!"

"Can't you just get the ABORTION, can't you just make it GO AWAY!"

Those words are out off my mouth and the Fish is SCREAMING inside me to get them back but they are escaped and their only answer is the slamming of the door as the Pear storms out of my apartment.

I sit down and light a cigarette looking at the glass of orange juice the Fish had poured for her.

Folic acid is very good for expecting mothers and orange juice has a lot of it.

I top it off with vodka and call into work.

That evening I call her and apologize. We talk it out a little bit. Her first clinic appointment is the day after tomorrow and she expects me to come. I ask her to come over for the night and she says no.

She says lets go out to dinner tomorrow night. She'll stay over and we'll head out together that morning for the appointment. I say yes and after she hangs up I finish off the bottle.

The next day is pretty fuzzy but I make it into work. It's not easy, but I get mostly reassembled by the time we meet for dinner. We go to a place we've never been to before and it's really nice. I have too much wine, but only a little too much.

The Pear doesn't say anything about it.

We're kind of on tip toes with each other avoiding anything contentious and kind of hiding in the details of what we'd usually talk past.

The atmosphere is kind of raw, but we both do a good job of not getting into it.

She stays over as planned. We don't make love, just sleep together without touching.

I am up an hour before the alarm and the Fish has a new glass of orange juice for the Pear. I've mixed a little vodka into mine. Not enough to give anything away, just enough to take the edge off it.

We finish those and get on the road.

The people in the clinic are fine. We fill out some paperwork.

They ask me if I am the father and I say yes.

They ask the Pear a lot questions before they get ready to do the physical. Then the Pear has to disrobe and get special gels spread across her tummy for the ultrasound.

I go outside and smoke.

I come back in and wait in the lobby. They have the day's paper there and I read about things and places meaningless and very far away from where I am.

My government is killing more people in the name of peace and democracy. The people that are getting killed just don't seem willing to get onboard with all the good that we are doing over there.

I wish I had brought the vodka with me.

Half an hour later they finish up. The Pear comes out and we both follow the nurse into a consultation room.

The Pear has a look on her face that I haven't seen before.

The nurse explains to us that we have a problem.

The union of sperm and egg seems to have gone fine, but for some reasons probably related to the genetic constitution of this particular union, the zygote hasn't thrived in the womb. It may be that it failed to embed correctly in the placenta or other unknown or unknowable reasons.

Some things we just can't determine.

The nurse explains to us that many pregnancies end in spontaneous miscarriage and that there isn't anything obviously wrong with either of us. She had some pamphlets for us to take home if we wanted to learn more about it.

The nurse said it all very kindly and with better words than mine.

She encourages us to try again.

When we're ready.

After the miscarriage.

I felt all the things that I had said come back to me like a whip across my face, and I know when it's too late to apologize.

The color of illusion is perfect blue.

We walked out of the clinic. We got in the car and drove back to my flat. We didn't say anything. When we got there the Pear made some tea and I mixed a vodka tonic. She didn't want me to touch her in any way except a way that was only holding her.

We cried for a while and she said, "Why are you crying, you're the one that got what you wanted."

All I could say was, "I'm sorry, I'm sorry, I'm sorry." Over and over and over again.

We've been together for a little over two years and we've had some challenges, but nothing like this.

The miscarriage will happen soon though we don't know when for sure. It's a small number, but its measured in days. She said that she wanted to be alone for a while and I told her to call me any moment night or day and I'd be there.

I walked her to her car.

I had a couple more drinks and then that bottle was empty too.

I smoked out my pack and bought another one. Then, I picked up the phone and tried a number from so long ago that I got it wrong on the first try, but I got it right on the second one.

I was sure when I called it that the line would be disconnected.

But it wasn't.

It's not too late to call, not at all.

Any chance your holding?

It's not a relapse, its just one fucking touch.

Just to help me make sense of things.

It's just a fucking sniff man.

The fucking week I've had.

It's just one little taste to bring things into focus.

That's all I need.

One taste and the edge is still there, in some ways even sharper than before.

Thats OK there's more where that came from.

fuck it

The Pear found me a few days later at my little café and by then I had really failed her for the last time.

I'm pretty sure I was unemployed by then and I was celebrating the occasion. You don't get to apply for unemployment when you tell your boss to fuck off.

I was glazed over with pharmies trying my best to come out of what I knew was only the beginning of something bad.

She stood over me and I must have said something sharp and clever to her because she slapped me full across the face.

The gypsy in her hair and eyes had already fled but there was still a little compassion left.

Looking into that compassion I realized that all the moments when I could have saved us had passed. Each of them finite and alive and then gone one by one until the last one was spent and thrown away.

She looked down on me with eyes full of sadness, pain and disappointment.

I looked up at her with eyes full of the end of us.

YOU KNOW

You know us pretty well now. You know that this is one of those moments of calm that is always forgotten. You have some idea of what's coming.

You have never tried hard drugs. You're pretty sure that they've been around, but you've never seen it. You think that there may have been a time when you would have tried it, but that time has passed. That could have been any time or no time. It doesn't matter now.

You're smarter than that.

You probably always have been. You did smoke some pot during your college days. You don't do it anymore, but some of your friends still do. You really don't see anything wrong with it. You don't like to be around them when they smoke it, but it's not really a big deal. You've never really felt the need to get high.

You do sometimes want a glass of wine though.

You can't imagine yourself going somewhere to buy drugs. It feels like a badly shot movie when you picture it and you think that even though it happens all the time that you would be the one that got caught or ripped off.

You trust your luck, just not too far and not too often.

You know what Hotrod wants.

You've seen it all before, haven't you? Well enough to have a good idea about what you know and what you don't know. You believe in the old adage that no one knows that you're a fool until you open your mouth.

You don't mind the winters here.

You don't drink or smoke excessively. You have a nice

job, decent car, and a great apartment. The apartment was a big decision, and you're happy that you got to decorate it yourself.

Most places won't let you paint, and you like to mention that when you have guests. You're not really a show off, but there are a few things your proud of.

You love your kitchen, but you don't cook at home as much as you'd like. You know how to cook. You just don't like cooking for one. You're hoping that will change though you couldn't say when.

You know what you want, though you're not exactly sure how to get it.

Today your boobs are a little swollen, tender to the touch. It always happens right before you have your period. You call menstruation, "the red days," and you find that cute. You're not wrong, when you say it, it is cute. You have never been one of those girls that need Midol and heating pads to get through it. You used to be proud of that, and now you just don't care.

You notice your body more around your period.

You feel good today, you like the way that your clothes fit you. You are a work out girl, treadmill slender, and you note with a personal irony that the swelling that comes with the period actually rounds out your figure nicely.

You have discipline and you don't like people that don't. It's not that you dislike them, that's too strong a word. It's more that you can't admire them. Just being here isn't enough. You need more than that out of someone if you're going to spend quality time with them.

You're starting to outgrow some of your friends from college.

You count your drinks even when you've had too many. You know exactly where your debit card and check book are. You know your balance to the penny. You lied about your weight on your driver's license, but you know by exactly how much. It's not that you're unhappy about it; it's just that you don't think anyone really needs to know.

You know which girls are prettier than you and you know which girls are only younger. That one, you'd say, is definitely on a fake ID.

You were too once upon a time.

You have met a few men that could've made a fine match, but none that were the one. You don't feel rushed at all about settling down. You know that it will happen when it happens and it will be with the right one. You're not nervous about ending up alone. You like to let guys make the first move. You don't mind beating a guy out for a promotion at work, but in the romantic sphere the man should carry the risk and the burden of proof

You're worth it.

You buy a pack of cigarettes for bar night, but you never smoke them all. You're always throwing away what's left on Monday morning. You had a friend that you used to give the leftovers to, but he quit. You supported his efforts even as you looked at that half pack of Marb Lights and thought, fuck.

You've been told not to smoke your entire life and the irony isn't lost on you.

You're going to quit for good soon, just not quite yet.

You read Harry Potter, and Dan Brown. You don't read Stephen King anymore. You dismiss Hemingway as too sexist, Buchowski as both sexist and depressing, and Faulkner as just too boring. You haven't read Kafka or Dostoevsky, and you're not being completely honest when you say you finished Anna Karenina.

You want to read more.

You read some women's magazines here and there, but without any level of seriousness. You don't want to be in the competition any more than you have to be.

Your education from chemistry to cosmetics wasn't wasted on you.

You're smart enough to take responsibility only for the things that you own. Those are the only things that you can control, change, improve or discard. The rest is beyond your power.

You have seen into the void, but not for long enough for it to see into you.

You're taking Hotrod home soon. You don't want anything more than what he has to offer and its ok to just get laid once in a while.

You never go to the boy's house. That's a little dangerous and a little stupid as far as you're concerned. You want to be in control and you want to walk them out the door in the morning. Plus, you hate the fucking mess that is almost guaranteed to be at his place.

You haven't taken *that* many home and you always lock the door after they leave.

You have dated on line and you are "done with the club scene," well maybe not completely, all the way, forever done with it. You might go once in a while when the mood hits, but it's not a lifestyle you want anymore. You'll let that mood come when it comes.

You're a little disappointed with the men of your generation. There are a few too many Peter Pans running around as far as you're concerned. They are a little too into video games, internet pornography, metrosexuality, and friends with benefits. You don't think that a real man that's willing to commit is too much to ask for and anyone less than that isn't one.

You dated outside your race and your parents silently disapproved. You don't really care about that when it comes to a man, how he treats you is far more important.

You don't need a man, you'd just like one.

You've thought about having a family as well. When it comes to having kids you just want to start with one and see how it goes. One could easily be enough and three feels like too many.

Things are coming together for you.

You're not angry. You're not shallow. You're not empty.

You belong, here, right here, where you are.

You really are in your moment even if your not sure what that means all the time.

You see your gynecologist once a year and you have good insurance. You believe in preventive medicine and routine checkups. You see the dentist twice a year for cleanings. You haven't had a cavity in a very long time.

You had a romantic fascination with European culture and social welfare in your college years and swore you'd live in the Belgium one day.

You've thought of learning French, when you can find the time. You have a lot of projects and plans, some you know you'll do and some are just fun to think about. You would really like to travel more. The destination isn't really all that clear. Somewhere warm or maybe it will be in Europe, maybe a summer of Dutch flowers is worth musing about. Maybe visit an old place where you can feel some of the history.

You get up and go to the bathroom. Your period hasn't started yet. It won't for at least a day. You know your cycle pretty well, and you're looking forward to having sex tonight. You always make the boy wear a condom even though you are on the pill. You had one "oops" a long time ago, and it was awful.

You won't go through that again.

You quickly check yourself in the mirror. The lipstick was really a good choice, and you like the way you did your hair, though it does smell a little too much like smoke.

You like the way that your new bracelet fits your wrist, just loose enough to play with, tight enough not to worry about it falling off. It wasn't expensive or cheap. It was just perfect.

The shoes, well they have lost their charm, but nothing else goes so well with the skirt, which you're sure will last forever. Ear rings are your personal struggle, what size, gold, silver, hippy or chic? Today is just fine with medium sized gold hoops and in the second holes diamond studs. You pull your hair over them for a moment and then pull it back.

The Adventures of Hotrod and Pilot Fish

You don't have a nose ring, but you've come close.

You smooth over your clothes and give a little lift to the bangs and you are out the door and back into action.

You have been in one fight in your life. It was with another girl. You were both sixteen. It was about a boy. You pulled her hair and slapped her. She did the same to you. You called her some awful names, and she said the same things back to you.

No one jumped in and no one got hurt. No one really won or lost. It was between fourth and fifth period in the hallway, and it was broken up pretty quickly. The girl and you made it up during your senior year and graduated without any lasting acrimony. It wasn't that serious.

You've forgotten about the boy.

You imagine she has too.

You're going to start saving money soon. You promised yourself, ten percent of the gross. Just not quite yet, you just got your first real job and you'd like to enjoy it a bit, upgrade the phone, and have some comforts. You've earned the right to enjoy the money a little bit and you still have the student loan and the car payment. You'll start saving when you're out of debt.

You're working on your credit score. You cut up all your credit cards except for one. The balance on that card is now at zero. That took some real work and discipline and your proud to be out of debt except for school and the car.

You keep the one card for emergencies, and you mean it.

You use your work e-mail for work and your private e-mail for friends. You check both whether you're at home or at work. Your personal one is cute. Your work one involves a last name followed by a number.

You adored your father when you were a little girl, but now you feel much closer to your mother. You call home every weekend. They are always happy to hear from you. They are very proud of you. The conversations always end the same with "I love you" getting exchanged and then hanging up.

Tom Nelson

Once about two and a half weeks ago you cried after hanging up. The tears came hard and fast and the storm lasted about twenty minutes and then it passed. You couldn't say why. You don't know where that came from.

Your commute isn't killing you, but it could be shorter.

You listen to the radio when you're driving to work, there's a morning show that you like. The rest of the time you listen to your iPod. You watch E-True Hollywood. You love Desperate Housewives. You think that reality TV has run its course. You don't mind the Simpson's.

Dave Mathews made you wild.

You are going to be okay.

You are going to be just fine.

DISINTEGRATION

The Pear has returned to her homeland to heal from the wound of me.

She told me the date, but not the time or flight. She made it clear that I was not to see her off. She was very kind about it being the last time that we would talk. I asked her for an address and she gave one to me, for a letter from the Fish that she promised not to open or destroy.

I stared at the sky guessing which plane was taking her away.

The Fish finished her poem and expressed what was impossible for me to do or say or write.

He rhymed beauty with elegance and the words came out her. He rhymed hurt with healing and the words came out her. He rhymed hope with love and the words came out her. He rhymed strength with quiet and the words came out her.

How he hated me as he did that. He hand wrote and mailed it. He cut our hand and signed the bottom of the letter with a thumb print of blood.

What happened next has been happening all along.

What was that line from my favorite book as a child?

It's getting less and less clear what is real or not.

Less clear.

Less real.

I think most of those moments were just an interruption, a detour along the way. I got lost in love for a little while you see, but that's over now. I found my way out of it.

My ambition to be something other than what I am has failed. It feels natural in a way to be back on course.

I had this idea, for a moment, that I was on my way to becoming someone else.

I was wrong, and by that I mean that I was right in the first place. I've been right about me all along.

All the way back in time to when I became what I am.

I have achieved equilibrium with the void and it stares into me now as freely as I stare into it. We are conjoined like a planet tidally locked to the pull of a black hole.

What was that line? I can't remember the line. It was my favorite line from my favorite book when I was a child.

My nose bleeds and bleeds. I do a rail and my left nostril bleeds and bleeds. It takes fifteen minutes to stop bleeding.

My nose bleeds and bleeds. I do a rail and my right nostril bleeds and bleeds. It takes fifteen minutes to stop bleeding.

I won't waste a sliver of glass. I tilt my head back after each rail and the blood and crystal rush down the back of my throat. It's burning and bleeding inside me all I am is blood and flame.

I dig around until I find my pipe.

I brownbag a forty and take to the street.

If glass is a liquid how does it burn?

What was that line?

What was that line?

Yes, the details stand stark and bold but what's around them I can't see. I can see the trees I just couldn't tell you if I'm in a forest or not.

No, nothings clear, nothings clear.

I've abolished love and life and fear.

I cup the pipe and smoke some more speed.

From this point on we are strangers all. This is the line, the border of the dawn and the darkness and I am finally dying and God that feels good. Really, I've wanted nothing else. I want nothing more than that.

No more concerns, no more decisions, no more thoughts.

The Adventures of Hotrod and Pilot Fish

I can see you!

What was that line? It was one of those stories told more by pictures than words. It was drawn more than it was written, but it had that one line. How did it go?

I can't reach back far enough in time to find it.

Time. I've seen enough of time. Time, time, time. Swallow me whole like Jonah's whale. Time is the jury that always convicts. Time stretched inside out is the void. Time found on a clock is a lost dream. Time started when a wrinkle in space blew up. Time in the infinite of introspection. Time is the riddle that solves us without ever telling us the answer. Time, the light that never goes out.

Where did it all begin?

I take a few drinks off the forty and burn some more crystal.

I remember!

LET THE WILD RUMPUS START!

Yes, that's it!

THAT'S IT!

EUREKA!!!!!

I grind my teeth.

I pull hard on the forty.

i GRIND my teeth!

I drink off the last of the forty.

i GRIND my TEETH!

I smash the empty bottle across the back of the head of the first guy I walk up on.

man DOWN!

We're going to need a clean up on the corner of Franklin and Chicago.

Oh Franklin Avenue you are my accomplice and my alibi, my muse and my excuse.

Apothecary, who doth mix my medicinal tinctures?

And people worry about whether or not I can handle my shit.

I cut back toward Nicollet and slip into a park behind

some apartment buildings. I find someone there. It's just a fight at first, but once he's down and I can really kick him, that's when the screams start.

THIS IS AS FUN AS PISSING THROUGH A HARD ON!

I kick him until my leg gets tired. He's covered up his head. I've mainly booted him in the guts and kidneys. He's soft there. He's moaning like a pathetic little bitch cunt. He moves one of his arms and looks up at me. His eyes are the eyes of homelessness and foster homes, and he dares beg for a reprieve after it was granted.

I spit at such ignorance.

I know that all of it happened inside my mind. I just don't know how much of it only happened there.

Let it be an orgy, let our physicality wear itself out in search of catharsis. Let the lie inside hedonism become our truth. Let us die mid stride, mid thrust, mid orgasm and in full ignorance of love.

And I'm off.

Ares and Aphrodite, how well you love and war inside of me.

I am dancing now, do you find me beautiful? Really, these are the moments that matter. Let life be a dream and each day a hallucination. Let go the dogs of war, let us live and fight and die and fuck in the fog of it.

There is no forgiveness and there is no mercy lest it comes from God and I doubt him greatly on this day. There is no choice and no coincidence, and how we live in the illusion of them. Let's dress the casual occurrences of daily living in beautiful language.

Let's lie some more.

Did I tell you my best lie? Did I tell you the one about how I reached up from the surface of the earth all the way out into space to the rings of Saturn? Did I tell you about the time I touched the rings of Saturn? They looked like diamonds when I started but by the time I got to them all they were was dust.

I can see Jani holding her guitar floating up and away on

a great column of wind and ash. Too far away for me to ever rescue or help again. Jani! Jani! Come back! I'm all alone again, come back! I'm all alone! I made myself alone!

Running now standing still and the visions rush and stop, crossing my mind like the stars across the heavens at the speed of light dwarfed by the distance of cosmos. All of us living in a slow destruction. All to come and all to go and all to wonder why and none of us to know.

I need a drink.

Now we begin the accumulation of regret. No, that's wrong, that was started long ago. Now is when we count them and hold them up and worship them. Now we manufacture our idols. Mine are: free will, morality, love and peace. Can someone smash them with a stone tablet made of rules?

It comes and goes, comes and goes. Rampant rushing rivers of rage and chemistry.

I am become a beast and lost of the tribe of man.

There can be no memory except that which is recorded, and still we'll see things differently. We can always reinterpret the words and the writers make no allowance for the future changes of language. I can feel it clearly now that there is an end in all things. I feel it better than I have ever felt it before. It is the truth of the void and I can understand it now.

I am complete with it.

I slip into a bar and head straight for the bathroom. I actually look much better than I thought I would. In fact I'm looking sharp! I'm way too spun to be affected by alcohol, but I'm going to give it my best shot anyway.

My beautiful dreams are bankrupted now, torn to shreds and spit out. My smile is a grinning skull staring back at me from the mirror.

For one moment I feel completely timeless.

Hold it.

Breath out.

It's gone.

"Etu Brute?" I ask and then push my fist through the

glass.

She could forgive things truly not like the fake fuck whores that say it's forgiven but are really only saving it for later. That was the miracle of her.

Oh my Pear, my beautiful sweet Prickly Pear, how I have failed you!

How I have failed.

Someone told me once that if you did enough meth that you'd start seeing things.

What a fucking joke. You don't see *things* on this much meth, you see EVERYTHING.

There is shattered glass all over the bathroom. A million reflections staring up at me, a thousand truths fractured with fictions. This broken plane holds all of me, the real and the unreal, the ideal and the actual, the intentions and the results.

Past, present, future, I grind it to powder under my shoe.

Truth is too much for us to grasp, only time can tell it.

If I told you that I've finally had enough would you call me selfish?

I am become Raskolnikov's heir attempting the messianic from what is only evangelical.

I am clay too long in the fire.

There is music playing, but I can't understand the words. I can't follow the tune or keep the time. Everything is suddenly unfamiliar to me.

The threads are all broken now. You never notice the first one. It's only through the compounding of errors that anything ever gets noticed. The first thread broke so long ago that I couldn't guess it, and still the tapestry held, but it's clear now that it's worn through.

Fuck Fuck Fuck

All of it has come together to become nothing.

In what's left of the broken mirror I can see Jani's father dying and all those lessons are for nothing, and all the pain we inflict on the people around us as we self destruct is just the cruel irony of multiplying something into nothing.

Nothing, nothing, nothing.

I am surviving this life against my will.

At the bar I encounter attitude, but he's seeing things from my perspective pretty quick. All it takes is force. After he goes down, I reach over the bar and snatch shit.

I gotta roll before the cops show. Let's bounce!

FUCK THE POLICE!

I am rage. I am disappointment. I am loss.

Bottles and blood, how much shit can sit on a dead man's chest?

What the fuck is this? GIN! Hell yeah!

LET'S PARTY!!

I dip into an alley and dig for my pipe, but it's gone. What the FUCK!

I pull hard on the gin and swallow the last of the crystal down.

GODDAMN!

I lean against the side of a building breathing heavily. I am fucking burning UP!

I take my shirt off. I want to take my pants off and get naked, I am on FIRE! But I force myself not too. Gotta hold on. Man, you gotta maintain! Just a few deep breaths and another pull on the gin, and then you'll be fine.

I look at the streaks of dried blood and broken scabs across my chest and along my arms from where I've been picking.

Oh man, oh man, oh man, that's no good man, that's no good at all.

The concrete of the building feels so cool, so nice and cool. I stretch my back across it waxing rhapsodic as I dream graffiti philosophy:

I saw the greatest minds of my generation getting wasted for the sake of being wasted. Stoned in slacker anhedonia, worn out with existential angst born of complacency and satiation instead of privation or suffering. In a void of purpose created from a climate of a constant reassurance of worth that became itself a need, in a landscape of cultural nothingness and personal cowardice, contemplating suicide.

Is there any meaning in my howl?

Does my barbaric yawp say that in being untranslatable I'm only the more alone?

Have I done nothing but ostracize myself?

Goddamn I swallowed a lot of that shit.

We must learn to embrace new ideas if we are to accept that we will never be enlightened, that we wouldn't deserve it if it happened to us.

I know the answer to this one! Pick me! Pick ME!

It's for us to make the waxen wings and show that we can fly and taste the singe of sunlight and high winds and then plunge and die. It's for us to live desperately. It's for us to break traditions so that others can enslave us with new ones. It's for us to swim against the current until we drown. It's for us to debase the public coin.

TEN POINTS!

My cup runneth over as it's spilled out

I am beauty. I am joy. I am magic.

Every girl that I have ever loved can tell you this, on every kiss that ever was there was also gin and cigarettes.

Sleep is for pussies. Sleep is the little death. Sleep is missing out. Sleep is what they make you do to control you with those fucking pills. Sleep, perchance to dream? I couldn't tell you the last time I slept.

Of all the flightless birds the Ostrich is the largest.

Angels and demons both dancing on the head of a pin. I can see them, I can count them. I'm not telling!

Yes, let everything that I ever touched or loved, or hated or called my own or despised, let it break. Let there be no record, let there be no evidence, let there be no nightmare, let there be no dream. Let everything go to pieces and blood and run to empty releases. Let me die next time.

Please God, let there never be a next time.

GUILT AND SHAME SHALL BE THE ARCHITECT OF OUR CONFORMITY! THE PURITANISM NEVER LEFT!

I take another pull on the bottle. The gin mixes well with the meth and I am fucking loving it. Need a little rest though and a plan.

Don't mourn me for me Antigone, I'm getting what I deserve. Don't honor me with burial sister, let me rot from the balustrade. Let my hanging corpse be the standard of my revolution.

Let it be my testament to my guilt and shame.

I step into a building and end up walking into some fucking hippi sit down. There are maybe ten people lounging on pillows listening to some fuck talk. I was hoping that this would be a bar, not some emo séance. My kingdom for a bar!

"I need some fucking lemons to go with this gin bitches!"

This small woman answers me, "This isn't a grocery store. This is a Baha'i service."

"A fucking what!" I scream at her. "I ain't leaving without some fucking lemons!"

"A Baha'i service. This is our church, where we worship."

I can see them seeing me and I have stared so long into the void that it now stares freely out of me into them.

I am the syllable that creates the rhyme, the sound that completes the stanza stretched out until it's lost its meaning attenuated to only the beautiful and forlorn sound of someone screaming.

All I ever wanted was to be someone that could be saved by love and could save others through love. That love could be transformational in power and palliative in substance. That I could be redeemed by love was all I ever wanted.

I am as disappointed as anyone by the knowledge that I can't.

She comes up to me and she has no fear in her eyes at all. She stares directly into the void of me.

She's fucking beautiful.

Tom Nelson

Then a memory comes back to me, something from so far away that I know in my heart that it can't be me, that I can't own it, that it must belong to someone else.

"Ich nicht spreche Deutsch!"

Then the floor surrounded by darkness rushes up and over me.

THE POEM

Beautiful Birds Singing Broken Tones

    I don't understand the character of women. A different balance of bend and break that I constantly confuse and consistently mistake. What it is to be a man still seems unplanned. What it means to combine the two I only care to understand through you.

    Knowing that the strength that came to me with time will gradually follow it away. That any resolve untested can even to the most innocent summon moments of anxiety and doubt.

    That every moment should matter, but how the moments outnumber the matter. The way that we remember based so much on temperament, a melancholy day recalls another, our shame hides away only to surprise us when we wish it least. And we re-write our memories making some more beauty and some more beast. Humor is our only defense against the past, but sometimes you have to wait so long to find it safe to laugh. Unable to comprehend the others, our happier times selfishly demand that they alone our memories remand and sadly we wear out the fastest what we wish would last the longest.

    When asked to remember love while in it I fled the task.

    Love, that poor and desperate word that everyone has said and everyone has heard. Hand in hand with a terror for its loss, holding all the jealousy and joy within that could destroy itself or pay off all its cost.

The things that we endured.

The fortuneteller's cards. The spells that were abjured. The placard of the princess and the bard. The serpent and the tree, the waterfall and moon. The river misted over with fog and gloom.

Our ghosts, our shadows, kissed in the meeting before being cast away. The sea, the sound, the never-ending night, the lighthouse to guide our way.

The driftwood on the beach, our reflection scratched into stuff sturdier than us already fallen to time. The ocean stole my secret before I could whisper it to you and stuck it in a seashell. Its meaning lost in the amplified echoes of rushing blood and paralytic against such sounds we listen determined of a meaning to be found.

Stepping along the seashore, our footsteps held in shallow depressions, with three waves already unmade. My memory, in ignorance of its fragility trying to measure out each grain, to know every touched piece of sand, to investigate them for evidence of a plan.

The little talk between us in the cadence of our walk, meaningless and wonderful, with nothing to do with why we were where we were arm in arm encharmed with every fifth wave strong enough to wet our feet and break our speech.

My vision, trapped in numerology counting out the ways of you seeing me. Selfish psychology built stone by stone and brick on top of brick laid by me on me around me, keeping trapped inside my horrible secret that it is I who undoes me.

Lying next to you in complicit ignorance of time. Asking if we suffer unnecessarily in each other's company. Sensing within you an uncertain sound, unremarkable but for its ability to confound.

Knowing that within me is the weakness and fear strong enough to destroy everything I hold dear, knowing that for everything I can be, what I am most in danger of is me, wishing to save you from myself, unable in some awful way to save us both by saving me, it was all too clear in the cards. It was all that the fortune teller could see, but she talked about the rising sun instead of the dying fire and she talked about the motion of the stars instead of the falling tower.

Our imprint seems so long on the shore of the sea. The dawn must not be long. A wayward hour of ghost and shadow. The taiga's finest flower, the desert's wayward son.

Stuck trying to picture out the shout.

But this, all of this is just one pathetic mirror of syllable layed along so edgewise, and leaving unexpressed is what we wanted and why we cried. How I failed and how love died. My darling, I tried, but a composition is just words collected with some care spent to how they're directed. Some attention to how they're effected.

A few errors that still need to be corrected.

AFTERMATH

I wake up in a hospital bed feeling the unreality of a fever dream.

I take stock of my circumstances slowly. I can see from the marks on my left wrist that I have had an IV and that the IV has been taken out, not too long ago.

I feel far, far, far, away. I have no idea where I am.

I guess this is what happens when you go through some madman type shit and get run down and have to take it easy for a while.

I hear a knock on the door and someone wearing scrubs walks in. I look at him and he looks at me. He recognizes me clearly and I have no idea who he is.

I find that unsettling.

I have no marrow, my bones are full of ground glass. With every turn they twist.

"That's mainly from the opioids, you was on a lot of pills."

"I was trying to land softly."

"Sure."

"Where am I?"

"You in the county detox."

It makes perfect sense once he says it.

"We've spoken before."

He nods.

"You been coming and going."

I wonder about throwing up, but realize that I have done enough of that already.

So here I am, here I have been, in detox, detoxifying.

The gap from what I remember last to now is a black hole in my mind that I can't see across. All I can say is that I wasn't through with it when I started remembering things again. Not that there is anything particularly memorable about it.

Mainly, I was cold as hell and shaking like fuck.

Time runs like rivers wild.

I saw Karen a few times though thankfully she was never my care giver. She looked both sad and unsurprised the first time she saw me. I guess I found the place that she volunteers at.

I was wracked with chills and then sweats and then chills for some time. I'd sleep and sleep and sleep and wake up too tired to get out of bed.

It took a while for all of that to pass.

My family came to see me and that was a shitty sequel to my first hospital stay. I can say without any doubt that I've broken my mother's heart. They love me, I love them, they help in ways that can't help and I appreciate it without letting any of the futility show. I disappoint and terrify them and they put a kind brave face on it all. They are really more than I have ever deserved.

They want to see me well and I've done my best to keep them out of it.

Part of being in treatment is going to AA and NA meetings. I did the forty meetings in forty days like a left behind animal watching the rising flood.

I expected to go to jail directly on exiting treatment, but nothing happened. I don't know if the victims of my violence went unreported in the greater violence of the city or if my spree wasn't pieced together and back to me. I didn't volunteer anything and I wasn't interrogated.

I had a sixty day commitment and then they turned me loose with a list of numbers to call if I am ever again in crisis.

My parents came and got me and with their support and some time and work I was able to get myself independent again. I may be the worst investment they've made, but I'm doing what I can with what I have left to make good on what they gave me.

NA and AA find me equally qualified for membership, but neither feels right.

I don't really think the meetings work. I don't believe in the sobriety system. I'm not convinced. I go and then stop and then go.

I slip.

I don't think that using was really ever the problem. I'm not saying that it helped anything. I'm just saying that the using was just a symptom of whatever it was that was really wrong. Whatever was really wrong is the harder question and the one I don't have a well prepared answer for.

Being that whatever it is, I have quit using all the hard drugs. I don't miss them and I am still paying the toll they have taken on my body and mind.

Sobriety in general is a pretty nice thing. Waking up in my bed instead of the closet certainly makes for more restful nights. I have much less stress being straight than spun. I still smoke. I still drink. I know that's not perfect, but that's how I'm doing it.

I really do need to quit the fucking cigarettes, but not this year.

We're picking our battles carefully these days.

I feel fear without cause. I feel guilt disconnected from crime. Sometimes I cry or get angry without reason. Anxiety spikes and valleys, but is almost always around. Sometimes, in small moments, I can't feel anything at all, and sometimes I am so overwhelmed with feeling that it paralyzes me.

I can't predict it. I can't control it.

There is no present pain.

I stare no longer into the void. The void goes on and on and on to the forever of entropy

I do not.

I end at the terrible limits of my skin.

I understand that now.

I am no longer mesmerized.

I still get what the French call l'appel du vide, here and there in little doses the allure to end it all overwhelms me for a moment and then fades away. That rush arrives in a mix of nostalgia and anxiety and fades out with little bumps of both. I don't know when those will come and I don't yearn for them after they've passed.

Understanding that has certainly helped a great deal in getting on with life. I am no closer to explaining any of that now than I was when it started. I have some theories about art and the destructive nature of creation, but it's all probably bullshit. Don't get me wrong, I appreciate the romance of the explanation, I just don't buy it.

If I'm asked I tell people that I fell into a bad way of thinking for a while, and that it took some time to get out of it. I would like to use the phrase spiritual crisis, but it's too loaded to really say it. I'd call it nihilism, but I don't know what to say after I say it. I just trail off and say, yeah.

I don't know what made me fall and I can't explain how I got back up.

When they ask me what I am thinking about now I shake my head.

I think about the great black holes in my memory and am grateful and ashamed. I think that some part of you always remembers even while the rest of you tries to forget.

Though for all of that I imagine I remember everything.

I've made some philosophical changes as I've moved along in my recovery.

I try to commit to each day as it comes. I tell myself that now is all that I have ever had and I am trying very hard to appreciate and treasure that. I am trying to wake up with that being the first thing that I think about and I am trying to take that idea to bed with me.

It's not easy. Ideas are slippery and hard to hold onto in all the noise of daily living. You can finish the day and not know where they've gone.

I've been trying to stay thankful for all the amazing things that have happened in my life. Being alive, being more or less whole after I've done my best not to be. The people that I have in my life, I love them so much and I am so grateful for their love. All of the little things and all of the big things, and most of all for the chance to still get things right. It's not over yet for me by a long shot.

I'm very thankful for that.

I'm getting my act together as fast as I can without rushing myself to pieces.

I graduated from the university.

I did something I had never done before. I scheduled the test, sat down with the books and studied. That's what I was supposed to have learned in college, to study, to care about these things. To achieve some discipline and set some goals. I should have learned it then and planned a life instead of holding those people in such contempt.

I passed by one question.

I guess I'm better at German now.

Doing that really made my parents happy.

I keep in touch with everyone.

I meet Wild for coffee every so often and that's really nice. She's in a good place in love and life. She is finishing her education to become an addiction counselor. She says going through what we went through will prove an invaluable experience for her future profession. She's looking forward to helping people like us, and I think she will.

She still hits the rink. We're going to watch the figure skating events at the next Winter Olypics together. That will be nice.

Wild and Jani could be friends now. The competition, the bullshit that had defined their relationship back then is completely meaningless now. The last time we were out Wild told me she thought the Pear and I were forever and I started crying on the spot.

And I thought I was such a tough guy.

I wear myself out with my thoughts and I'm worn out with how I am and how people are. I'm tired. Sometimes I get really tired and the depression slips in. I have to be careful when that happens.

I have no one to call me to bed.

That is a miserable thing.

I get really lonely sometimes.

I'll meet a girl and be overwhelmed by what it could mean to share time with her, what kind of a treasure it is that two people can spend time together instead of watching it pass by alone.

I don't pursue it though, not now.

I won't do the plant thing, or the pet fish thing. I'm not into that bullshit. I don't give a fuck about the sobriety steps for when you are well enough to try and be with someone again.

I only know that right now I can't be with anyone.

I only know that right now will not last forever.

It will happen when it happens and I'm looking forward to when it does.

I know it won't be easy when it does happen and that's just how life is.

I'm never really alone anyway. I have the Fish and we're doing pretty well. Just because we've tried to kill each other doesn't mean that we don't care. We are one, though how we are still confuses me. Sometimes I feel relief when he takes over and sometimes I'd prefer to be in charge. We are learning how to share better.

Flesh and spirit divide me.

How they push and pull at each other in the short battle that is life. Sometimes it's more than I can stand.

I call Jani every so often. She is still making music in New York. She is doing well. We'll talk for two hours and it feels like ten minutes have gone by. There are some things that we don't talk about, but I've told her everything.

I try not to take anything for granted.

I try not to take anyone for granted.

Sometimes I still get overwhelmed. I look at the fake fucking smiles, the celebrity magazines in the checkout lines, the cute little actors on TV, the constant consumption of shit and our pathetic little dramas, and my scars start to look lonely and I long for the fire, but if I wait a while it passes.

I'm making progress.

I did do one of those AA step things. The one about accountability and amends.

I went back to that church. The Baha'i one. I apologized for breaking up their service. They were nice about it, not uncomfortable or embarrassed at all. The lady I yelled at was there and she told me never to do whatever it was that I had done again. She told me that I had the power to destroy everything beautiful in my life and that it's up to me not to do that.

She filled in some of the blanks for me: After I screamed at her I fell down and went into a seizure. I had one seizure after another for minutes. She put a pillow under my head while I thrashed around on the floor and everywhere she touched me, I burned.

I thanked her for the pillow.

I guess all in all the last year has been two steps forward and one step back. I am improving though crawling is a fairer description than walking. It's been slow going that's for sure.

I've been spending time with Hotrod in the way that you should just hang out with your best friend. We haven't done anything self-destructive. Sometimes I think that we're like veterans adjusting to peace time, but that's a little dramatic and we're really just friends finding our way to fine. Last Friday we watched a baseball game. We had some brandy Old Fashioneds and we were just two kids from Wisconsin grown up. The game went into extra innings and we called it a night.

It's a shame you couldn't have seen it, there was a lot of laughter. We really do bring out the best in each other.

That's been really nice.

If you shake a Polaroid photo three times the color

starts to come in, on the fourth you can just kind of see us, a girl wearing black jeans and an Evanescence t-shirt, me in a wife beater and shorts, both of us smiling.

Just smiling.

I put a stable address in with the letter if she ever opens it and replies it'll get to me.

If she does she does, if she doesn't she doesn't.

You have a lot of life left after your done being young and my door is never closed.

I just hope she is happy wherever she is and I pray her life is turning out well.

I don't have the words for what it would be like to see her again.

Bonk has healed as much from his damage as he ever will. That's not much better, but it's something. We talk on the phone, and email each other zombie stories. I'll visit him again. Where he is in the world of me, I freeze there still.

All that aside we're just good friends and life goes on.

I see a shrink and a psychologist here and there depending on job and insurance and need. Most of that time is probably wasted, but I get a few good things out of it. One thing I learned from a psychologist that I saw for a while that stuck with me that is that part of the process of surviving with mental illness is realizing that you are sometimes a passenger of your own life.

Oh look, I've been going through money fast lately, might be getting a little hypomanic, oh look my emotions are irrationally amplified between euphoria and despair, might be getting into a bit of a mixed episode, oh look I'm flying through outer space.

Again.

Oh look, I'm traveling backwards in time.

Again.

It's kind of like being on a hard acid trip, it's your lived experience, it belongs to no one but you, but really you're just along for the ride.

I practice letting loose the reins while staying balanced on the horse.

When I'm not doing psychiatry or psychology I'm doing psycho-history with the Fish. He has been explaining heroism to me now that we have some time and I am together enough to listen. I think he's glossed over the history a bit, and maybe embellished on the psychology, but I'm not interested in fighting about it.

He says that the heroes of Antiquity were typically just killers and thieves on the good side of the story tellers. They killed monsters and rescued princesses. The treasure they got usually never left their possession. They got wasted and did terrible things when they lost their temper.

They revenged.

The next phase in the evolution of the hero was the formation of a code, a social contract, chivalry or honor, internalized or externalized and often with some specific relationship to some kind of religion.

The relationships that heroes had to people in the stories were paralleled by the relationships of individuals to their realms, kings, countries.

This birthed the monster that no hero could kill: nationalism and it grew out of this until nothing else was left. That monster dug the trenches of World War One. That monster built the gas chambers of Auschwitz. That monster flies through the forests and mountains of the Balkans today. That monster screams from the minarets that the youth of Islam should suicide.

The Fish dates the end of the romantic hero to Agincourt when the peasant archer proved more valuable than the knighted horseman. The unnamed killed the named in great numbers that day, and that ushered in a whole new order of things. The idea of individualism in combat took a mortal wound and from there it was just a matter of time before the engineering made it possible for men to kill each other anonymously and in great numbers and to die for the most abstract of causes.

In many wars the line between civilian and soldier disappeared.

Things had to change if heroes were to survive. The social codes didn't work anymore. It was difficult to distinguish a hero or even the relevancy of being one amidst all the death. Heroes became isolated, internally rigidified because the outside world couldn't be trusted or predicted.

The Fish says a new space for heroism manifested in the rejection of the murderous collective.

We want there to be heroes.

We want to be at least two of those heroes and we agree on that point.

Our way of doing that is having a vigilance to do good in the world with the selflessness to leave people to their own destinies.

Our perspective is that life can be a simple and beautiful thing, if you let it, but how you go about living it we'd just as soon leave up to you. Outside of that, we're just trying to do some nice things without making a crusade out of it.

Give someone the benefit of the doubt, look past how someone looks, re-examine your own perspective periodically, stop the noise that makes you feel so self-important in your life for just a moment, and listen.

Mind your own fucking business once in a while and don't walk past someone in need.

I'm not asking you to sleep with anyone or sign over your paycheck.

That and you should always open the door for the person behind you, but that's just common fucking courtesy.

That's how the Fish and I are trying to do it, but you're welcome to come up with your own way, just try to be aware of the consequences of your intentions.

When we're not talking about heroism we argue about life and literature.

We wonder about our story, how it's being written and

how it will turn out.

We argue over the approaches of our favorite writers.

The Fish leads in with a bit from Maugham about how the story always ends in death or marriage. The story is buried with its protagonists or inherited by their children, as though the story is something that you can pass like the turn in a game until the game is over.

But, I reply.

I am not dying and I am not getting married. I'm not through with the story. The story is through with me. There is always a before and after. This isn't the ending. It's just the last chapter.

And he replies that poetry can only be felt.

I come back with a bit of Fitzgerald. Wouldn't it be nice if life was something like Gatsby. Nine perfectly paced chapters that flow together nicely, that concludes with elegance and grace. It wouldn't matter if the ending was happy or sad so long as everything was tied up cleanly by the time it was over and with such beautiful language.

It's not though says the Fish.

We go back and forth and back and forth, and after some more argument we agree.

For our story, history and life, Kafka is our author. Our world is best defined by its missing chapters, incomplete ideas, lost conclusions, and broken threads. Moments of intense genius and a lot of burned notes. The best answers just leave us with more questions and the real struggle isn't getting what we have, but keeping it or thinking after some time that any of it ever mattered anyway.

It matters, well the important things matter, whatever the hell they are.

To figure that out we lean on some Nietzsche. He advises that to come to peace with it all we need to accept that we live forever in the pendulum's swing between Apollonian Reverie and Dionysian Revel. That we can't help but yearn for one from the throes of the other is our enigma and our beauty.

We content ourselves with the knowledge that some mysteries just explain the limits of what we can know.

The Fish and I are going to get out of Minneapolis soon. We're due for a trip. I expect us to cross a border or two along the way to wherever it is that we end up.

It's not exile.

There's nothing to run from and there is no place we have to go.

We're going to take our time with it.

I was of age when this started, but the maturity that seems to go on and on and on.

The destination of our journey is to put our philosophy into action. The aim of our proselytizing is to listen to everyone we meet on the way. The dream of our action is to do what heroes do, in each town and city that we pass through. We're going to do some good things, and we're going to be human about it. Hotrod's bound to be around for some of it.

Keep an eye out for us.

EPILOGUE

We are come at last to the ending of us back to where we started so long ago in the deep of the desert. The Fish and I are Joyce fans. We couldn't end it without at least a nod to circularity. Maybe all of us, each chronicler since the modern era began are just paddling in the wake of Finnegan, or in the Fish's case swimming.

We are at last, all of us, well met.

The last rays of the sun are fighting their way over the mountains. I told you it would get cooler. I'm not even sweating anymore and the night air here is very calming.

It feels very nice after all the heat that we have been through.

The wind refreshes instead of punishes as it threads its way through the mountains down and across the desert valley. You can see storm clouds building up over the mountains as the sun slides away behind them. They trade places slowly casting everything into shades of purple, red, orange and gray in the alpine twilight. It's a soft darkness pregnant with the forces of life even as it tip toes in death.

It's really quite beautiful.

I'm glad we got to share this.

We stand where once we knelt in prayer and our prayers have all been answered individually even as none have been answered collectively.

Such is life.

The Fish is chipping our names into a stone.

It's all that we could ask for in an epitaph. We'll lay it

down here as a memorial and a guidepost for anyone who happens to come along. Many ways lead to here and from here there are many ways to go. We leave our names as a marker against isolation. We leave our names here to balm the ostracized and the alone. However you got here, we're happy you came, wherever you're headed, good luck on your way.

For us though, our road ends here.

It's almost time.

The Pilot Fish, Hotrod and I take in one of our last breaths and let it out without wishing to hold it in any longer than it needs to be. I light a cigarette and Hotrod does the same, we're indulging now that the need to preserve time has passed. I pull out my flask and take a pull and hand it to Hotrod.

Cheers.

Welcome to our requiem.

Please, shed no tears for us and make no lament. We are where we belong and time has finally come for us. There is a stillness here that youth can only hate in its willful ignorance of death, but that we in age find comforting. Indeed, like an old friend that we haven't seen in a very long time, not since before we were born, coming back to us.

It's been awhile.

The circle is complete.

We're not leaving with many regrets.

We're not leaving with much undone or left unsaid.

We learned from our errors and we tried to live always in the motion of reaching for something.

We kept our word and we ended at our intended destination. We wandered as warriors and lovers and healers through the world. We were other things as well as we were needed to be, but no matter what or where we were, we were always poets.

The world makes for a grand stage and our parts were many.

We've been on both sides of loving and being loved and

found both sides sweet with as much as we could give and as much as we received. That's been the most important journey for us, and I hope everyone finds a way to know all those roles and more as they live their lives.

There is a hero inside each of us often only waiting for the challenge of life to stir it. It's not always pleasant to meet a challenge, but it's always worthwhile. Spiritual and emotional growing pains are bound to occur as you go through the great process of learning who you are.

It's a good hurt.

There are a lot of pitfalls and hazards along the way and many opportunities to be overwhelmed with bitterness or regret. It wouldn't be worth it otherwise.

For us it's been nothing short of miraculous.

We've had our turn as son and father, friend and lover, husband and grandfather. We've walked on four legs, two and three. We've shared life with many and in many ways. We've told our stories along the way and we've made our way into other's stories as we've passed through. There are many to remember and be remembered by and in many ways.

We've tried to live with our aspirations and inspirations closely related and even if we couldn't reach them all in full it's been everything we could hope for to live in the pursuit of meaningful things.

We're not sad that it's coming to a close. We've written some good poems about it, and found that our philosophy for life has been as dynamic as our process of living it.

We learned along the way and all the way was a teacher to us.

There's nothing wrong with life coming to a close and in many ways we've earned a rest. That's the part the existentialists leave out of it all, they write about the crisis of finding meaning within the constraints of mortality while in the full flush of youth and never let you know how tired living is going to make you. There is an end in everything, and once you accept that than you can just acknowledge it without a mad desire to embrace it or a mad desire to escape it.

I'm not afraid of it anymore.

Coming to terms with it isn't very easy. You can always find a reason to stay a little longer. There's always something to fear in the unknown. It's a tough courtship to become a companion of the inevitable, but I think that in the end you must. In the beginning though you should fight it, make it earn your respect.

Besides, if the eternal reoccurrence isn't just a dream then we must all move towards an end so that the cycle can repeat. I believe in it without justification, and I mean it with all my heart when I tell you that I can't wait to see you again.

After the universe turns over.

Again and again and again.

I'm so thankful that the Fish can travel in time.

I've had such incredible adventures with him.

We crossed a lot of borders and learned a lot of new words. Sometimes we didn't know any words for where we were and the only way that we lived and ate was through the expression of good will.

Thank you, all of you, for that.

The bread and wine have been fantastic.

Some years ago we were in Germany and there were flags waving everywhere. From the tops of all the buildings, flags waving in the schools, all the youth of Germany were waving flags, girls had German flags painted on their cheeks, even on the bumpers of police cars there were flags, there were flags waving from the Reichstag. The rest of the world got nervous for a moment and then the soccer tournament began.

It was finally ok to be German again.

I want to wave my countries flag around here in the desert. I'd like to march south and wave it around where the bombs were tested. I'd like to climb the mountains and wave my flag from the summit, but here there are no flags to wave. Here there is no one to see, no one to participate in the nationalism.

All I can do here is run the sand of war through my hands again and again and again.

I want to take all that international nervousness that came with all those German flags and show my compatriots how that feeling is mirrored onto our flag in many parts of the world for the things that we are doing and the things that we have done. I want to take the lessons home to us without acrimony or judgment. I don't want to be a sanctimonious cunt about it. I want to talk about the terrorist attacks and the torture and the wars. I want to talk about them without using them, and I want to shame those that do use them.

I want to show that we can still change the course.

I want to say that it's not too late, and there's no reason to wait until it is.

I want to make it clear how long the memory of those flags can remain, and how in our accelerated culture what we consider a minutes worth of news here can spawn acrimony that stretches across generations somewhere else.

I wish I could make it clear how long that after can be.

I want to show these things, but it's impossible. My country hasn't learned the lessons of Germany. It takes a catastrophic defeat to make these things clear and we haven't had one, until we do I don't think anything that can be said will be understood.

I don't know if it's fair to call the USA an empire yet, if it is one then it's a peculiar one. It's not particularly imperial, but quite keen to war.

I look at it more as the King on the chessboard in the Great Game for the World.

It's trying very hard to stay on top and it's trying very hard to order everything around it.

I wonder how the game will end.

Not every kingdom ends in blood and ash and bankruptcy, but many do.

It will be China's turn next, and I wonder how they will do. I wonder about what will happen in South Sudan, Iran, and

North Korea.

I look at Tibet and Taiwan.

The Fish has traveled in time to Rome when it was 52 B.C. and 476 A.D. He told me that the more things change the more they stay the same. People are people in all places and through all of time to our glory and shame.

The Fish and I watched the United States take a step forward on race and representation after the soccer games were over and we saw the disappointment when everyone realized it was just a step and more symbol than substance.

The tribe of man goes on and on and on. It's so diverse that it can never get along with itself. It's so broad that it can't recognize its members. It's so careless that it crushes its children and abandons its elderly. It threatens its individuals with ostracism and condemns its conformers with anonymity.

If it weren't for its beauty and art it would have no redeeming quality whatsoever.

It's been that way for as long as it has been and I don't know if it can change, but I've tried to do my part to make the boundaries seem less stark and the commonalities more clear. I have a feeling that may help, but I have no idea what really works or even if anything can. I wonder about our natures, if we're programmed to be this way. To what extent and can such things be unmade? Can a social evolution of the tribe occur? What would it look like? How long would it take?

Do we have that kind of time?

It seems like every time someone starts talking like that there is a disastrous war. Can we do it without a war? Can we do it without prison camps and blood lust? Can we do it with liberty and dignity?

I don't know if it can be done or how to go about it, but I'd like to be remembered as someone who carried a candle in the wind and the darkness instead of as someone who blew one out. A gadfly stinging a stallion, a swimmer who knows the river is different with every swim, a man overcome.

I have no idea really, but I take solace in this, every time you jump the whole world moves just a little, little bit.

Please, stay light on your feet.

Listen with me a moment, sound carries so well in the desert.

You can hear them crying now. A new generation born as we speak and they are crying just as we did and they don't know what else to do just like we didn't. We're going to pass the world to them and for all our ambitions it will be about the same.

We'll arrest their fears with the same mantras that our parents used on us. The ones that were passed down to them. That most people are basically good and decent, at least most of the time, so always be careful and watch your back. And that's pretty much true.

They'll have their tragedies just like we did.

They'll have their comedies just like we did.

We'll have to let go of them as we were also set free.

They'll bury us one day, hopefully with tears, as we buried ours, hopefully with tears.

They'll join the great and perpetual argument of Apollo and Dionysius. They'll experience the impossibility of wishing for permanence while caught up in the vibrant celebration of our temporal existence. They'll fight similar battles of heart and mind, and they'll face the same conundrums of finding resolution in the irresolvable that we all have gone through. We're the first one's they'll listen to.

Let's choose our words carefully.

Finally, the end is coming across the desert. The clouds have broken over the mountains and the rain is nearly here.

The Pilot Fish has finished chipping our names into the stone. He throws it down at our feet for a final inspection.

It looks fine to me, let's leave it lay.

We pick up some of the sand that held the afterbirth and the blood from so long ago, running it through our fingers, feeling time like hourglasses gone awry. Where we began and where we end and the wind blows lightly on us with the promise of eventual disintegration as it scatters the grains falling from our hands.

We offer it to Hotrod, but he won't touch it, says it's disgusting.

We can see the great-great-great-grandchildren of those scorpions. We can see the lonely soldiers of love and memory, the orators that remember Diogenes and the quiet multitudes of honest men and women that understand integrity is the only possession we have that travels.

We honor them all as we take our place at the end of the line.

The last of the sun has disappeared and our day is finally over.

The stars come out gradually and beautifully. The night sky here is untainted by civilation's progress and shines fully and brilliantly.

There are still places in the heavens unimagined by man, and we guess new constellations here and there.

A girl with a guitar, a muscle car, a figure skater, a fish bowl, and a pear.

We watch the procession of the Equinoxes. The age of Pisces has finally ended.

Listen as the clouds burst over the desert and the rains rush down upon us.

Aquarius come at last.

I told you that there was water after the blood.

We're in luck, the phacelia are blooming. Life is erupting here.

The Fish blows a kiss out across the desert. One last look as we fade into shades in starshine, legends now, all of us, become comedy and anguish, laughing and crying over all of it as we pass the flask back and forth between the cigarette drags that give us away in the night.

Made in the USA
Coppell, TX
25 January 2020